W9-BDS-990

The Deadly Embrace

ALSO BY ROBERT J. MRAZEK

Stonewall's Gold
Unholy Fire

The Deadly Embrace

A Novel of World War II

Robert J. Mrazek

VIKING

VIKING
Published by the Penguin Group
Penguin Group (USA) Inc., 375 Hudson Street, New York, New York 10014, U.S.A.
Penguin Group (Canada), 90 Eglinton Avenue East, Suite 700, Toronto,
Ontario, Canada M4P 2Y3 (A division of Pearson Penguin Canada Inc.)
Penguin Books Ltd, 80 Strand, London WC2R 0RL, England
Penguin Ireland, 25 St. Stephen's Green, Dublin 2, Ireland (a division of Penguin Books Ltd.)
Penguin Books Australia Ltd, 250 Camberwell Road, Camberwell, Victoria 3124,
Australia (a division of Pearson Australia Group Pty Ltd)
Penguin Books India Pvt Ltd, 11 Community Centre,
Panchsheel Park, New Delhi – 110 017, India
Penguin Group (NZ), Cnr Airborne and Rosedale Roads, Albany, Auckland 1310,
New Zealand (a division of Pearson New Zealand Ltd)
Penguin Books (South Africa) (Pty) Ltd, 24 Sturdee Avenue, Rosebank,
Johannesburg 2196, South Africa

Penguin Books Ltd, Registered Offices: 80 Strand, London WC2R 0RL England

First Published in 2006 by Viking Penguin, a member of Penguin Group (USA) Inc.

1 3 5 7 9 10 8 6 4 2

PUBLISHER'S NOTE

This is a work of fiction. Names, characters, places, and incidents either are the product of the author's imagination or are used fictitiously, and any resemblance to any persons, living or dead, business establishments, events, or locales is entirely coincidental. In certain instances where the author makes references to historical events and real persons, those references are made solely in a fictional context.

LIBRARY OF CONGRESS CATALOGING IN PUBLICATION DATA

Mrazek, Robert J.
The deadly embrace : a novel of World War Two / Robert Mrazek.
p. cm.
ISBN 0-670-03478-9
1. World War, 1939–1945—England—Fiction. 2. Mistresses—Crimes against—Fiction.
3. Americans—England—Fiction. 4. London (England)—Fiction. 5. Women soldiers—Fiction.
6. Conspiracies—Fiction. 7. Treason—Fiction. I. Title.

PS3563. R39T73 2006
813' .54—dc22 2005042400

Printed in the United States of America
Set in Nofret
Designed by Elke Sigal

To Carolyn, with Love

And, after all, what is a lie?
'Tis but the truth in masquerade.

Lord Byron

I regret to say that I learned too late that
it was not what a person did, but what he got
the credit of doing that gave him a reputation.

Major General George Crook (1864)

The Deadly Embrace

CHAPTER 1

It was snowing hard as the blacked-out coach carrying Lieutenant Elizabeth Marantz arrived at Victoria Station shortly before dawn. The sixty-mile trip from Southampton had become a nine-hour ordeal as the unheated troop train was forced to wait in darkness while successive waves of Luftwaffe bombers attacked London.

Above the strident wail of air-raid sirens, she could hear the rhythmic staccato bark of anti-aircraft cannons and the thunderous roar of the German armada passing overhead. Inside the dark car, a match would flare at the end of a cigarette, momentarily illuminating a restless young American face.

Two days earlier, she had arrived at Southampton aboard the *Empress of Scotland*, a converted British passenger liner transporting a fully equipped battalion of the American Third Infantry Division to its new base of operations in England.

Lieutenant Marantz shared the railroad coach with more than a hundred officers and enlisted men. Most of them were only boys, just eighteen and nineteen years old. They packed every compartment as well as the floor space along the connecting corridors.

All the windows had been screwed shut, and cigarette smoke soon turned the confined space into a choking yellow haze. A number of soldiers had managed to buy liquor before boarding the train, and they became raucously drunk.

As the train came to a grinding halt at Victoria Station, Lieutenant Marantz pulled a haversack from under the seat bench and wearily followed the line of men out onto the open platform. Although the air was stingingly cold and invigorating, it reeked from the fires caused by the Luftwaffe incendiaries. A biting wind sent grit and ashes swirling into their exhausted eyes.

Shoulders hunched low under the weight of their overseas bags, the new arrivals were greeted by a gigantic white canvas banner that hung askew from the stanchions of the rusty iron roof that soared a hundred feet above their heads. It read,

WELCOME ALLIED ARMED FORCES—HAPPY CHRISTMAS 1943

After two nights without sleep, the young Women's Army Corps officer longed for nothing more than a long, hot bath. As the line of soldiers snaked its way slowly toward the station, another snow-clad train arrived in a cloud of coal smoke and began disgorging its passengers. The crush of people made it almost impossible to move.

"Do you have a place to stay, Lieutenant?" came a low voice over the distant shriek of a train whistle.

Marantz turned to see a tall British officer standing near the open door of the newly arrived train. He was no more than thirty, his clean-shaven face deeply tanned. Just above the white silk scarf that circled his throat, livid burn scars puckered the skin up to his jawline and across the right cheek. Colonel's tabs adorned the epaulets of his greatcoat. The empty sleeve where his right arm should have been was pinned to his side.

"Yes, sir," she said. "I have orders to report to the Officers' Replacement Depot to receive my billet."

"Well, I could do better than that, Lieutenant," he said. "I would be happy to share my suite with you at the Dorchester."

Speechless, Lieutenant Marantz stared up at him as the line began to move slowly forward. The young colonel's face softened into an apologetic grin and he said, "Please forgive me for being so bloody obvious. I've spent the last two years in the Burmese jungle with the Chindits. Forgot my manners, I'm afraid."

Lieutenant Marantz nodded tentatively.

With a casual bow of his head, the Englishman said, "Colonel Henry Livingston, known to one and all as Hal . . . formerly of Cambridge by way of the Fourth Armoured Division of the Royal Tank Corps, and more recently a brigade commander under the somewhat legendary Orde Wingate."

She couldn't help smiling.

"Second Lieutenant Elizabeth Marantz," she replied, "known to one and all as Liza, formerly of Barnard by way of New York Medical College, and more recently the Women's Army Corps. I once met the somewhat legendary Artie Shaw in the lobby of the Biltmore Hotel."

"You have the best of me, I'm afraid," he said, suddenly coughing into a white handkerchief. As Liza watched the edge of it turn crimson, he added, "I assume you know that you are a stunningly beautiful girl."

He had obviously just been released from a hospital. The last thing she wanted him to think was that his battle scars were somehow hideous to her.

"I'm confident you'll have no trouble making new conquests, Colonel Livingston," she said with a sympathetic smile, "but, regretfully, I won't be one of them."

"Pity," he replied as she disappeared through the entrance door into the station.

Dawn had paled the gray, snow-filled sky when she joined several other American officers waiting for transportation to the same temporary housing billet on Grosvenor Road in Pimlico. A few minutes later, a dilapidated bus pulled up with a loud, clattering growl. Its only heating source was a small, sputtering coal stove in the back, and Liza shivered as the damp chill penetrated her coat and uniform skirt.

"The Jerries are coming almost every night, like in '41," the red-faced driver shouted back at them as soon as they were under way. "And just like the last time those posh bastards in Whitehall have moved their families out into the country again . . . leavin the rest of us here to take it in the throat."

The window was coated with a grimy mixture of snow and fire ash. Trying to see through it reminded her of swimming underwater. She fell asleep to the throb of the engine as they waited for a long caravan of military vehicles to pass by. Later, she awoke to the noisy downshifting of gears as the ancient vehicle came to a halt outside a small hotel.

While unpacking in her room, her mind drifted back to the maimed British officer who had propositioned her at the train station. In truth, she had never considered herself beautiful and saw no reason to change her mind now. Glancing into the mirror, she saw no more than the essential features so many other women shared. Slim figure, dark complexion, green eyes, black hair. Perhaps it's the hair, Liza concluded: it still flowed thickly down her back.

It struck her that wartime England was not the place to be worrying about her hair or its possible effect on men. After borrowing a pair of scissors from the clerk at the front desk, Liza went back up to her room and cut her hair off to collar length. Without ceremony, she picked up the soft black heap at her feet and deposited it in the wastebasket.

"To my new life," she said into the mirror.

Early the next morning, she checked in at the crowded Officers' Replacement Depot to see if her new orders had been cut. Like the others who hadn't received their assignments, she was told simply to wait.

She occupied her first days in London walking the crowded streets and gazing at the sandbagged monuments and buildings. Aside from the meals she ate in the hotel dining room, her evenings were spent alone in her room. It faced onto the Thames, and she enjoyed watching the river traffic of transport ships gliding silently toward the East End docks, which were the principal target of the nightly bombing raids. Late at night, she would lie awake listening to the comings and goings of the other officers.

One evening, she was sitting in her darkened room listening to the radio when the BBC broadcast a live speech of Joseph Goebbels, Hitler's propaganda minister. He was addressing a screaming crowd of Nazis at the Reich Chancellery in Berlin.

"ROOSFELT," he raved in German. "The paralytic Roosfelt and his Jew bankers will be punished for their crimes."

With her childhood knowledge of Yiddish, Liza could understand many of the demagogue's words and phrases, punctuated by the fawning audience's screams of "SIEG HEIL . . . SIEG HEIL!"

As Goebbels's braying voice ranted on in the darkness about the evils of international Jewry, the faint orange glow of the radio dial cast a yellowish tint on her trembling hands.

That night, she dreamed of her family for the first time since she had left home. In the dream, she was a child again in the big mahogany bed at their summer cottage in the Catskill Mountains. Her older brother, Nate, was asleep beside her, a contented smile on his boyishly handsome face.

A peal of thunder rattled the bedroom window. She dreamed that the storm was moving fast, roaring toward them from across the Allegheny Mountains. A jagged shaft of lightning erased the darkness. In the blinding glare, Nate sought to calm her with a reassuring grin as the room suddenly shuddered under a brutal concussion.

She bolted awake to the agonizing truth that Nate was dead, killed in action while fighting with the Fifth Marines at Guadalcanal a year earlier. Someone was screaming in the street below her room.

Liza stumbled to the blackout curtain and swept it away from the half-open casement window. Looking up into the rain-filled sky, she saw column after column of Luftwaffe bombers flying in disciplined formation up the river.

They came in low under the clouds, lit up by the blue-white searchlights from the hundreds of artillery batteries deployed across the city. With an earsplitting roar, the planes began to drop their payloads. The bombs fell to earth in a long, shrieking chorus.

As Liza watched from the window, one stick of incendiaries exploded in the neighborhood directly across the river from her. A few seconds later, the house shook under her feet as a bomb landed less than a block away down Grosvenor Road.

A massive chunk of ceiling plaster collapsed onto her bed, and she could smell the acidic stench of cordite. As the piercing human screams below her receded to a moaning wail, she felt an intense wave of heat blow past her face through the window. A cloud of black, greasy smoke wafted across the opening, blocking her view.

Her uniform coat still lay on the small end table where she had tossed it before falling into bed. Draping it over her shoulders, she ran down the carpeted stairs. An officer was slowly backing out of his room on the ground floor. Its front windows were blown in, and his hands were bleeding.

The entrance door to the hotel lay flat on the floor in the hallway of the foyer. She walked over it and outside into the pelting rain. Fires were raging out of control in the mansions directly across the river. Twenty yards down Grosvenor Road, a military lorry and an ambulance had collided head-on in the middle of the street. The driver of the lorry was trying to crawl through the shattered windscreen.

Liza heard what sounded like the groan of a wounded animal. In the glare of the fires, she could see two dark figures on the broad sidewalk in front of the hotel. She didn't linger at the first one. The corpse was wearing the uniform of a U.S. Army Air Corps officer. It was headless, and lay spread-eagled on its back in a small lake of blood. Farther on, a young woman was down on her knees at the edge of the paving stones.

The girl's pale-white hands covered her face as Liza knelt beside her. A chain of quick impressions raced through her brain as she tried to determine if the young woman was seriously injured or had simply become hysterical at the sight of her friend's gruesome death. After gently pulling the girl's hands away from her face, Liza unbuttoned her woolen overcoat and slipped it off her shoulders.

The girl was wearing a tight-fitting pink satin dress, mended carefully at the collar and shoulders. Around nineteen, she wore no wedding ring or other jewelry. Liza's eyes took in Cupid's-bow lips and an apple-cheeked face crowned with curly red hair.

A prostitute? Liza wondered, as she began her examination. Definitely not a streetwalker, she decided. Aside from lipstick, the young woman wore no makeup, and her skin tone was unspoiled. She smelled fresh and clean. The slightly scalloped fingers of her hands, however, bore the roughness of hard physical work.

Liza found the first wound, a deep, slashing cut below the right elbow. Not life-threatening. She continued searching, pulling away the lower half of the girl's overcoat.

"My God," said a trembling voice behind them at the entrance staircase. It was one of the American staff officers from the hotel.

"It's Major Slattery," said Liza without turning away from the girl.

She had immediately recognized the headless corpse from the handmade alligator-skin boots he had been wearing when he had tried to pick her up that morning at breakfast.

He had obviously been bringing the young woman back to his room. It was right above Liza's, and she was already familiar with Slattery's nightly routine. The strains of Tommy Dorsey's "Embraceable You" on the Victrola, followed by slow-moving dance steps across the groaning floor, leading finally to the unholy chorus of his shrieking bedsprings.

The young woman began falling over to one side as Liza's fingers found a second wound. A piece of shrapnel had sliced through the coat into her abdomen. Blood was pulsing out of the narrow slit, and flowing down the side of her dress. She gently lowered the girl's head to the paving stones.

Without instruments, it was impossible to tell if the metal fragment had torn through a vital organ. Liza pulled a clean handkerchief from her coat pocket and pressed it firmly against the girl's stomach. Staring up at Liza with shock-deadened eyes, the girl moaned again, and Liza smelled the aroma of scotch on her breath.

A kitchen maid, she concluded, probably from one of the nearby mansions, lonely and anxious to meet a dashing American flyer.

"Doctor Boynton is coming," the staff officer said as he folded the girl's coat and placed it under her head. "He's bringing his medical kit."

A blaze of light lit the sky above them. Liza looked up to see one of the German bombers hurtling earthward like a flaming meteor. A few seconds later, she heard an explosion when it plunged into the neighborhood across the river.

Still using her left hand to compress the wound, Liza saw something she thought deeply poignant. Using an eye-shadow pencil, the young woman had meticulously drawn an intricate mesh pattern of tiny intersecting lines on her shaved legs to simulate stockings. The pattern ran from her thighs down to her ankles, and it must have taken her hours to do it. As Liza watched, the lines were slowly dissolving in the rain.

The red-haired girl continued to stare up at Liza, her big luminous eyes seemingly studying the American's face. At one point she raised her head a few inches and actually smiled up at her. By then, Liza's fingers and right hand were warm from her seeping blood.

"It's going to be all right," said Liza, using her free hand to shield the girl's eyes from the merciless rain.

A minute later, someone knelt beside them on the sidewalk. It was Boynton, the elderly cardiologist who was supposedly treating General Eisenhower's heart condition. Like Liza, he was coated in plaster dust and looked like a snow-frosted version of Father Time.

Boynton unzipped his bag and removed a stethoscope and a small flashlight. Leaning over the girl, he focused the light into her open eyes and pressed his fingers to her neck at the carotid. In the small cone of light, Liza saw that the girl's eyes were bright blue.

"She's gone, I'm afraid," Boynton said apologetically.

Staring down at her, Liza saw that the young woman's face still held the same enigmatic smile with which she had greeted Liza's pathetic attempt to save her life. As an all-clear siren began to wail, Liza could hear the bombers' deafening roar begin to fade into the distance. Several more officers had cautiously ventured out of the building onto the sidewalk.

"I know that girl . . . Slattery's latest conquest," said one of them. "She was a scullery maid in that big brick mansion down the road."

Liza headed back inside the hotel. Two more staff officers were standing in the wrecked foyer when she came in.

"What's the score out there?" demanded the first one with a nervous laugh. A colonel in the Supply Corps, he was wearing a yellow silk smoking jacket over matching pajamas. Liza brushed past without acknowledging him.

"Did you see that? A goddamn female officer," said the other one. "That's what's wrong with this war."

The remainder of the ceiling had come down in Liza's room, and her bed was covered with wood lathing and horsehair plaster. Dropping onto the narrow cushioned bench under the bay window, she stared out at the burning city, finally falling asleep as a greasy dawn crept over the eastern horizon.

CHAPTER 2

Liza awoke with a blinding headache to the sound of rain dripping on the sills of the shattered window. Wind whistled through the cracks in the broken glass. Rubbing her temples, she closed her eyes and tried to forget the face of the young woman on the sidewalk.

She found a clean towel in the closet, and headed down the hall to the cold, drafty bathroom that she shared with the three other officers on her floor. Thankfully, it wasn't occupied. When she turned on the hot-water tap, the pipes began clanking and groaning in their usual manner. Glancing into the mirror, she saw that her eyes were rimmed in red.

A few minutes later, the tap had produced five inches of lukewarm water in the base of the chipped enamel tub. She lowered herself into the bath, carefully washing the dried blood and plaster dust from her hair and body as best she could.

The telephone began to ring in the hallway one flight down. She heard footsteps coming up the stairs, and then the grumbling voice of Pete Meadows, a former P-47 ace who had been grounded for recklessness and was waiting for a staff assignment.

"Everyone still alive up here?" he called out.

"As far as I know," another voice replied.

Liza had left the door to her bedroom open. From the sound of his footsteps, Meadows headed first in that direction. Then, she heard him arrive at the bathroom door.

"You in there, Lieutenant Marantz?"

"Yes," she said.

"A major named Samuel Taggart wants you at his office in SHAEF at 0900. He is sending a staff car for you."

"Thank you," she said through the closed door.

Liza climbed out of the tub, toweled herself off, and went back to her room to assemble a presentable uniform. The rain had finally stopped when she came out on the street again, through the wrecked front entrance of the hotel. Streamers of black clouds scudded low across the still-smoking city.

The bodies of Slattery and the young red-headed woman had long since been removed from the sidewalk, and an elderly charwoman was making an attempt to wash away their blood with a bucket of water and a long-handled brush.

A black Humber was waiting at the sidewalk with the engine running. She gave her name to the young driver, and he came around to open the rear door for her. Sinking back into plush leather upholstery, she wondered who Major Taggart was, and why he wanted to see her.

At Aldford Street, a long convoy of military trucks was passing by in an unbroken stream. On the next corner, a team of laborers was clearing a gigantic pile of rubble from the roadway where an office building had collapsed.

"When do you think the balloon will go up, Lieutenant?" asked the young driver as they sat waiting in the car. "I hear we're going to invade at Calais."

He pronounced it "Ka-LACE." No more than eighteen, he spoke with the flat nasal cadence of the Great Plains.

"If you know that, you must be driving General Eisenhower," she said.

"No sir, he's got himself an Irish girl driving him," he said, turning around with an innocent smile. "She's prettier than Dorothy Lamour."

Everyone knew that the invasion of Hitler's Fortress Europe was coming. The island was practically sinking under the weight of millions of combat soldiers, most of them Americans. Liza had read in *Stars and Stripes* that a new infantry division was arriving in a fast convoy from the United States every week. Outside the car window, the sidewalks thronged with uniforms of every color and design—Czechs, Free French, Americans, Poles, Dutch, and English.

Ten minutes later, she got out of the Humber in front of a massive brick building on Saint James Square. An imposing sign above the main entrance read,

SUPREME HEADQUARTERS–ALLIED EXPEDITIONARY FORCE

A squad of armed British sentries stood guard along the sidewalk in front of the building. Double walls of ten-foot-high sandbags flanked the doors. Men in a variety of colorful Allied uniforms were waiting in line to gain entry past a sergeant who was checking their identification from inside a small kiosk next to the wall of sandbags.

"I'm here to see Major Taggart," she said, presenting her identity card when she arrived at the head of the line.

The sergeant matched her card against a list of names on his clipboard.

"Military Security Command," he said. "Fourth floor."

Once inside, she saw that the place was a madhouse of nervous energy. Through the open doorways in the dark-paneled corridors, she saw tired-looking secretaries clattering away on typewriters while clouds of cigarette smoke billowed above their heads. Officers and enlisted men surged up and down the halls as if victory over the Germans hinged on their every step.

Reaching the fourth floor, she encountered another sign at the top of the staircase: "Military Security Command—No Unauthorized Personnel." Two uniformed American soldiers guarded the entrance to the hallway. Liza presented her identity card again to the first one. He took it over to the logbook lying on a small table and found her name on another list.

"Major Taggart is in the last office on the right," he said in a slow Texas drawl.

The big walnut door at the end of the hallway stood open. When she stepped inside, Liza thought for a moment that she had to be in the wrong place. The room was barely larger than a freight elevator. Aside from a small desk and two side chairs, an old leather couch occupied most of the remaining space.

Her first thought was that the man lying on the couch looked like an incredibly seedy version of Humphrey Bogart in *The Maltese Falcon.* Unshaven and smoking a cigarette, he was wearing a ratty bathrobe, red flannel pajamas, and carpet slippers. Looking up from the report on his chest, the man said, "I assume you're Lieutenant Marantz."

"Yes . . . sir," she said, as he pushed himself up from the couch and tossed the report over to the desk.

He looked like a football player, all solid mass, slab chest and powerful legs—an aging fullback with a full head of slate-gray hair and morose brown eyes. His nose looked like it had been broken more than once.

"We're a little pressed for space around here," he said, pointing at the chair in front of the desk. "Want some coffee?"

"No sir," said Liza, sitting down in one of the side chairs while he poured himself a cup and carried it over. She wondered whether he was living in his office.

A thick stack of reports and documents rose from the blotter on his desk. Lying next to it was a pack of Chesterfield cigarettes, a box of kitchen matches, and a bar of Hershey's chocolate.

"If you want to know the truth, coffee and cigarettes are fueling the war effort right now, not tanks and gasoline," he said, sifting through the papers.

He found another folder and began to scan the first page. When the right sleeve of his pajama shirt slid back to the elbow, she saw a white gauze bandage on his wrist and discarded the notion that he was living there.

"I was wearing these clothes when my billet took a direct hit last night," he said, as if divining her thoughts. "But this is nothing compared with what the Brits went through in '41. The little man in Berlin had a temper tantrum after we firebombed Hamburg. This is his personal retaliation."

Her eyes dropped to the folder again. Even upside down, she recognized the capitalized letters of her last name at the top of each page inside the standard personnel jacket.

"I'm thinking of offering you a job," he said, glancing up at her again.

She waited for him to continue.

"Let's see.... Twenty-five years old... Enlisted in the Women's Army Corps a week after Pearl Harbor... Eighteen months of training at a military pathology unit in Philadelphia before assignment to Valley Forge Army Hospital... Applied three times for overseas duty," he muttered before flipping back to the first page. "It also says here that you studied forensic medicine at New York Medical College."

"Yes sir, although I left school to enlist when the war began."

"According to this professor—Dr. Brubaker—you have superior, even remarkable powers of scientific deduction."

"He... exaggerates."

"Yeah, well, he claims that while your anatomy class was dissecting an anonymous cadaver, you concluded after a twenty-minute examination that the woman had been poisoned."

"That would have been discovered by any competent pathologist if there had been an autopsy," she said.

"It also says that the case was reopened, the corpse was identified, and a man was actually charged with the crime."

He took a last deep drag on his cigarette and stubbed it out.

"And convicted," she added as he partially unwrapped the chocolate bar and extended the open half toward her.

"No thank you," she said.

"What can you deduce about me?" he asked with a caustic grin.

The question took her aback. Was he playing some kind of game with her?

"Come on—go ahead," he said gruffly.

His hands seemed to be in constant, nervous motion. As he lit the tip of another cigarette, her eyes roved to the broken knuckles holding his nickel-plated lighter, then up to the lumpy bridge of his nose.

"I grew up in a place called Sheepshead Bay.... In those days it was a good thing if you learned how to fight. And you can see how good I was," he said, pointing at his damaged nose. "Aside from that."

She stared back into the well-lined poker face.

"You're... you were a police officer," she said.

"Well, that's a stunning piece of deduction.... Yeah, I was a New York City homicide cop—fourteen years. Then I got fired and went private. What else?" he demanded, seemingly all male life force and toughness.

"Why were you fired?" she blurted out.

"What do you think?" he came right back.

She thought for a moment and said, "You were too docile and mild-mannered."

He smiled again.

"She has a sense of humor. Deduce again."

"Insubordination," she said.

"Close enough. What else?"

"You went to college," she said.

"Yeah . . . City College."

"The first in your family," she went on.

He nodded.

"Why do you try to mask it?"

"What?"

"Your intelligence," she said.

"What else?" he demanded again.

She was still trying to process the jumble of confusing images he presented to her. The magnificent ruin of a face, the restless mind, the heavy pouches under his seemingly disillusioned eyes, the weariness, the strain. All of it could simply be the pressure of his job, or what had just happened to him in the bombing raid.

"This is silly," she said.

"No, it isn't. Say what you think," he said.

"I think," she began, "I think you've recently suffered a serious emotional blow, the loss of someone very dear to you."

For a moment, his brooding eyes dropped their guard. She saw a spark of anger followed by a momentary look of desolation. He shook his head disdainfully and said, "After three years of war, who hasn't? I could probably say the same thing about you."

He saw the sudden distress in her face. His eyes softened as she stared down at her lap.

"Have you ever heard of the code name Overlord, Lieutenant Marantz?"

"I doubt if I was supposed to, but I've been staying at a hotel full of army staff officers since my arrival in London. It's the code name for the campaign to open the second front in France."

He nodded and said, "I work for General Ernest Manigault, the head of the Military Security Command here at SHAEF. My job is helping to provide security protection for Overlord. I've been asking for a forensic pathologist for months now to complete our investigative unit. You are the closest thing the paper pushers could come up with. You'll start work here tomorrow morning."

"Here?" she said, glancing around the tiny office.

He laughed.

"In one of the offices downstairs."

"What will I actually be doing?" she asked.

"Right now, there are no active investigations pending, but I don't expect that to remain the case. In the meantime, you can start with a sensitive task that we all have to share around here—reading each other's mail."

"You mean censoring people's personal letters?"

He finished the chocolate bar.

"In a nutshell, the Germans know we're coming," he said. "The question is where and when. That invasion plan is the most important secret we have over here, and we're responsible for its protection. So far, General Manigault's command has provided security clearances to four hundred and sixty-two officers and support staff who are involved in planning the invasion. Presumably, none of them are security risks. All of them were thoroughly checked out. But every one of those people knows the proposed target date, and they also know where we're going in. Do you understand?"

"Yes, of course," said Liza.

"If just one of them were to betray that information, perhaps inadvertently or unknowingly to German agents, Hitler would put enough panzer divisions behind those landing beaches to drive us right into the sea. The whole invasion force could be wiped out on the first day. So we read everyone's mail."

"I understand," she said.

"Maybe you can use your deductive powers to help plug any leaks," he added almost kindly.

"Yes, sir."

"Just a couple more things," he said.

For the first time, he sounded a little unsure of himself.

"I don't know exactly how to say this. . . . Look, you're young and you're pretty. Around here that usually means you're being used as a mattress by somebody . . . and those somebodies usually have 'General' or 'Admiral' in front of their first names."

"You don't have to worry about that," she said emphatically.

"I won't, but you should be prepared for it, and the fact that you may receive propositions that . . ."

"I understand."

"One more thing," he said, softly, as she stood up to leave.

"Yes sir?"

"Sit down," he said, and she did.

"You're Jewish."

She waited several moments for him to continue.

"So?" she said, finally.

"How important is your religion to you?" he demanded.

She imagined her gray-haired father looking over her shoulder, thin and rumpled, with his metal-rimmed spectacles perched on the tip of his nose, a gentle smile on his face.

"My father is a rabbi," she said.

"Yeah . . . I saw that in the folder. Conservative, right?"

She nodded.

"I caused him great pain when at seventeen I told him I was no longer a practicing Jew and wouldn't be going to temple."

"And what did he say?" asked Taggart.

"He was wise enough to say that he respected my decision as an honest questioning of my faith. . . . And why is any of this relevant to my job?" she demanded, with rising color in her cheeks.

"What do you think about a homeland for the Jews in Palestine?" he asked.

"I haven't thought about it," she said.

"What about all the rumors of Hitler massacring the Jews?"

"I think they're probably true," she said. "That's one of the reasons my brother and I volunteered after Pearl Harbor."

Taggart nodded and said, "You should know that the top brass doesn't trust Zionists. If it turns out you're an agitator, you'll be transferred out of here in a heartbeat. For your own good, I suggest that you keep matters like that to yourself."

"I'm not an agitator," she said.

CHAPTER 3

At five the next morning, Liza walked to work along streets hazy with the acrid smoke of burning buildings. There had been another Luftwaffe attack the previous night, although none of the bombs had landed near her hotel in Pimlico. The morning sky was still dark when she arrived at Saint James Square. After passing through the heavy security detail in front of SHAEF, she went searching for her new office.

The massive building was a rabbit warren of dark corridors, all of them lit every twenty feet with bare lightbulbs hanging from tin conical shades. She found her subbasement office buried at the end of a long, dank hallway about twenty feet below ground level.

The room smelled of stale cigarette smoke and was about fifteen feet square, with brick walls painted a glossy white. An overworked iron radiator clanged in the far corner, vainly attempting to battle the cold and dampness. Four wooden office desks were clustered in the center of the room, each topped with a brass table lamp. Banks of wooden filing cabinets covered two of the walls.

Three of the desks were already occupied. A young British Army officer sat at one of them with his chair tipped backward, his feet resting on the blotter, and a cigarette dangling from his wide, fleshy mouth. He looked up from his copy of the *Times* and said, "Welcome to the dungeon. I hope you've brought some new whips and chains. We've worn out the old ones."

"Something is worn out, Charlie, and it's your jokes," said a buxom woman with blue eyes who was applying her makeup at the desk closest to him. She was wearing a Women's Army Corps uniform just like Liza's and spoke with an American accent. A second woman sat at the desk opposite the young man, typing a document with calm proficiency. She wore the blue naval uniform of a British Wren officer.

When the young man stood up and came toward her, Liza saw that he was enormous, at least six and a half feet tall, with broad, powerful shoulders and a large head covered with a shock of prematurely white hair.

"Charles Wainwright, resident misogynist," he said with a leering grin, extending his hand. She took it in hers. It was heavily calloused, as if he had been a day laborer in civilian life.

"Liza Marantz," she said. "I believe I'm supposed to be working here."

"Another American," he said, absorbing her accent. "Thanks to General Eisenhower, we are all one big happy family, British and Americans shoulder to shoulder in common purpose to rid the world of Nazi tyranny. All except the Frogs. We can't trust the Frogs, can we?"

"The Frogs?" repeated Liza, confused.

"The French, my dear girl, the frog eaters," he said in a disparaging tone. "They've packed it up, sitting around drinking wine and smoking Gauloises until we come over to save them."

"Charlie's just jealous because the Free French officers in London are so attractive to the Englishwomen," said the large-breasted American girl as she applied bright-red lipstick. Behind her false lashes and face powder, Liza could see signs of premature aging in the faint ridges around her eyes, mouth, and forehead. Although she was still in her early twenties, there were already gray streaks in her hair, at the temples. In spite of her brassy manner, Liza sensed something oddly tragic about her.

"My name is Janet Barnes," she said, snapping her compact mirror shut and pursing her new red lips into a tissue. "Call me J.P."

"Hello," said Liza.

"And this sweet young example of English virtue is Lieutenant Jocelyn Dunbar," said Charlie. "Unfortunately, the lovely Joss focuses on work to the exclusion of all else."

"You just say that because she won't go out with you," said J.P.

Joss was boyishly slim, with short blond hair and a lovely, innocent face. Her desk was piled with handwritten notes that she was transcribing into formal documents. She had not looked up from her typing since Liza arrived.

"I have forsaken all women," said Charlie. "Love is a disease."

"Oh, Charlie likes women, all right," said J.P. "It's just that women don't want anything to do with him, even after he tells them all he was a champion rower at Oxford."

That explains the callused hands, thought Liza.

"No, it's true," shot back Charlie. "As Gauguin said, or maybe it was Maugham actually, women are strange little beasts. Treat them like dogs, beat them till your arm aches, and they'll love you all the more."

Looking up at his liquid, spaniel eyes, Liza decided he was totally harmless. She sat down at her desk and began organizing the office supplies she found in the drawers. She was putting a new ribbon in her typewriter when a downy-cheeked military courier came through the open door carrying a large green canvas sack.

Looking at the three women in turn, he asked, "Lieutenant Marantz?"

"That's me," said Liza.

He fished a sheet of onionskin paper from his uniform blouse and extended it toward her along with the key to a small padlock that secured the top of the sack.

"Please sign here, ma'am," he said.

She signed the form and handed it back to him, then opened the padlock and emptied a portion of the bag's contents on her desk. Carefully sifting through the pile, she discovered that it contained the personal letters and private communications from almost two hundred officers involved in planning the Overlord campaign.

"Another paragon of censorship, I see," said Charlie Wainwright.

"I didn't ask to be," mumbled Liza as she began sorting through the pile.

Major Taggart had told her to read every letter as thoroughly as possible, flagging with an adhesive sticker any passage that might represent a potential security breach. Someone further up the intelligence food chain would then review the cited material and determine if it warranted elimination.

"How do I decide what a potential security breach might be?" she had asked him, having absolutely no knowledge of the Overlord plan.

"Just imagine that you're a German Abwehr intelligence agent looking for compromising material," said Major Taggart. "Deduce it."

After reading the first few dozen letters, Liza began to feel almost voyeuristic, learning the most private thoughts of people working alongside her in the offices of SHAEF. Particularly graphic were the love letters, filled not only with words of longing, but with detailed descriptions of the lovemaking that could be anticipated upon that officer's arrival home.

Even more shocking to her was the amount of gossip routinely included in letters going back to wives, fathers, and other family members. Although few of the writers revealed anything embarrassing about themselves, they exhibited no reluctance in betraying the peccadilloes of others, particularly the most senior officers.

One of the first letters she read was five single-spaced pages long, and written by a U.S. Army Air Corps officer on the staff of Air Chief Marshal Sir Arthur Tedder, the deputy supreme commander to General Eisenhower. The American was writing to his wife about the air marshal's girlfriend, who was nicknamed Tops.

"The air marshal is besotted with her and bends to her every wish," he wrote. "Here he is with a whole army quaking at his feet, and he is like putty in her hands. I saw something just before we flew up here from North Africa that you wouldn't have believed. There we were on the runway, four lieutenant generals and all the staff cooling our heels, waiting for old Tops. Finally, a two-ton truck pulls up next to the plane and she gets out. Would you believe that the truck was filled with antique furniture, Persian rugs, drums of olive oil, and a load of other things blacklisted in England according to the King's regulations? Well, it was, and she was bent on smuggling it all back. Sir Arthur stood there begging her to relent, but when she threatened not to go he had me round up some enlisted men to load it all into the cargo bay. I just hope the IG doesn't get word of it."

In another letter, a senior staff officer declared to his wife that General George Patton had been having an ongoing affair with his niece, Jean Gordon, ever since he had been stationed in Hawaii before the war. According to the officer, she was on her way over to England to work as a doughnut girl at one of the canteens and to resume her affair with the general.

Still another letter revealed that General Eisenhower was romantically involved with his Irish limousine driver, Kay Summersby.

It was astonishing to Liza that Americans were apparently so guileless about keeping secrets. After considering the matter, Liza decided not to flag any of the passages, concluding that gossip was probably endemic in every army, and that it was of no strategic value to the Germans. Besides, if she began flagging all the gossipy revelations, she would have run out of the adhesive stickers before lunch.

As the day wore on, she learned that Charlie liked the room very cool, and J.P. liked it very warm. Depending on which one had last adjusted the hot-water intake to the radiator, the room alternated between a dank chill and stuffy airlessness.

At lunchtime, two elderly ladies came down the corridor with a large tea cart loaded with urns of tea and coffee, along with a selection of lunch items, including soup, pork pies, Cornish pasties, cut sandwiches, and bread, all of it available for a few shillings.

J.P. invited Liza to join her at lunch in the canteen upstairs, but Liza decided to stay and work at her desk after buying soup and a beetroot salad from the trolley. She read letters all that afternoon, taking one more break at four o'clock, when the trolley came back down their corridor laden with tea and scones.

At six o'clock, people started filtering down the corridor and heading home in the London darkness. At seven, Liza was the only one left in their office. She thought about going back to the hotel, but there was nothing of interest waiting there for her. She decided to stay and work.

As the hours passed, it became a matter of personal pride to watch the tall stack of unread letters slowly melt away on top of her desk. She was in the middle of a long missive about the romantic yearnings of a Brooklyn dental officer when she looked up to see a two-star American general staring at her from the doorway. He was the first general she had ever met, and she leapt to attention.

"Can I help you, sir?" she asked, not sure whether to salute him, since he was holding his cap in his hand.

"Just continue your work," he said gruffly, in a voice used to command.

Even with the poor illumination from the corridor, Liza could see the simian quality in his excessively long arms and prognathous jaw. She watched his eyes slowly train down the front of her uniform. Sitting back down at her desk, she picked up the last letter she had been reading. Even without looking back toward the doorway, Liza knew he hadn't left. A few seconds later, she heard one of the office chair legs squeak as he brushed past it.

"Do J.P. and Joss work in here?" he asked in a low, guttural voice, trying to make the words sound casual.

"Yes, they do," said Liza, looking up at him again, "but both of them have left for the evening."

His shaved head gleamed in the harsh light of Charlie's desk lamp. The darkly tanned face looked like it had been chiseled out of polished granite, but his menacing demeanor was undercut by his wide, matronly hips.

"Can I give them a message for you, General?" asked Liza.

Without a word, he turned on his heel and walked out of the room. She tried to resume reading her letter, but began yawning uncontrollably. Glancing at her watch, she saw that it was nearly eleven o'clock.

For the first time since her arrival in London, she found herself looking forward to sleep. Before leaving the office, she locked all the letters in her desk, then gathered her coat and handbag and headed toward the front entrance. Outside, it was a raw, blustery night, and rain spattered the sidewalk. After trying without success to hail a cab, she walked back to her hotel through the damp.

The next morning, Charlie looked up from his *Times,* took a sip of his tea, and said, "We've got that bullet-headed American general here again. The two-star. Kilgore. He's just back from Ike's old headquarters in North Africa."

Liza was watching J.P. as he spoke. The other woman's ears pricked up like a fawn's. The sound of Joss's clattering typewriter abruptly stopped at the same time.

"Who is Kilgore?" asked Liza.

"Another West Pointer," said Charlie. "One of Patton's old roommates, I'm told . . . but different than his sort. In spite of the bloodthirsty name, I gather Kilgore's not a warrior. He's supposed to be the kind of indispensable fellow who can lay his hands on ten cases of good whiskey when he needs to—and that's a man who will go places in this war."

Charlie buried his face back in the *Times.* As Liza watched, J.P. got up from her desk, adjusted her uniform blouse, and left the room. Joss resumed her typing. A minute later, Charlie gave out with a low whistle.

"Another young woman was found murdered last night in Belgravia," he said. "Just like the last two, apparently."

"The last two?" asked Liza.

"The last victims—young and attractive . . . They suspect one of your oversexed American chaps, I gather."

Liza went back to work on the slowly dwindling mountain of correspondence. By the end of her second day on the job, she had a much better idea of what her officemates actually did in the war effort.

Joss Dunbar worked on the staff of British Admiral Sir Thomas Jellico, who was responsible for assembling the fleet of ships necessary to deliver the Allied invasion force safely to France.

She was reserved to the point of deep shyness, but carried herself with elegant grace. Very efficient in her job, she was almost paranoid about the security of the papers she was entrusted with transcribing at her desk, and never left the office without locking her work in the desk drawer. Several of her unpainted fingernails were bitten to the quick.

J.P. had already served on one of the military staffs in North Africa. Now she was involved with the routing of enlisted WAC support staff to England, everyone from stenographers to the doughnut girls at the London canteens. Noticing at one point that Liza was staring at her wedding ring, she said, "My husband . . . Lloyd . . . is an army officer in the Pacific. He . . ."

Her voice stopped in mid-sentence as copious tears flowed silently down her cheeks. "Lloyd . . . was captured by the Japanese at Corregidor, and is now a prisoner of war. The last word I received about him was almost two years ago."

"It must be very hard," said Liza. J.P. nodded, dabbing at the corners of her eyes with a Chanel-scented handkerchief before resuming her work.

She still wasn't sure exactly what Charlie did. He would spend half the morning sitting around reading the *Times* or playing chess against an imaginary opponent on the board that occupied a corner of his desk. Then he would receive a written message and bolt out the door, disappearing for hours at a time before returning to resume the same indolent schedule.

Charlie waited until they were alone one afternoon and made a halfhearted play for her. She told him firmly but in a kindly way that she wasn't interested. He retreated with the look of a chastened puppy.

The first few days passed in the same predictable but reassuring routine. Each morning, she would awake in the darkness, walk to SHAEF in the darkness, leave to go home in the darkness, and go to sleep in the darkness as soon as she had undressed and taken her nightly bath in unheated water. There was an air raid almost every night, but the bombers were again focusing their attacks on the docks of East London.

She happened to be in the ladies' bathroom at work one morning when Joss Dunbar came in and went straight to one of the sinks. After removing a handkerchief from her blouse, she ran cold water over it and held the cool compress to her forehead.

"Are you all right?" asked Liza.

"Just a touch of influenza, I think," she said, her eyes tightly shut. Liza was standing alongside her when the girl uttered a sigh and her knees buckled. Liza caught Joss as she fell, eased her to the floor, and then felt for her pulse. It was slow and steady. The girl regained consciousness a few seconds later.

"What happened?" she asked, looking up at Liza, her blue eyes muddled with confusion.

"You fainted, Joss."

"I've never done that before," she said, moving to sit up.

Perspiration dotted her forehead at the hairline.

"Have you been eating?" asked Liza.

"Yes. I'm always hungry these days," said Joss.

She swayed unsteadily in Liza's arms after regaining her feet.

"I still feel quite nauseous," she moaned.

With a tremulous shudder, she turned and vomited into the sink. Liza held her shoulders until she had finished and rinsed out her mouth.

"Have you considered the possibility that you're pregnant?" Liza asked gently.

As she watched, the confusion in the young woman's eyes turned into a look of wonderment, followed by a smile of unbridled happiness.

"Could it be possible?" Joss's face turned giddy. "Please don't tell anyone. Oh, that it could be true. I only . . . Swear you won't tell anyone, Liza—swear to me."

"Of course I won't tell anyone," she said, noting that Joss wore no rings on her delicate fingers, and no jewelry of any kind except for a small gold locket on a thin chain. Joss's fingers now flew to it and clasped the locket tightly.

"Do you have a doctor?" asked Liza.

"Of course . . . except . . . Don't worry, I'll have a test."

Back in the office, Liza buried herself in the remaining pile of letters for the rest of that day and the next. By Thursday evening, she had finished the last letter. Dozens of them were separated from the others, all flagged with neatly organized adhesive stickers. Calling for a courier, she sent the separate padlocked bags back upstairs.

On Friday morning, she received a brief note from one of the junior officers who served under Major Taggart in the security command. It expressed his appreciation for her "gung ho" spirit in helping with the mail, and praised the thoroughness with which she had reviewed the correspondence. Accompanying the note was another mailbag, fully as large as the first one.

She plunged right into the next batch, privately hoping that something would happen to relieve her temporarily of the monotonous drudgery, but still glad to have work to fill her waking hours. She had already come to embrace fully the English notion of teatime, and was enjoying that respite on Friday afternoon when Charlie turned to Joss and said, "I'm heading down to Rawcliff for the weekend. Sure you wouldn't like to join me? Country air might do you some good."

Joss looked up at him from across her typewriter, gave him a polite smile, shook her head, and returned to her work. Charlie's eyes slid past her to Liza, obviously hoping for a positive reaction from her.

"What is Rawcliff?" she asked, neutrally.

"One of the finest estates in England," said Charlie with renewed enthusiasm, and clearly desperate to find a weekend date. "It's the country place of a friend of mine from Oxford. One of the greatest rowers in Oxford history, actually—heart of oak and all that."

"Perhaps J.P. might be interested," Liza said.

"She has other plans," said Charlie forlornly. "She always does."

An hour later, what was apparently a regular weekend stampede began with the early exit of the SHAEF support staff from the below-ground corridors. Liza watched them jauntily milling along the hallway, clearly excited to have a day or two free from the drudgery of staff work.

Joss had already left the office and J.P. was gathering her things to go when a young RAF officer poked his head through the door. She saw that he was walking with a slight limp. Almost as tall as Charlie, he was more slender, with corn-colored hair that fell past his right eye, and a broad insouciant smile. Scooping back the lock of hair, he called out, "So how is the old misogynist? Ready to go, Charlie?"

Charlie looked up at him and grinned.

"Of course, my lord," he said with exaggerated courtesy.

Liza's attention was momentarily drawn to another man, who was standing out in the corridor. Wearing civilian clothes, he was short and well built with dark-brown hair. As she watched, he removed a cigarette from a silver case and lit it with a silver Ronson.

"They are threatening to tow my car out in the square," said the RAF officer, with suppressed mirth. "We've got to get cracking."

"Yes, my lord," said Charlie, with mock deference, as he threw together his gear. Glancing over at Liza, he motioned to his friend and said, "Meet the new Yank."

The RAF officer looked over and his eyes connected with hers. A moment later, he was limping toward her, the startling blue of his eyes matching the uniform he was wearing.

"Hullo," he said. "I'm Nick Ainsley."

It was only when he reached out to shake her hand that she saw the red-patched skin grafts on his cheeks and neck. She was fairly sure that his nose had been rebuilt by plastic surgeons. The terrible injuries hadn't erased his cleft chin.

"Hello," she replied, somewhat amazed to find herself so gripped by a man's physical presence. He seemed reluctant to remove his eyes from hers.

"I'm ready, my lord," said Charlie, smiling from across the room.

"Well, we must be on our way, then," said the young officer.

He followed Charlie through the door. A moment later, she could hear them laughing as they headed down the corridor. J.P. was still standing by her desk, her eyes shining with aroused luster.

"What's all that 'my lord' stuff?" asked Liza.

"Lawd Nicholas Ainsley," said J.P., pronouncing the words as if she had just become an English duchess. "What I wouldn't do for that man, even with all those hideous scars." She let out a coquettish sigh and said, "He has one of the oldest titles in England . . . huge mansions all over the place."

"His left leg was amputated below the knee," said Liza.

J.P. nodded and said, "He was a Spitfire pilot in the Battle of Britain. One of Churchill's cherished few. His plane crashed and burned."

As she was going out the door, J.P. looked back at Liza with an appraising eye.

"If you're not doing anything tomorrow night, I could find you a date for dinner," she said as if lonely for female company. "Have you ever eaten at Claridge's?"

Liza shook her head and said, "Thanks, but I have other plans already."

She didn't elaborate on the fact that the plans consisted of doing her laundry and reading another chapter of Jane Austen.

"Maybe some other time then," said J.P.

Liza walked back to her hotel through another rainy downpour. Even to a new arrival from the States, it was obvious that Londoners were almost worn out. The city newspapers kept referring to the new Luftwaffe bombing campaign as the "baby blitz," but exhausted city dwellers did not find it amusing. The victories at El Alamein and Stalingrad had receded into distant memory, and the inescapable monotony of dull rationed food supplies had finally begun to erode their spirit. They moved listlessly through the streets, their barely suppressed anger spilling out if their bus was late or there was no meat at the market.

It was different for the Americans, Liza concluded. There was nothing listless about them. Having taken over the best hotels and restaurants, they strutted along the avenues with the arrogance of conquering heroes, even though she knew that very few of them had ever seen battle. To most of them the war was still a great adventure.

As she stared up at the barrage balloons floating lazily in the sky above London like immense children's toys, Liza thought about everything that had happened during her first week in the new job. Although one of the tiniest cogs in the machine being constructed to destroy Hitler's Third Reich, she was grateful to be finally playing a part in that vital undertaking.

She was troubled by only one thing, the knowledge that, after reading less than a week's worth of private correspondence, she already knew the two most important secrets of Overlord, including the planned invasion date at the end of May, and the fact that the assault was to be made against a series of landing beaches in Normandy.

If she could find out that information so easily, how hard would it be for the Germans to learn the secrets? she wondered. She decided to talk about the situation with Major Taggart on Monday morning. Of far less importance was the knowledge that at least twelve of the top Overlord commanders apparently had mistresses, and three of them were sharing the favors of J.P.

CHAPTER 4

That Sunday night, the Luftwaffe launched the biggest attack of their new bombing campaign. Hundreds of aircraft rained down tons of block-buster bombs indiscriminately across the city, forcing Londoners to seek out the corrugated tin shelters that had sat unused in backyards since the nightly bombing raids ended back in 1941. The number of civilian casualties was enormous. On Monday morning, Londoners were again digging themselves out of a landscape strewn with rubble and oily smoke.

Sam Taggart's new billet near the Strand had barely escaped another direct hit, and he was now down to wearing his rumpled uniform coat over a pair of borrowed oatmeal-tweed pants. He was still soaking his badly sprained ankle in Epsom salts when a staff corporal came in to say that General Manigault had called from upstairs and wanted to see him right away.

Sam put on his socks and shoes, and hobbled painfully down the corridor and up the two flights of stairs to the general's suite. As he came through the outer office, Staff Sergeant Grossman cupped his hand over the telephone next to his ear and whispered, "He's madder 'n hell, Major Taggart."

"He's always madder than hell," Sam replied, knocking on the interior door.

The general was sitting ramrod-straight in a leather armchair in front of the polished-enamel coal stove, gazing into the fire. His shoes were resting on the grate, and steam was rising from the wet cuffs of his starched khaki pants. He had on the short uniform coat that American newspapers were already referring to as the Eisenhower jacket. After Ike had started wearing it, most of the staff officers at SHAEF had run out to their tailors to have one made.

"When does this foul weather ever end?" the general demanded, his voice husky from chain-smoking Cuban cigars. He glared up at Sam as if he were personally responsible for it. "If it isn't raining, it's threatening rain. Dull gray, pale gray, charcoal gray—that's the entire weather pattern in this fucked-up country."

Ernest Manigault was fifty-four years old, and from Los Angeles, California. A West Pointer, he had commanded a division that got chewed up at Kasserine Pass, in North Africa, before being relegated to the post of security commander for Overlord.

That was when he had sent for Sam Taggart. Five years earlier, Taggart, then still a detective lieutenant on the New York City homicide squad, had helped him out of a predicament that could have wrecked his military career when he was stationed at Fort Hamilton in Brooklyn. At the time, Manigault thought that Detective Taggart had performed a miracle. Now he wasn't so sure.

"You look like shit, Sam," he said. "That so-called uniform is a disgrace."

"My billet took another near hit last night," said Taggart, sitting down in one of the armchairs clustered around the stove.

"That's your excuse after every raid," the general retorted, his thick, bushy eyebrows knitted together. "You're always a mess. In fact, you have the worst military bearing of any officer it has ever been my misfortune to command."

"I'm not happy with it either," said Taggart.

"You shouldn't even be an officer in this army."

"No," he agreed.

"The only reason I keep you on my staff is that you're good at what you do," Manigault said, running blunt fingers through his salt-and-pepper hair.

"Issuing parking permits and censoring mail?" asked Taggart.

"That was Colonel Baird's doing. You know he can't stand you. As soon as I found out, I . . . Look—I don't have to explain myself to you."

Kicking the bumper of the stove, he stood up and stretched himself to his full height of five feet seven. He grabbed a scuttle and poured a few more chunks of coal into the stove.

"Did we know the big raid was coming last night?" Taggart asked.

Manigault nodded. "The ULTRA intercepts told us. Basically, it was another Coventry problem. We can't allow the Germans to know we've broken their codes. Next to Overlord, ULTRA is the most important secret we have to protect over here."

Back in November 1940, Churchill had learned through his code-breakers that the Luftwaffe intended to fire bomb the city of Coventry, but ordered that no warning be given for fear that the Germans would suspect that the Allies had broken their most secret transmission codes. The English code-breakers had nicknamed the intelligence breakthrough ULTRA, for ultrasecret. Hundreds of civilians died in the Coventry attack to preserve it.

"A lot of people paid the price for ULTRA again last night."

General Manigault walked over to his inlaid Regency desk and held up one of the morning newspapers. A banner headline screamed "BABY BLITZ CONTINUES."

"They've been warned to take every precaution."

"I'm sure that will be a comfort to those who died," said Sam, dragging on his cigarette.

"We have a serious problem," the general said, coming back to the chair and dropping heavily into it. "The Metropolitan Police have found a corpse in one of the buildings in Cromwell Park."

He pointed toward the window that faced onto Saint James Square. From where he was sitting, Sam could see the tops of mature elm trees, denuded of leaves and black with rain. Beyond the trees were the slate roofs of several large buildings.

"At this moment there are probably a thousand corpses lying in buildings across this city," he said.

"Yeah, but this one is different."

Taggart waited for him to continue.

"She worked for us," Manigault said. "Based on the identification they found, it appears to be Lieutenant Jocelyn Dunbar."

"The young blonde Wren officer?"

"Yes."

"Admiral Jellico's . . . ?"

"Yes," he interrupted, rubbing his forehead. "It looks like she might have committed suicide. . . . At least that's what the British seem to think. One way or another, we need to know the truth. Although she wasn't officially cleared for ULTRA or Overlord, she may have been in possession of . . . sensitive information."

"Through Admiral Jellico."

He nodded.

"In bed."

He nodded again. Taggart had already reported the relationship to Manigault, after monitoring private communications between the two over the previous months.

"Why me?"

"You're the best criminal investigator I have around here. At least you used to be, Sam. God, I never thought it was humanly possible for anyone to unravel that mess I was in at Fort Hamilton."

"You were innocent," he said. "I just proved it."

"Yeah . . . well . . . you saved my life. I hope that counts for something."

Taggart didn't respond. He could now hear the low rumble of powerful aircraft engines coming from the west. As it grew progressively louder, Manigault stood up and walked to the window. Sam followed him. Although they couldn't see anything through the dense gray cloud cover, Manigault obviously knew what it was.

"The Krauts won't like today's entertainment program," he said with a feral grin. "That's more than a thousand Fortresses and Liberators on their way to Adolf's favorite city."

"Since when is his favorite city one of our military targets?" asked Taggart.

"An eye for an eye," said the general as he headed back to the fire.

"So . . . about Lieutenant Dunbar," said Sam, sitting down again. "If you haven't read the reports, there appears to be a murderer running amok in the city who has killed at least three young women in recent weeks."

"To my knowledge, none of them worked for us. Anyway, I want you to find out what happened to her. Let me know as soon as you do."

"I will."

"There's a police inspector named Drummond waiting for you. I asked that his people not touch anything until you get there. My car is waiting outside."

"I'll let you know what I find out," said Taggart, heading out of the office.

On his way down the stairs, he remembered that Liza Marantz worked in the same office that Jocelyn Dunbar had. Favoring his bad ankle, Taggart hobbled down to the subbasement. He found her standing in the corridor outside her office, ordering a cup of tea from the trolley women.

"I need you," he said, as J.P. came out of the doorway to the office, looked up, and smiled at him.

"Good morning, Major Taggart," she said, swiveling past in a wave of Chanel.

Without a word, Liza went back into her office to grab her coat and purse. Rain was falling hard again when they got outside. General Manigault's Humber was waiting for them at the curb. They rode across the Strand and past a long block of impressive public buildings, until they reached another small park surrounded by large mansion houses.

Taggart had already decided not to tell her the name of the victim. There was always the possibility that there had been a mix-up. If it was Joss Dunbar, he wanted to see how she reacted to the situation.

"Where are we going?" she asked, looking out at the fallow gardens in the center of the square.

"To see a dead body," he replied.

The driver stopped in front of a four-story white brick mansion enclosed by an eight-foot-high gold-painted iron picket fence. A British soldier brandishing a Sten machine gun waved them through the open gate.

The majestic edifice had big marble columns in front of it. An imposing second-story balcony with matching marble railings projected out over the circular driveway. The buildings on both sides had received direct bomb hits in recent raids, reducing them to thirty-foot-high mountains of smoldering rubble.

Taggart saw that, although most of the mansion's side windows were shattered, it was otherwise unscathed, as if fate were preserving it for some higher purpose. Waiting under the marble balcony, out of the rain, was a gaunt white-haired man in a rain-slicked rubber overcoat. He stepped forward as Sam and Liza walked toward him.

"Major Taggart?" he said uncertainly, staring at Sam's uniform coat and tweed pants with his tired brown eyes.

"That's right," said Taggart. "This is Lieutenant Marantz."

"I'm Inspector Drummond, Scotland Yard."

Taggart took in the inspector's gin-blossomed cheeks and bulbous red nose. Stepping forward to shake hands, he sniffed the scent of licorice breath mints. They didn't mask the powerful odor of gin.

Turning back to the mansion house, Drummond led them toward the shelter of the marble balcony. The January air had all the sharp bite of midwinter, and Liza shivered involuntarily from the vicious punch of the wind.

"Bit parky this morning," said Drummond as he stopped under the exterior balcony. The trembling of his hands had nothing to do with the cold, thought Sam, watching the inspector remove a pack of Camels from his coat pocket and extend it toward them.

"Fag?" he said, looking at Liza.

She shook her head. It was still awkward for her to hear English words that meant something totally different back in the States. Two peoples separated by a common language, Churchill had said, and it was true.

"I'm still not sure why your general has demanded your participation in this investigation," said Inspector Drummond. "We have the matter well in hand. There is really no need for you to go in there. Why don't you and the lieutenant stay warm inside your car while we tidy up."

"The victim had a sensitive job at SHAEF," Sam replied. "I'm sure you understand."

Drummond nodded. "Just following orders," he said resignedly. "I told him it wouldn't do."

Taggart wondered who the "him" was as he followed the inspector across the driveway toward the huge oak entrance door. Pausing outside it, Drummond turned and pointed up at the marble railing of the second-story balcony.

"You might be interested to know that King George the Third stood up there to publicly read the dispatch from the Duke of Wellington that he had defeated Napoleon at Waterloo."

"When was that?" asked Taggart.

"Eighteen fifteen," he said with obvious pride as they went through the entrance door into a marble-and-gilt vestibule.

To Liza, it seemed even colder inside the building than it had been under the balcony. She could hear the wind moaning through the shattered window frames at both ends of the marble hallway. Another man stood waiting for them in the rear of the vestibule.

"This is Colonel Reginald Gaines of His Majesty's security staff," said Inspector Drummond.

Around sixty, the colonel had a thinning head of marcelled silver hair, small gray eyes, and a beaked nose. He was wearing a scarlet riding jacket with polished brass buttons down the center, cream-colored breeches, and black thigh-length riding boots.

Looking from Taggart to Liza, he shook his head disdainfully and said, "Didn't Inspector Drummond inform you that this matter is already closed?"

"I am here under direct orders from General Manigault at SHAEF Security Command," said Taggart. "If you want him to reverse the order, be my guest and get him on the phone."

Colonel Gaines thought about it for several seconds before wagging his head again with obvious distaste.

"If indeed this is absolutely necessary, I will accompany you," he said in a tone that implied he was worried they would steal the silverware.

"Are we riding to the hounds today?" Sam asked as they headed down another marble staircase.

"I serve the King in many capacities," Colonel Gaines said curtly.

They went down a wide corridor lined with gold-framed life-sized oil paintings of men and women dressed in ermine robes and Elizabethan collars. Liza recognized the regent's face in the last painting. It was the current King of England, George VI. A courtier was fitting the British crown on his head.

"What is this place?" she asked.

"It is the Royal Natatorium," pronounced Colonel Gaines gravely.

"Sure," said Taggart. "I should have guessed."

Two etched-glass doors loomed up ahead in the shadows. Flanking the doors were glass display cases. Inside each one of them was a four-foot-high stuffed penguin standing in a white plaster snowscape. Liza stopped to gaze at the bird on the left. He stared back at her with a hurt, puzzled look on his face.

"Emperor penguins . . . *Apterodytes forsteri*," said Colonel Gaines, as if the birds were still enjoying themselves in their natural habitat. "Captain Robert Falcon Scott brought them back for the Queen from the Antarctic . . . before his last, tragic voyage, of course."

They went through the swinging glass doors into the next room.

It was no ordinary swimming pool. The gigantic high-ceilinged room was a hundred feet long and sixty feet wide, the pool itself measuring around seventy-five by forty. The colors in the chamber were a kaleidoscope of red, purple, and orange. It appeared to Liza that the walls and floor were made up of tiny ceramic tiles, each one no more than an inch square.

Seeing her staring down at them, Colonel Gaines said, "Mosaic tiles—there are more than three million of them here in the natatorium. They are a thousand years old and once graced the Mesopotamian palace of Genghis Khan."

Taggart didn't ask how they had gotten there, but was fairly sure a lot of Mongols had died in the process. He imagined all the sweating British soldiers it must have taken to pry them out of the looted palace. Across the room, two men in gray coveralls were standing by the far edge of the pool.

"The natatorium has served the royal family for over two hundred years," said Colonel Gaines as they walked toward the pool. "The King enjoys these waters on a regular basis, along with the Princesses Elizabeth and Margaret. Queen Victoria swam here as well."

"These waters?" asked Liza.

"New shipments are brought down to London every few months in railroad tanker cars from Loch Lomond," he said. "Loch Lomond is the King's favorite."

"He never swam in the East River," said Taggart.

The water no longer had the blackness of a deep Scottish lake. It was tinged a pinkish red. The men in coveralls were draining the pool, and the water level was down to four feet at the deepest end. The shallow end already lay exposed. Halfway between the shallow end and the deepest part, Taggart could see something solid emerging from beneath the surface of the pink water.

"Where is the rest of your investigative team?" whispered Taggart to Inspector Drummond as they began walking toward the pool.

Looking distinctly uncomfortable, he responded, "So far . . . Colonel Gaines is conducting it personally."

"Why am I not surprised?" said Taggart as his eyes were drawn to several objects sitting on the foot-wide marble apron that bordered the edge of the pool. They appeared to be lying almost directly above the dark solid mass below the surface. The objects were surrounded by a large red puddle. As he walked toward them, his nose took in the familiar metallic odor he had encountered at dozens of violent-crime scenes over the years.

Stepping across the blood pool, he crouched beside the objects. The first one was a carved pewter goblet, six inches high and embedded with brightly colored gemstones. A dried brownish crust stained the pewter handle. An inch of amber liquid still lay inside. Taggart smelled the aroma of good brandy.

Sitting next to it on the marble apron was an unlabeled brown glass apothecary bottle. It was empty. One yellow pill lay a few inches away from it, next to a cork stopper. Taggart picked up the loose pill and touched the edge with his tongue. It was a strong barbiturate.

The final object was an ivory-and-silver-handled straight razor, its polished grip coated with more of the brownish crust. The razor lay spread open next to the edge of the blood pool.

"I would think it is obvious, even to you, Major," said Colonel Gaines with condescension in his voice.

"That this is a suicide?" asked Taggart.

"Of course," he said.

Taggart grinned.

Inspector Drummond said, "While we're waiting, you'll want to see what we found in the changing rooms."

He led Sam and Liza across the vast chamber through two more swinging pebbled-glass doors. It was no ordinary locker room. There were eight individual rooms in it, all of them facing onto a circular marble courtyard. Each one was the size of a railway compartment and furnished with a gold-inlaid dressing table, matching ballroom mirror, and carved walnut armoire. The dressing tables were adorned with vases of fresh flowers, combs, hairbrushes, and vials of various perfumes and ointments. Privacy in each room could be achieved by closing a matched set of painted Chinese screens.

Only one of the rooms appeared to have been in recent use. A British Wren officer's uniform lay on the floor inside it. A matching navy greatcoat was draped over the dressing-table chair. Liza could see the two embroidered gold rings of a Royal Navy lieutenant sewn into the cuffs of the uniform coat on the floor. A gold brassard signifying staff rank was attached to the right shoulder.

The uniform skirt lay in a circular heap next to the dressing table, as if the owner had simply stepped out of it. A black lace bra, matching black panties, and two nylon stockings were strewn in a broken line toward the swinging doors that led to the pool.

"No one has moved anything?" asked Taggart.

"Just this," said Inspector Drummond, handing him a thin leather wallet. "Colonel Gaines found it lying on the dressing table. It is Lady Jocelyn Dunbar's."

Liza's eyes widened as she heard the familiar name.

"Lady Jocelyn Dunbar?" she repeated, trying to keep her voice steady.

"Of course," replied Colonel Gaines with irritation. "She is a Windsor on her maternal side . . . a second cousin to the Prince of Wales. Otherwise, she would not have received privileges from the King to bathe here."

"Did you check the wallet for fingerprints before picking it up?" asked Taggart.

"Why would I?" said Gaines. "It's clearly a case of suicide."

"Brilliant," said Taggart. "I guess that's how you got to be head of the King's security staff."

Colonel Gaines's face colored as Taggart opened the billfold. Inside was Joss Dunbar's Royal Navy identity card, along with an unused ration book, an expired driver's license, two five-pound banknotes, and a roughly cropped photograph of a young blonde girl in riding clothes on a chestnut horse. After putting on his glasses to examine the ragged edge, Taggart handed the picture to Liza.

"It's Joss," she said, her voice cracking as she handed it back to him. "She was probably no more than fourteen at the time."

"The other half of the picture is missing," said Taggart, holding it out to Gaines. "You can see that it was recently torn in half."

"Well, I certainly didn't do it," declared Gaines heatedly.

One of the men in coveralls came through the swinging doors that led back to the pool.

"We're almost done in there, Colonel," he said.

Liza fought to control her emotions as she followed the others back into the pool area. The water level had dropped much farther, and she could now see the outline of a dark form just under the surface near the sidewall, about ten feet from the deepest end.

"Aside from the damage from the bombing raid, were there any indications of forced entry?" asked Taggart. "Damaged locks on the doors?"

"Not that we have determined," said Drummond, glancing warily at Colonel Gaines.

Sam and Liza stood on the white marble apron, staring down at the surface of the pool as the blonde girl emerged from the pink water.

"Sweet Jesus," called out one of the men in coveralls, his eyes bulging in disbelief.

"Quiet there," barked Colonel Gaines.

Naked, she was actually sitting up, her back resting against the wall of the pool, arms at her sides, her lovely mouth drawn downward in seeming resignation, blue eyes wide open, staring blindly forward into the distance. Her body was pure white.

"Exsanguinated," said Inspector Drummond.

"Bled white," agreed Taggart.

But that wasn't what had caused the man in the coveralls to cry out. It was a stark image that had nothing to do with her naked body.

Coiled around the dead woman's stomach like a black snake, was six feet of heavy-duty electrical cable. It was attached to a macabre-looking machine that was resting on its back farther down the pool.

"It's the tile clopper, sir," called out the second workman. "We was replacing the tiles along the back wall there with it just yesterday morning."

Liza walked over to a cabinet at the end of the pool and removed a clean towel from the stack on top of it. Without asking for permission, she took off her shoes and socks and rolled up her uniform skirt before dropping down into the ankle-deep water at the far end of the pool. Taggart and Drummond stood looking at her from the marble pool apron as Colonel Gaines craned out over the edge and said, "What do you think you're doing, young woman?"

"She is conducting a preliminary investigation under my authority," said Taggart.

Gaines said nothing further as Liza slowly made her way toward the body through the pink water. By the time she reached it, the area around it was almost dry.

In death, Joss looked to Liza like the young girl in the photograph rather than the grown woman she had become. There was very little muscular definition in her arms and shoulders. Her breasts were barely developed. Aside from the long blond mane, the body was absolutely hairless, including the pubic area, which had obviously been shaved.

"How old was she?" asked Taggart.

"Twenty-two, I believe," said Colonel Gaines.

Gently pulling her body away from the wall, Liza removed the electrical cord from around her waist, and then grasped Joss's shoulders to lay her down on her back. Picking up her left wrist, Liza took in the three separate slashing wounds about two inches from the base of the palm. Two appeared superficial. One of them had gone deep to the bone.

The right wrist was unmarked, as well as the rest of her upper body. Turning her to the side, Liza briefly examined her back. It was unblemished. When she spread Joss's hair away from the nape of the neck, Liza saw a small bruise close to the hairline.

"You're still treating this as a suicide?" said Sam Taggart to Gaines.

"That's exactly what it was," Colonel Gaines said, as if daring him to object.

"I want a complete autopsy done at the SHAEF hospital on Curzon Street," said Taggart. "If you have any objections, take it up with General Manigault at command headquarters."

Colonel Gaines glared at him in pursed-lip silence as Liza made a quick examination of Joss's vaginal and anal cavities, then her ears and hands. Several of her fingernails had been bitten to the quick. None were painted or polished.

"You don't see anything odd about this scene?" Taggart said.

"Odd? Not at all," said Colonel Gaines.

"So it's your view that she came here alone to take her life . . . that she then drank a pint of brandy, consumed a bottle of barbiturates, tied the machine cord around herself, slashed her wrist three times, and shoved the tile machine into the pool?"

"As I said, it's obvious," persisted Gaines.

Liza climbed out from the shallow end of the pool, dried her feet with the towel, and put her socks and shoes back on.

"Did anyone see her arrive?" asked Taggart.

"No," replied Colonel Gaines. "The staff leaves at nine each evening."

"Then how did she get in here?"

"With her key," he said. "Each person chosen by the King to have natatorium privileges receives a silver key."

"How many are there?" asked Taggart.

"I don't keep a list," he said.

"Fewer than a thousand?" asked the American.

Gaines laughed harshly.

"Fewer than fifty," he said imperiously.

"Well, that shortens the list," Taggart said.

"What list?" demanded Gaines as two men wearing the white coats of laboratory technicians appeared at the doorway by the dead penguins. They stopped in their tracks, apparently waiting for further instructions.

Taggart led Liza back to the locker room. Gaines and Drummond followed them.

"Do you see her clothing?" asked Taggart, pointing at the garments and underwear spread across the floor. "It's flung in every direction."

"Perhaps she was in a hurry to get into the pool," offered Gaines. He frowned as Liza began going through the drawers of the dressing table. "You have no right to do that, you know," he said to her admonishingly.

"She was in a hurry, but it wasn't to get in the pool, Colonel. It's obvious that she came here to meet someone," said Taggart, starting to go through her uniform jacket and greatcoat.

"I don't know what you're insinuating, Major."

"She was obviously here to engage in some privileged fucking," said Taggart, removing two foil-wrapped condoms from the side pocket of her greatcoat.

"Fucking?" said Gaines, as if he had never heard the word before.

"A tryst, then," said Taggart. "In your parlance, a rendezvous . . . an assignation."

The colonel's beaklike nose seemed to curdle.

"Lady Dunbar would never have chosen the natatorium for something like that," he proclaimed.

"You don't think there's been some good fucking in the natatorium over the last two hundred years?" said Taggart.

"You are crude and insolent," declared Colonel Gaines. "If you didn't have General Manigault's misplaced confidence, I would demand . . ."

"Anything else in her clothes?" asked Liza.

Taggart shook his head.

Colonel Gaines's cheeks had become as red as hot coals.

Taggart turned to Inspector Drummond.

"Isn't the Yard investigating the murders of several other young women in this city over the last few weeks?"

The old man looked at Gaines, as if waiting for him to speak. When he didn't, Drummond said, "Very different circumstances, I assure you."

"I would like to see those crime-scene reports," said Taggart.

"We'll take your request under advisement," said Colonel Gaines.

"Anglo-American cooperation," said Taggart. Turning to Liza, he asked, "Anything else?"

She nodded. "I would like to participate in the autopsy when Joss is moved to the morgue."

"So ordered," said Taggart.

Colonel Gaines glared at the two of them with a contemptuous sneer and said, "Many of us rightly believe that an occupation by the German Wehrmacht would have been preferable to having you Americans here."

"You wouldn't have liked their cigarettes," said Taggart. "Or their coffee."

He picked up an empty, silver-capped glass vial from the dressing table and headed back into the natatorium. Stooping next to the marble apron, he dipped the vial into the inch-deep pool of Joss's blood and covered it.

As they were going out the door past Captain Scott's penguins, he said, "Get this on ice and take it to the military hospital on Curzon Street for analysis."

"She was pregnant," whispered Liza as Taggart continued hobbling up the first marble staircase on his bad ankle.

"You deduced that from your three-minute examination?"

"She told me," said Liza.

"Uhmm," he muttered, breathing ever more heavily as they climbed the last set of stairs to the entrance vestibule.

"And her locket is missing," said Liza. "She had a small gold locket that meant a great deal to her. There is an abrasion on the back of her neck from when it was ripped free."

As Taggart paused to rest at the top of the staircase, Inspector Drummond caught up with them. He moved fast for a drinker, thought Taggart, lighting another cigarette.

"What are you going to do now?" asked the old man.

"Did Colonel Gaines send you up here to ask me that?"

"No," he said.

"We're going to try to find that girl's murderer," said Taggart.

"I'll try to help you in any way I can," said Drummond, his knowing brown eyes apparently sincere. "Here is my card, with my work and home numbers."

"Thanks," said Taggart, taking the card and handing it to Liza. "We'll be in touch."

The strident sound of air-raid sirens began an ugly whine outside as they went through the front door.

"You had better find yourself a safe haven," Drummond called after them.

CHAPTER 5

"How do you know she was murdered, Sam?" demanded General Manigault, removing a twelve-inch Romeo y Julieta Cuban cigar from his mouth.

"Fourteen years of looking at crime scenes," said Taggart.

"I just got a call from some Limey colonel named Gaines who sounded like he had the King's fork up his ass," said Manigault. "He says the Dunbar girl took her own life."

Taggart nodded and grinned. They were in the walnut-paneled anteroom of the large conference hall where General Eisenhower had just convened a meeting of the top British and American commanders of Overlord. Liza waited at the door about ten feet away, but she could hear every word.

"They don't want the murderer to turn out to be someone with a silver key to the Royal Natatorium."

"What's that?"

"The royal swimming hole," said Taggart.

Manigault shook his head and growled, "So you looked at the crime scene. That's all you're going on?"

"That's all I went on when I got you off the murder charge five years ago."

Manigault's eyes found Liza's for a moment before they returned to Sam.

"Get rid of her," he whispered.

Taggart motioned to her to leave. Liza went out the door, closing it behind her.

"That was different," said Manigault.

"How was it different?" asked Taggart.

"I was innocent," said the general.

"As I recall, you were the only one who thought so," said Taggart, "aside from me. . . . Look, General, this one would have been obvious if it was my first homicide case. I don't care what the royal ass-kisser has to say about it. He would try to conceal the truth if Jack the Ripper was back in business and it involved the royal family."

"All right," said Manigault. "If Lieutenant Dunbar was in a position to compromise Overlord, we need to know it. Otherwise, I don't care what she was doing or who she was sleeping with."

"Or who murdered her?"

"I didn't say that."

"I'll need to interview Admiral Jellico," said Sam.

Manigault took another puff of his cigar and exhaled a cloud of bluish aromatic smoke.

"Listen to me, Sam," he said. "There are eagles and sparrows in this war. The eagles soar, the sparrows fall. In other words, this requires delicacy."

"You want me to be delicate? I'm as delicate as a fist," said Sam.

"Jellico's a goddamn Limey admiral," Manigault growled again. "Just try to be discreet."

"Has he been told yet?"

"They are trying to locate him now. To my knowledge, he hasn't been informed."

"You want my opinion, General?"

"Of course," he said.

"It will be a miracle if the Nazis don't find out about our Overlord plan. When it comes to spying, they may be dense, but they could still be handed the golden goose. There are Nazi sympathizers all over England, and half of them are in the so-called aristocracy. If General Eisenhower knew how many . . ."

"Cross yourself when you say that name."

Taggart shook his head and said, "I don't have to tell you that the Dunbar girl is only one of the many young women around here who are in a position to learn our most important secrets from across the pillow."

For a second, Manigault's eyes reflected the enormity of the danger, as well as its impact on his own job as the head of the Security Command.

"Just try to look at these girls as slumming angels, Sam," he said with resignation. "They're basically good kids, doing what they do best in the war effort. When the war is over, most of them will go back and get married and live happily ever after."

"Yeah," said Taggart with sarcasm.

"You just don't get it, Sam," came back Manigault. "These men are responsible for planning and executing the greatest military invasion in history. The whole goddamn war might be at stake. Roosevelt and Churchill are riding them like bulls—Marshall and Ernie King are, too. In the meantime, the testosterone level around here is . . . Most of them need companionship. They need to swing from the tree now and then. Can't you understand that?"

"Yeah . . . they need companionship. They have the world on their shoulders. So what do you want me to do?"

"I want you to find out the circumstances of this girl's death. In addition to Overlord, Admiral Jellico is cleared for the ULTRA intercepts. We need to know if he leaked anything through her."

"He probably wasn't her only lover," said Taggart. "She was young and beautiful, even if she looked like an altar boy."

"Follow it wherever it leads, as long as it has to do with security of Overlord. Just try to keep your big mouth in check. If you screw up, Sam, I won't be able to protect you."

There was a knock on the connecting door to the conference hall, and an overweight WAC sergeant came in wearing an Eisenhower jacket identical to General Manigault's. Unlike his regulation trousers, her khaki skirt wasn't regulation. Form-fitted across her broad hips, the hem revealed two inches of thigh, as well as a pair of silk stockings that weren't painted on her tapered calves.

"They need you in the conference right away, General," she said. "I told them you would be right along."

Her wide hips rolled under the tight skirt as she moved back to the door and closed it behind her. Manigault avoided Sam's gaze.

"Does she have Overlord clearance, too?" said Taggart, deadpan.

The general's face mottled with anger.

"You're a real ball-breaker, Sam. You don't give a shit about anything. I don't know what happened to you after I left Fort Hamilton, but you're not the same man I knew then. I didn't even know that you left the police force until Baird found out. After what you did for me, I never even bothered to check when I asked for you to come over. But it isn't working out for either of us. I'm sending you home when this is done."

Taggart felt his words like a blow in the pit of his stomach. He watched Manigault's retreating back as the general stalked to the door, swung it wide, and disappeared into the conference hall.

CHAPTER 6

Vice-Admiral Sir Thomas Vivyan Jellico, M.C., D.S.O., O.B.E, was sixty years old and clean-shaven, with a long ascetic nose and pallid, somber face. His pomaded silver hair peaked in the middle of his broad forehead like the prow of a ship.

Taggart and Liza had waited an hour in a corridor filled with British and American staff officers before they were finally ushered into his office on the top floor of the Admiralty Building in Whitehall.

Admiral Jellico was standing in full dress uniform in front of a twenty-foot-high painting of Sir Francis Drake. To his left was a shiny mahogany conference table with elephant-tusk legs. A slim, attractive woman in a pale-yellow dress was seated at the nearest end of the table. Sam and Liza came to attention and saluted. The admiral returned their salutes with a casual flip of his fingers to his oak-leaved hat.

"Good afternoon," he said, the mordant face momentarily creased by a curt smile. He removed his hat and pointed to two chairs opposite the woman at the table.

The far end of the table had been set for lunch. There were two place settings. Sterling silver and cut-glass wine goblets flanked fine old china. A ripe wedge of cheese sat next to a plate of freshly cut tomatoes and fresh basil. Taggart was tempted to ask him where the admiral got fresh tomatoes in January, but he was trying to be on his best behavior.

"Thank you for taking time to see us," he said after they had sat down. "May I smoke?"

"Of course," replied the admiral, sitting down next to the woman.

His uniform was impeccably tailored, with six inches of heavy gold braid on each elbow.

"I regret that I only have a few minutes for you," said the admiral, removing his rimless steel glasses and rubbing his eyes. "I have an exceedingly busy afternoon."

Although she had seemed more youthful from a distance, the woman beside him was in her late thirties, with delicate, angular features. Her large amber eyes were flecked with gold. Liza noticed the narrow bands of red puffiness underneath them, and wondered if she had been crying. She sat in the carved chair with a trim, graceful bearing.

"I gathered from General Manigault's telephone call that this was important," said Admiral Jellico.

"Yes, sir," said Taggart, glancing momentarily at the woman. "It is also highly confidential."

"Helen Bellayne is my personal aide and secretary," he replied. "Anything you have to tell me can be said in front of her. She has a top-secret clearance, just as I do."

The woman smiled politely at Taggart.

"This matter is highly personal," persisted Taggart. "I wanted to give you a private opportunity to . . ."

"I said I only have a few minutes, Major Taggart. Get on with it."

Taggart nodded and said, "I assume that you have been notified about the death of Lieutenant Jocelyn Dunbar."

"Yes, I was. It's most unfortunate. She was a very efficient girl," he said, as if the loss had only been a typewriter.

"We have every reason to believe she was murdered, Admiral."

"I understand that Joss took her own life," said Helen Bellayne in a voice steeped with upper-class cadence. Her amber eyes filled with tears as she added, "Colonel Gaines called an hour ago to tell me."

"He is entitled to his opinion," said Taggart, "but he is not in charge of the investigation. I am."

"I gather you are some kind of policeman," said the admiral, looking at Taggart as if the job was as disreputable as his uniform.

"Not any longer," replied Taggart. "Now I work for General Manigault in military security."

"And why did you leave police work?"

"I was fired," said Taggart.

"I see. And now you're over here."

"That's right."

"Well, I have no idea how she died," he said. "Is there anything else?"

"Admiral Jellico, I will be very blunt. It would appear that your relationship with Lieutenant Dunbar went well beyond the military chain of command," said Taggart.

The admiral glanced momentarily at Helen Bellayne before training his eyes again on Taggart.

"What are you implying, Major?"

"That you were involved with Lieutenant Dunbar in a sexual relationship," he said evenly.

"That is absurd," pronounced Admiral Jellico very calmly. "Jocelyn was younger than my own daughter. On what basis do you make such an accusation?"

Taggart debated for a moment whether to be frank about the private communications he had read over the past several months. This was worse than matrimonial work, he thought silently.

"I'm not at liberty to discuss that right now," said Taggart. "However, I was hoping to enlist your cooperation so that you're immediately removed as a potential suspect. Can you please tell me where you were last night from nine o'clock until dawn?"

"This interview is at an end," the admiral said, standing up from the table. "I plan to call General Manigault immediately and tell him that you have made a totally unsupported allegation against me."

"A young woman is dead . . . murdered," said Taggart. "We know that you and Lieutenant Dunbar were close enough to have spent . . ."

"I am ordering you to leave," Admiral Jellico said, his voice becoming shrill. "If you do not do so voluntarily, I will have one of my marines escort you out of the building."

"Fine," said Taggart, before heading toward the door. "But this won't end it. There is too much at stake . . . as you should know, Admiral."

They came out of the side entrance of the Admiralty Building into bright sunlight.

"And the Lord parted the heavens," said Liza, looking up at blue sky for the first time since she had arrived in London.

"I'd forgotten the sun actually rises over here," said Taggart. "The Germans will have a bomber's moon tonight."

He paused on the crowded sidewalk.

"Well, that went about as good as I expected," he said. "He is not about to admit to an affair with her unless presented with the evidence of her letters. Even then he would probably deny it as some kind of delusion on her part."

"I think her death hit him hard," said Liza.

"Maybe . . . Listen, I want you to arrange for Joss Dunbar's autopsy to be done at the SHAEF hospital," he said. "Start putting to work all those forensic talents you learned."

"I'll do my best," said Liza.

"Find out all her secrets," said Taggart, grinning.

"All her secrets," repeated Liza. "Done."

"What did you think of Helen Bellayne?" asked Taggart as he hailed a taxi.

"I think she may be related to Joss in some way," said Liza. "Also—you probably noticed it, too—she may have the early onset of a minor thyroid disease. . . . You can see it in the lagging of her eyelids."

"Where I come from we call those bedroom eyes," said Taggart, holding the door of the cab open for her. "I think she's gorgeous."

When Liza arrived back at her office, Charlie was standing in the corridor outside talking to two other men. She recognized one of them as his friend Lord Ainsley. The other man was a member of the security detail permanently stationed at the end of their corridor.

Lord Ainsley turned and saw Liza as she came toward them. Grinning, he removed his flight cap and said, "I'm not sure if you remember me, Lieutenant. I'm Nick Ainsley."

"Of course," she said, smiling up at him. "What is happening here?"

"Apparently, you've had a bit of thievery in the office," he said.

Charlie was speaking to the military policeman in hushed tones.

"I know it sounds crazy, but someone broke the lock on my desk," he whispered.

"Is anything important missing, sir?" replied the policeman.

"I don't keep anything important in my desk," he replied.

J.P. was applying lipstick in front of a compact mirror perched on her desk when Liza went inside. Going straight to her telephone, she dialed the number on Inspector Drummond's card. As she waited for it to ring through, J.P. said, "Why would anyone break into Charlie's desk? All he does is sit around and play chess with himself."

Inspector Drummond came on the line.

"Yes, Lieutenant?" he said after she identified herself.

"I wanted to schedule the autopsy of Jocelyn Dunbar," she said. "Major Taggart would like it to be done at the SHAEF hospital on Curzon Street."

Liza looked up to see J.P. staring at her intently.

"I'm sorry, but they took her straightaway to Golders Green," said Drummond.

"What is that?" she asked as J.P. continued staring.

"It's a hospital in North London," he replied.

"Why wasn't she brought to the SHAEF hospital?" asked Liza.

"You will have to take that up with Colonel Gaines," he said, apologetically. "He ordered the transfer of her body."

"Do you know when the autopsy will take place?"

"I wasn't told," he said.

There was a burst of static on the line, and then silence.

"Are you still there, Inspector?" she asked as J.P. resumed applying her makeup.

"I'm here," he said wearily. There was another pause before he added, "You should know that Golders Green is also the city's largest crematorium."

"Oh no," she said.

"I will probably be fired for telling you this, but I would strongly advise you to hurry."

As she headed toward the door, Nicholas Ainsley was standing at Joss Dunbar's desk.

"Look here," he called out to one of the military policemen in the corridor. "This desk has been jimmied, too."

Joining him behind Joss's desk, Liza could see that the metal lock bar on the right bank of drawers had been gouged away. Turning to the sergeant of the security detail, she said, "I want this room sealed off until I return. No one is to touch anything."

"Under whose authority?" demanded the sergeant, looking at her with obvious skepticism.

"Major Sam Taggart," she said.

"Yes, sir," he said.

CHAPTER 7

Traffic slowed to a crawl near Buckingham Palace and came to a complete stop at Green Park. British military police had blocked all civilian traffic to allow passage of another seemingly endless military convoy. Although Liza's driver was a native Londoner and claimed to know several alternative routes to Golders Green, his efforts were to no avail. Most of the residential neighborhoods in the north of the city were choked with fire engines and rescue vehicles

"Please hurry. . . . Please hurry," she kept repeating as they inched past scores of indistinguishable streets filled with identical row houses, many reduced to charred ruins from the recent bombing raids.

"I'm trying the best I can, Lieutenant," he said, "but it is four bloody miles any way you slice it."

Nearly an hour after they started, the staff car pulled up at the side entrance to what looked to Liza like a Charles Dickens–era prison. Twelve-foot-high soot-covered walls surrounded two enormous brick buildings. As she approached the entrance, Liza glanced up to see black, oily smoke wafting skyward from a circular brick chimney that towered over the roof of the second building.

When she stepped inside, her nose was assaulted by the overpowering smell of a bleach-based disinfectant. It could not mask the cloying odor of decaying corpses coming from a large holding room off to the left. Liza headed straight for the front desk, where an elderly woman with a white doily pinned to the front of her rose-colored dress was fanning her face with a folded newspaper.

"Sorry, dear," she said, "but we just got another delivery from the raid two nights ago. Poor lads was trapped inside a ship they was unloading that took a direct hit."

"I'm Lieutenant Marantz, and I'm here to participate in an autopsy," said Liza, showing the woman her identity card. "The decedent's name was Lieutenant Jocelyn Dunbar."

"If it's military, dear, you've gawt to see Captin Sleeves," she said. "'E's down that 'allway over there."

"Thank you," said Liza.

As Liza started down the hall, the woman called after her: "A piece of advice for a girl as pretty as you are, dear . . . 'E's got loose hands, if you know wot I mean."

Liza smiled back at her and said, "Yes . . . thank you."

An officer was standing in a shadowy doorway about halfway down the corridor. As Liza approached him, she saw that he was talking to the young scrubwoman who was mopping the floor of the office.

"Captain Sleeves?" she asked, coming up to him.

Over his shoulder, Liza could see that the girl's blouse was unbuttoned and her cheeks were red with apparent humiliation.

"What is it?" he demanded without turning to look at her. Although he wore the uniform coat of a British Army officer, there were no badges or campaign ribbons on it.

"I am Lieutenant Marantz," she said, holding out her military identity card, "and I am here to participate in the autopsy of Jocelyn Dunbar."

"That autopsy has already been concluded," said Captain Sleeves, his eyes still on the young scrubwoman as she backed away down the hall. "According to the family's wishes, she is being cremated."

"I need to examine that body," Liza said forcefully, stepping in front of him.

The man had brown close-set eyes and a little upturned nose. A heavily waxed mustache extended across his upper lip like a propeller blade.

Seeing her for the first time, he stepped back as if he had received a jolt of electricity. After studying her identity card for several seconds, he looked back up at her and smiled, revealing a row of ferretlike teeth.

"Are you a licensed pathologist, Miss . . . Marantz?" he asked, his eyes dropping to her breasts.

"No, I'm not . . . and it's Lieutenant Marantz."

"Yes, I can see that," he said, his body inching closer to her.

"Elizabeth Marantz," he said, "very pretty name . . . beguiling, in fact."

"Captain Sleeves, it is imperative that I see Lieutenant Dunbar's body," she said. "My orders are to . . ."

"Marantz . . . German, isn't it?" said Captain Sleeves.

He had already moved close enough for her to smell the stale coffee on his breath. Liza decided to humor him for the last time.

"Yes . . . German," she said.

His thick eyebrows rose to meet one another above his eyes like two caterpillars.

"I thought so," he said.

Farther down the corridor, a young man came out through a pair of swinging doors. He was wearing a blood-smeared gray lab coat. Striking a match against the red brick wall, he lit a cigarette.

"German of the Hebrew persuasion?" asked Captain Sleeves.

"Yes, I am Jewish," said Liza. "Now . . ."

"I thought so," he declared again, with the hint of a smirk.

"Are you going to allow me to examine the body of Jocelyn Dunbar, or do I need to see your superior officer?" Liza demanded loudly.

"I am in full command here at the present time," he said, as if holding the beachhead at Dunkirk. "Of course, you can always contact Major Faulks in Supply and Administration."

"Where is he?"

"Haven't the slightest," said Captain Sleeves. "Probably on his rounds of the city facilities."

Liza watched him glance at his wristwatch before his eyes swept over her again.

"If you're trying to keep me occupied while they destroy Lieutenant Dunbar's body, then know this," she said, fiercely. "By allowing it to happen, you may well be compromising the security of Operation Overlord. I assume that even someone like you knows what that means. I am here at the direct command of General Ernest Manigault, the head of Military Security Command for Overlord," she lied. "If I am not allowed to examine Lieutenant Dunbar's body right now, I promise you, Captain Sleeves, that instead of your comfortable little post here in Golders Green you will be spending the next thirty years in a military prison."

The caterpillar eyebrows began oscillating up and down.

"Corporal Moncrief?" he cried out as if calling for reinforcements.

The young man down the corridor dropped his cigarette and stubbed it out with the toe of his boot.

"I'm afraid you're too late, Lieutenant," he said, coming toward them. "She went to the fire. Those were my orders."

"From whom?" she demanded.

"From him," he said, pointing at Sleeves.

The captain was slowly backing up into his office.

"Who ordered you to destroy her body?" demanded Liza.

"I must follow orders, even as you must . . ." he began.

"Who gave you the order?" she demanded.

"Colonel Gaines . . . called to say that Lady Dunbar's family wanted her cremated as soon as possible after the autopsy," he mumbled.

"It's possible she could still be in the holding area over there," said the young corporal. "They've had a lot of business today."

"Where is it?"

"I'll take you," he said.

As she followed him down the corridor, Captain Sleeves retreated back into his office and shut the door.

"What do you do here?" she asked the young man as they rushed together through darkened hospital corridors to the crematorium building. He smelled like human ordure.

"I work in the pathology lab," said the corporal.

"Were you present for Lieutenant Dunbar's autopsy this morning?" she asked.

"I don't know them by name," he said.

"She was young and blonde . . . very pretty."

"I was there," he said, leading her down a set of stairs and out the door into an open courtyard.

"Did you hear any of the doctor's conclusions?"

"I heard the doctor tell Captain Sleeves that she drowned," he said as they headed into the next building.

Victims of the recent Luftwaffe raids filled the hospital rooms and lined the hallways on temporary cots. Many people with less serious injuries simply sat on the floor waiting to be treated. Their collective moaning sounded like an unholy dirge.

"The doctor said that there were air bubbles in her heart and water in her lungs," said Corporal Moncrief as they flew down another corridor and came to the entrance of the crematorium.

"Who keeps the paperwork from the autopsies?" asked Liza.

"Captain Sleeves," he said as they pushed through the door.

The smell of decomposing flesh almost made her gag as he led her through another door into a large, open holding area. Scores of bodies lay scattered across the bloodstained concrete floor. Some lay on rolling gurneys under soiled sheets. Others had simply been dumped on the floor, naked. Many of them were burned black. A number were missing heads and limbs. Liza began removing the sheets from the corpses on the nearest gurneys as the corporal skirted the room, briefly eyeing each body.

Two burly men in leather aprons came through a door off to her left and began transferring bodies onto what looked like a rolling coal car.

"Wait," shouted Liza as they picked up a young female body she hadn't had time to examine.

"I found her," shouted Corporal Moncrief from across the room.

He was standing by a gurney next to the door that led into the coal-fired incinerator. As she watched, he covered Joss's naked body with a sheet and began wheeling the gurney toward her.

"We'll bring her back to the lab," said Liza, following him out of the holding area.

When they returned to the pathology suite in the basement of the hospital wing, Captain Sleeves was waiting for them.

"That will be all," he said, summarily dismissing Corporal Moncrief. Turning to Liza, he said, "I will allow you fifteen minutes to examine the body."

From his renewed bravado, it was obvious to Liza that he had been in contact with Colonel Gaines again. Clutching the pathology notes from the autopsy, he sat down at a metal desk in the corner.

As she prepared to remove the sheet covering Joss's body, Liza felt a familiar surge of pure adrenaline, just like when she was about to run a race back at Great Neck High School. This was what she had been trained to do, to use her forensic talents to help find out the truth surrounding a young woman's death.

Joss was lying on her back, the thick blond hair covering most of her face. When Liza finished pulling away the sheet, it was all she could do not to recoil in shock. "Oh God," she said softly as her eyes took in the condition of the young woman's body. Liza had watched or participated in more than a hundred autopsies, almost all of them with experienced pathologists, but she had never seen a cadaver so violated in a routine set of autopsy procedures. Considering that Joss had suffered no traumatic injuries except to her left wrist, it seemed almost nightmarish, more like the work of a butcher than a doctor, and she wondered whether it might have been purposely done to prevent her from discovering the true circumstances surrounding her death.

"Who conducted this autopsy?" she asked.

"Not one of our regular chaps. Didn't know him," said Sleeves.

"Was he a doctor?"

"No idea, I'm afraid. He came in with the corpse."

Seeing the anger in her eyes, he added, "We're a bit overworked here, as you can imagine."

"I would like to see his pathology notes," she declared.

"I'm not authorized to give them to you," he replied. "Colonel Gaines said that if you want a copy of the autopsy report it must be officially requested through him."

For a moment she considered the idea of snatching the notes out of his fat fingers, but managed to suppress her anger. Whoever had performed the autopsy had incised the back of Joss's head at the nape of the neck, and then pulled Joss's scalp forward over the skull, covering her eyes. Instead of cleanly sawing off the top of her skull, he had apparently used some kind of chisel to cleave it open in order to expose the brain. The brain cavity was empty.

"Where is her brain?" demanded Liza. "I would like to check it for trauma and hemorrhaging."

"I'm afraid . . ."

"Afraid of what?" she demanded when several seconds passed in silence.

"It was sent to the crematorium in the viscera bag, I believe."

"I see," she said. "Are there any references to its condition in the pathologist's notes?"

"Let me check," said Sleeves, scanning the two hand-scrawled pages.

A sixteen-gauge needle was protruding from Joss's neck above the tracheal tube. Lower down, the pathologist had made a broad lateral chest incision, hacking through her rib cage with what appeared to be the same crude instruments.

"No references to the brain at all," said Sleeves, getting up from the desk and starting to come toward her. "It concludes that the cause of death was drowning, either by accident or at Lieutenant Dunbar's own hands."

Joss's heart had been removed, along with the lungs. Her stomach lining had been peeled back to remove the stomach. The liver was also missing.

"Where are the rest of her organs?" she angrily demanded.

"The organs?"

"Her heart, the lungs, the liver, her vital organs. If drowning was the probable cause, I need to examine the pericardial sac."

"They must have gone over in the viscera bag with her brain," he said, now standing beside her. "Sorry about that. Who could have known?"

"What did they find in her stomach?" she said, beyond outrage.

He looked down at the notes.

"Some sort of brownish fluid, it says here. Apparently, she hadn't eaten in at least six hours."

He was standing uncomfortably close to her again.

"I need room to work," she said, glaring at him with unmasked hostility.

"That kind of tone won't get you anywhere," he said, his voice taking on a husky quality as he stepped back a few inches.

Liza began a systematic examination of what was left of her body. Using a small penlight and her own magnifying glass, she began carefully to scan every inch of the girl's skin, slowly working her way from the face, mouth, and neck down the arms and shoulders to her hands.

If Joss had been murdered, there were no indications that she had tried to defend herself, concluded Liza. Aside from the slashing wounds in her left wrist, there were no contusions or abrasions on her hands or arms to suggest that she had tried to fight for her life.

Liza carefully examined the three parallel slits in her wrist. Two of them were very shallow, as if Joss had only been half serious at her purpose, perhaps just testing the whole idea, or performing a charade for whoever had been with her. The third one, almost certainly the last, had been sliced deep with great force. In the process, the razor actually grooved the wrist bone, which lay exposed in the overhead light.

She briefly considered whether Joss would have had the strength to slash herself after consuming both alcohol and barbiturates. She looked forward to receiving the blood analysis from the SHAEF hospital, knowing that Colonel Gaines or his people could not have tampered with those results.

Almost unconsciously, she found herself silently reciting the words of the Kaddish in memory of her young co-worker. Somehow, the phrases she had learned so long ago from her father gave her a small measure of comfort. At one point, she happened to glance up at Sleeves, who remained standing behind her. A look of almost indecent revelry animated his flushed face, and Liza was repulsed by the thought that he might actually be sexually stimulated by her violated body.

"Stand back," she shouted, jostling him away from Joss's body. As if he had been caught by his mother in an indecent act, the officer's face flushed with embarrassment before he returned to the desk and sat down.

Joss's pubic area had been carefully shaved, probably no more than a day or two before her death. Why would she have done it? Liza wondered, before considering the possibility that someone else might have shaved her, perhaps with her consent.

As Taggart had pointed out to her after his meeting with General Manigault, her undeveloped breasts, tiny feet, narrow hips, and lack of muscular tone left the indelible image of nothing so much as a beautiful young altar boy.

"Maybe Admiral Jellico enjoyed buggering boys at sea," Taggart had said to her cynically. "Maybe she was a throwback to his glorious youth."

Liza put her arm behind Joss's neck and gently turned her over on her back. A deep lateral incision had been made between the shoulder blades. It was connected to another that ran down to the pelvic bone.

Liza found almost immediate signs of intercourse in the form of swollen tissue around the vagina as well as the anal ring and a distension of the sphincter muscle. She took double swab samples of both passages before concluding a meticulous inspection of Joss's lower extremities.

Liza concluded her examination with the certain knowledge that whoever had conducted the autopsy had effectively obliterated any chance for her to confirm the cause of death. Perhaps the blood tests would reveal some answers. In the meantime, she wanted to make sure that the body was not destroyed.

She covered Joss with the sheet, then placed the swab samples in a specimen jar and put them in her handbag before walking over to Captain Sleeves.

"As soon as I get back to headquarters," she said, "I will have Major Taggart issue immediate orders to transfer this body to the morgue at the SHAEF hospital on Curzon Street. Lieutenant Dunbar better be here when they come to transport her."

Seeing the smoldering menace in her eyes, he just nodded in agreement.

CHAPTER 8

At five o'clock that evening, Liza met Sam Taggart at the SHAEF hospital to learn the results of Joss's blood workup. They were informed at the desk that the testing protocol had been given to a Dr. Cabot, who was still on duty.

Inside the basement laboratory, they found a stocky, boyish-looking man wearing a long-billed fishing cap over his army fatigues. Sitting in an armchair with his feet on the desk, he was surrounded by three young English nurses in starched white uniforms.

"Call me George," he said with a brash grin. "I've just arrived from Philadelphia, girls, and I definitely need some help to find my way around the city."

"I'll help you," growled Taggart, coming up behind him as the nurses hurried off.

Momentarily crestfallen, Dr. Cabot glanced up at the two of them before quickly focusing on Liza. He removed his feet from the desk, stood up, and gave Taggart a casual salute.

"We need the results of the Dunbar blood tests," said Sam Taggart without bothering to return it. "We're in a hurry."

"Sure," said the young doctor, blowing a perfect bubble through the wad of chewing gum in his mouth. Leaning over his desk, he quickly riffled through a disordered pile of folders, removed one from the stack, and handed it to Taggart, then popped the bubble, revealing perfectly formed white teeth.

"Are you a pathologist, by any chance?" asked Taggart, scanning the file.

"Uh . . . no," he replied, grinning at Liza.

"What is your field?"

"Um . . . reconstructive surgery," he said.

"What do you reconstruct?" demanded Taggart.

"My practice was largely cosmetic," said Dr. Cabot. "Female anatomy, mostly."

"I just wanted to make sure you knew how to test a blood sample," said Taggart.

"No problem . . . This person is dead, right?" he said, chewing his gum.

"Why do you ask?" said Taggart.

"Because whoever she was had enough yellow jackets in her system to kill a rhinoceros," he said.

"Yellow jackets?" asked Taggart.

"Phenobarbital," said Liza. "Sleeping pills."

"How long could she have lived with that concentration of drugs in her bloodstream?"

"She was probably already unconscious when she died . . . definitely close to it," said Cabot. "It wouldn't have taken more than another hour or two for her to lapse into a coma. She also had a blood-alcohol level of point two four. Not a fun date."

"Anything else?" asked Taggart. "Did you screen for anything else?"

Cabot's eyes were still on Liza's. As if hoping to impress her, he blew out another two-inch bubble and snapped it back in his mouth.

"Everything else looked normal," he said. "I assume you knew she was pregnant."

The image of Joss's fainting spell in the bathroom played back in Liza's brain. This was the confirmation of what she had then deduced.

"Yeah . . . thanks," said Taggart, turning to go.

"You interested in dinner, Lieutenant?" asked Dr. Cabot, taking off the long-billed fishing cap to uncover an amazing thatch of carrot-red hair. "I'm about to go off duty."

"No thank you," said Liza, although she was ravenously hungry.

Back outside, night had fallen and it was pouring rain again.

"Let's eat," said Taggart, trying to hail a taxi. "We need to talk."

After standing in the cold downpour for several minutes, Taggart gave up trying to get a taxi and started down the sidewalk with Liza in tow. Without a reservation, they were turned away from the first three restaurants they entered, each of them already packed with Americans. There were even lines of people on the sidewalks waiting outside the pubs. They ended up walking four more blocks to Taggart's apartment on Jermyn Street.

It was at the top of a set of sagging stairs above a saddlery shop. A hand-tooled English saddle sat in the store window, along with two stuffed foxes and a female mannequin dressed in tan riding breeches and a scarlet jacket.

The apartment consisted of a parlor, two bedrooms, and a small kitchen. Taggart lit a coal fire in the parlor, and Liza warmed her hands in front of it while he disappeared into one of the bedrooms. She glanced at the few pieces of simple furniture and two overstuffed chairs. An old Empire couch rested under the bay window.

Sam returned a few moments later with a large towel.

"Well, this is cozy," she said, drying her hair while standing at the bay window. People were scurrying up and down the sidewalks, heads bent against the driving rain. "How do you rate an apartment?"

"By getting bombed out of the two billets where I was living. I share this with a navy commander who does Atlantic convoy routing," said Taggart, hanging their trench coats to dry on two hooks near the coal fire. "We both work odd hours."

He led her back to the kitchen, bending down in front of an oak icebox to check its contents.

"Tea or coffee—that's all there is to drink," he said, apologetically.

"Tea," she said.

He lit the stove and put water on to boil.

"Are you hungry?" he asked.

"I would eat my mother's pickled herring at this point," she said.

"How does poor man's Stroganoff sound?" he asked, removing several articles from the icebox.

"Good," she said. "Whatever that is."

"It will be done in fifteen minutes."

He lit the burners on the small gas stove with a kitchen match. After putting a tea kettle on one of the burners, he dropped a large dollop of butter into a skillet pan. Waiting for the tea water to boil, Liza sat down at the kitchen table and watched him unwrap a pound of ground beef from a roll of brown butcher paper. He placed it in the melted butter, over low heat.

"It's a good thing we're not on the civilian rationing plan over here," he said, with a taut grin. "This would be our entire meat allotment for the week."

After sprinkling the meat with salt, dried basil, paprika, and ground pepper, he expertly peeled and chopped two small onions on the black stone countertop.

"Are you sure you found your right calling?" she asked.

"Yeah, but I've always loved to cook, too. My mother was Italian," he said, pulling three cloves of garlic from a string above the sink, and mincing them with practiced virtuosity.

He started the onions and garlic in another saucepan with some more butter and dried parsley. After pausing to light a cigarette, he threw a small handful of tea leaves into a clay teapot and poured in boiling water. Then he took a packet of GI coffee grounds, dropped them in a separate pot, and added the remainder of the hot water. It was wonderfully warm in the little kitchen, and Liza felt herself beginning to relax for the first time that day. Closing her eyes for a moment, she savored the delicious aroma of the sautéing onions.

"Why would Lieutenant Dunbar have been carrying condoms if she was already pregnant?" he asked, offering her sugar and cream.

Stirred out of her reverie, Liza said, "I don't know. It makes no sense."

"Murder cases rarely make any sense until they're over and the murderer is caught," said Taggart. "Then they always make sense, no matter how many mistakes are made in the investigation along the way."

Liza thought back to the obvious signs of both vaginal and anal intercourse she had witnessed under the magnifying glass on Joss's body. "She may have used condoms with certain partners and not with others," she said.

Using a wooden spoon, Taggart stirred the contents of the two saucepans and said, "It could have been her regular practice to use condoms with the man she was meeting at the pool. Maybe she didn't want to change her routine for him."

He picked up a small bowl full of raw mushrooms from the window ledge.

"That would be logical," she said, "particularly if it was someone like Admiral Jellico. I think he is the type who would notice any change in routine."

"Tell me what you discovered during the autopsy," he said, breaking up the clumps of mushrooms with his fingers and adding them to the onions and garlic.

Liza spent ten minutes describing everything that had occurred at Golders Green, including the butchering of Joss's cadaver and the very limited physical data she had been able to gather without the benefit of the vital organs. "It would help if we knew Admiral Jellico's sexual proclivities," she said, "although I heard him tell you he has a daughter older than Joss."

"So what," said Taggart. "I once had a murder case where the father of six girls murdered his homosexual partner and then cut off the man's testicles."

"When is dinner going to be ready?" said Liza, with a note of sarcasm.

"Sorry," said Taggart, stirring the browning meat. "Do you think she was intimate with a lot of men?"

"I'm not sure," said Liza.

"At this point we know she was involved with her boss," he said. "And, according to you, she might have been in love with the man who made her pregnant. We can assume that wasn't Jellico. And you also said that an American general was asking about her and J.P."

"General Kilgore."

Taggart remembered Kilgore well. The general had been a dinner guest at one of Manigault's parties. He had been bragging about his friendship with General Patton and complaining that "Georgie" had been given a raw deal after the slapping incident in Sicily.

"We'll have to talk to him, too," said Taggart.

The room filled with the fragrance of the browning sauce.

"I have to cheat a little here," said Taggart as he opened a can of peeled tomatoes and slowly stirred them into the onions, mushrooms, and garlic.

"So, with what little you have to go on . . . how do you think she died?" he asked.

In her mind's eye, Liza tried to reconstruct everything she had observed, both at the death scene and after examining the body.

"Joss almost certainly drowned," said Liza. "But that begs the question of why she would have employed three different methods to kill herself when any one of them would have succeeded. Based on the blood results, she would have died from the phenobarbital overdose . . . and by then she would have already bled to death from the wrist wound."

"She didn't kill herself," said Taggart.

"I agree," said Liza. "You should have seen her face when she first realized she was going to have a child. This was a young woman who wanted to live. She was crazy about someone, and I believe it was the man she was convinced was the baby's father. He was almost certainly the one who gave her the gold locket she wore around her neck."

"Maybe his picture was inside," said Taggart. "His face could also have been removed from that torn photograph we found in her wallet."

Liza nodded. "The lover and the murderer could well be the same person."

"There is always the chance that the man she loved didn't want the baby . . . or even her anymore," offered Taggart. "It could have been a duet."

"A duet? What do you mean?"

"Maybe she started down the suicide trail for leverage, threatening to take the pills unless he married her. Perhaps she never meant to finish it that way. Lieutenant Dunbar was already drunk. Maybe she expected him to stop her. And then he didn't. Maybe he just laughed at her. So she went and got the razor. And that didn't work either. And then he might have just helped."

"What kind of man would do something like that?"

"Are you kidding? We're at war with millions of them right now, although the predators are not limited to Germany and Japan," he said. "Think of something closer to a more elemental form of life—a crab, maybe."

"A man with the moral convictions of a crab?"

"You asked me," he said.

"That's awfully hard to believe," said Liza.

"Yeah, well, something tells me that whoever did this might have done it before," he said. "Or tried to . . . You know . . . the monster child who starts out removing the wings on a fly, moves up to a sparrow, and then on to gouging out the eyes of a kitten with a penknife. Of course, the good ones don't usually provide indicators. On the outside, they are all sunny smiles and a perfect disposition. Those are the hardest to catch."

He held up a pint of sour cream.

"This is the secret," he said, slowly adding half of it to the sauce.

"There could be something else going on here," said Liza, as Taggart added the sauce to the well-browned meat. "Someone broke into Joss's desk early this morning, and Charlie Wainwright's, too."

"What does he do?" asked Taggart. "Wainwright, I mean."

"I'm not sure, exactly."

"I'll check him out," he said, stirring the aromatic mixture, while Liza laid out his meager inventory of plates and utensils.

"You only need a spoon," he growled as she looked for knives and forks.

"What if the murderer found out something from her that had nothing to do with the two of them?" she asked. "What if it was something involved with Overlord?"

"That's what we have to find out," said Sam, cutting several thick slices of dark, crusty bread from a loaf on the window ledge, and carrying the skillet over to the table.

"So what's next?" she asked.

"Even if Gaines and his people have already gone over it, I want to make a careful search of Lieutenant Dunbar's apartment," said Taggart. "He doesn't impress me as particularly thorough."

After carefully ladling a large portion of the Stroganoff onto her plate, he watched Liza intently as she took her first spoonful.

"How is it?" asked Taggart, as if the fate of the war hung on her answer.

She smiled and said, "It's the best meal I've had since arriving in London."

"Where have you been eating?" he asked, and she laughed.

They both made short work of the simple supper. As Liza dipped the last of her bread into the gravy, Sam said, "So your father is a holy man."

"A holy man?"

"A rabbi."

She chuckled.

"Not really. Not a holy man in the sense of a Catholic priest. A rabbi has no special privileges, no rank or holiness. When it comes to God, he is simply a scholar in the law . . . the Jewish law."

"Well, I've seen plenty of rabbis marching in the Saint Patrick's Day parade," said Taggart.

"Yes. Well, there are community obligations for any religious leaders," said Liza.

In her mind's eye, she could see the image of her father in his study at home, poring over his well-thumbed copy of Caro's *Shulchan Arukh*. He was so very different from other rabbis she had met growing up, men with egos worthy of Moses who were convinced that they stood at the right hand of God. Her father was just the opposite—thin, rumpled, and bookish. With his metal-rimmed spectacles and tangled gray hair, he looked exactly like the scholar he was.

"My father is more of a teacher . . . an interpreter of the most complex questions and traditions of Jewish law."

"Traditions of faith?"

"No," she said. "Not of faith in the sense of Christianity. Jews don't believe that this life leads anywhere. Essentially, they believe that virtue is its own reward."

"What about heaven?" he asked.

"There is no heaven or hell. Every Jew is made to feel responsible for his own actions and life decisions. He has only one chance to make a difference, and that is here on earth in his or her own lifetime," she said.

"So what happens when you die? Nothing?"

"If you're a believer, then your spirit lives on through your children, or in the legacy of what you have accomplished, or in the fact that people remember you and what kind of person you were."

"I prefer eternal paradise," said Taggart.

She smiled and said, "Well, I hope you get there, Major."

"Sam," he said.

"Sam," she repeated, sipping another cup of tea.

"I gather you separate yourself from your father's religion," he said.

"Well, let's just say I don't practice it," she said.

"Why not?" asked Taggart, lighting another cigarette.

"I guess I question things too much. Mostly, I question the existence of an all-seeing, benevolent God. How could a just God stand by while someone like Hitler unleashes the greatest suffering in the history of the world?" she asked.

"Yeah . . . and, according to the Jewish religion, Hitler faces no penalty beyond the grave, right?" asked Taggart.

"Aside from the belief that evil diminishes the evildoer, no," she said softly.

"So what do you think?" asked Taggart.

"I hope he burns in hell," said Liza.

CHAPTER 9

The rain had finally stopped shortly before dawn. Standing in the darkness, Taggart pulled the scrap of notepaper out of his trench-coat pocket and rechecked the address. It matched the elegant brick apartment house across the street, in the center of Belgravia's Hamilton Row. An apartment in the building was far beyond the means of a Wren lieutenant, but well within the family expectations of Lady Jocelyn Dunbar.

Liza had learned from a co-worker that Joss lived on the top floor. Taggart glanced up at the apartment. The windows were dark and the blackout curtains weren't drawn. He decided to try the building's front entrance first. It was always possible that Colonel Gaines had not yet sent a team to search the apartment.

When he walked across the street, an old man in a royal-blue porter's jacket was standing in the darkness in front of the vestibule, smoking a cigarette. Taggart flashed his identity card and said, "Military Security Command . . . I'm here to check Lady Dunbar's apartment."

The old man dropped his cigarette stub and crushed it with a scuffed boot. When Taggart offered him another one from his open pack of Luckies, his wrinkled face lit up in pleasure.

"The Metropolitan Police have come and gone already," he said, tucking it behind his left ear. "They left a bloody lock on her flat that belongs in the Tower of London."

"Glad to hear it," said Taggart. "Well, good night, then."

Taggart sauntered back down the sidewalk. When he turned again, the porter was disappearing inside the dark vestibule. He waited in the shadows to make sure the street was empty before slipping down the narrow, brick-lined alley that separated Joss Dunbar's apartment house from its stately neighbor.

It was pitch-black in the narrow passageway. He could smell bread baking in one of the buildings. Removing his flashlight, he pointed it ahead of him on the cobblestone path until he turned the corner and came to the rear entrance.

Three overflowing garbage containers stood along the wall next to it. As he stepped toward the door, an orange cat leapt from inside of one of the receptacles, tipping it over with a noisy crash. Taggart switched off the flashlight and stood silently in the darkness, waiting to see if someone came to investigate. Except for a bus chugging by on the next street, he could hear no sound of movement.

Taggart turned the flashlight back on and focused it on the small glass panel in the rear entrance door. It was secured from the inside by a stout metal bar. Continuing along the rear wall, he came to an iron fire-escape ladder bolted to the façade in the far corner. The lowest rung was only four feet above the cobblestones. In New York, it would have been an invitation to plunder. Londoners were a more trusting people, he concluded, at least until the Americans had arrived.

He began to climb up into the darkness. At the second floor, a wood-sash window revealed itself in the darkness less than a foot away from the ladder. Looking up, he saw that there was an identically spaced window on each of the next two floors.

The smell of baking bread grew stronger as he passed an open window on the third floor. Reaching the underside of the slate roof, he switched on the flashlight just long enough to see that Joss Dunbar's window was securely locked. He pulled out his pocketknife, inserted the blade between the two sashes, and tried to force open the fastener. It refused to budge.

He waited in the darkness for the sound of several vehicles passing by in the next street before using the butt of the knife to smash the small windowpane above the fastener. When he had unlocked it, he carefully removed the broken shards of glass and put them in his coat pocket. Then, raising the bottom sash, he went through the dark opening headfirst.

He found himself in the kitchen. As he knelt on the floor, Taggart could hear the regular tap-tap-tap of water as it dripped into the kitchen sink. An upright refrigerator hummed against the far wall. In the murky darkness, he could make out a door at the other end of the room.

After closing the kitchen blackout curtain, he switched on his flashlight again and went to the door, slowly turned the knob, and swung it open. The narrow beam revealed the edge of a thick Persian rug, then the arm of an elegant sofa and a matching side chair.

Taggart thought he smelled licorice. A moment later, the cone of someone else's flashlight pinned him in its beam, and he heard a low, guttural laugh.

"I've been sitting here salivating over the smell of that baking bread for almost an hour," came the voice of Inspector Drummond from a comfortable armchair in the corner. "In another five minutes, I was going to head home for breakfast."

"Sorry to take so long," said Taggart. "Who were you expecting?"

"A murderer, perhaps."

"Well, that's progress," said Taggart. "Scotland Yard actually believes a murder might have taken place. If I'd known that, I would have just asked for the key."

"I assume you've come to search the flat," said Drummond, sucking on his licorice.

"Yeah . . . before Gaines destroyed all the evidence that exists in the case."

"You don't have to roast that chestnut anymore. He now agrees there was foul play."

"With your help, I assume."

The old man nodded and said, "If there is a murderer preying on young women in this city, he just doesn't want it to be a member of the royal family."

"No one is off limits to me," said Taggart.

"I told him that you were the hard-boiled type," said Drummond. "Now, why don't you close the rest of those blackout curtains so I can turn on the lights and we can go through the flat together—that is, unless you would like me to just sit here and watch the great American detective at work."

When Taggart drew the curtains in the living room, Drummond switched on the floor lamp sitting next to his chair.

"Where would you normally begin?" asked Taggart.

"When the victim is a woman, I always start in the kitchen," said Drummond, struggling to climb out of the chair. "So many good hiding places . . . sugar, cornstarch, flour, and so forth. Perhaps I'll write a monograph about it someday."

"Yeah, well, send me a copy," said Taggart, heading into the bathroom.

"Why the loo?" asked Drummond.

"For a young woman, it's the place of intrigue," said Taggart, surveying the interior. The window above the claw-footed enamel tub was covered with a fitted piece of painted wood instead of a blackout curtain. A small clothes hamper stood next to a large painted washstand. There was a medicine chest behind the mirror over the sink.

"For me, it's the most useful indicator of how she lived, the extent of her personal needs, what medications she was taking . . . the place where she created a new personality each morning in front of the mirror . . . all the idiosyncrasies."

"Fascinating," said Drummond with a hint of sarcasm.

Taggart removed the top of the toilet tank and peered inside. There was nothing in it but brackish water. He searched the back of the tank in case something might have been taped to the polished enamel surface. There was nothing there either. The bathtub was immaculate, with no hair strands, soap residue, or any other evidence of recent use.

Taggart went through the drawers of the painted washstand. They held towels, washcloths, toilet paper, soap, and a powdered cleaning product. After turning each object over, he waited for Drummond to step aside so he could search the sink area and the medicine chest.

"You're big—even for an American," said Drummond, leaning away from him.

The cavity under the sink yielded nothing, and the contents of the medicine chest seemed to put the final lie to Taggart's thesis. A new razor sat on the top shelf. It was still in its original packing container. Aside from a single tube of lipstick, there was no makeup of any kind on the three glass shelves. The only medication was a small paper roll of a popular stomach antacid.

"So what would you conclude about Lady Dunbar's little idiosyncrasies here in her secret lair, Mr. Hammett?" asked Drummond smugly.

"Obviously, she didn't spend a lot of time here," said Taggart testily. "Why don't you show me the kitchen, Bulldog?"

In the kitchen, Drummond turned on the overhead light. The small enamel sink was as immaculate as the bathtub. The refrigerator and ice chest held nothing but an empty ice-cube tray.

He watched Drummond go down on his knees with the flashlight to examine the base storage cupboards on either side of the sink. In one of them, he found a water glass and a broken china cup. From another, he pulled out a dusty mixing bowl and two settings of sterling-silver flatware. Only an empty wastebasket occupied the space directly under the sink.

"Maybe she hid everything in the cornstarch," said Taggart.

"Ahhh," replied Drummond, opening one of the cupboards above the counter.

A jar of raspberry jam sat on the bottom shelf, next to metal canisters of tea, salt, and baking soda. Two paper sacks appeared to contain sugar and flour. On the top shelf, an intricate spider's web connected two bottles of Napoleon brandy. One bottle was unopened, the other half full.

Drummond removed a folded newspaper from his side pocket and spread it out on the counter. Then he picked up the flour sack, poured the contents onto the newspaper, and began sifting through them with his fountain pen. Finding nothing but flour, he refolded the newspaper and carefully emptied the powder back into its sack. He checked the contents of the other containers with the same result.

"So much for the kitchen," he said, wearily.

Together, they headed into the apartment's sole bedroom. The canopied double bed was crowned by a carved walnut frame, which was bordered with crocheted lace. They stripped the bed, lifting the mattress to examine its lining as well as the box spring underneath it.

The Chippendale chest of drawers next to the bed held sensible cotton undergarments, socks, and handkerchiefs. After examining every article, Drummond removed each drawer and turned it over, just as Taggart had done in the bathroom.

"Odd—she has no jewelry," said Drummond.

"Either she didn't like the stuff, or else she didn't keep it here," said Taggart, without mentioning Joss Dunbar's missing locket.

The last place in the bedroom to be searched was the large walk-in closet. An assortment of fine women's clothing hung from one of the two closet poles, dresses and ensembles for every season. On the other side of the closet, three large full-length garment bags hung from the second pole. The shoe rack underneath the bags held women's dress shoes. Most of them looked new.

"Formal gowns . . . the kinds of things she would have worn to Buckingham Palace," said Drummond as he went through the first garment bag. "Also prewar, from the look of them."

While Drummond continued searching each garment, Taggart ran his flashlight over every inch of the walls, and flooring in the closet and bedroom, just as he had in the other rooms they had searched. Ten minutes later, Drummond came out of the closet, shaking his head in frustration.

"Nothing," he muttered.

Back in the living room, they spent another thirty minutes examining the furniture, rugs, walls, and flooring. Wheezing from exertion, Drummond dropped into one of the easy chairs as Taggart went into the kitchen and retrieved the open bottle of brandy and a water glass. He poured a generous helping of brandy into it and offered the glass to Drummond.

"You're not drinking, Major?" asked the Englishman before taking his first swallow.

"There was only one glass," said Taggart with a taut grin.

"Reformed?" asked Drummond knowingly.

Taggart nodded. "I wish I could stay that way," he said. "My wife died last year."

"Always something, isn't it," said Drummond. "Well, I'm afraid you're right about this place, Major. Apparently, she spent very little time here."

"Then the obvious question is this," said Taggart. "Where did she spend her time when she wasn't on duty?"

"I'll make some inquiries," said Drummond. "We'll interview her co-workers on Admiral Jellico's staff. Perhaps one of them knew."

Taggart walked over to the built-in bookshelf in the corner of the living room. Above the shelves, a large map of the world was fastened to the wall. There were multicolored pushpins all over it, each set denoting the relative positions of Allied and Axis forces in the many fighting theaters. Since the beginning of the war, he had seen similar maps in parlors and living rooms all over New York. In looking at the force dispositions, Taggart concluded that the pins had not been updated for at least a year.

The bookshelf under the map consisted of four shelves, each holding about a dozen volumes. Taggart scanned the titles on the top shelf. They were all war poets, including Wilfred Owen, Dorian Saint George Bond, and Vincent Mai. Taggart picked up the first one, by Rupert Brooke, and began thumbing through it.

"So how did you convince Colonel Gaines that Joss Dunbar was murdered?" he asked, putting back the book and picking up the next volume.

Drummond let out a wheezy sigh.

"He already suspected it," he said, taking another swallow of brandy.

"Then why did he put us through that charade at the swimming pool?"

"Have you ever heard of the Duke of Clarence?" asked Drummond.

"Is he related to the Duke of Wayne?"

Drummond shook his head, wearily.

"Another attempt at Yank humor, I expect," he said.

"Yeah."

"Well, the Duke of Clarence was actually Prince Albert Victor, the grandson of Queen Victoria. His father was King Edward the Seventh. They called the boy Prince Eddy."

"So the kid had a lot of names—very impressive," said Taggart, thumbing through the next book of poems. "So what?"

"So Prince Eddy was a principal suspect in our infamous ripper murders," said Drummond.

Taggart stopped and stared at him. "Jack the Ripper?"

"The same."

"Was there any proof?" asked Taggart.

"Rumors of there being some," said Drummond, finishing his first glass of brandy and then pouring another measure. "If there ever was any, it was destroyed forty years ago. A predecessor of mine at the Yard once told me that he had seen papers written by Sir William Gull that claimed Prince Eddy was suffering from syphilis."

"Who was Gull?" asked Taggart.

"The royal-family physician," said Drummond. "According to his papers, Prince Eddy contracted the infection while carousing with a coterie of local whores aboard his yacht in the West Indies. When he finally learnt what he had contracted, his rage and dementia supposedly led him to commit the ripper murders. Later on, Sir William allegedly informed the king that Eddy was not only dying of syphilis but had admitted to being the ripper. Eddy was then taken away to a private sanitarium, where he was locked up until he died."

"Do you believe it?" asked Taggart, moving on to the books on the next shelf.

"I wouldn't disbelieve it."

"What has that got to do with Colonel Gaines? And why would he try to cover up the murder of Jocelyn Dunbar? Isn't she a member of the royal family?"

"I should think it would be obvious to you, Major Taggart: to protect another member of the royal family . . . perhaps more highly placed," Drummond came right back.

"What about the other murders of young women here in London recently?" asked Taggart.

"We know of at least three."

"Who were the victims?"

"All young women, single and attractive, but there was no other common thread between them. One was a shop girl, another just arrived from the country, the third a student nurse."

"How were they killed?"

"They were all criminally assaulted. Two were strangled. The latest one was killed with a stab wound to the chest."

"I doubt they're connected to Joss Dunbar," said Taggart.

"I agree with you," said Drummond. "With so many foreign troops stationed in and around the city, these types of crimes are inevitable."

"So what is your theory?" asked Taggart, picking up still another volume.

"I think Lady Dunbar was killed by someone who thought she could incriminate him in something," said Drummond.

"Something?" repeated Taggart.

"That's your department, isn't it?"

Taggart was about to respond when his thumb suddenly found an extra space between two of the pages. Looking down at it, he saw a piece of cream-colored stationery folded into the bookbinding. Using his handkerchief, he nudged the paper from its resting place and carefully unfolded it. The handwriting at the top looked as if it had been written in rusty brown ink.

"'My God, you shall pay for this,'" Taggart read aloud. "'I'll wring that obstinate little heart.'" It was signed, "Noel."

Another passage was written below the first. Although it was also written in brown ink, the handwriting was definitely different. The letters were so small that Taggart couldn't read them in the shadowy light. Holding the edge of the page with his handkerchief, he carried it over to the lamp next to Drummond's chair.

"'9 August,'" he continued reading aloud. "'I asked you not to send blood but Yet do—because if it means love I will have it. I cut the hair too close & bled much more than you need—I pray that you put not the knife blade near where quei capelli grow.'"

In one of the fold lines, Taggart noticed what appeared to be sandy-colored hair cuttings. He pointed them out to Drummond, who put on his spectacles and took the page from him, still using the handkerchief to grasp it.

"What book did you find it in?" he asked, holding the page up to the light.

Taggart brought the book over from the shelf.

"Prometheus Unbound," he said, reading the title before starting carefully to leaf through the rest of the pages.

"Percy Shelley," replied Drummond as he inspected the stationery under the lamp. "These are definitely hair clippings."

Taggart opened the book to the flyleaf, and began going through it page by page, searching for any handwritten inscriptions.

"This isn't brown ink. I believe that both these notes were written in blood," said Drummond.

Taggart put down the book. "That notepaper could have been inside the book for years," he said. "The words sound like they were written a hundred years ago. Hell, the book may not even have been hers."

"I would assume it was," said Drummond, rubbing his eyes.

"Yeah," agreed Taggart. "We need to find out if she was ever close to someone named Noel."

"Leave it to me," said Drummond.

"After your lab boys examine it, I want Lieutenant Marantz to have a look at this, too."

"The Jewish lass?" said Drummond.

"Yeah. You have a problem with her?"

"Only that I wish I was forty years younger and single," he came back with a tired smile.

CHAPTER 10

Liza's office at SHAEF was still locked and sealed when she returned in the morning, accompanied by a crime-scene technician from the SHAEF military-police detachment. He was a fingerprint specialist, and Liza had him start with Joss's desk.

After he had unpacked his leather kit bag and begun to dust, she carefully examined the broken lock on the right bank of drawers, where Joss kept all her confidential documents.

The top two drawers, which were usually crammed with hand-inscribed notes from Admiral Jellico, now stood empty. So was the drawer in which Liza knew that Joss kept her address book and personal items. Based on the tapered gouges around the keyed lock, she concluded that it had been forced open with a screwdriver or small pry bar. The same gouges surrounded the broken lock on Charlie's desk. For some reason, the thief had not tampered with the lock on J.P.'s desk or her own. The lock bars on the file cabinets were also untouched.

As Liza was completing a search of her own confidential papers, J.P. arrived. Without a greeting, she went straight to her desk, turned on the snake lamp, and pointed it directly toward herself. She wasn't wearing makeup, and in the harsh light of the naked bulb her face looked haggard. Opening her handbag, she took out her hand mirror and an array of small cosmetic cases.

"Please don't touch anything on the desk until the crime technician is finished over there," said Liza.

"Sure," said J.P., glancing over at her with a surprised look before beginning to apply foundation to her cheeks.

Liza wrote out a requisition order for Joss's service record from the records unit, and called for a courier to run it upstairs to the file clerk's office. She happened to glance up at one point, and found J.P. gazing at her with new curiosity.

"Are you a cop?" she asked, moistening the tip of an eyebrow pencil with her tongue.

"Something like that," replied Liza. "Do you know yet whether anything is missing from your desk?"

"There isn't," said J.P. "I checked yesterday, when I saw that they had broken into Charlie's desk, too."

Her wording struck Liza as odd.

"Why did you say 'they'?" she asked.

"I have no idea," said J.P., darkening her eyebrows in contrast to her bleached blond hair. She stopped when she realized that Liza was still staring at her. "Really, I don't."

The crime technician was taking prints off every surface on which he found them, pausing only to photograph the two broken locks.

"Are your fingerprints on file upstairs?" asked Liza.

"Ummm . . . I'm not sure," said J.P.

"Well, we need to have a set of yours, mine, and Charlie's, to screen them out from any others the technician might find."

"Fine," she said.

"I also need to ask you some questions about Joss," said Liza.

J.P.'s hand stopped in midair, a powder puff poised an inch from her chin.

"I really didn't know her . . . outside the office," she said.

"That's all right," said Liza. "One never knows what might be helpful. We need to find out everything we can—people who came to visit her, things like that."

"I really don't know anything," said J.P. "She was a very quiet girl, as you know. We never went out to lunch or anything."

Liza grabbed a steno pad and pencil from her desk and sat down in the chair next to J.P.'s desk.

"How long have you worked here?" she began with a reassuring smile.

"Umm . . . three months, I guess," J.P. said nervously.

Within a few minutes, Liza knew that she was either badly frightened or hiding something. Her manner became uncooperative to the point of hostility, and her answers to the most innocuous questions were needlessly evasive. Liza wondered whether it might have something to do with her relationship with General Kilgore.

"I don't know if I should be talking like this," said J.P. finally, standing up from her chair.

"I am fully authorized to conduct this interview, Lieutenant," replied Liza firmly.

"I know—I understand that," said J.P. "Maybe it's because it's all happened so fast. It's still hard for me to believe that Joss is really dead."

Her face contorted for a moment, and tears started to flow, smudging the makeup she had applied.

"I think I should go home," said J.P., picking up her purse and walking straight out the door.

Liza waited ten minutes to see if she would return, and then went upstairs to the records unit. Joss's service record was waiting for her. She took the thick folder back to the office, opened it to the first page, and began to read.

The first five documents were a summary of Joss's family background and education, obviously prepared as part of a background check by Naval Intelligence. Apparently, she had grown up shuttling between a London mansion, a country house in Devonshire, and a castle in Normandy.

Her father was a viscount, and her mother a Huguenot of both French and German extraction. At the age of seven, Joss had been sent to a boarding school in Switzerland, followed by two more in France. She was at the Sorbonne in Paris when Germany attacked Poland in 1939 and war was declared by England.

Looking up at the clock, she saw that it was already eleven, and Charlie had not yet checked in at the office. Concerned, she picked up the phone and called the security office, which monitored the schedules of the entire staff. After asking to be connected to Captain Wainwright, she was told that he was attending a conference at Field Marshal Montgomery's office.

Calling up to the records unit, she found that copies of Charlie's,

Joss's, and J.P.'s fingerprints were already on file, along with her own. She asked to have them sent to her right away. When the crime technician was finished, she gave them to him. He told her that he would review all the prints and report back to her the following morning.

Having not taken time for breakfast, she was about to order lunch from the food trolley when Sam called to give her an update on his search of Joss's apartment. He said that Drummond's office would be sending over the handwritten note he had found after the hair clippings were forensically analyzed at Scotland Yard. Liza told him about the rifling of Charlie's and J.P.'s desks, as well as her unsatisfactory interview with J.P. Sam said that he would schedule an appointment with General Kilgore as soon as possible.

"I also checked on what your friend Captain Wainwright does," said Sam. "He is in code analysis."

"You mean he's a code-breaker?" she asked.

"No, analysis is different," said Sam. "He's an Oxford whiz kid, brains off the chart, with a degree in Germanic culture and civilization. He's one of the people they bring in to flesh out the meaning of Kraut military traffic after it's decoded."

That explained why he would disappear for hours at a time, thought Liza. He only parked himself at his office desk with his chessboard when there was nothing important for him to do.

"You should know that he is one of a handful of people who have access to information requiring the highest security clearance we've got," said Sam. "I can't tell you any more than that, but he may be some kind of target in this whole thing. Try to keep a close eye on him."

She knew he was talking about the highly secret intercepts that she had learned about after reading hundreds of privileged communications in her first week on the job. Obviously, Charlie was one of the people assigned to help interpret them.

"I understand," she said, the secret unspoken between them.

Liza went back to Joss's service folder.

She had joined the Wrens in June of 1940, shortly after France had surrendered to the Germans, and just before the Battle of Britain. After four months of training, she had been assigned to British Coastal Command in Scapa Flow, where she worked in the convoy-routing office for the Murmansk runs. In 1943, she was assigned to Admiral Jellico, and spent more than a year on his staff as he helped plan Operation Torch, the Allied invasion of North Africa. When the admiral was given his new post in Overlord, she had returned with him to London.

It was almost four that afternoon when Charlie trudged listlessly into the office. His eyes were red and puffy. After removing his greatcoat, he slumped down in his desk chair and stared at Joss's desk. As she watched, his eyes overflowed, the tears streaming down his cheeks and dripping onto the desk. He didn't physically react when Liza walked over and placed a reassuring hand on his shoulder.

"It's the young men who are supposed to die in war," he said, looking up at her. "Not Joss."

"I need to talk to you about our investigation into her death, Charlie," Liza said, gently.

"I'll help in any way I can," he said, slowly regaining control.

"Did you keep anything sensitive in your desk, Charlie?" she asked.

"Sensitive?"

"Matters of military intelligence . . . things like that," she said.

"No. I never bring my work back here."

"Was anything missing when you returned yesterday afternoon?"

He thought about her question for several moments.

"I know it probably sounds crazy," he said, "but the only thing missing was the copy of *Mein Kampf* that I kept in the side drawer."

"Is there any reason why someone might have taken it?"

He shook his head no.

"Did you ever make notes in it?"

Charlie shook his head again.

"How well did you know Joss?" she asked next.

"I'm not sure . . . now," he said.

"Did you ever see her outside the office?" she asked.

"Recently, you mean?"

When she nodded, he shook his head no again. His swollen eyes sparked another female intuition.

"You knew her before the war, didn't you, Charlie?" she said.

He slowly nodded his head.

"Her parents and mine were close friends. . . . I mean when the Dunbars lived in London—before the Viscount died and her mother moved back to Devonshire."

"Were you two close?" she asked gently.

His eyes drifted over to the photograph of King George VI on the wall opposite his desk, and then came back to hers.

"I was in love with her," he said. "I didn't think I would ever get over it."

Liza still had her hand on his shoulder.

"Did she have the same feelings for you?" she asked.

"No . . . but she was very kind about it. I made an ass out of myself, I guess. She just finally sat me down and said, 'Charles . . . I don't love you in that way.'"

"It's pretty remarkable that the two of you ended up working in the same office," said Liza.

"No, it isn't," said Charlie. "I asked if I could work out of here when I wasn't needed in the lair."

"The lair?"

"Oh . . . sorry . . . that's hush-hush."

"I understand."

He happened to look up at the wall clock and immediately stood up.

"Could we possibly continue this at the Savoy?" he said. "I'm meeting my friend Nicholas there. You're welcome to join us for dinner."

Liza was surprised to see that it was already six o'clock. While they had been talking, a courier had delivered the notepaper that Sam had discovered in Joss's apartment, which he had asked her to look at as soon as possible. At the same time, he had suggested keeping a closer eye on Charlie. The gnawing grumble in her stomach was a reminder that she hadn't eaten anything besides a breakfast scone since the dinner in Sam's apartment.

"All right, Charlie," she said, finally, "but only for an hour or so. I have a lot more work to do."

He stood up and began looking around for his greatcoat.

"It's over here," she said with a smile, carrying it to him from the chair where he had dumped it. Before she left, Liza took the envelope containing the handwritten note Sam had found down to the security detail at the end of the corridor, and asked them to put it in the document safe along with Joss's service folder.

It was snowing when they came out onto the street and headed down Pall Mall toward Trafalgar Square. As they walked along the slushy sidewalk, Charlie kept trying to flag down a taxi. As usual, it was impossible to find an empty one in inclement weather.

At the Savoy, they were forced to wait outside the entrance as a wedding party of Grenadier Guardsmen emerged through the doors, the bride dressed in a canary-yellow taffeta gown. After throwing a bouquet back to her female consorts, she followed her new husband into a shiny black Rolls-Royce, and the crowd on the sidewalk erupted in loud applause. Liza and Charlie stood behind them in melancholy silence.

"Buck up there, you two," came a voice through the throng of well-wishers. Liza glanced up to see Charlie's friend Nicholas Ainsley limping toward them.

Covered with a thin coating of snow, he was wearing his RAF uniform under an unbuttoned navy topcoat and white silk scarf. Together, they pushed through into the lobby. Inside, Nicholas took off his flying cap and shook the snow off it, his corn-colored hair gleaming in the light of the wall sconce above his head. An orchestra was playing in the ballroom as he led them upstairs to the piano bar.

The room was small and intimate, with a wood fire roaring in one corner, and candle lamps on all the polished ebony tables. A grand piano sat in the center of the room. The walls were covered with cleverly drawn caricatures of famous people who had frequented the bar before the war. As in so many other public places in London, its once-exquisite trappings had clearly suffered from four unrelenting years of war and bombing raids.

The use of candles could not hide the fact that the plaster ceiling had fallen in several places and the remainder of it was being held in place with lengths of unpainted planking. The cream-colored walls displayed countless spider marks from past bomb concussions, and three of the big plate-glass windows overlooking the street were cracked and patched with tape.

Two elderly waiters were standing forlornly at the bar. The bartender behind them looked like a seventy-year-old Mr. Pickwick, with a fringe of silver hair around his shiny bald head. All of them visibly perked up as Liza and the others entered the empty room.

"Welcome, milord," called out the bartender, greeting Nicholas with a friendly wave.

"Good to be back, Jameson," said Nicholas.

One of the waiters escorted them to a table near the fireplace.

"So what shall it be?" said Nicholas to Charlie. "You look all in."

"I don't know. . . . I'm feeling a bit ragged," he said.

"Gimlets, I think," said Nicholas. "We need a tropical remedy to battle this blasted weather."

"May I have some water?" asked Liza.

"Certainly," said the waiter.

Returning immediately with a carafe and a glass on a silver tray, he set her glass down and poured it full. Even in the paucity of the candlelight, Liza could see that it was badly discolored.

"Some fresh water, I think, Barrett," said Nicholas, eyeing it with distaste.

"Yes, sir; sorry, sir," said the waiter, picking up the glass with a look of horror. Bowing to Liza, he said, sadly, "It's the war, you see."

"So—what is a gimlet?" she asked, watching the snowflakes melting against the plate-glass windows.

"She's led a sheltered life," said Nicholas. "The gimlet is the great unheralded secret of the British Empire, my dear girl. It is made with Rose's Lime Juice, the elixir that has sustained our colonials in every distant and deadly corner of the globe—brewed in wooden vats from an ancient mixture of spices and juices from our conquered lands."

Across the bar, Liza could see the aged bartender tossing a mixture of liquid and ice in a large silver cocktail shaker. As the snow continued its assault outside, it felt good to be there by the fire. Barrett brought the shaker over to their table and poured out three equal measures in stemmed champagne glasses.

Liza took her first sip.

"This is wonderful," she said.

"Now you know why we're called Limeys," said Nicholas.

When he smiled at her, it transformed his terribly scarred face. For a moment, he looked young again, and Liza was surprised to find herself thinking that he was the most beautiful man she had ever seen.

At Barnard, she had been taught by one of her professors that character was often molded into a person's features. Over time, she had learned that there was truth in his words.

With Nicholas, she was struck successively by the lingering pain in his war-crippled face, the irrepressible humor in his large blue eyes, the determination in his purposeful jaw, and the assurance in his full lips and mouth. What came as a surprise was that, for the first time in her life, Liza knew she wasn't making these instinctive character judgments dispassionately.

Charlie finished his gimlet in two long swallows, and slowly put his glass down on the table. Within moments, the waiter reappeared with another frosted shaker to refill it.

"May I top you off, milord?" he asked.

"Of course," said Nicholas. "We are here to celebrate the living."

With a tortured grimace at the reference to the living, Charlie quaffed the second one as if it were only fruit juice. Not having had time even to move, the waiter refilled his glass again. Although she found the drink delicious, Liza had watched the bartender making the second round, and knew that each drink contained at least two fingers of gin.

"Any chance for some music, Barrett?" asked Nicholas of the waiter.

"Yes, milord," he said. "Mrs. Soames will be playing in a few minutes."

Nicholas nodded, and then turned to Liza. "What kind of name is 'Marantz'?"

"German," she said.

"Really . . . I'm part German, too."

"On his mother's side . . . the Windsor side," added Charlie.

"The House of Windsor?" asked Liza.

"Afraid so," he said, almost apologetically. "Of course, that name only came into being in 1917. My great-uncle, George the Fifth, changed it to 'Windsor' by royal decree. Our name used to be Saxe-Coburg-Gothe—that is, until another great-uncle, Kaiser Wilhelm, started the last war. That was when our German moniker became very unfashionable."

"Do you speak it?" asked Liza, finishing her gimlet.

"German? Not a word . . . No—two, actually—Marlene Dietrich. You?"

"A little," she said with a laugh. "Yiddish, in fact. The two are very similar in certain ways."

A thought suddenly struck her as she felt the gimlet going straight to her head on an empty stomach.

"Have you ever visited the Royal Natatorium?" she asked before she could stop herself.

Smiling, he reached into the side pocket of his tunic and pulled out a small leather key ring. Separating out a polished silver key, he held it up and said, "In the mood for a swim?"

Liza felt the hair lift up on the back of her neck as she shook her head no.

"Another drink?" he asked, solicitously.

"I really need to eat something or I'll soon be lying under the table."

"Jameson," Nicholas called out to the bartender, "may we have our supper served up here?"

"Of course, milord," he said, dispatching the waiter to bring up menus from the dining room.

Charlie turned to Liza, his eyes already unfocused.

"You know that Nicky here is the holder of the Military Cross for shooting down seven Hun bastards," he said.

"Judas Priest, Charlie," said Nicholas, visibly embarrassed.

"Well, Nicky," said Charlie, ignoring him, "I just wanted you to know that Liza has had her share of heroics, too."

"What are you talking about?" asked Liza.

"Now, don't ask me how I know it, but this young lady sitting beside you went through a ship torpedoing in the freezing wastes of the North Atlantic," said Charlie. "Her transport was sunk halfway across the pond from Halifax, and she survived for three days on a piece of floating wreckage."

"How did . . . how could you possibly know about that?" began Liza, but he was already moving on to her brief ordeal on the raft before she and the other survivor were picked up by the *Empress of Scotland*.

In her muddled state, she couldn't imagine how he had possibly learned of the story. She had talked about the sinking only once, and that was to an American naval officer right after her arrival in Southampton. How could Charlie have gotten hold of it? And why? Nicholas was looking at her with renewed curiosity and seeming admiration. Acutely embarrassed, she attempted to divert the subject.

"What was it like?" she asked him, taking a sip of her new gimlet.

"What was what like?" he replied.

"Fighting in the air . . . during the Battle of Britain," she said.

"I bodged it," said Nicholas with a shy grin.

"Bodged it?" she asked.

"Lost control for a few moments at the end. No second chances up there."

"How did it happen?"

"You really want to know?" he said, as if it were the most boring and commonplace thing he had ever done.

"Yes," she said, truthfully.

"One must be very quick about it all, you see," he said, his eyes coming alive. "When it starts, there is no time for contemplation of your next decision. It must be instinctive and it must be right. The Germans usually came at us out of the sun, you see."

As he continued to talk in vivid word pictures, she could see a blue sky full of fighter planes darting high and low with their guns spitting flame. Unconsciously, he raised his badly burned hands from the table and clasped them together, to sweep upward in concerted motion, simulating the flight of his Spitfire.

"The good ones feel the flow instinctively," he said. "The rest of us, well . . ."

His words became more deliberate.

"One mistake in the intricate pattern and you've bought it. That's what happened to me. I wasn't very good, I'm afraid."

"After shooting down seven Huns," repeated Charlie.

Her heart went out to Nicholas for the disfiguring wounds he had suffered. She had to fight the impulse to reach out and stroke his maimed hands. At that moment, the waiter arrived with their menus.

In compliance with strict rationing, the fare was limited to four choices, including roast mutton, Lord Woolton's vegetable pie, broiled salmon, and Colchester oysters. As they finished ordering, she looked up to see a young man enter the room and advance toward the bar. He ordered a drink and then turned to look over at them. For some reason he looked familiar to her.

"Thought I might find you here, Nicky," he called out.

Hearing his voice, Charlie looked over at him and then back at Liza, rolling his eyes disparagingly as Nicholas responded, "Des . . . come join us."

Pulling a chair from the next table, the man sat down between Charlie and Nicholas. Unlike the two of them, he wasn't in uniform, and wore an expensive double-breasted suit and a red patterned tie.

"Des, meet Liza Marantz," said Nicholas. "Liza . . . my old roommate at Trinity, Desmond Sullivan."

Physically, they were very different. Whereas Nicholas was tall and slender, Des Sullivan was short with a deep chest and broad shoulders. In looks, he was probably as handsome as Nicholas had once been, with thick, wavy brown hair and a thin, aristocratic nose.

"How's the boy?" he said to Charlie, who merely grunted in acknowledgment.

"Barrett," Nicholas called out to the waiter, "another round of gimlets, please."

Des pulled a silver cigarette case from his breast pocket, removed a cigarette, and lit it with a silver Ronson. As soon as he did, Liza remembered him. He had been the man standing in the hallway when Nicholas came to pick up Charlie for the country weekend during her first week at SHAEF.

"I'm heading over to the Palladium to see that new dance revue," he said with a distinct Irish brogue. "There is a new girl from Istanbul with an ass that . . ."

"Don't get yourself in a lather, Des," interrupted Nicholas. "Anyway, we were just about to have dinner. Perhaps we can catch up to you later."

"Suit yourselves," he said, gazing at Liza for the first time.

Over his shoulder, Liza saw an elderly woman in a long white dress sit down at the piano. A few moments later, she began to play a slow, melancholy version of "Something to Remember You By."

"And what do you do?" asked Des Sullivan, continuing to stare at her with his intense black eyes.

"Hands off," said Nicholas. "She works with Charlie."

"Yes, of course . . . old Wainwright," said Sullivan, as if he had just heard a new joke and wanted to pass it along. "If you haven't heard already, your friend Bobby Machem resigned his commission in the Irish Guards."

Although Charlie showed no visible reaction, Liza saw his hands clench into fists under the rim of the table.

"Wasn't he at Eton with you two?" asked Nicholas.

Charlie nodded.

"I gather he was always dropping out from some kind of infection, poor chap," said Des, his lips curling disdainfully. "Then he missed his posting for some reason or another—stomach virus, toe infection, that sort of thing."

"You mean he flaked out?" asked Nicholas.

"Not so anyone could take notice and do something about it," said Sullivan.

"At least he volunteered to serve," said Charlie, almost belligerently.

From the way Charlie was glaring at the Irishman, Liza was afraid he might actually punch him.

"Would you like to dance?" asked Nicholas, breaking the tension.

"I would love to," said Liza.

He stood up and began limping toward the piano, remarkably graceful in spite of the prosthetic leg.

She was about to follow him when Des Sullivan said, "Pity about Joss . . . Tasty piece, that."

Charlie picked up Nicholas's half-full glass and downed the entire contents.

After crossing the floor, Liza stepped into Nicholas's arms. In spite of his injuries, he danced with self-assured confidence, holding her casually and smiling down into her face as they moved around the room. When the song ended, the pianist effortlessly segued into "Moonlight Serenade."

"You dance magnificently," said Nicholas, holding her closer.

"You, too," said Liza, feeling totally relaxed in his arms.

The first course of food was waiting when they finished the dance and returned to the table. Charlie and Des Sullivan were embroiled in a heated discussion about the state of European politics. Without waiting for the others, Liza picked up her spoon and began eating the savory mushroom soup with relish.

"We should have stopped Hitler at Munich in 1938," said Charlie, his voice rising. "Instead, we sold the Czechs out when they had a steel ring of fortified defenses in the mountains and the best-trained army in Europe. . . . Hell, even the bloody Frogs were ready to fight. . . . We could have strolled into Berlin and put the match to his house of cards once and for all. Instead, Chamberlain went to Berchtesgaden and got down on his knees to the bastard."

"It would appear that someone is ravenous at this table," said Nicholas, grinning at Liza.

"It's delicious," she said, smiling back at him.

"I'm surprised at you, Wainwright," said Sullivan with a laugh. "Tell me the difference between Germany taking Czechoslovakia, and England invading Ireland or annexing Scotland. It is all about survival of the fittest. England invades India. Hitler invades Russia. Empires come and go. Read your Hegel. Hitler is no different from Caesar or Napoleon."

"You're still a cynical bastard, aren't you?" said Charlie, starting on another gimlet. "I remember you holding a similar brief for Hitler back at Trinity. I can't believe you're still pushing it now, considering everything he has done since."

"The ruling dynasties in Europe are finished once and for all," said Sullivan, "and as the rot of that old order fades away, it gives birth to a new type of leader—men capable of cleaning out the rot."

When he finished his soup, Nicholas dabbed at his mouth with a starched napkin. "Des is right about one thing," he said. "The old Europe has disintegrated. After two centuries of rule by the Hapsburgs and Hohenzollerns, along comes Adolf Hitler—a small-minded, bigoted Austrian who was nothing more than a tramp, a vagabond living in a flophouse in Vienna, begging on the street, and eating in a soup kitchen. Yet, a decade later, he was riding in triumph through the streets of Berlin. Remarkable."

"He is an unmitigated monster," said Charlie, heatedly. "The personification of evil in its most malevolent form."

"Hitler has committed crimes on a monumental scale, that's true," said Nicholas calmly. "But Stalin takes the prize as the greatest mass murderer of the century, at least so far, and no one raised a peep when he slaughtered millions of Kulaks. Now he's our stalwart ally. Actually, there's not a shilling's worth of difference between them. National Socialism . . . communism . . . they're just words to mask a ruthless drive for total world domination. Is there any difference between Hitler's concentration camps and Stalin's concentration camps?"

He was looking at Liza, apparently waiting for her to answer, but she was finding it hard to pay attention. Not used to alcohol, her normally active brain had slowed to a crawl.

"I don't know," she said, dully as the main course was served. "Thank goodness, we don't have any concentration camps in America."

"Oh, really," came back Sullivan in his lilting brogue. "What do you call the places where you sent your American Japs after Pearl Harbor? And what about your so-called Indian reservations? Your founding fathers systematically slaughtered the red men to take over the whole continent in the name of Manifest Destiny. Americans should be the last to talk."

"What we did to the Nisei is horrible," said Liza angrily. "But there is no national policy to murder them."

"She makes a good point, Des," added Nicholas. "We English aren't all that different either, after two thousand years of so-called advancement."

"I'm not bloody English," growled Sullivan as Liza sampled her salmon.

"Nobody's perfect," said Nicholas, grinning at him. "Anyway, do you think we would allow a Jew in our best clubs here in London? Or allow them to mingle with our daughters?"

"You Americans are the worst hypocrites," said Sullivan, going after Liza again. "Roosevelt has been president for ten years. How many

Jews did he allow across your borders back in the thirties, when they could still have escaped the whirlwind?"

Liza's appetite had disappeared. She only wished that Sullivan had never shown up to spoil the evening. Looking at her watch, she realized that she needed to get back to the office anyway.

"Well, the war's almost over now," said Charlie, his words as thick as pudding as he stared at his empty cocktail glass. "Another year at the most, and the monster will be gone . . . defeated by sheer numbers."

"That's what Montezuma probably said before the whole Aztec Empire was plundered by Cortés and his handful of dedicated butchers," said Nicholas. "And how big was Macedonia when Alexander conquered the known world?"

"The Germans can hold on for years, especially if the invasion fails," said Sullivan, "and at some point Hitler will use those rocket weapons he keeps talking about. Anything's possible."

"Sheer numbers," repeated Charlie, slurring his words badly. "That and the fact that we bloody well know what they're going to do before their own generals do."

Liza was watching Des Sullivan, who now began gazing at Charlie with a quizzical expression.

"Charlie, we have to go," she said. "I need to see you back at the office."

"Sure, happy to go with you . . . anywhere," he said, unsteadily rising to his feet.

As she was about to leave, Nicholas reached out and took her hand.

"May I ring you?" he asked.

His hand felt warm and soft.

She nodded her head a fraction and said, "Yes. Please do."

CHAPTER 11

J.P. stumbled out of the seventh-floor suite in the Dorchester Hotel at three o'clock in the morning. She was still wearing the white silk sheath that General Kilgore had bought her at Bergdorf Goodman, although it was now ripped at both shoulders.

When the elevator door opened on the ground floor and she stepped into the ornate lobby, several doormen and porters were clustered near the front desk. None of them moved to get the door for her as she crossed the lobby and went out into the night.

Standing on the sidewalk in the bitter cold, she began to cry. Her already swollen cheeks were red and aching by the time she flagged down a taxi on Park Lane and gave the driver her address.

J.P. knew right after meeting him for dinner that she didn't want to sleep with him. She was so tired of it all. Kilgore had said, "I need you to be real nice to him, baby. Phil Gramm's only a supply officer . . . but he keeps track of the booze and does Ike's laundry. He's also one of the guys reviewing the recommendations for Georgie Patton's D-Day assignment, and this could help get him out of the doghouse."

Like most of the officers Kilgore had arranged for her to sleep with, he was just another arrogant desk jockey, already drunk when they met for dinner. For staff officers, the war seemed nothing more than a never-ending party.

He wouldn't stop pawing her, even at the dinner table, in front of dozens of people. Up close, she saw that his teeth were stained greenish-yellow from the cigars he constantly smoked. Every time he smiled, she felt nauseous.

Concerned that someone from work might see them together, she was almost grateful when he finally suggested that they go upstairs. In the lobby, she tried to beg off, claiming a headache, but he had cruelly squeezed her hand and whispered, "I know you can be had, baby. Kilgore told me so. He says you've seen half the hotel ceilings in London."

As they headed into the elevator, she happened to glance toward the front desk. A young blonde woman was standing with her back to the lobby, and for a moment J.P. thought it was Joss Dunbar. No, it couldn't be, she realized a second later. Joss was dead.

While they rode up to the seventh floor, the tiny fragment of a lost memory began gnawing at the back of her mind. She knew it had something to do with Joss. Like a small, elusive fish, it darted back and forth as she tried to reel it into her brain with no success.

At one point, Gramm stopped the elevator between floors, taking his cigar out of his mouth before attempting to kiss her. As she tried to repel him, red cinders dropped from the cigar, burning a hole in the silk bodice covering her breasts.

He was too drunk to notice or care. And then they were in his room. Without any preliminaries, he told her to take off her clothes. When she didn't move fast enough, he began ripping at the straps of her dress. In bed, he used her like a Filipina whore. The worst part was when he repeatedly taunted her with the words, "This is for your husband, baby."

She wondered whether Gramm might have known Lloyd in the old army before the war, and had harbored a grudge against him. Lying there after he was finished, she tried to imagine Lloyd in his Japanese prison camp, gaunt and emaciated, wondering where she was and what she was doing at that very moment. When she started to cry, the general had ordered her out of the suite.

In the corridor, she realized her topcoat was still inside. When she knocked on the door, he refused to open it to give it back to her. In the taxi, she began sobbing again, almost hysterically. The driver pulled over to the side of the road.

"You all right, miss?" he said.

"Please, just get me to my apartment."

The cab moved slowly along the blacked-out London streets until it reached her address near Charing Cross Station. It was dreadfully cold in the street as J.P. paid the driver and headed across the sidewalk. She was pulling out her key when a little man in coveralls walked past her carrying a canister tray full of milk bottles, his breath wreathed in a small cloud of steam. She unlocked the door and stepped inside, locking it behind her.

The fragment of the elusive recollection about Joss flickered in her brain again. Joss hadn't looked like a girl who lived on the wild side, but she was into things that made even J.P. blush. When Kilgore confided some of it to her, J.P. had refused to believe it. Joss was so poised and intelligent. And she was royalty, too.

But J.P. had learned for herself that the stories were true. She hadn't told anyone about those nights. If Kilgore found out, he would have probably sent her home. And there was no one waiting for her at home.

When they first arrived in London, Kilgore had found her the little apartment near Charing Cross. The kitchen was nothing to speak of, but she rarely cooked anyway. There was a quaint living room, with ancient wooden beams running across the ceiling and a cozy brick fireplace. On the mantelpiece, she was able to showcase the collection of hatpins Lloyd had found for her during his travels before the war.

Kilgore had hated the apartment's bathroom on sight. He loved to stretch out in an oversized tub, and there was just a shower stall in the tiny room. Right after moving her in, he ordered one of his army contractor friends to knock down the wall of the spare bedroom, which more than doubled the bathroom's size.

The enormous pink enamel tub, along with the sinks and matching toilet, had been shipped over from the States in one of the B-17s assigned to SHAEF. Kilgore had also ordered a U.S.-made hot-water heater that, unlike the English models, allowed him to fill the tub with steaming water.

The army contractor had spent almost a week reconstructing the bathroom to Kilgore's personal design. When his men were finished, the walls and floor were tiled in white and red, and there was a glossy white cabinet to hold his thick, luxurious Afghan towels, plus all the creams and perfumed ointments he had bought her.

Once she had removed her necklace and earrings, J.P. put them in the lockbox sitting on the sink. She pulled off her torn dress and tossed it in the wastebasket. After washing off her tear-blotched mascara, she thoroughly rinsed her mouth with a strong mouthwash. She took her aromatic bath salts from the cabinet, poured two full measures into the tub, and began running a hot bath.

Standing naked in front of the mirror, J.P. took stock of herself. She was probably a few pounds heavier than the last time she had been with Lloyd in Manila, but J.P. was confident he would never notice the difference. Her "best feature," as Kilgore referred to them, showed no signs of sagging, and her legs were as firm and lovely as ever.

She tried to ignore the new age lines in her face. God only knew what Lloyd would look like after years in a Japanese prison camp, but it didn't matter. She would make him the best wife he could ever hope for when the war was over.

Turning off the hot water, J.P. climbed into the tub and dropped down into its fragrant warmth. After shampooing the cigar stink out of her hair, she sank back up to her neck, luxuriating in the solace of its restorative power, and slowly cleansing away the reek of the man she had been with.

The phone began to ring in the bedroom. It was probably Kilgore, she concluded. The general rarely slept more than two hours at a time, and he was probably looking for an update on the "Georgie" situation. Well, it could wait until morning. That was when she planned to tell him she was through being his tramp.

The phone stopped ringing. Ten minutes later, she turned on the hot spigot again to add a few inches of hot water to the bath. She was starting to nod off in the blissful warmth when a sudden jet of cold air came through the half-open bathroom door, chilling her shoulders. From past experience, she knew it always happened when someone opened the front door of the apartment. But she had locked the front door behind her. She was sure of it. A moment later, the stream of cold air abruptly stopped.

"Everett, is that you?" she called out.

There was no response. This is ridiculous. I'm not in an Alan Ladd movie, she thought. She imagined Kilgore in the bedroom, taking off his uniform, then suddenly yanking the door open and leaping naked into the tub. He had done that before, and scared her half out of her wits.

"Everett, I know you're out there. Stop playing your childish games and get in here. I have something important to tell you."

When there was still no response, she became mildly concerned. What if it was the kind of prowler that Kilgore had warned her about when he had given her the little automatic that was sitting in the drawer of her bedside table?

She heard the creak of the old pine flooring in the living room. She even knew exactly where it creaked like that—right in front of the fireplace. She was about to climb out of the tub to lock the bathroom door when she recalled that the lock was broken.

She felt a tremor of irrational fear and looked around the bathroom for something to defend herself. The only things that registered in her frantic eyes were hairbrushes, powder jars, tubes, oils, talcum, and towels. Then she saw Kilgore's razor sitting on the cabinet shelf. It wasn't a straight razor, just one of the new nickel-plated kind, with a double-edged blue Gillette blade.

Vaulting upward, she grabbed the razor and dropped back into the tub, sloshing soapy water over the side onto the tile floor. She unscrewed the handle of the razor and removed the blade.

The water suddenly seemed cold. Her skin began to quiver. She sat there motionless, as if being silent might make her invisible. The lights went off in the bedroom.

God . . . someone was definitely with her in the apartment. She dropped down into the water up to her chin. Too late, she remembered that the light switches for the bathroom were on the wall just outside the door.

"Everett, stop this," she loudly demanded.

When the lights went out, she suddenly remembered the elusive fragment of memory that had bothered her all evening. Her body began to shake uncontrollably, and the blade slipped from her fingers. A flashlight beam found her terrified face.

"Please don't hurt me," she begged into the darkness.

CHAPTER 12

"My God, you shall pay for this. I'll wring that obstinate little heart. . . . Noel."

Using a magnifying glass, Liza studied the handwriting segment on the piece of cream-colored stationery. She concluded it must have been written with some form of quill pen, with the writer frequently dipping the point into a blood pool. The letters were consistently thick, and of approximately the same height and width. None of them were smudged. She slowly moved the magnifying glass down to the second handwritten segment.

"9 August. I asked you not to send blood but Yet do—because if it means love I will have it. I cut the hair too close & bled much more than you need—I pray that you put not the knife blade near where quei capelli grow."

She decided that the writing instrument for the second segment wasn't a pen of any kind. For one thing, there was no consistency to the blood flow. Some of the letters were thick and pudgy, others slivery and barely registering on the paper. A pin, she thought, possibly a long hatpin.

The lab at Scotland Yard had already examined the notepaper, finding no latent fingerprints on it. They had also done an analysis of scrapings from the written segments, as well as the hair clippings that had been folded into the paper. Both segments had been written in blood. The first was written in AB negative, the rarest blood type found in human beings. The second passage had been written with type 0 positive blood, which was a match for Joss Dunbar, and the most common type.

Liza removed a short letter from Joss's service record that had been written in her own hand. When she put it side by side with the second passage on the notepaper, she used her magnifying glass to compare the script in both documents. Although she was not a handwriting expert, there were enough common features to the letters for her to be fairly confident that Joss had written the second note.

"That's great," said Taggart when he learned the results of the blood work. "Assuming our killer wrote the first segment, that only limits the potential suspects on this island to about a million people."

After the Yard technicians compared the hair clippings folded into the paper with hair samples from Joss's body, they had concluded that almost half of them matched her own unique characteristics. The other half were from another human source, as yet unidentified.

Liza tried to remember the many lectures she had attended that dealt with blood attributes. One thing she knew was that it tended to fade very quickly. Although Sam had suggested to her the possibility that the notes might have been written a hundred years earlier, she knew that was impossible: the writing would have disappeared long ago. She concluded that the notes were probably no more than five years old. Liza copied the words of the first segment onto a blank index card.

"My God, you shall pay for this. I'll wring that obstinate little heart. . . . Noel."

Were the words possibly written in jest? she wondered. What kind of person could have written them, if indeed they were original to the author? The line suggested someone passionate, possessive, and cruel. Perhaps Sam was right, and Joss's death had resulted from a combination of factors—a girl threatening suicide, and the man she was in love with becoming a willing and sadistic accomplice.

She copied the second passage onto a separate card.

"9 August. I asked you not to send blood but Yet do—because if it means love I will have it. I cut the hair too close & bled much more than you need—I pray that you put not the knife blade near where quei capelli grow."

She tried to imagine Joss as the author of the words, but found it hard to imagine her writing them. Joss had received her education in France and Switzerland, and she was probably fluent in several languages. But the words had an archaic construction, one that harkened back to a different time. She decided to ask Taggart and Drummond where she might send the lines for another opinion, perhaps to an Oxford don with a knowledge of the classics.

Next she turned her attention to the hair samples. They were in a clear cellophane bag. To the naked eye, they all appeared to be the same color, but the Scotland Yard technicians had examined the hair under a microscope and concluded that the cortex contained slightly different pigment granules, which confirmed it came from at least two different sources. In both cases the granules were evenly distributed, indicating Caucasian hair. The words suggested that the two lovers had each contributed pubic hair. But why? she wondered. She was writing another reminder to herself when a courier entered the office and walked straight up to her desk.

"This is marked 'urgent,' Lieutenant," he said. "I was told to bring it straight to you."

The note was from Sam, hastily scrawled on the back of an envelope.

"Order a staff car and come immediately to the following address," it commanded.

Twenty minutes later, her car was inching through the fogbound London morning. From the side window, she watched people on the sidewalks emerging and then quickly disappearing into the ghostly pale. The driver pulled up at a small row house off Charing Cross Road. Two English bobbies were standing guard at the front door.

After presenting her identity card to one of the policemen, she was ushered inside. An old Persian carpet runner led to an open doorway at the rear of the ground floor. A half-dozen crime technicians were swarming through the living room when she stepped through the door.

"Is Major Taggart here?" she asked one of them.

He pointed to the bedroom. Through the open door, she saw the backs of Sam and Inspector Drummond. Both were standing at the foot of a brass double bed. They looked up and nodded as she joined them. It was very hot in the room, and she smelled the faint reek of fecal matter. It was much stronger near the bed.

"The cleaning lady found her at a little after eight o'clock this morning," said Inspector Drummond.

Liza did not recognize the woman lying naked in front of them. One of the technicians was taking photographs of her, and the bloated face flashed incandescently in the glare of the flashbulbs, the eyes bulging out like some monstrosity in a freak show, before receding again into shadow.

"It's Janet Barnes," said Taggart, noting the confusion in Liza's eyes.

"J.P.?" she said, uncertainly.

She forced herself to stare at the corpse. What had once been human and distinctive about her had completely disappeared. The fact that another person she had worked so closely with was dead almost took her breath away.

"Seems a bit more than coincidence that two young women working in the same office have died under such mysterious circumstances," said Drummond.

J.P. was lying on her back, her left arm flung away from her chest, the right bent back toward her chin. A small semi-automatic pistol was loosely clenched in her right hand. There appeared to be an entry wound in her right ear. It had already turned a glutinous black. Liza saw that there was no exit wound. The hydrostatic pressure of the bullet inside her brain had transformed her face into a clownish nightmare of doughy pulp.

"Any sign of forced entry?" asked Sam.

Drummond shook his head.

"The front-door lock has a spring mechanism. It engages automatically when the door shuts. The cleaning lady said it was locked when she arrived, although the dead bolt wasn't shot home. There is no back door."

Liza went around the side of the bed and placed her fingers against J.P.'s cheek, gently massaging the surface of her skin.

"Rigor is already setting in," she said. "Is there any preliminary estimate of time of death?"

Drummond shook his head and said, "No one in the house knows when she came home, or if she even went out last night at all. The woman upstairs is a sixty-year-old spinster. She told me somewhat disapprovingly that Lieutenant Barnes entertained several different men in her apartment. At least one of them is a high-ranking American officer, possibly a general. Apparently, there were a lot of your army chaps in here doing the whole place over from stem to stern before she moved in."

"Has anyone taken her internal temperature?" asked Liza.

Drummond nodded. "You'll have it for the autopsy."

Taggart looked down at the grotesquely distorted face. In his fourteen years as a homicide detective, he had seen hundreds of violent-crime scenes, and many had delivered a serious jolt to his nervous system. But, in spite of the old truism that a cop eventually became desensitized to violent death, it wasn't true, at least for him. He felt only deep sorrow that a woman so young had to die. Slumming angels, General Manigault had called girls like her. Like they were disposable refuse.

One of the technicians came toward them from the bathroom. He was carrying a white dress.

"I found this in the trash, sir," he said.

When Drummond held up the dress, Liza saw that both of the shoulder straps were torn. There was a brown-edged burn hole on the bodice, and the dress smelled of stale cigar smoke.

Stepping around the corner of the bed, Liza leaned close to the crimson-stained pillow. J.P.'s dull eyes stared back at her. The puffiness around both eyes as well as her reddened lids suggested a recent bout of crying.

Liza looked at each of the fingers holding the pistol. Two of her manicured nails were cracked, and one of them was broken. She remembered how careful J.P. had been with her nails and makeup.

There was some slight skin discoloration around her left wrist, and a definite bruise on the nipple of her right breast. Liza noticed more discoloration above the subcutaneous tissues on both knees.

"These could be possible defensive injuries," she said, "although it's possible the bruising might have occurred earlier." She pointed at the deep-purplish-blue area on J.P.'s breast. "It takes several hours for capillaries to bleed sufficiently for the blood vessels to rupture this way."

Seeing the two parallel scratches along the inside of her left thigh, she added, "And we need to determine whether she might have been assaulted. We'll know better after a thorough examination at the autopsy."

"Anything else?" asked Taggart.

"I'm a little surprised at the small blood loss. It's less than I would have expected from a gunshot wound," said Liza.

"You never know with head wounds," said Taggart, coming around to the other side of the bed.

The drawer of the nightstand by the headboard was partially open, and he could see the base of a framed color photograph peeking out from it. Using the heel of his hand, he drew the drawer open farther.

Smiling up at him were the faces of a young man and woman. The man's arm was tucked possessively around the woman's waist. He wore the uniform of a West Point upperclassman.

The young woman was gazing up at the handsome cadet with almost reverent awe. She was wearing a frilly white cotillion gown, the epitome of voluptuous innocence. It was a young Janet Barnes.

"Any idea who this man might be?" he asked, picking up the photograph by the edges and showing it to Liza.

"I think it's her husband, Lloyd," she said. "She told me he was captured by the Japanese at Corregidor."

"What a war," said Taggart disgustedly, laying the photograph down on the bed.

"So you're suggesting she might have been sexually assaulted somewhere else," said Drummond, "and then returned here, where she either committed suicide or was murdered."

"It's only a possibility at this point," said Liza, "but, yes, it could have happened that way."

One of the English bobbies who had been guarding the front door came up to Drummond.

"We found the milk delivery boy, sir," he said. "He is waiting out in the front parlor."

"We'll be right in."

Turning to Taggart, Drummond said, "When I arrived here, there was a fresh bottle of milk lying in the box on the stoop. I asked for the delivery boy to be tracked down as soon as possible."

"Good work," said Taggart, as he and Liza followed him into the living room.

A diminutive man in white overalls stood next to the policeman, looking around the room with curious eyes. He was no longer a boy.

His face was marked with several livid scars, one of which tracked straight across his mutilated nose. His right ear was missing.

"This is Reg Dockery," said the policeman. "He delivered the milk to this address on his regular round this morning."

"Thanks for coming in," said Drummond with a weary smile. "Do you remember what time you reached this house?"

"Right . . . it was about three-thirty . . . same as usual," he said in a harsh Cockney accent. He was keeping his head canted to one side so that he could hear Drummond with his good ear.

"Did you happen to notice anyone entering or leaving this house when you were making your rounds?"

"Just the lady," he said.

"The lady?" repeated Drummond.

He nodded. "Never talked to her, but she got dropped off out in front when I was picking up the dead bottles."

"By a taxi?" asked Taggart.

"Yes, sir," he said, "but don't ask me what kind it was, 'cause I don't remember. I was looking at the lady."

Across the living room, Liza found the control thermostat for the apartment's heating system. It was pushed all the way to the highest setting.

"This was at approximately thirty minutes past three in the morning?" said Drummond.

"Right," said the Cockney.

"Any particular reason you remember her?" asked Taggart.

"She wasn't wearing no coat," said Reg Dockery, cocking his good ear toward Taggart. "Just the fancy white dress . . . And it was bloody cold out."

"Is that all?" asked Taggart.

"She was crying," said Dockery. "Crying like there was no tomorrow."

"Do you think you could identify her if you saw her again?" asked Drummond.

"For sure," he said. "She was a real looker."

Drummond turned to the policeman standing next to him and whispered, "Cover her with a sheet . . . up to the neck."

"Yes, sir," said the policeman, heading into the bedroom.

"Mr. Dockery, I should prepare you for the fact that the woman in the bedroom is dead," said Drummond. "From violent causes."

"That's all right, sir. I fought with the Desert Rats at Tobruk. That's where I got this," said Dockery, pointing proudly at the wreckage of his face. "I seen plenty of dead Jerries. Our chaps, too."

"All right, then," said Drummond, leading the way back into the bedroom.

The little man walked straight up to the edge of the bed and looked down into J.P.'s face. Without flinching, he turned to the others and said, "I never seen this woman before in my life."

Taggart joined him by the side of the bed and picked up the photograph of J.P. and her husband from the silk coverlet. Still holding it by the edges, he held it up to Dockery.

"Yeah . . . that's her," said the little man.

In the living room, Liza was drawn to the grinning visage of a familiar figure sitting on the mantelpiece over the fireplace hearth. It was a moon-shaped head of Winston Churchill. Drawing closer, she saw that it was actually a pincushion, the famous Churchill head fashioned in tan leather and stuffed with some kind of soft material.

Sticking out of it in all directions were hatpins, at least a dozen of them. They were about six inches long, the heads mounted with gemstones, some gold, some filigreed silver. A Churchill voodoo doll, she thought, grinning at J.P.'s humorous touch.

"We need to know as soon as possible whether this death was self-inflicted," said Taggart, coming to her side. "I want you to schedule the autopsy immediately . . . and no mistakes this time."

"Yes, sir," she said. "May I use the phone over there?"

Drummond nodded, saying, "It was already dusted for fingerprints."

While she attempted to reach the SHAEF hospital administrator, Drummond motioned Taggart to the chairs in front of the fireplace. He removed his notebook and said, "You might be interested to know that I interviewed three senior members of Admiral Jellico's staff yesterday. All of them professed to know nothing about Lady Dunbar's death. None of them have ever heard of a man named Noel. One of them, a Mrs. Helen

Bellayne, stated that Lady Dunbar was a frequent overnight guest at her home."

"I've met Mrs. Bellayne," said Taggart.

"Yes . . . very lovely woman. Apparently, she is related by marriage to Lady Dunbar," went on Drummond. "She lives in a once-imposing home in Belgravia."

"Once-imposing?" asked Taggart.

"Fortunes come and go," said Drummond.

"I've never had one come," said Taggart.

"Pity . . . Me either . . . Incidentally, I had the strong impression she was hiding something . . . never deciphered what it was."

"Who isn't?" asked Taggart.

"Well, perhaps you can try to crack that safe," said the grinning inspector.

"I'll make an appointment to speak with her."

"So what is your view, Sam?" asked Drummond. "Are we looking at a homicide or a suicide here? And if it's homicide, is it the work of the same killer?"

"I don't know," said Taggart. "The first murder scene was as gaudy as any I've ever investigated. This one actually looks like it could be suicide, but I don't believe it. As you said, it's too big of a coincidence that two women working side by side are both suddenly dead."

One of the crime technicians came out of the bedroom.

"We're finished in there, sir," he said, handing Drummond a tally sheet of articles they had found in searching through the apartment. "Do you have any instructions for the body yet, sir?"

Liza put her hand over the mouthpiece of the telephone and said, "They can fit in an autopsy right now at the SHAEF pathology unit."

"Good," said Taggart. "Let's move her."

They stood up and headed back into the bedroom.

"I'd like to have a look at the gun," said Taggart, as the technicians prepared to move J.P.'s body onto a rolling gurney.

He saw that the dead woman's fingers were only loosely clenched around the butt of the pistol. Using his handkerchief, Taggart gripped the gun by the barrel and slid it free. He held the muzzle up to his nose.

"Recently fired," he said. "I'm surprised no one heard the shot."

"The spinster upstairs was probably the only one who could have heard it, and she's practically deaf," said Drummond. "My men talked to the three tenants on the opposite side of the house. None of them heard anything unusual last night. To be on the safe side, I've sent men to question everyone in the adjoining houses, too."

J.P.'s body was gently shifted onto the gurney. After they covered her with a sheet, the orderlies strapped her down and rolled the gurney outside to a police ambulance. Gazing down at the pistol again, Taggart saw two initials engraved into one of the ivory butt plates.

"E.K.," he said aloud.

"Strike a chord?" asked Drummond.

"Everett Kilgore comes to mind," he said.

"General Kilgore?" asked Liza.

"The same, I imagine," said Taggart.

"I'm going in the ambulance with J.P.," said Liza, almost protectively.

"Fine," said Taggart. "I'm heading back to the office. Call me there as soon as you're finished."

"Yes, sir," she said, then stopped to turn around once more as she reached the door.

"Did they happen to find any of her jewelry?" she asked.

Drummond put on his glasses and perused the tally sheet he had been given.

"No," he said.

"She had nice things," said Liza. "Very good jewelry. She usually put it on when she was leaving the office to go out for the evening. If you haven't found any, then it raises the possibility of a robbery motive. That or she had a good hiding place."

Taggart and Drummond looked at one another.

"I'll try the kitchen," said Drummond with a raised eyebrow.

Liza was mystified when Sam replied, "The bathroom for me."

As they headed in opposite directions, she shook her head and went out to the ambulance.

The bathroom was still filled with the lingering aroma of fragrant soap and good perfume. Unlike in Joss Dunbar's apartment, there were personal possessions everywhere Taggart looked. A douche bag was hanging from a hook on the back of the door. In the drawers of the glossy white cabinet, Taggart found soft, flimsy lingerie, silk stockings, bras and panties in every hue and shade. The drawers of her dressing table yielded an assortment of makeup, hair curlers, and beauty aids, along with a second douche bag.

The medicine chest was full. Several of the prescribed medications had been issued from a U.S. Army pharmacy and were made out in the name of Everett Kilgore. A safety razor sat on the top shelf, next to a mug of soft soap and a whisker brush. Taggart noticed that it was missing its blade. He emptied the various jars and bottles on each shelf into the sink. There was nothing inside them except the labeled contents. Drummond joined him as Taggart was unscrewing the ceiling fixture. It yielded three dead flies.

"No joy here," Drummond said. "I'm chagrined to report that there is no jewelry hidden in the kitchen, and no hiding places to have secreted a jewelry box or anything else. I tend to doubt she ever set foot in it."

"No luck here either," said Taggart. "Perhaps this did start as a robbery."

Standing up from the dressing table, he walked over to the massive bathtub.

"This room must have cost a small fortune," said Taggart. All these fixtures are American-made . . . top-of-the-line. Who owns this building?"

"Local fellow . . . I spoke to him before you arrived. He said this work was all done by the army—your army."

"I can guess who ordered it done," said Taggart.

Taking his flashlight, he began to examine the four-inch tiles that covered the walls and floor. They were white and red, the spaces between them grouted with pink cement. The work was obviously recent and done by a skilled joiner. The patterns were straight and perfect.

He was on his knees with the flashlight trained on a section of wall beneath the sink when he found a small irregularity. Instead of solid pink grouting around the tiles, the cement appeared to be black. He then saw that the black grouting was actually a series of tiny gaps surrounding two four-inch tiles behind the nickel-plated drainpipe.

Drummond was standing over his shoulder when Taggart said, "Bingo."

"What is that?" asked the old man.

"One of our national pastimes," said Taggart, placing the flashlight on the floor.

Using his fingers, he began applying modest pressure to the first tile. When nothing happened, he moved to the second one. Employing the same pressure, he felt the tile spring back toward his hand.

"Pressure switch," he said, removing his hand and allowing the little access panel to swing open.

The hole in the wall was about eight by four inches.

"She obviously had the tile joiner install this for her," said Taggart, reaching into the space behind the tile-covered door. His hand came out of the darkness holding a small felt-covered jewelry box. He handed it to Drummond and reached in again.

"Well, it wasn't robbery, Sam," said Drummond, sifting through the pieces.

Taggart held up another object. It was a U.S. Army overseas cap, prewar issue, sweat-stained and obviously well traveled. Stenciled inside the band was the name "BARNES, LLOYD, 2LT."

"The husband?" asked Drummond.

Taggart nodded before his fingers found one more object in the hiding place.

The book was the size of a small business ledger, the bindings made of cheap red fabric. He opened it to the first page. The handwriting was in large capital letters.

"MY DIARY," it read. Under that was written the words, "JANET PATRICIA RITTENHOUSE."

"Still a bingo?" asked Drummond.

"Yeah," said Taggart.

CHAPTER 13

Taggart got up from his desk, shut his office door, and then sat down again. He took a sip of the fresh hot coffee and opened the diary back to the first page. It was dated June 4, 1939. The words were written in a girlish hand, with little curlicues punctuating the letters.

> *I guess it's hard to believe that a farm girl from Kinderhook is going to be the wife of the most handsome cadet at West Point, but that is the God's honest truth. I've decided to put all my new experiences down in this book to be saved for when I am old and looking back at our life together and want to remind myself of everything that happened along the way.*
>
> *It all started when Lindsay asked me to go with her to the cotillion. I almost fell over when she told me. Lindsay had been working behind the counter in her dad's store when a young man had come in to ask for directions. The next thing she knew, he said he thought she was real pretty and could she go to the movies with him sometime. Lindsay's dad came right over to put an end to it, but when he found out the young man was a cadet at West Point, he became all smiles. One thing led to another, and after he invited her down to the Point for the winter cotillion, it turned out he had a friend who needed a date, too. I told her I didn't have one good dress to my name. Lindsay said her mother would sew one for each of us, and she did. Lindsay's was red chiffon and mine was white organdy. All the girls at school were green I can tell you. When our train pulled in at West Point, there were about thirty cadets waiting there on the platform for their dates. My eyes found Lloyd right away. I think I fell in love with him before I even knew he was my date.*

Taggart skimmed through the rest of the early entries, which recounted her falling in love with Lloyd Barnes during that snowy weekend in February 1939, followed by his ardent courtship. Each page reflected the gushing enthusiasm of an eighteen-year-old high-school girl in the throes of first love. The last page in the first section culminated in the words:

We are married!

Wearing a green surgical gown, Liza stood at a stainless-steel counter in the SHAEF hospital operating suite, setting up a row of test tubes and specimen jars, as she waited for the autopsy to begin. After arriving with J.P.'s body in the ambulance, Liza had been excited to discover that the pathologist assigned to do the postmortem was none other than Dr. John Forbes Channing, one of the most renowned forensic pathologists of the early twentieth century.

Liza heard movement in the corridor, and turned as the double entrance doors swung open and an elderly little man in a blood-spattered white lab coat shuffled into the operating room. He was hunched over like a land crab and carrying a leather satchel in each hand. The man has to be almost ninety, Liza thought as he glanced briefly in her direction before going straight to J.P.'s sheet-covered body in the center of the well-lit room. He dropped the bags down on the gurney next to the operating table and turned back to her.

"Are you assisting me?" he squawked in a high-pitched voice.

"Yes, Doctor," she replied in an awestruck tone.

Pulling away the sheet, he looked down at J.P.'s body.

"She's in full rigor," he said without touching her.

"Yes, Doctor," agreed Liza. Staring at his back, she said, "Dr. Channing, I read your treatise on poisons and horology when I was a student at New York Medical College. It was absolutely brilliant."

When he didn't respond, she assumed he hadn't heard her.

Stepping around to face him, she said, "Sir, I read your treatise on horology and . . ."

"I may look decrepit to you, young lady," said the old man as he ran hot water into a pan, "but I am not deaf."

His body was actually skeletal, reduced to sinew and bone. However, his keen brown eyes were still young and vital in the ancient, craggy face. The large bald head was crowned with one tuft of white hair.

"And that was a long time ago," he said, not altogether unkindly, as his hands and fingers moved nimbly to clean the area around the entry wound in J.P.'s ear.

After wiping his hands with a clean towel, he went over to one of the cracked leather satchels and removed a brass-framed lamp connected to ten feet of coiled electrical cord. When he inserted the plug into the wall receptacle behind the operating table, a powerful cone of light lit up his path back to the examination table.

"Hold this for me," he demanded, handing her the powerful spotlight.

His tone reminded her of all the times at medical college when a male counterpart treated her with thinly veiled disdain. In those early days, it had occasionally caused her to cry. Not any longer.

Taking a probe in one hand and a small mirror-headed instrument in the other, Dr. Channing began to carefully examine the skin around the entry wound, as well as the subcutaneous membranes just inside the bullet track, where it entered the brain.

"What do you make of this?" he said, waving her closer.

Following his bloody index finger in the glare of the spotlight, her eyes focused on the mutilated tissue just inside J.P.'s right ear.

"Ancillary damage from the bullet track?" she said, after picking up a magnifying glass with her free hand and examining the tissue more closely.

"Could be," he said, "but it doesn't entirely comport. . . . Do you see how the periphery of this membrane is subluxated here . . . and the rupture of these blood vessels in the impact area? This reddened tissue appears to be just outside the path of the bullet. Of course, I could be wrong. That did happen before, you know—I was wrong once in 1923."

Grinning impishly, he paused to wipe his hands on the towel again, then went back to his satchel and returned with a thin, straight copper rod. It was etched with tiny engraved measurements along its entire length.

"Created this myself," he said as he attempted to determine the exact trajectory of the bullet's flight through her right ear by carefully probing along its track. Next he used a probe and forceps to extract the small lead slug from deep inside her brain, and dropped it into a metal tray.

"I requested that the pistol this woman was holding be test-fired into a cadaver's brain. We'll see if the bullets match later."

Taking the spotlight from her, he began a thorough external examination, spending almost five minutes on the fingers and palm of her right hand before scrutinizing the scratches on her upper thigh, and the chafing near the ventral and anterior areas of the pelvis. With almost limitless patience, he explored every inch of her body in the glare of the lamp. When he was finished, Liza wisely refrained from asking him for his preliminary conclusions.

"Well, let us begin our work inside the divine mystery, young lady," he said, moving to part J.P.'s hair at the back of her head.

He picked up a scalpel in his left hand and made a long incision across the neck, using his fingers to pull the scalp upward to expose her skull. He took a large bone-saw from the rack on the edge of the table and tested its sharpness with his thumb.

"You might be interested to know that I also wrote a monograph for the Livestock Association on how much more tender their beef would be if they waited to butcher the animals until there was full leakage of the lysosomal intracellular digestive enzymes," he said, putting the bone saw back on its peg.

"I never read that one," she said.

"Pity," he replied.

Frowning, he went back to his leather satchel and removed a small sharp-toothed butcher's saw. Coming back to J.P., he placed the edge of the blade next to the dome of her skull and began to saw.

Lloyd and I are headed for the Philippines. Now that my mom is all alone, I'm a little worried about being so far from home. But she is selling the farm and moving up to Albany, where Aunt Viv lives.

Her handwriting had subtly changed since the early diary entries. She was a young wife now, and the pages dealt with her life in Manila after Lloyd Barnes had become commissioned as a second lieutenant.

For two weeks in July, I was sure that I was pregnant, but it didn't turn out be true. I so much want a baby, and Lloyd does, too. I hope we have a boy first, although he says he wants a girl. We'll see. For now, he is doing infantry training and exercises with the Philippine soldiers under the overall command of General MacArthur. We have a little cottage on Lieutenant's Row, and I've done my best to make it seem like home.

He flipped through a dozen pages until he came to an entry in big letters.

I'm pregnant! It is the most incredible thing that has ever happened to me, and I pledge to you that I will be the best mother I can possibly be.

There was a black-trimmed mass card stuck between the next two pages.

Lloyd knows the accident wasn't my fault, but it doesn't make it any easier to see his face each morning when he passes by the room we had fixed up as the nursery. Maybe I didn't tell you this before, but she was a girl. A beautiful little blue-eyed girl. I'm going to see the doctor tomorrow. Say a prayer that I'm going to have another chance to give Lloyd his daughter.

Taggart put down the diary and rubbed his weary eyes. Reading the new entries, he realized that the diary had become a kind of talisman for her, an animate object to share her thoughts with, to consult with, and to log in her prayers, an amulet with the power to affect her life.

Using his scalpel again, Dr. Channing made a quick "Y" incision in the torso, cutting J.P. open from her shoulders down to the sternum.

"Yes . . . quite possibly a suicide," he squawked as he began to expose her organs. "There is ample powder residue on her fingers. Based on where the bullet ultimately lodged inside the brain, it was probably fired at a distance of no more than three centimeters. Although the vast majority of self-inflicted gunshot wounds are through the temple, a fair proportion of them are fired through the ear. This bullet's trajectory is certainly consistent with that possibility."

The Japanese have invaded the Philippines. They could be in Manila in a few weeks, and all the married dependents have been ordered to leave. Lloyd says that the army has arranged for many of the wives to be quartered at Fort Sill in Oklahoma until the men return. They already have some kind of job lined up for us working at the base.

As Dr. Channing was about to examine her vital organs, the door to the autopsy suite swung open. Dr. Cabot, the red-haired Philadelphia plastic surgeon whom Liza had met on her last visit to the hospital, slouched into the theater, carrying a folder in his hands. He was still wearing the long-billed fishing cap over his fatigues. When he saw Liza, his face broke into a convivial smile.

"Well, if it isn't the lovely Lieutenant Marantz," he said, chomping his ever-present gum like a healthy calf.

Dr. Channing looked up and glared at him.

"Do you have a function in this hospital?" he demanded, testily.

"Unfortunately, I'm still assigned to the laboratory," said Dr. Cabot, observing the ancient, crablike pathologist with distaste. "Someone said they wanted this blood workup immediately."

"And?" came back Channing, holding up J.P.'s heart between his hands.

"Completely normal," said the former plastic surgeon. "And the oxygen level was fine—no suggestion of hypoxemia."

"Why would we care about hypoxemia, pray tell?" growled Channing.

"I told him to check for it," said Liza, as the old man stared at her, perplexed.

I am working for the base commander. His name is General Everett Kilgore. I know from the way he stares at me through the connecting door to his office that he likes me that way. I also know it could be dangerous. This morning he said that I had a way of looking into his eyes that felt like a sock in the jaw. As far as I can tell, that's exactly what he needs—a good sock in the jaw. But he has also become my only source of information about Lloyd. Since my beloved surrendered with the others at Corregidor, I haven't heard a thing from him—even whether he is alive. General Kilgore was the one to finally break the news to me about the Bataan death march. But he says he will do everything he can to help me find out if Lloyd survived it. Pray that my darling is all right.

Stuck between the next two pages was a wrinkled and faded card. Taggart pulled it out of the diary. It was one of the Red Cross cards distributed to American soldiers held by the Japanese and Germans. Dated September 12, 1943, it consisted of just one line: "J.P. Am still alive. I love you, darling. Lloyd."

I can't even send him letters or keepsakes. All the official army types will tell me is that he is in a prisoner-of-war camp somewhere in Japan. I have decided to go with the rest of General Kilgore's staff to North Africa. He has promised to do his best to help Lloyd and me from there. And I'll be a couple thousand miles closer.

Kilgore had waited almost three months before making his move. They were in North Africa by then. He was on the Allied senior staff—one of the commander-in-chief's "eyes and ears." It was apparent that J.P. now only wrote in the diary when in the clutches of despair.

Algiers, November 2, 1943 . . . There is no one else I can tell these things to. My life may just as well be over. I got awfully drunk last night and not for the first time. But this time he helped me up to one of the guest rooms at Ike's compound. I don't remember a lot of what happened after that, but the following morning he apologized and offered me money. In my anger I took it, figuring that it was money that would help Lloyd and me make a new start after the war. What have I become?

"I would like you to check for evidence of water in her lungs," said Liza to Dr. Channing.

He looked at her as if she were an idiot and muttered, "Are you daft?"

"No, Doctor, I'm not," she replied firmly. "Based on her rectal temperature at eight-thirty this morning, her state of rigor, and the room temperature in her apartment, one could have safely speculated that the time of death was somewhere around midnight. Yet we know that she didn't even return to her apartment until three-thirty this morning, which means that something dramatically depressed her body temperature after death. As you know, water conducts body heat away up to twenty-six times faster than air of the same temperature. So I asked for a blood screening that might reveal hypoxemia, and I would now ask that you also check for signs of a petechial hemorrhage in the brain."

Dr. Cabot was gazing at her with a goofy smile on his face.

"Holy shit," he said, admiringly.

For the first time since the start of the postmortem, Dr. Channing looked at her with a glimmer of professional interest.

"A submersion injury is largely secondary to hypoxia and ischemic acidosis," he said, bringing his miner's lamp to bear on J.P.'s fully exposed heart. "Fluid aspirated into the lungs should have also produced vagally mediated pulmonary vasoconstriction and hypertension. Let's have a look."

I am a different woman from the one Lloyd left behind. Kilgore is now finished with me. I knew it from the minute that the new blonde arrived in the office. She can't even type or take dictation. He said that he had found another important use for me. I am to become an even more invaluable member of "the team," another set of "eyes and ears." "You never know what kind of information you'll pick up, honey," he said. From now on, he will tell me who he wants me to sleep with, when, and where. When I said no, he became very angry. He even suggested that Lloyd might find out what I have already done. My head aches and I can no longer write.

"No indication of hypoxemia and resultant acidosis," said Dr. Channing, switching off the spotlight and wiping his hands again with the towel. "No signs of asphyxia or water in the lungs . . . Nothing to suggest cardiac arrest consistent with even dry drowning. No petechial hemorrhaging." The door to the suite swung open again, and an orderly came forward with a small brown envelope.

"I was told to bring a .25-caliber bullet here," he said. "It was just fired."

"Give it to him," said Dr. Channing, pointing at Dr. Cabot.

Picking up the bullet he had removed from J.P.'s brain, Channing tossed it to Cabot, who caught it in midair. "I want you to see if they match under a microscope."

"I'm not a trained ballistics expert," said Dr. Cabot.

"I doubt if you're even a competent surgeon," Channing replied, "but you don't have to be. A good microscope will tell us all we need to know for now."

"Fine," said Cabot angrily. "Just don't ask me to make you look young again."

Taggart finished his coffee and read the last entry in the diary.

> *Another part of me died this morning. I am so tired of these brass hats with their pompous arrogant staffs throwing their weight around on people who can't fight back.*

Utterly enraged, Taggart slammed the heel of his hand into the side of the desk. He only wished that he had his old heavy bag in the office so he could release the surge of anger that threatened to consume him. Maybe he was a throwback to a different time, but he found the way she had been manipulated by Kilgore, pimped by him, and then thrown away contemptible.

The phone began to ring on his desk. It was Liza.

"I will have a full report for you by tonight, but here are our preliminary findings," she said. "Although there is a troubling question about the time of death, the pathologist and I agree that J.P. probably took her own life, and that the weapon was the .25-caliber revolver she was holding in her hand. The bullet in her brain matches the gun."

Taggart already knew that he would be going after Kilgore one way or the other.

"As far as the contusions on her nipples and the other superficial injuries, the pathologist and I concur that these occurred several hours before her death—certainly before she came home at three-thirty," she went on. "They are consistent with either a sexual assault or violent sex. There were only small traces of male semen inside her vaginal canal, but that is probably because she douched upon her return home and then took a bath."

Taggart had stopped listening to her. He was remembering the initials he had seen engraved on the ivory butt-plate.

"E.K."

He felt the furies rising inside him again.

CHAPTER 14

From deep inside the labyrinth of the SHAEF building on Saint James Square, Taggart thought he heard a roll of thunder as he headed down a dark hallway and stopped at the big mahogany door. A polished brass nameplate identified the occupant of the office suite as Major General Everett Kilgore.

Taggart opened the door and stepped inside. A plump blonde WAC with Shirley Temple curls was painting her nails at the reception desk. She was alone in the outer office.

"I'm here to see General Kilgore," he said. "I called earlier for an appointment."

She looked up at him and smiled.

"I'll see if he is receiving, Major," she said, displaying glistening white teeth. The meaty solidarity of her was undercut by a thin, shrill voice.

After standing up from the desk, she took a moment to smooth the front of her uniform skirt before crossing the room to the door of the inner office. The curls bounced in poetic rhythm as she walked away from him. She knocked once and went inside, closing the door behind her. She was back out in less than a minute.

"He must have left while I was down at the canteen," she said, slowly ambling up to him. "Would you like to wait?"

"Yeah," said Taggart, wondering if this was the blonde that J.P. had written about in her diary.

"You're real good-looking," she said with a simpering smile. "I bet you know it, too."

"It's the uniform," he said. "The uniform makes the man."

She had a little button nose. Some men might have thought it was cute. Seeing her nostrils flaring up at him, Taggart thought it looked piggish.

"No, it's not the uniform," she said, unfazed. "So what do you do around here?"

She was standing no more than a foot away from him, her sculpted hips cocked in a provocative cant. He smelled good perfume.

"I'm Ike's golf pro," he said.

"You are not!" she said, her eyes wide. "Really?"

The door to the inner office swung open, and two officers came out. One was a colonel and the other a captain. They both had aiguillettes hanging from the shoulder straps of their uniforms, identifying them as staff aides. The colonel picked up a briefcase from the conference table and headed toward the door. He stopped a few feet from Taggart.

"Do you know how to salute a superior officer?" he demanded.

Taggart came to attention and saluted him. Frowning, the colonel returned it with crisp precision. When they left, Taggart walked over to a chair under the window and sat down. The WAC went back to painting her nails, her tongue extended between her teeth as she concentrated on the task. Occasionally, she would glance over at him with open interest and then smile.

Thirty minutes passed with no one coming in or out. Considering how busy the rest of the headquarters was, Taggart wondered what General Kilgore really did. Through the window, he watched as the pelting rain drubbed the sentries standing in front of the sandbagged entrance to the building.

He thought of J.P.'s diary, and it made him angry all over again. Like her, Taggart knew all about loneliness and unabated guilt. He was trying to clear his mind when the outer door opened and General Kilgore strode in. There was a physical heft about him, an aura of carefully cultivated dominance. Looking neither right nor left, he disappeared into his office. The WAC followed him through the door, closing it behind her.

Five minutes passed. The WAC came out again. She was no longer smiling.

"You can go in now," she said nervously.

Kilgore was standing at the window of his large office with his back to the room. His hands were clasped behind his back. Dramatically turning to face Taggart, he pointed to the chair in front of the big polished desk.

A silver-framed photograph sat on the edge of the blotter. It showed a solemn General Kilgore with his arm around a portly, gray-haired woman, the two of them surrounded by four teenaged children.

As he sat down, Sam looked up at Kilgore closely for the first time. The shaved head and fleshy nose were vaguely reminiscent of Mussolini, but the small, close-set monkey eyes undercut any appearance of imposing intelligence. His carefully pressed uniform was obviously tailored. There was no disguising the barrel chest, linebacker's neck, and long powerful arms. He used his physical menace to full advantage.

"I've made a little time to see you, Major," said General Kilgore in his baritone voice. "I'm not sure why. I don't like policemen."

From across the desk, Sam picked up the scent of his strong aftershave. He remembered smelling the same cologne in one of the bottles in J.P.'s bathroom. The thought of it made him furious again.

"Yeah . . . we're real popular wherever we go," replied Taggart. "I assumed it was because I made it clear to one of your aides that if you didn't see me I was going straight to General Manigault."

"Didn't you forget something, Major?"

"What's that?" asked Taggart.

"Sir," commanded Kilgore.

Taggart forced a lazy grin.

"Sir," he repeated.

"Staff cooperation within the security command is vital," pronounced Kilgore, his jaw rigid. "We need to make sure everyone is on the same page. As I'm sure you know, there is an invasion coming."

"Yeah . . . and I'm sure you know that Lieutenant Barnes is dead," said Taggart, adding, "sir."

The general's silver eyebrows suddenly arched in a steeple of sympathy. When he stepped away from the desk again, Taggart's eyes strayed down to his feet. His polished black boots had two-inch lifts.

"I was deeply sorry to hear about that," he said, as if fondly recalling a good soldier fallen in battle. "I gather it was a suicide."

"A suicide?" said Taggart.

"I just assumed. . . . I'll confide something to you," he said. "She wasn't very happy with her life. Her husband survived the Bataan death march and is being held prisoner by the Japs."

"Yeah I know," said Taggart. "But that's pretty gamy coming from you, General, isn't it, sir?"

Kilgore was staring out the window as if the fate of the invasion hinged on his continued delivery of well-aged steaks and Johnny Walker Red to the top Overlord commanders.

"What did you say?" he demanded, pivoting to face Taggart.

"You'll be sorry to learn that she was killed with your gun."

"My gun?"

"The bullet they took out of her brain is a 6.35-millimeter slug. It matches your pistol—the one engraved with your initials."

Kilgore stared at him for almost ten seconds.

"I gave that weapon to Lieutenant Barnes some time ago . . . for her personal protection," he said, beginning to pace slowly back and forth in front of the window. "We were in North Africa at the time. There was a constant danger from street criminals. I was worried about every female member of my staff."

"Because your heart is pure, is that it?" asked Taggart. "Sir?"

Kilgore's mouth went hard.

"I won't take that from you," he said.

"Two young women from the same office have died in less than a week. Lieutenant Marantz says that you knew both of them."

"I don't know any Lieutenant Marantz," he said.

"She worked in the same office," said Taggart, "and said that after your return from North Africa you asked for them both by their first names."

The general's hand rose from the desktop. He extended it toward Taggart as if quieting an obnoxious heckler.

"You would be wise not to take this any further, Major."

Taggart felt the rage steadily rising in him again, like a blazing fire.

"Where were you last night, General—say, from around three o'clock to five?"

"Asleep in my bed," he came right back.

"Really? Which bed?" asked Taggart.

"I swear I won't take any more insolence from you," said Kilgore.

"You don't have to, General. Someone else can ask you the questions—Ernie Manigault, maybe."

He stopped pacing and came back to the desk.

"Ernie would understand this," he murmured, as if testing the proposition.

"Why don't you tell me who paid for the bathroom, General?"

"What bathroom?"

"The one in the apartment you arranged for Lieutenant Barnes, the one with the brand-new fixtures shipped over from the States . . . the one where all the work was done by U.S. Army contractors."

"I haven't got the slightest idea."

"Lieutenant Barnes didn't have the money for it."

"How do you know?" he said without pausing. "I don't like to pry into the personal lives of my former staff members, but I understand she got around."

"By getting around, you mean she turned tricks for extra money?"

"You said it, Major. Not me," he replied.

"So where were you last night, General?"

A glint of cunning appeared in the back of the monkey eyes. He gave Taggart a suddenly expansive smile.

"At the right time, that can be accounted for to Ernie Manigault's satisfaction," he said. "Being an officer and a gentleman, I'm sure that you understand even generals need a little rest and relaxation."

"I found two douche bags in Lieutenant Barnes's bathroom, General. I guess you kept her working overtime when it came to your rest and relaxation."

A vein began to pulse at Kilgore's left temple.

"I've taken all of this I'm going to," he said. "Keep pressing your luck and you'll find out how the army deals with troublemakers like you."

Taggart grinned back at him.

"I could kick your ass from here to Sunday," said the general, sizing up Taggart with a sneer.

"Try it," said Taggart. "You don't look all that tough to me. Besides, you'd get that new uniform all wrinkled."

"Just continue on this track and you'll find out how tough I am. People get hurt in wars. Things even happen behind the lines," said Kilgore.

"Behind the lines . . . You'd know all about that, wouldn't you, General?"

Pulling open the center drawer of his desk, Kilgore removed a brown service folder. Without opening it, he dropped it on the blotter. "You were pegged as a troublemaker months ago. I know how to deal with men like you."

He began tapping his index finger on the closed file.

"You're some piece of work, General," said Taggart.

"Colonel Baird prepared a full report on you, Taggart. If I were to show this to Ike, you would be on the next plane to the Aleutian Islands. I gather you can be very tough to live with . . . can't you?"

"So what does that mean?"

"Your wife committed suicide, didn't she?"

Taggart suddenly felt himself starting to lose control, unconsciously clenching and unclenching his fingers on his lap. He imagined the general's neck between his hands.

"And we know why as well. We have her suicide note. Very interesting reading."

Taggart suppressed his rage and said, "You know what I think? I think you murdered Lieutenant Barnes, General, or you had somebody take care of it for you. J.P. was about to become an embarrassment, wasn't she?"

"Go ahead—keep it up," Kilgore said, grinning almost merrily. "Dig your own grave."

"She kept a detailed diary, General, and you are the man of the hour in it. Very interesting reading, as I guess you can imagine. Maybe we should both show what we have to General Eisenhower."

As Taggart watched, the general's demeanor subtly changed, the look of the predatory animal slowly melting away as uncertainty crept into his eyes.

"If you weren't with her last night," said Taggart, "I want the name of the man you told her to sleep with. I will also need to interview the people who can vouch for your whereabouts at three-thirty."

Kilgore's gaze was now centered on the framed photograph of his wife and children.

"General? I'm speaking to you. We believe that Lieutenant Barnes was sexually assaulted before she died."

"I have never assaulted a woman in my life," he said woodenly.

"Yeah... I guess you didn't have to, did you? You just get them drunk and helpless. And when you finish with them, you throw them away like paper plates after the picnic. You're a lousy pimp in gold braid, General."

"I had nothing to do with her death," Kilgore said, his voice starting to quake. "I..."

"We found deep scratches on Lieutenant Barnes's thighs. There should be traces of her skin under the fingernails of whoever did it to her. I need to take a scraping of the material under your fingernails. It can be typed... just like blood."

General Kilgore continued to stare at the photograph on the desk, his cheeks mottled a deep red. Removing his pocketknife, Taggart opened the blade and came around to Kilgore's side of the desk. He was prepared for a fight, but there was no resistance when he grasped the general's right hand and took the scrapings. Taggart swiped the blade inside an evidence packet and put it in his breast pocket.

"One final question... Did Lieutenant Barnes have either direct or indirect knowledge of the invasion plans?"

Kilgore was now gazing at the far wall, seemingly oblivious, but Taggart could see the hatred in his eyes.

"Yeah... how could she not?" said Taggart disgustedly.

The blonde WAC in the outer office was in the process of filing her newly painted nails when he came past, her tongue still projecting through her front teeth. She stared up at him as he went out the door, slamming it behind him.

The room was silent for several seconds.

"Tell Colonel Baird to get up here immediately," called out the general from inside his office.

CHAPTER 15

Alone in a dank, evil-smelling room within the pathology wing of the hospital, Liza glanced nervously up at the wood-framed clock on the wall. It was almost midnight. She took comfort in the occasional laughter that came from the night staff in the morgue, farther down the corridor.

It had taken her almost two hours to decipher Dr. Channing's hastily scrawled and bloodstained postmortem notes. While waiting for J.P.'s fluid analyses from the laboratory, she found herself nodding off to sleep several times before she could finish the typewritten report. Then, after collating the original and two carbons, she carried one copy down to Dr. Channing's empty office and left it on his desk.

"Death by probable suicide," was the inescapable conclusion they had jointly reached after Dr. Channing completed his internal examination and Dr. Cabot came back to confirm that the grooves of the two bullets were an identical match under the microscope. Once Dr. Channing had left the autopsy suite, the young doctor grinned broadly at her and said, "We make a good team, don't we?"

She could only laugh at his relentlessly obvious approach.

"Yes, we do," she agreed, bone-weary and suddenly famished.

"So—how about dinner?" he asked. She found herself saying yes.

They went around the corner to a small Italian restaurant he recommended and enjoyed a simple meal of pasta and red wine. Liza was surprised to find that she actually enjoyed his company, not in a romantic sense, but in the casual way he had of making her laugh, something she had sorely missed in recent weeks. It turned out that he had also gone to the New York Medical College, and they compared notes on several of the professors.

When they returned to the pathology unit, she fended off his advances without hurting his feelings, and shooed him after a pretty nurse who came into the lab to drop off a supply of fresh towels. By then, she felt thoroughly worn out. As soon as she completed the postmortem report, she decided to go straight back to her room on Grosvenor Road.

As she headed out the front entrance of the hospital, air-raid sirens began their strident wail all over the blacked-out city. After so many hours in the smelly pathology unit, the thought of spending the rest of the night in one of London's foul-smelling shelters seemed intolerable. Besides, she assured herself, the recent raids had concentrated on the East End dock facilities.

Knowing there would be no chance to find a taxi, she struck off for the Thames Embankment on foot. Within minutes, she heard the low, sinister drone to the east signaling the arrival of the first Luftwaffe bombing formation. She sped up and turned onto one of the narrow cobblestoned streets that led toward Horse Guards Row and the Thames Embankment beyond.

One by one, the powerful searchlights mounted near the rooftop anti-aircraft batteries began to light up the sky over London. She moved into a slow trot as the anti-aircraft spotters probed the sky for the first German pathfinders.

In the street ahead of her, a dozen people were running from their homes to one of the many air-raid shelters identified by a big white-painted "S" over the doorway. Most of them were already dressed in their nightclothes.

The concentrated gun batteries near Battersea and Holborn opened fire with a great booming roar as the German bombers appeared in the distance. While Liza continued running, she tried to occupy her mind with something that Charlie had told her when the "baby blitz" had begun a few weeks earlier.

Employing the tone of a condescending professor, he had explained that the German bombs fell at a speed of 150 miles per hour, and that based on the German's usual bombing altitude of twenty thousand feet, it took the bombs ninety seconds to land. After providing her with a needlessly technical explanation for how increased air resistance created the whistling noise, he said that the distinctive wail began one minute after their release through the bomb bays.

"So that gives you thirty seconds to find shelter after the initial wail turns into a mortal shriek," he said, giving her his lopsided grin.

Still jogging along the sidewalk toward the Embankment, she realized that his scientific reasoning was absurd. A direct hit would mean instantaneous death, and, based on her past experience, there was no way to tell from the whistling noise whether the bomb was dropping directly on top of you or would land two streets away.

Parliament Square was looming up in the distance when several bombs exploded off to the northeast, momentarily lighting up the horizon. She felt the concussion through her shoes, and the pavement trembled menacingly beneath her feet.

Beginning to sprint, she looked up to see the roving searchlights on the roof of Parliament. Far above them, one of the huge, sausagelike barrage balloons floated in and out of the swirling beams.

With her energy almost spent, Liza came to a sudden stop on the sidewalk, her chest heaving madly. She drew in great gulps of air as several more bombs landed a block or so closer. It was when she turned to watch the glare of the explosions a few streets behind her that she saw the man: a dark figure in a broad-brimmed fedora and long overcoat, about thirty yards behind her, running from the direction she had just come.

Liza's first reaction was one of almost detached curiosity. She assumed that he was doing precisely what she was, trying to get home without having to sit out the raid in a smelly shelter. That thought was immediately followed by the nagging recollection that she had seen the same man on the sidewalk outside the hospital. What if he had been following her? Without knowing why, she sensed deadly danger, and not from the bombs falling out of the sky. It was the primal fear of a hunted animal.

As she began to run again, the hideous images of Joss and J.P. raced through her brain. A rush of pure terror seized her as she desperately looked for a policeman or air-raid warden who might be patrolling the street ahead. She glanced back to see that he was still coming after her. Although now breathing as heavily as she was, he was slowly gaining ground.

Liza came to the next corner. Left or right? She had a fraction of a second to make her choice. She turned left, away from the Embankment and in the direction of Westminster Abbey, where there were sure to be more people. Over the approaching din of the bombers, she could hear the sharp tapping of the man's boot heels as they struck the pavement behind her in quick succession.

"Footsteps have a rhythm as uniquely characteristic as fingerprints," she suddenly remembered one of her criminology professors declaring as he droned on through a boring lecture at Barnard. But of what value is the information if you're already dead? her mind silently screamed.

A moment later, there was a tremendous clamoring roar as the gun batteries around Parliament opened up in a cacophony of earsplitting noise. She felt another concussion beneath her feet as bombs landed a block or two away, near Whitehall. The last tremor shook her violently.

Running on, she could see a chemist shop on fire and passed through a cloud of pungent black smoke. Straight ahead, she saw a white-painted "S" above the doorway of a tall brick building opposite Westminster Abbey, and began to run toward it.

The shriek of falling bombs penetrated her ears as she ran though the opening between the five-foot-high walls of sandbags surrounding the entrance to the shelter. Grasping the bronze handle of the massive metal-studded door, she pulled hard. It was either jammed or blocked from the inside. She turned and saw that the running man was only ten feet behind her. In the glare of a wildly spinning searchlight, she saw something metallic glint in his hand.

There was a brilliant flash of light and she felt a cataclysm boiling beneath her feet. The earth seemed to splinter upward before it slammed her back down to the pavement. She clapped her hands to her ears as a deafening explosion concussed the sandbags next to her head amid eruptions of pink-and-yellow flame. She opened her mouth to scream, but found she could not draw breath. Frantically, she groped closer to the edge of the nearest sandbag.

All about her, the street was raked with bits of glass, brick, and stone. Acrid bomb grit filled her nose and mouth as a section of the sandbag wall collapsed across her back. Horror-struck, Liza waited for the air to clear, feeling like a trussed animal.

A hurricane of anti-aircraft fire was still raging into the sky above her when she finally dislodged the weight and rose to her knees. The first thing she saw was the blazing façade of the building across the street. As she watched, it came tumbling down like a descending stage curtain. In the middle of the roadway, a fountain of black water was spewing high in the air from an exposed water main that lay in the middle of a vast bomb crater.

A cloud of choking smoke hung low over the street. In the glare of the searchlights, she suddenly glimpsed the man who had been running after her. He was lying on his back in the gutter at the edge of the sidewalk, his legs splayed out in two impossibly different directions, like a broken marionette.

Her ears were still aching from the bomb concussions when the door to the air-raid shelter screeched open behind her, and an elderly man with a grimy face slowly came out. His light-blue air warden's uniform was covered with plaster dust. From the dark, cavernous shelter behind him issued a series of terrified screams.

The warden made his way slowly toward her through the haze. After stooping to help her up, he spied the body lying in the street and shone his flashlight into its face. As the earth beneath them continued to shake with bomb tremors, he said, "Sad . . . he almost made it. A friend, miss?"

She stared down at the corpse. His hat had fallen away, and she could see him clearly in the flashlight beam. The face was no longer human. One eye peered out of a hideous scarlet mask.

"No? I guess his own mother wouldn't recognize him now," the elderly warden murmured. He bent down next to the corpse and briefly searched the pockets of his suit jacket.

"It says he worked for the Irish Consulate," he said, examining the man's identification under the flashlight.

Liza looked down at the man's right hand. Whatever he had been grasping in his fist was gone. She wondered whether it might have been a knife or gun. What if she had been wrong? It might have been anything. The whole idea of his stalking her suddenly seemed absurd.

Two sobbing women came out of the air-raid shelter behind them. One was obviously pregnant and clutching her abdomen. She lurched out into the street, pleading to be taken to a hospital. Liza calmed the woman down and stayed with her until an ambulance arrived a few minutes later.

It began to rain again as she walked home amid the carnage of smoking wreckage and damaged buildings. A wing of Buckingham Palace had been hit and was on fire. One of the Luftwaffe bombers had crashed into the woods fringing Green Park and was still a raging inferno. On almost every side street, firefighters were battling the spread of dozens of blazes as rescue workers dragged survivors from the rubble of their former homes.

The rain became a downpour, running down her collar and chilling her to the core. Somehow the icy water was a calming influence, serving to numb her brain and partially soothe her raw nerve endings. The distant drone of the last bombers faded away as she reached the Thames Embankment and saw that her hotel was undamaged.

In her room, Liza took off her wet, bloodstained uniform and fell exhausted into bed. Yet, as much as she willed it, sleep would not come, the events leading to her narrow escape continuing to play over and over in her fevered mind.

Power was out in most of the city, but one of the American engineers at the hotel had rigged up a generator on the ground floor to provide temporary electricity. The engine was very loud, and as she stared up into the darkness, it felt as if the room were part of some great machine moving slowly through the night.

CHAPTER 16

Taggart was forced to stand in the driving rain outside the Admiralty Building while a South African military policeman personally checked the identification papers of every person seeking entrance. As each minute passed, the crowd became louder and more belligerent. A man in a bowler hat suddenly began shouting that his Member of Parliament would soon hear about it.

Taggart was already fifteen minutes late for his appointment with Helen Bellayne when he finally passed through the checkpoint. Inside, an English military policeman informed him that, thanks to a continuing power outage, the elevators weren't working.

Still favoring his sprained ankle, Taggart joined the herd of people slowly making their way up the stairs. The bombing raid had caused jagged chunks of plaster to shake loose from the ceiling of the stairwell, and several times he was forced to dodge falling debris while making the long climb to the seventh floor. He paused for a minute outside her office to regain his breath before stepping inside.

"I have an appointment with Mrs. Bellayne," he huffed to the wizened navy petty officer manning the front desk.

"I'm sorry, Major, but she never came in this morning," he said. "I believe her street took several hits in the raid last night."

"Shit," said Taggart, fuming at his useless odyssey.

"Try to keep a stiff upper lip, sir," said the petty officer. "I'm sure she's safe."

"Yeah, thanks," said Taggart.

As he trudged back down the stairwell, echoing in his ears were Drummond's words after the old inspector had interviewed Helen Bellayne himself: "I had the strong impression she was hiding something," he had said.

Taggart needed to find out what it was and why. By the time he got back down to the lobby of the Admiralty Building, he had decided to go straight to her home. After calling the inspector's office to get her address, he hailed a taxi and gave it to the driver.

"A posh one, that is," the driver said, before heading out into the inevitable crush of military traffic.

The war-ravaged city was at its most gray and dismal as Taggart watched people digging out from the previous night's raid through the grimy side window. Twenty minutes later, the taxi pulled up short in front of a bomb crater in the middle of a residential street in Belgravia.

"The place you want is up along there," the driver said, pointing farther up the lane. "It looks like they took a real pasting last night. Sorry, but I can't get you no closer."

Taggart paid him off and went ahead on foot in the driving rain. Beyond the bomb crater, there were magnificent brick mansions on both sides of the avenue, relics of the golden eras of the British Empire.

Farther up the street, relief workers were sifting through what remained of one of them. Taggart smelled the sour odor of smoldering wood and rain-soaked plaster. As he walked by, several men were vainly trying to pry up a massive support timber from the largest section of rubble.

"I think there's someone still alive down here," screamed one of them with a voice like a macaw. Taggart was climbing toward them to help when another voice called out, "She's had it, lads. Stand easy."

Helen Bellayne's address was farther up the block, at that end of the avenue. There the houses had sustained cracked and broken windows, but none appeared to have taken a direct hit. The last property on the street was surrounded by an eight-foot-high brick wall and had an ornately carved iron gate in the center. A dull brass nameplate was embedded in the wall. It read, "BELLAYNE."

Taggart pushed the gate open and headed up the long gravel driveway toward the front entrance. He saw that the grounds were overgrown with thornbushes and strewn with weeds.

The central wing of the mansion was probably a few centuries old and had been constructed with monument-sized blocks of white granite and polished stone columns. Two imperious brick wings extended away from the central structure like a miniature version of the U.S. Capitol.

He recalled Drummond telling him that the house had once been imposing. Now he understood the full meaning of his words. Even without the benefit of German bombs, the place was slowly falling to ruin. The roof on the left wing had begun to settle badly in the middle, like a swayback horse. White paint was peeling off the windows like mange on a dog's back. A number of the window frames had rotted away and been replaced with raw boards. Pigeons were roosting in the crevices behind them. Sheltered from the cold rain, they silently watched him pass by.

Taggart arrived at a covered stone portico and pulled the bell chain next to the front door. Although it was nine o'clock in the morning, none of the blackout curtains had been drawn away from the ground floor windows. After waiting almost a minute, he pulled the chain again. It rang faintly behind the massive oak door.

He was just about to leave when he heard the sound of a dead bolt sliding in the lock, and the door slowly swung open. A slim figure was standing in deep shadow in the foyer. From her faltering movements, he thought she must be old and very frail. As she came tentatively out of the gloom, Taggart was shocked to discover that it was Helen Bellayne. A hint of recognition registered on her pallid face when she looked up at him.

"Oh, it's you," she said, her voice seeming to come from a great distance. "I thought you were . . . Well . . . come in."

She slowly closed the door behind him. For a few moments, they stood awkwardly together in the dark, high-ceilinged foyer as his trench coat dripped rainwater onto the black-and-white marble tiles. Taggart could feel no heat in the house, and he shivered involuntarily.

"Please come with me," she said, walking toward another closed door. "It's warmer in the library. I have a fire there."

The high-ceilinged library faced onto a back garden. Its four bay windows had white lace curtains, trimmed on each side with maroon satin drapes drawn away from the windows with braided tassels. One of the blackout curtains had been pulled away, allowing in a pale, filtered, greenish light.

The walls of the library were lined with floor-to-ceiling bookshelves, most of them crammed with books, photographs, and small family objects. The room was decorated with rosewood furniture. Comfortable chairs and couches were grouped together in each corner. Persian carpets covered the wide plank floors. A seven-foot-high grandfather clock stood silently against one wall.

As she led him toward the small coal fire, he could see that the furniture coverings were worn and frayed, the carpets cracked with age and water damage. There was an empty space over the fireplace where a large painting had recently hung. A thin coating of plaster dust covered everything in the room. He took off his wet trench coat and laid it next to the warm hearth as she slowly turned to face him.

"Forgive me, Major," said Helen Bellayne. "I'm afraid I've just been wandering around here like Miss Havisham. I must really try to clean up this mess."

She was wearing a gray cashmere sweater over a medium-length charcoal skirt. Despite the reference to the eccentric Dickens character, Taggart thought she was the loveliest woman he had met since arriving in England. Her gold-flecked amber eyes accented the heart-shaped, delicate face. In truth, she reminded him of his wife, even down to the slender body and tapered legs.

"You have blood on your clothes," said Taggart gently.

Her eyes followed his own down to the dried stains on the front of her gray sweater.

"That is Gwendolyn's, I'm afraid," she said with a suggestion of stubborn weariness. "She . . . died last night. . . . One of the bombs caught her on her way back here from her daughter's flat. They brought her home after the all-clear sounded. I thought you would be the person from the undertaker's coming to get her."

In the dim light, Taggart noticed an inert human form lying on a couch below one of the tall bay windows. The body was covered by a blue afghan.

"A relative?"

"No," she said with a fragile smile. "But she worked for my mother and then me for almost forty years. Very much part of the family."

She began to totter to one side.

"I'm sorry, but you'll have to excuse me," she said, sagging backward into the chair near the hearth. The small coal fire had done nothing to remove the chill from the room.

"Have you eaten anything today?" asked Taggart.

She shook her head.

"Yesterday?"

Her eyes began to flutter, and one pale hand rose slowly to her throat. As he moved toward her, the arm dropped to her side and she fainted. When he picked her up in his arms, she was completely limp. He carried her back into the foyer, momentarily stopping to regain his bearings.

The two wings of the mansion headed off to the left and right. Along the passageways he could see open doorways to what were probably formal entertaining rooms. He assumed the bedrooms were upstairs. A wide marble staircase led up into the darkness, and he began to climb.

Taggart carried her into the first bedroom he found on the second floor and placed her on the canopied bed. Although the room appeared to have been in recent use, there were no personal items to indicate who might have occupied it.

Her hand was very cold, and he began to chafe her wrist. Feeling for her pulse, he found the heartbeat tremulous and elevated. He removed her shoes and covered her with a heavy feather tick that was rolled up at the foot of the bed.

A few moments later, the front-door chime began to peal downstairs. He went back down to the foyer and opened the big oak door. A man was standing under the portico, holding an open umbrella in one hand and a greasy bowler hat in the other. His pomaded hair was parted in the middle, and he was wearing a long black frock coat. A pimple-faced boy in blue coveralls was standing behind him, holding a folded canvas stretcher.

"I'm Mr. Feith," the man said with a grisly smile. "I was called about a loved one who needs to be removed from these premises." Over his shoulder, Taggart could see a dilapidated Black Maria backed up to the curb in the street.

"She's in the library," said Taggart.

After the undertaker and the boy had carried the body of Helen Bellayne's servant out to the hearse, the man returned to present him with a bill for the service. Taggart thought the amount was probably enough to bury three or four people before the new German bombing campaign. Supply and demand, he realized.

"It will need to be paid before we begin all the necessary arrangements," said Mr. Feith firmly. "I'm sure you understand."

"I understand," said Taggart. "You're a vulture."

After closing the door in his face, he left the bill on a table in the foyer and went looking for the kitchen. Heading down the hallway that led through the right wing, he passed a large formal dining room and a butler's pantry before reaching the kitchen.

A big iron cookstove sat under a copper hood against the far wall. It was a wood-burner, just like the stove he grew up with in his family's Yorkville tenement. Taggart quickly set a small fire with paper and wood chunks under the stove plates.

Except for a small pitcher of rancid cream, the refrigerator was empty. The cupboards contained nothing but a wide assortment of crockery. He walked into the large cold pantry off the kitchen. He found only some small burlap bags containing moldy onions and potatoes.

Taggart went back into the library, put on his trench coat, and headed out to the rain-slicked street in front of the mansion. A few blocks to the east, he found a busier crossroad that led to a small food shop. Most of the shelves were empty, but Taggart collected a fresh loaf of bread, one jar of homemade currant jam, a small round of butter, some packets of brown sugar, a pint of milk, and six ounces of tea.

When the shopkeeper asked for his ration coupons, Taggart told him he didn't have any. Scowling, the man began to remove the items from the sack. Taggart took a twenty-dollar bill out of his wallet and laid it on the counter. After the man glanced in both directions, he replaced all the items in the sack.

"We call these Yank coupons," said the storekeeper, putting the bill in his pants pocket.

The mansion house was silent when Taggart returned. He went straight back to the kitchen. The stovetop was hot, and he put a kettle of water on to boil. Ten minutes later, he headed upstairs carrying a pot of tea and some toast rounds slathered with butter and jam on a silver tray.

He could hear her gentle breathing through the partially open bedroom door. She opened her eyes as he approached the bed. Putting the tray down on the nightstand, he gently clasped her wrist and took her pulse again. It was slow and steady.

"How long was I out?" she asked.

"About an hour," he said. "They came for . . . your servant."

"Thank you," she said. Seeing the food on the tray, she said, "That smells exceptionally good."

"I gather you've been running on nerve for a while."

"A bit, perhaps," she said.

She sat up in bed as he poured the tea. When he handed her the mug, she added a full spoon of brown sugar to it, along with a dollop of milk. Between sips, she ate the toast and jam with obvious relish. Within minutes, a hint of color began to suffuse her pallid cheeks.

"You're hired," she said with a shy smile.

As he poured her a second mug of tea, an electric light suddenly came on above their heads.

"Power is restored," she said. "The British Empire endures."

The light was coming from a cut-glass chandelier in the center of the room. Taggart noticed that of more than twenty flame bulbs on its arms all but two were burned out. Helen's eyes met his when he turned back to her.

"You've seen enough to know that I live in genteel poverty, Major Taggart," she said icily.

"I only know about the other kind," he said. "I grew up in a cold-water flat. At the age of five, my first winter chore was to hunt for chunks of coal at the railroad yard."

"Genteel poverty is not much better," said Helen Bellayne. "One tries at all costs to appear proper and refined while selling off the good silver and paintings . . . never letting friends and relatives see how far you have sunk. It was particularly difficult for my mother. She worked so hard to keep up the pretense of wealth without having any money to do it."

"My mother spent all day sewing button sets onto pasteboard cards," said Taggart. "She earned a penny a card."

"Perhaps a nip of this tea would improve your humor," she said with a puckish grin.

Taking it from her outstretched hand, he sipped from the mug.

"So what happened to the family fortune?" he asked.

"It is now part of the Greater Asian Co-Prosperity Sphere," she replied evenly.

"The Japs?" he said, and she nodded.

"My father inherited rubber plantations in Malaya, tea plantations in Ceylon, and textile mills in Shanghai. They had been in our family for generations. All his wealth was intertwined with the fortunes of the British Empire. As the empire died, so did our family holdings. The Nipponese took everything we owned. My father was murdered eight years ago in Shanghai, trying to save the Chinese who worked for us there. My brother Edward died trying to protect our interests in Malaya. I am the only one left."

Taggart examined her amber eyes for a sign of self-pity. There was none.

"Forgive me," said Helen Bellayne. "I don't usually prattle on like this, I assure you, Major Taggart. Perhaps it was Gwendolyn's death last night. She was my last connection to the past . . . or maybe it was the thought that one of those German bombs last night would eradicate everything I have ever known. You know, I wasn't entirely sure it would be such a bad idea."

"Where is your husband?" asked Taggart.

"Colonel Roderick Bellayne. There is a good painting of him by Linklater over the mantelpiece in my bedroom. My Roddy . . . he is dead, too . . . killed very early in the war. He was commanding a battalion in Tunisia when we denied Mussolini his new African empire."

She had said it all so casually that Taggart wondered if, like him, she had accomplished the very difficult task of walling off any emotion from her daily life.

"What about you, Major? Are you married?"

He nodded and said, "She's dead, too . . . she took her life. . . . That's what living with me for eighteen years will do for a woman."

"I'm sure there was more to it than that," said Helen Bellayne, obviously waiting for him to say more.

Instead, Taggart stood up next to the bed and glanced at his watch.

"So what is it you want of me?" she asked. "In spite of your obviously fine qualifications, I assume you did not come to my home this morning to play the role of my butler."

"I was told that Jocelyn Dunbar stayed here often," said Taggart, his voice becoming harder.

"Yes, she did," said Helen Bellayne. "In fact, this was her room."

"I wonder if you wouldn't mind my looking through her things when we finish talking," he said.

"Not at all. She was my niece by marriage, you know. Her father married my cousin Angela."

"I didn't know," said Taggart.

"I feel so horrible about her death," she said. "She had a very difficult time growing up. Of course, she had the Dunbar blood, which made long life problematic anyway."

"The Dunbar blood?"

"Her father was a Dunbar. Very good lineage, but a streak of madness has always run through the family. My mother once said that they should never have had children—end the line, if you will."

"Who might have wanted to kill her?" asked Taggart.

"I have absolutely no idea. When Colonel Gaines called me to say that she had committed suicide, I wasn't terribly surprised."

"Why not?"

"For one thing, she had tried it once before . . . with sleeping drafts."

"Do you know why?" asked Taggart.

"She fell in love with someone when she was very young. It apparently turned out badly. I never learned who it was. Our family was very good at keeping secrets, particularly of the heart."

"Do you know if it might have been someone named Noel?" asked Taggart.

She thought about it and said, "Inspector Drummond asked me that same question. I don't recall her having any friends with that name."

"Who were her friends?" asked Taggart.

"Growing up as a child in the country, she was a wild spirit—she loved horses more than boys back then. Recently, I know she spent time with Charles Wainwright and his crowd . . . Lord Ainsley, of course, and several other RAF types. One of her boyfriends was killed early in the war at Benghazi."

"Any other affairs?" asked Taggart.

"It's fair to say that Joss had difficulty maintaining relationships. She . . ."

Helen paused in mid-sentence, seemingly lost in thought.

"Go on," said Taggart.

"Joss had a troubled upbringing," she said. "Her father had the pronounced strain of erratic behavior that was so prevalent in the Dunbar line. It's entirely possible that he abused her as a child . . . in a sexual way."

Taggart decided to come right to the point.

"I'd like to ask you about Admiral Jellico," he said.

"I have no direct knowledge of their relationship," she said without a pause. "Joss never told me about it. I have never asked Thomas about it."

"As I told the admiral when we first met, I have proof that he was engaged in a sexual relationship with her."

"So?" she replied. "What of it?"

"He's a married man, and he is old enough to be her grandfather. Those could be motives for murder if she decided to expose their relationship," said Taggart.

She shook her head as if he were a naïve schoolboy.

"You don't understand the English, I'm afraid," she said. "Joss was a free spirit, Major Taggart—like Cathy in *Wuthering Heights.* She did as she pleased. Besides, the admiral's wife had full knowledge of it. In fact, she encouraged the affair. She happens to prefer younger men."

"And it didn't bother you as her aunt?"

"That was a choice Joss made as an adult. We all have to live with our life decisions when we are no longer young."

"You're right. I don't understand you people," said Taggart.

She removed the feather tick covering her and stood up. Taking the silver tray from the table, she began walking toward the door.

"Thank you for the tea and toast," she said. "I mean it."

"You're welcome," he said, watching her go. At the door, she turned and said, "Why don't you conduct your policeman's search now, Major. I'll see you downstairs before you leave."

Taggart spent almost an hour systematically going through Joss's room and the bathroom that adjoined it. The closet was full of her uniforms, shoes, and other personal clothing. The bathroom contained her makeup and medications. But there were no letters, notes, or personal items that offered even the hint of a clue to her death.

When he appeared again at the bottom of the stairs, Helen Bellayne was waiting for him in the foyer. She had changed into a conservative black woolen suit, her hair was newly brushed, and she had applied fresh lipstick.

"Any luck?" she asked.

He shook his head. "I'm afraid not."

"Well, I need to get back to work. Is there anything else you want of me?" she asked, looking up at him with the hint of a smile.

"A woman as beautiful as you shouldn't have to ask a question like that," he found himself saying.

She slowly raised her chin almost defiantly toward his.

He leaned down and kissed her. Her mouth was uncertainly responsive. She parted her lips for a moment before slowly pulling them away. He felt a warm, sweet exhalation against his throat.

"Thank you again for the tea, Major. That was pleasant."

"Yeah," he said, turning to go out the door.

CHAPTER 17

Liza bolted awake in the semidarkness, her brain still racing with the vivid nightmarish images. For several moments, she could not remember where she was. Then she heard the familiar sounds of vehicle traffic down on Grosvenor Road.

A narrow patch of daylight was leaking through the frayed lower corner of her blackout curtains. She could just make out the hands of the small travel clock next to her bed. It was almost ten.

Drawing open the curtains, she barely noticed the remarkable sight of an English battleship gliding silently down the narrow river toward the East End repair docks. All she saw was another dreary morning with a harsh wind that rattled the broken frames of the bomb-damaged windows.

As she headed to the bathroom, her mind was still sorting through the possibilities that had begun to coalesce in her mind. Upon reflection, the lurid idea seemed fantastic, even if it did fit the facts. But it could have happened that way, she concluded, sitting naked in the cold bathwater.

After putting on a bathrobe back in her room, Liza walked downstairs to the telephone box in the first-floor hallway. Ten minutes later, she had reached one of the two men whose help she needed to prove the hypothesis.

As soon as she was dressed, she went out and hailed a taxi, giving the driver the address of J.P.'s apartment near Charing Cross Station. The sidewalk was deserted as she came up to the front entrance of the row house. Before she could knock, the door swung open to reveal Inspector Drummond standing in the hallway.

"Well, are you going to tell me who or what we're looking for?" he asked, smiling at her in an almost fatherly way.

"Winston Churchill," she said, moving past him down the hallway.

He had already unlocked the door of J.P.'s apartment. The airless rooms still smelled rank as she went directly to the fireplace. The round Churchill pincushion was sitting in the center of the mantelpiece.

Holding the bulbous leather head between her two index fingers, she carried it into the bathroom and set it down on J.P.'s dressing table, then stepped back into the hallway and switched on the bright bathroom lights. Inspector Drummond stood in the doorway, watching her with sleepy eyes and scratching his head.

Using a paper tissue from the top drawer of the dressing table, she pulled one of the hatpins out of the cushion and held it up to the light. The large garnet on the head of the pin glinted smoky red in the lamplight.

The six-inch pin was made of burnished steel and looked as if it had never been used. After a thorough examination, she put it down on the dressing table and drew out another pin. One after another, she removed all of them from Churchill's head and studied the shafts carefully in the light. When she was down to the last two, her frustration became evident.

"Damn," she said. "Perhaps I was wrong."

"Could you enlighten me as to what it is we're looking for?" asked Inspector Drummond.

As she pulled out the next hatpin, Liza's lips arched upward in a grim smile.

"This," she said, holding up a pin that was crowned with a polished brass knob.

Drummond could see a brownish discoloration at the pointed tip, as well as along the shaft.

"Do you have a car, Inspector?" she asked.

"Certainly," he said.

"I would like to go to the pathology unit at the SHAEF hospital right away."

"May I assume this is important?" he asked.

She nodded. After carefully wrapping the pin in a towel, she placed it in her handbag. On their way to the hospital, she explained what she thought had taken place on the night of J.P.'s murder. He listened patiently. When she was finished, he said, "Do you think you can prove it?"

"We'll know in a little while," she replied.

After stopping briefly at the laboratory to have the stains on the shaft scraped for analysis, they headed to the pathology suite. Liza asked one of the nurses if Dr. Channing was still on duty.

"He rarely leaves the hospital," she said. "You'll find him in the storeroom at the back of the morgue."

Liza found a closed door just beyond the refrigerated lockers. A hand-lettered sign on the front of it read "Medical Supply." She opened the door, stepped inside, and turned on the light. Wooden shelves held unopened vats of formaldehyde and an assortment of surgical tools and supplies. Beyond the last rack, a metal-framed cot sat snug against the brick wall. Something was lying on it, covered by a blanket. Leaning over the cot, she pulled back the blanket.

The old man's eyes flickered open and stared up at her.

"Even at my age, young lady, sleep is sporadically valuable," he muttered. "What do you want now?"

"I need your help, Dr. Channing. It involves the postmortem you conducted yesterday on Lieutenant Barnes. Do you remember your initial examination of her entry wound?"

"I am not yet fully impaired with senility," said the pathologist.

He slid back the blanket and slowly sat up, rubbing his eyes.

"Do you know how to brew a respectable cup of tea?" he asked querulously.

"I do," said Drummond, who was standing in the doorway.

"You will find the burner and empty pot out there behind the meat lockers," said Channing. "Please use fresh water."

A few minutes later, he took a sip from a steaming mug, licked his lips, and said, "How can I be of help?"

"As I told you yesterday, Doctor, there was something abnormal about her body temperature when it was recorded the morning after her death," said Liza, the words pouring out. "Based on the temperature of the room she was in, it suggested that she had died at around midnight, but we know that she was alive several hours later, which is what led me to believe that she might have been immersed in water."

"I remember the question," he said, "but there was no evidence to support any form of hypoxia. There was a bullet in her brain."

"Correct," said Liza. "But I would like you to consider the hypothesis that she was already dead when the bullet was fired—that she had been murdered by a different instrument while sitting in her bath."

"And what instrument would that be?" he asked.

"Do you remember the reddened tissue you showed me that was just outside the bullet track? You conjectured about it at the time."

"A bullet can do peculiar things," he said.

"Of course," she agreed. "I am merely asking you to reopen the inquest to investigate that one curious element."

Dr. Channing led them into the morgue, asking one of the attendants to retrieve J.P.'s body from its locker.

"That one's already gone, sir," said the attendant.

"By whose authority?" demanded Liza.

"Colonel Baird sent orders that the body was to be shipped immediately back to the United States at the urgent request of her husband."

"That's a lie. Her husband is in a Japanese prison camp," said Liza, seething with outrage.

Dr. Channing patted her gently on the back.

"Perhaps all is not lost," he said.

She and Drummond followed him back to the pathology unit. Channing walked over to a long row of specimen jars on one of the wooden shelves. Grasping a large formaldehyde-filled jar, he brought it over to an examination table.

"We still have her brain," said Channing. "That will give us the answer, one way or another."

With a wheezy sigh, he dragged out his brass lamp and switched it on. For the next fifteen minutes, he carefully studied the tissue just inside the wound with a magnifying glass. At one point, he retrieved a small scalpel and incised the wound from the point of entry, parting the two sections with forceps. He spent another five minutes focused on the exposed gray-pinkish brain matter.

"It could be a separate wound," he said, finally.

"Possibly made by this?" Liza asked, holding out the polished brass hatpin.

Channing took it from her hand and held it up to the light.

"Let's find out," he said. Before fitting it to the secondary wound, he asked, "Have you already checked it for blood type?"

"We dropped off several scrapings at the laboratory on our way here."

Channing used the scalpel again to extend his incision deeper into the brain, tracking every millimeter of damaged tissue under the brilliance of his spotlight.

"I can't be certain this was the actual weapon, but it's entirely consistent with the size, shape, and track of the wound," said Channing. "The murderer almost certainly attempted to obliterate it with the gunshot."

"Thank you, Doctor," said Liza.

When she gave him a hug, the wizened old man actually came out of his crablike slouch and beamed. Liza and Drummond headed back to the laboratory, where the blood analysis was waiting for them. She placed an immediate call to Sam Taggart in his office at SHAEF.

"J.P. was murdered, Sam," she said. "The murder weapon was a six-inch-long hatpin. Apparently, she collected them. The murderer killed her while she was taking a bath, and left her there until he arranged the scene of the fake suicide in the bedroom. The blood on the tip of the pin matches J.P.'s."

"Very good," said Taggart, his mind racing.

"Two other things," said Liza. "First, the scrapings you took from under General Kilgore's fingernails contained no other skin tissue."

"What else?" said Taggart, disappointment obvious in his voice.

"Colonel Baird had her body removed from the morgue before we got here," she went on. "He apparently claimed that her husband was requesting its return to the States."

"They're covering their tracks just in case," said Taggart.

"Who is Colonel Baird?" she asked.

"One of Kilgore's hatchet men. He ran a military prison before the war. The Alcatraz of military stockades. Anything else? I'm calling Kilgore's office as soon as we hang up."

For a moment, Liza debated whether to tell him about the man who might have been chasing her during the bombing raid.

"It will wait," she said.

CHAPTER 18

The blonde secretary in Kilgore's office put Taggart on hold for over a minute before coming back on the phone to tell him that General Kilgore was out of the office and wouldn't be back until later that afternoon.

Taggart got a fresh cup of coffee, lit a cigarette, and lay down on his sprung leather couch to ruminate over what they had learned so far in the two investigations. "Couch time" was what he used to call it back at the homicide-squad office. "Loafing" is what the commander used to call it before Taggart was fired.

Two young women had been murdered in the same week. They had worked in the same office. Both were in possession of highly classified information. In Joss's case, she was familiar with virtually every facet of the Normandy invasion plan, as well as the even more secret ULTRA intercepts. J.P. had indirect access across the pillow to the invasion plans and God knew what else.

Both young women had been sexually intimate with high-ranking Allied officers who knew the Overlord plans. Based on the diary she kept, J.P. had slept with at least a half-dozen top generals. But would one of them have had a motive to kill her? And Joss?

Taggart knew that some killers possessed the hunting instinct, enjoying the chase more than anything else. For others it was the kill, cherishing the moment when they could look into the eyes of their prey and watch its life ebb away. The lust to kill was in many men, and many of them were soldiers. But these two crimes had clear sexual overtones. Even if they had something to do with war, there were other elements involved as well.

As he went over the evidence they had amassed in investigating Joss Dunbar's death, his mind kept returning to the note written in blood he had found in her apartment. Was the man named Noel no more than a red herring? And what of Drummond's view that the royal family was concerned that one of its own might be a serial murderer?

His mind drifted back to Overlord. The most important question was whether Overlord had potentially been compromised. That had to be the central focus of his investigation.

The proposed invasion date was still a few months away, but with millions of men involved, the supreme commander's planning staff had grown exponentially in recent weeks. According to the last count he had seen, more than seven hundred Allied officers were cleared to know that the invasion target was Normandy and that the projected attack would take place in late May or the first week of June. If even one of them betrayed those plans to the Abwehr, the war could go on for years. And if the rumors were true about Hitler's secret weapons, they could still lose. Or old Joe Stalin could strike a separate peace with Hitler, as he had done before the war.

Taggart had to wrestle with yet another problem. He personally hoped the murderer was General Everett Kilgore, whom he detested for what he had done to J.P. after her husband had been captured at Corregidor. What defenses did she have when he made his move on her? What does the deer say to the point of the rifle?

But he had also learned the hard way through his years as a homicide detective that hate was like an empty .45. Taggart always had to battle his inner demons. But what he felt now was a different emotion, almost out of control. It was more like a disease of the soul. He wasn't sure if he could harness it. He knew he had to try.

As he sat on the couch staring out at the park, the image of Helen Bellayne suddenly came into his mind, her sad heart-shaped face, the shy smile, and the amber eyes. The image of her was enough to drive away the demons momentarily. She was the first woman he had desired since his wife died.

Barbara. His wife. How had General Kilgore learned about the circumstances of her death? And how had he learned the contents of her suicide note? To Taggart's knowledge, only two men aside from him had ever seen it—the judge at the inquest and the commander of the homicide squad.

"Major Taggart?"

He looked up to see Lieutenant Rusty Courtemanche, one of his criminal investigators, standing in the open doorway. Only twenty-two, he had yet to subject his fair skin to the regular stroke of a razor. Before the war, he had been a police patrolman in Saint Louis. His only ambition when it ended was to go back into the city department as a plainclothes detective.

"Yeah?" Taggart replied from the couch.

"I found out where Lieutenant Barnes spent at least part of the night she died, sir," he said.

Taggart stood up and stubbed out his cigarette in the ashtray on his desk. "Where was she?" he asked.

A day earlier, Taggart had given him a list of London hotels along with an enlarged copy of J.P.'s prewar photograph, and told him to interview the desk clerks, bellboys, doormen, and any other hotel employees who might have remembered seeing her on the night of the murder.

"She was at the Dorchester," he said, pulling out a small notebook to review his notes. "The headwaiter in the restaurant remembers seating her with an officer that night as a guest for dinner. He isn't familiar with all the different American military uniforms but he thinks it was green."

"Army," said Taggart, and the young officer nodded.

"And he remembered something else," said Rusty Courtemanche with a satisfied grin. "He said the officer had a star on his collar."

"A brigadier general," said Taggart.

"The reservation was made in the name of someone called Gramm. I've never heard of an army brigadier with that name."

"They're thicker than fleas over here," said Taggart. "Anything else?"

Courtemanche nodded again.

"One of the doormen thinks he saw her. . . . He couldn't be sure, but he said a woman that looked like her left the hotel alone at around three o'clock. He remembers because he said she wasn't wearing a coat and it was bitter cold outside."

"Did you ask him what she was wearing?"

"A white dress."

"I think you might need a promotion, Lieutenant," said Taggart.

"Thank you, sir," said Courtemanche, grinning broadly.

As soon as he left, Taggart walked downstairs to the personnel office and checked by grade the names of all those ranked above colonel currently serving in the European and North African theaters. He found the name on the active roster. Brigadier Philip Gramm served in the Supply Corps, and was stationed at the quartermaster detachment in Southampton. Taggart wrote down his office designations and contact information.

He requested General Gramm's service folder, and a clerk brought it out to him a few minutes later. A small black-and-white photograph of the man was attached to the cover page. To Taggart, he looked like a life-insurance salesman pretending to be Black Jack Pershing.

He saw that Gramm had graduated from West Point in 1940. The date sparked another flash of recognition. J.P.'s husband, Lloyd, had graduated from the Point in 1940, too. They had to have known one another. Yet he had taken his brother officer's wife.

Shaking his head, he gave the service record back to the clerk, and returned to his office. It was almost five o'clock. He called Rusty Courtemanche and brought him up to date on what he had learned about Brigadier General Gramm.

"Try to find out if he spent the whole night in that hotel," he said.

Putting on his uniform coat, he went back up to Kilgore's office. The blonde was typing at her desk in the front reception room. Though she looked up at Taggart, her fingers continued to strike the keys for several seconds. When she looked back down at the typewriter, a scowl contorted her face.

"Shit," she muttered, yanking the page out and tossing it in the wastebasket.

"I need to see General Kilgore," he said.

"I awreddy told you over the phone, Major. The general isn't here."

Taggart looked past her to the inner office door, which was wide open. He could see Kilgore's desk. It was unoccupied.

"Give him a message for me when he checks in, sweetheart. Tell him that Lieutenant Barnes was murdered, and he is now a material witness in my investigation."

"Yes, sir," she said, as if whispering in church.

Leaving SHAEF, Taggart started back to his Jermyn Street apartment on foot. That night, General Manigault was hosting a dinner at Claridge's in honor of his British counterpart in the security command, and he had ordered Taggart and the rest of the senior staff to attend in dress uniform. The evening sky was already black when he unlocked the door next to the saddlery shop and headed upstairs to change.

The light fixture was out at the top of the stairs. If he hadn't been tired, Taggart might have considered the possibility that someone had intentionally unscrewed the bulbs. Not doing so was his first mistake.

The man came out of the darkness behind the railing of the second-floor stairwell. Taggart heard a harsh groan in the old floorboards and instinctively ducked to the left. He felt the hard blow glance off his left shoulder. As it went numb, he realized the man must be wearing brass knuckles.

Circling back toward the stairwell, Taggart could barely discern the man's outline in the faint light coming up from the street. Still down low, he locked his elbows in front of him and lunged forward at the dark mass.

The brass knuckles slammed into his rib cage as Taggart drove at the man's thighs, knocking him off balance. The man went back several steps and plummeted headfirst down the long staircase. A few moments later, his body crashed into the door at the bottom of the steps. He moaned once and was still.

As Taggart regained his balance and turned around, another man came at him from the alcove just beyond his apartment door. Again, he heard rather than saw him coming across the creaky plank flooring.

Stepping out of the murky glow near the stairwell, he waited blindly for the next attack. The first punch landed on the edge of his jaw, but it was ill-timed and grazed past him. Taggart sensed that this man was shorter, no more than five ten, but squat and very strong. He smelled the man's stale sweat as they grappled at one another in the darkness. The attacker hit him twice in the belly—short, hard punches that rocked him backward as he waited for an opening.

The heel of the man's left hand was suddenly lodged under his chin. It was callused and hard. He slowly forced Taggart's head back, exposing his Adam's apple to what Taggart was sure would come next—a sharp, powerful blow using the base of his right hand. This one has commando training, he thought as he pinioned the attacker's right wrist and they silently continued to circle one another in the darkness.

Releasing the man's wrist, Taggart struck at the side of his head with a straight right hook. The man didn't go down, but he staggered backward a step, and Taggart brought his knee up hard between the man's legs. As his head came forward, Taggart chopped down on the back of his neck, and he dropped to the floor with a raspy grunt.

This time he was prepared for another attacker, but the corridor remained silent. Taggart could hear nothing except the automobile traffic going by in the street below. The pain in his left shoulder was aching like a gunshot wound, and he felt blood running down his neck. He reached into the pocket of his trench coat for the flashlight he always carried.

The third man must have been standing right behind him. A white blossom of pain erupted behind his eyes as something smashed into the back of his head. He felt himself starting to fall. A second blow detonated inside his brain, and he hit the floor face-first.

Tiny fragments of memory hurtled through his brain in quick succession—images of his mother from when he was a little boy, the sight of his dog after she had just been run over in the street—a jumble of images that made no sense at all.

He could hear voices. They came from way off as if in a liquid fog. He thought that one of the voices was somehow familiar, but he didn't know why. His brain felt like pork suet—good for feeding birds. He was suddenly sick to his stomach, and began to vomit. After a while, he slept.

He came awake again to the kick of a boot being driven into his left side. He heard a voice cry out. The sound was utterly strange, like a cawing bird. He realized that the voice was his. His rib cage ached as if it had been cracked wide open.

He was very cold and realized he wasn't wearing his uniform any longer. Someone pried his mouth open. He felt liquid going down his throat and gagged, spewing it out. They forced his mouth open again. This time he swallowed some of it. The fluid filled his mouth and burned his sinus passages as it came back up. He knew the smell of it. He knew what it was. He gagged again. They left him alone.

He heard voices. Someone was lying next to him. She was cooing at him, as if the whole affair had been a wonderful idyll. At one point, he reached up to touch the back of his head. He felt soft, hot stickiness and was sick to his stomach again.

Someone laughed.

"Be sure to remove the lens cover," said a familiar voice.

He felt tiny spikes of light behind his closed eyelids. It was quiet again. He slept.

Someone began hauling on his shoulder.

"Wake up, buddy," came a rough voice.

"He's out for the count," said another voice. "Let's haul him in."

CHAPTER 19

Charlie Wainwright lay almost supine in his office chair with his feet splayed across the desktop, reading the *Times* and smoking his favorite Dr. Watson briar pipe. He had just come back from the lair after spending most of the night analyzing a long, desperate message to the high command in Berlin from a major general commanding a German SS panzer division in Russia. His troops were being overrun near Kharkov, and he was requesting orders to retreat before they were wiped out.

Charlie had written a detailed analysis of the tactical implications and sent his report upstairs to the supreme commander's office. With the incredible advantage of the ULTRA code-breaking intercepts, Eisenhower and Churchill often knew what was happening on the Eastern Front before Hitler did.

Still half asleep, Charlie took a sip of strong tea and said, "Looks like the war on our front is entering a critical new phase."

Liza glanced up from the revised postmortem report she was typing and glanced over at him. He was wearing a ratty blue bathrobe over his favorite orange Hawaiian shirt, khaki shorts, and desert boots.

"The new German bombing campaign?" she asked.

"No," he said with a cynical grin. "Our vaunted security command has decided to crack down on the evils of prostitution here in the London den of Sodom."

She smiled.

"How are they going to do that?" she asked.

"Last night they made a sweep of the most notorious houses of ill repute and arrested all the unlucky patrons," he said, yawning. "Thank God, I was otherwise occupied."

Liza returned to J.P.'s postmortem report. She wanted to get it up to Sam before leaving for Cambridge, where she had arranged an interview with a history don to explore the possible origins of the notes written in blood between Joss and the mysterious "Noel."

She was removing the last page from the typewriter when the door banged open and three men swept into the office. Two of them were wearing American uniforms. The third was English. One of the Americans was a captain. His arm patch identified him as a member of the Joint Security Command.

"Stand away from your desk," he said, coming to a halt in front of her.

"What the hell is going on here?" Charlie demanded, getting to his feet.

"Just stay out of it, pal," said the American captain.

His two subordinates were carrying empty cardboard boxes in each hand. As soon as Liza stepped away from the desk, one of them sat down in her chair. Opening the top desk drawer, he began emptying its contents into the first box. The second man went straight to the file cabinet that contained her case files. She wondered how he knew which one was hers. There were six cabinets lined up against the wall. He left the others alone.

"I demand to know on whose authority you are doing this," said Liza.

The captain removed an order from his uniform coat and handed it to her.

It was on security-command letterhead, and ordered the confiscation of "all pending case materials in the possession of Lieutenant Elizabeth Marantz, currently assigned to the Office of the Joint Security Command, Supreme Headquarters Allied Expeditionary Force."

It was signed by Colonel Lyman Baird. Underneath his signature, the order was endorsed by General Ernest Manigault. By the time she finished reading it, the two enlisted men were already heading for the door with full cartons. She looked back at her desk. The drawers stood empty.

"You're being reassigned, Lieutenant," said the captain, taking back the written order before turning to leave. "You will remain at this duty station until your new orders are cut."

As soon as he was gone, she headed upstairs to find Sam. The two guards at the head of his corridor were checking each person who attempted to pass. Without slowing down, she smiled at the first one and held up her identity card. The young guard grinned back, letting her through.

Sam's door was shut. Opening it, she stepped inside his office and stopped short. The room was bare. Sam's desk was gone, along with his file cabinets and the big Atlas safe that had stood in the corner. They had even taken his old leather couch. She glanced back at the door. Someone had removed the nameplate that read "Maj. Samuel Taggart."

The young guard from the security post appeared in the open doorway.

"Ma'am, I'm sorry, but this office is off limits to everyone."

"Where is Major Taggart?" she asked.

Under her direct gaze, the young man's cheeks flushed. He could not have been more than eighteen.

"I ain't supposed to say, ma'am," he said. "We was ordered not to."

The look of concern on her face seemed to soften his resolve. Quickly glancing up and down the corridor, he whispered, "He was arrested last night, ma'am. They got him over in the military stockade."

A mile away, in North London, Taggart slowly came alive to the loud clanging of steam pipes. Each jarring clang was like another sharp blow to the back of his head. His eyes felt glued shut.

As he raised his fingers to clear them, the right side of his chest erupted in a jolt of fiery pain. From his boxing days in the Golden Gloves, he knew that one of his ribs was cracked or broken.

He rubbed away the mucuslike material that covered his eyes and opened them warily. Nothing was in focus at first. He found that he couldn't look at anything straight on. Images were clearer off to the side. It was like trying to see around a corner.

He saw that the door was made of heavy-gauge iron mesh, the walls of concrete block. There was no window in the room. He was lying on an iron-framed cot that was bolted to the concrete floor.

There was a thin mattress beneath him. Someone had covered his chest with a green woolen blanket. A ceramic chamber pot sat in the far corner next to an open bucket of water. He realized that he was in a jail cell.

He was very thirsty. Sitting up, he slowly turned his body to the right and brought his feet down to the floor. The simple movements were agonizing. He paused to regain his strength. They had taken his belt and shoelaces. His watch had also disappeared. He had no idea what time it was.

The cellblock was very hot, the mattress rank with the odor of sweat and dried urine. He knew the odors well. After fourteen years as a homicide detective, he was a connoisseur of jail smells. But this was the first time he had found himself inhabiting a cell.

Feeling a hundred years old, Taggart slowly levered himself off the cot onto his knees and crawled over to the bucket. A tin ladle was hanging from the edge and he drank several swallows of the tepid water.

After rinsing his face, he used his fingers to explore the back of his head. There were two lumps behind his left ear. The larger one was the size of a walnut. On his way back to the cot, he glanced through the wire mesh at the cell opposite his. A man sat staring at the wall. He was wearing a U.S. Army Air Corps uniform, and tears were running down his face. From farther down the cellblock, Taggart could hear another man retching.

After carefully climbing back onto the cot, he fell asleep again. The next sound he heard was a key moving in the lock of his cell door. A small bandy-legged private came in carrying a metal tray. He set it down on the floor and left.

Taggart looked down at the tray. It contained a plate of runny powdered eggs and a slice of burned toast. Next to the plate were an empty china mug and a small metal pitcher filled with black coffee.

He got up for the coffee. It tasted surprisingly good, even better than the stuff they brewed back on Generals' Row at SHAEF. It picked him up considerably. He only wished he had a cigarette to go with it. As his brain began to function again, he considered how and why he had ended up in the stockade.

Obviously, he had been set up. Taggart had a vague recollection of lying in a bed somewhere with flashbulbs going off. Maybe this whole murder investigation was too big for him after all. Who knew how high it went and where it finally stopped? He remembered Kilgore opening the file on his desk that included all the details of his wife, Barbara's suicide. How had they gotten hold of her handwritten note? It had been sealed in a District Court case file in Manhattan.

An hour later, the guards came for the air-force officer in the cell across from him. He was still crying when they walked him out. More hours passed, he had no idea how many. He slept a good part of the time. He awoke again to the sight of the bandy-legged private, standing in front of the wire-mesh door.

"You have a visitor, Major," he said.

Taggart slowly followed him down the cellblock and into one of the stockade holding cells. Liza Marantz was sitting in a straight wooden chair next to a scarred oak table. Her eyes were creased with worry when she looked up and saw him.

"Thanks for coming," he said. "What time is it?"

"Three o'clock," she said, glancing at her watch.

"In the morning or the afternoon?" he asked.

"Afternoon," she said, realizing there were probably no windows in the cellblock. "I went up to your office. It's empty, Sam. They took everything out of it . . . even your old couch."

"They wanted to make sure they got it," he said.

"What?"

"J.P.'s diary," he said.

"Where is it?"

"I left it in the safe. I doubt they can crack that old Atlas very easily."

"They didn't have to," she said. "They just took it with them."

He nodded and said, "When it comes to their own hides, they can be pretty thorough," he said.

"All my case files were confiscated as well," she said. "And the order was endorsed by General Manigault."

Sam's badly puffed eyes showed surprise for the first time. Slowly shaking his head, he said, "I guess they've gotten to him, too. It's all over, then."

"I was told that I am being reassigned," she said.

"They'll probably send you back to the States," he said. "God knows where I'll end up. I know too much for them to allow me to walk around anywhere."

She took his hand in hers, and gently stroked his swollen knuckles.

"You're a good man, Major Taggart," she said softly. "And you tried to do the right thing."

"Yeah," he replied. "And look where it got us."

They took him back to the cell. He was soon asleep again. Some time later, he awoke to the sound of the cell door being unlocked once more. When he opened his bleary eyes, Rusty Courtemanche was standing by the bed.

"I'm sorry about this, Major," said Courtemanche.

He was in full uniform, with a .45-caliber Colt strapped to his hip.

"So where do we go from here, Rusty?" asked Taggart as he followed him out of the cell block.

"My orders are to get you cleaned up and then escort you to General Manigault's office," he said. "After that, I don't know what happens."

"Have you ever been to the Aleutian Islands?" asked Taggart, deadpan.

Courtemanche looked at him with his jaw wide.

"Tell me," said Taggart. "Did you find out whether General Gramm spent the night at the Dorchester?"

"I was ordered not to discuss any pending investigations with you, sir," said Courtemanche as he signed the release book at the front desk.

"Sure. I understand," said Taggart.

A staff car was waiting for them outside the stockade. The night sky was clear for a change, and full of stars. When they were alone in the back seat, Courtemanche turned to him and whispered, "Gramm was there all night. According to the night porter, he ordered a bottle of booze from room service at around four. The waiter who brought it to him told me he was fast asleep in his bed when he delivered it to the sitting room of the suite."

Taggart nodded.

"You're the best man I've ever served under, sir," said the young soldier.

"You're still young," said Taggart.

They drove first to Taggart's apartment. When he reached the top of the stairs, Taggart saw that the bulbs in the ceiling fixture had been replaced. There was no hint of what had happened except for a small bloodstain near the second-floor railing. Whoever had orchestrated the attack had cleaned up after it very well.

Inside the apartment, Courtemanche waited while Taggart shaved, took a quick bath, and put on his best uniform. When they arrived at SHAEF, Taggart almost felt like a visiting congressman as they whisked him through Manigault's outer office past a brigadier who was cooling his heels with his entire staff.

The general was waiting for Taggart behind his desk. He didn't stand up.

"Thanks. You can go now, Lieutenant," he said to Courtemanche. "I can take it from here."

"Yes, sir," said Courtemanche, saluting crisply before he left.

"Sit down, Sam," Manigault said with a grim smile. "You know, for the first time since you got over here, you actually look like a soldier—just in time for your court-martial."

Still woozy, Taggart dropped into one of the chairs in front of the desk.

"Well, this is the end of the line, Sam," said the general, shaking his head sadly. "I told you to be careful when you started this thing. First you riled up half the senior Overlord command. A week later, you get dragged out of a whorehouse dead drunk. And just yesterday you were giving me grief about . . ."

"It was a setup, General."

"That's a honey, Sam," Marigault said, his voice stiffening. "If I wanted to listen to that kind of bullshit, I'd ask for a meeting with Montgomery."

"How long ago was it planned?" asked Taggart.

"Was what planned?"

"That crackdown on prostitution last night."

"How the hell do I know?"

"Tell me who was behind it," said Taggart.

"Colonel Baird spoke to me about it yesterday afternoon," said Manigault.

"The whole thing was a setup to nail me."

Manigault picked up a file folder from the out box on his desk. He quickly scanned the cover page and said, "You're telling me that a raid on twenty-six whorehouses that resulted in more than a hundred arrests was carried out so that they could get you in a compromising position? You have a problem. It's called imaginitis. Aside from that, you're a ball-breaker, Sam. You resent authority."

"Well, it accomplished its purpose, didn't it?"

"What purpose?"

"I'm being court-martialed while the murders of Joss Dunbar and J. P. Barnes go unsolved."

"There's your imaginitis again, Sam. Colonel Baird says that the autopsy on Lieutenant Barnes proved she committed suicide because she was distraught about her husband, who I gather is a prisoner of the Japanese."

"It's not imaginitis, General," said Taggart. "And that information is out of date. She was murdered, maybe by the same man who killed Joss Dunbar. You should know that Lieutenant Barnes's murder could prove embarrassing to Everett Kilgore and his cronies. That's why they set me up."

"They've got pictures of you with a prostitute, Sam. Do you want to see them?"

"Who took the pictures?" demanded Taggart.

"How would I know?" said Manigault, his voice rising in anger. "MPs, I guess."

"Why?"

Manigault's cheeks reddened.

"That's not all, Sam," he said angrily. "When they searched your office, they found that your petty cash was missing. Colonel Krieger found a whole stack of illegal vouchers you signed."

"He's Kilgore's stooge. I've never taken a dime in any job I've ever had, General, and you should know that better than anyone. Do you remember the night at Fort Hamilton when you tried to bribe me to let you go?"

Manigault stared hard into his eyes before turning away.

"I never thought you were a thief, Sam."

"Thanks for that at least."

"Look . . . my hands are tied on this. I just wanted the chance to tell you myself. I owed you that much. This isn't going to be easy for either of us. Everyone around here knows you're my man."

"I'm sorry to have put you in an embarrassing position," said Taggart.

Manigault stood up and walked over to the coal stove to warm his hands. Returning to the desk, he paused as he reached toward the transmit button on his office intercom and said, "You'll probably be going to a maximum-security prison, Sam, at least until the invasion is under way. At this point you know everything the Germans would love to have."

"And so does the whoever murdered Joss Dunbar and Lieutenant Barnes," replied Taggart.

Manigault's finger remained stopped in midair.

"What is that supposed to mean?"

"It means that Lieutenant Barnes was murdered because she knew something that would have incriminated the man who killed Joss Dunbar."

"If you think this is going to save you, Sam, I . . ."

"Just listen to me, General. I don't know who committed these murders, but there is no doubt that the answer involves either the ULTRA secret or our D-Day plans or both. And that was what you wanted me to find out when you first ordered me to investigate Joss Dunbar's death."

"I suppose you learned all that lying dead drunk in the whorehouse," said Manigault, his voice laden with sarcasm.

"Will you let me tell you a story, General?" said Taggart, pulling out a pack of Luckies.

Manigault glanced at his watch.

"Tell me why I should," he said, harshly.

"You have to ask that?"

Manigault's eyes bored in again for several moments.

"All right . . . five minutes, then," he said, coming back to the fire.

Taggart lit a cigarette and inhaled deeply. He had never talked about it with anyone before. That was part of his nature. He remembered looking down at his dead father after they had poured him into his coffin. He had never said more than a dozen words about himself in his whole life.

"Colonel Baird reported to you that I was drunk last night," he said, keeping his hands steady. "You know, General, I recently told someone that eighteen years of living with me drove a woman to drink herself to death, and that wasn't far from the truth. You asked me what happened back in New York. I'll tell you what happened, but it isn't pretty."

Part of him still wanted to stop, even if it meant prison.

"I said five minutes," declared Manigault coldly. Taggart nodded.

"You never met my wife, Barbara, but we had a good marriage. It only got better when our son, Johnny, was born. He was the best of both of us. You would have liked him, General. At eleven, he contracted yellow fever and we almost lost him. After that, Barbara became very protective of him."

Manigault was already furrowing his eyes, obviously regretting his decision.

"I thought she was overprotective," said Taggart, his voice stronger as he committed himself to finishing it. "At school, she wouldn't allow him to play any contact sports—she treated him like he was still an invalid. It was the one thing we argued about. I finally gave up. A few years later, the Japs struck at Pearl Harbor. Johnny was seventeen by then. Like a lot of his friends, he wanted to fight. He said it was the most important time to fight in human history . . . and that he wanted to make a difference."

Manigault's eyes softened slightly.

"So he enlisted in the Marine Corps. But because he was only seventeen, he needed one of our signatures to do it. Barbara wouldn't sign the form. I could probably have talked him out of it, but I didn't. He had thought it all through. I signed the paperwork. Nine months later, he was killed at Tulagi."

"I'm sorry, Sam. I didn't know," said Manigault, but glancing down at his watch again.

"Barbara couldn't come to terms with his death," Taggart went on, his throat dry. "She never forgave me. She began drinking in the morning and she stayed drunk all day. She tried to commit suicide twice before she finally succeeded. She left me a note. 'It's all your fault,' she wrote."

Manigault looked pained about something.

"I have a confession of my own to make, Sam," he said. "Baird told me about that note. He said it proved you were responsible for your wife's death. He said you drove her to take her own life and Kilgore called you on it, which was why you were drunk when they picked you up."

"Barbara didn't blame me for what she decided to do that night," said Taggart. "What she was trying to say was that it was my fault Johnny died."

"But it wasn't," said Manigault. "Young men die in combat. He was old enough to make the choice for himself."

"Thanks for saying that, General," said Taggart. "But that's not the reason I told you all this."

Manigault waited for him to continue.

"When Kilgore and Baird set me up, they didn't know one thing after they sprung the trap. I don't drink, General. I haven't had a drop of alcohol since Barbara died. The only reason I'm over here, General, is to make sure that her death and Johnny's have at least some meaning in this goddamn war. They had to pour the booze into me . . . and that was after they sapped me twice back here," he said, pointing at his head.

Manigault reached over and felt the two contusions behind Taggart's left ear. He sank back in his chair, shaking his head.

"I'd like to tell you what I've learned," said Taggart.

The general nodded, no longer bothering to check his watch, as Taggart outlined the things he had learned so far, including the revelations in J.P.'s diary.

"Jesus Christ," Manigault said. "I can't take on Kilgore right now. He's wired all the way to the top."

"I'm just asking you to let me stay here, General," he said. "The murderer, whoever he is, is still in a position to compromise Overlord."

"I can't let you take over the investigation again," said Manigault. "They'd put my tits in the ringer for that."

"And you have such beautiful tits," said Taggart.

Manigault gave him a sour grin.

"Put me on your personal security detail, then," said Taggart. "I don't care what the job is. Maybe something will turn up that will allow me to find out what we need to know."

Manigault stared glumly into the fire.

"All right" he said finally. "I'll tell Baird you're off the investigation—that should cool him off for now. He knows that I'm loyal to my people. Besides, he and Kilgore would have to go directly to Ike to overrule me. They won't want to open the can of worms involving Lieutenant Barnes."

Manigault stood up and headed back to his desk.

"That prima donna Montgomery is setting up an Overlord planning conference in a few weeks, for all the senior commanders, at his old boyhood school. . . . I think it's called Saint Paul's," he said. "As of now, you're part of the security team for the conference—you'll be working directly under me."

CHAPTER 20

The German bombers still came almost every night, wreaking havoc in neighborhoods all over London. The first official day of spring arrived with a blustery snowstorm that temporarily coated the war scars of the bomb-ravaged city with a soft mantle of white.

Walking to work at five each morning, Liza could hear the great roar of the American Flying Fortresses massing in the sky over southern England as they took the war back to Germany in daylight, devastating their industrial centers with the same ferocity the Luftwaffe was visiting on London at night.

Her new life had settled into a dull, repetitive routine. At first, it had seemed truly miraculous that Sam Taggart was able to save himself from being sentenced to a military prison. And he had somehow managed to keep her from being shipped home as well.

But reality set in within twenty-four hours of his release. For one thing, she learned that she no longer reported to Sam. And she was no longer a member of the criminal-investigations unit of Military Security Command. Even though she remained at the building on Saint James Square, her new duties consisted of arranging the rotating duty schedules for the lowest-level security staff at the new SHAEF offices in Bushy Park.

General Eisenhower had moved most of the Overlord planning staff there after one of the buildings across Saint James Square had taken a direct hit. The new headquarters was outside central London and less vulnerable to the German bombers. It was also closer to General Eisenhower's personal quarters in Telegraph Cottage, which he often shared with his driver, Kay Summersby.

Taggart had called Liza after his release to tell her they could no longer directly communicate with one another. Kilgore's people were looking for any opportunity to get rid of him once and for all, and would almost certainly be watching both of them. He promised to get in touch with her again if he heard of any important break in the two murder investigations.

Taggart had not exaggerated. When she left Saint James Square at the end of each day, someone invariably followed her home. As the weeks passed, Liza came to recognize several of the young men in the surveillance detail. Occasionally, she would smile at them when they met accidentally in a crowded shop or riding home on a bus.

She still worked in the same office with Charlie Wainwright, but rarely saw him anymore. He spent most of his working hours in the code-breaking lair. When he did come back to their office, it was to relax with the *Times* or to nap in his chair. Gray lines of fatigue soon etched his big, homely face. The one time they went out to lunch together, he fell asleep in the middle of the meal.

Two Wren privates were assigned the desks that had once been occupied by Joss and J.P. Both had attended vocational school and were assigned to the secretarial pool. When they weren't typing routine orders and paperwork, the two of them chattered endlessly about the American boys they met, giggling together at the slightest opportunity.

Liza continued to read and censor personal mail, but it was now limited to the correspondence of junior officers, none of whom had security clearance for Overlord. Nevertheless, she could discern from the tone of the letters that the invasion date was rapidly approaching. No one in southern England needed a letter to know that. Every road and train station was clogged with the men and equipment being moved to the staging areas south of London.

The murders of Joss and J.P. remained unsolved. In early April, Inspector Drummond had telephoned her to ask if she had retained a copy of J.P.'s autopsy report. He was still in charge of both investigations at Scotland Yard, but was no longer receiving cooperation from the Joint Security Command. After she informed him that all her records and files had been confiscated, he confided his doubt to her that either case would ever be resolved.

In late April, Liza's hotel in Pimlico was badly damaged by a fire, and she was forced to move to a billet for female officers in North London. By then, she was certain that no one was bothering to follow her any longer.

To escape her boredom, she went out on dates several times with Dr. Cabot, the red-haired plastic surgeon. One night he took her to the Palace Theatre to see a revue hosted by Bob Hope and several other American entertainers. General Eisenhower was the guest of honor. Gazing up at the honorees, she saw General Kilgore sitting in one of the royal boxes with a young blonde woman. From a distance, she looked like a pudgy Shirley Temple.

Liza had retained only one small connection to the murder investigations, and she was careful not to share it with anyone at SHAEF. The link involved the two pieces of evidence that had not been confiscated with the rest of her case files after Sam's arrest. These were the two index cards on which she had written the lines that had been inscribed in blood on the stationery found in Joss's apartment. Both cards had been in her purse.

Whenever she met someone outside SHAEF who seemed to possess a knowledge of English history or literature, she would ask the person to look at the two cards. So far, her queries had proved fruitless.

On a weekend trip to Oxford in late April, she visited several of the college libraries, asking each research librarian whether he recognized the passages. One librarian thought there might be something vaguely Shakespearean about them, and spent an hour with her thumbing through a Shakespeare concordance before declaring himself stumped.

One morning, she was having a cup of tea at her desk when an elderly gentleman wearing a formal black morning coat and a starched white neck-cloth appeared in the open doorway. The sight of him immediately generated a fit of giggling from the two young Wren secretaries.

"Lieutenant Elizabeth Marantz?" he asked solemnly.

"I am she," said Liza.

"I was instructed to deliver this to you," he said, placing a large buff envelope on her desk.

He was carrying at least a half-dozen more envelopes in his left hand.

Her immediate reaction was to wonder how he had gotten past the security detail. Before she could ask him where he had come from, he was gone.

The envelope stock was actually heavy. Engraved in gold on the wax-sealed flap was the figure of a roaring lion, standing on its hind legs. The lion was holding a sword in one paw and a mace in the other.

She slit the envelope with a letter opener and removed the card from inside it. A matching gold lion was embossed on the front of the card. It contained an engraved invitation to visit Rawcliff Castle. Turning it over, she found a personal note written in royal-blue ink.

"Liza . . . Please forgive me for not getting in touch sooner, but I was in hospital for some touch-up work at the Beauty Shop. Would you consider joining us at Rawcliff for the weekend? There will be other guests. You won't be lonely. With fond regards, Nick."

"Other guests," said Charlie with a laugh when he returned to the office and she had time to ask him about it. "Several hundred, more than likely," he went on. "It's a big show, Liza—the biggest and most luxurious house party of the year, for the elite of the realm. Always takes place in mid-May. The Ainsleys have been famous for these affairs for two hundred years."

"Does Nicholas host them?"

"Someday he will," said Charlie. "But for now it's still Lady Ainsley, Nicky's mother. She was a famous beauty in her day."

"And Nicholas's father?"

"He is . . . dead," said Charlie.

Liza thought he was about to add something, but he didn't.

"Are you going?" she asked.

"Probably won't be able to break away, but I would love to go down with you. I have a standing invitation," he said, clearly proud of the privilege.

"Well, I'll go if you go," she said.

"Have you been out of this godforsaken city since you arrived?" asked Charlie.

"I went to Oxford once," she said with a smile.

"That's it?"

She nodded.

"Isn't it about time, then? Might do you some good, considering everything that . . ."

He stopped in mid-sentence.

"Only if you go," she repeated.

"Look . . . I'll go if I can. Believe me, Liza, I want to," he said, gazing at her longingly. She immediately felt guilty, knowing he still had a crush on her. It wasn't fair to hold out any hopes there.

"I'll give it some thought, too," she said.

Lying in bed later that night, she decided to go. For one thing, there was nothing important to keep her in London any longer. It would finally serve to break the dull routine. And Nicholas would be there.

CHAPTER 21

Sam Taggart stood in front of the walk-in closet wearing only his white boxer shorts. He had just drawn the blackout curtains before turning on the lights in the bedroom.

"Do you mind if I try on one of these suits?" he asked.

"Go ahead," said Helen Bellayne with a smile. She was lying naked on the bed gazing up contentedly at him. "Roddy was about your height. You're a little fuller in the chest . . . and at least one other area."

Taggart removed a double-breasted charcoal suit jacket from the closet pole and tried it on.

"Not bad," she said. "Now come over here and let me take it off you."

"I want to go out tonight," said Taggart.

"Anywhere special, darling?"

"The Ritz Bar," he said.

"Exclusive, aren't we?" said Helen Bellayne, sitting up in bed and stretching like a contented cat.

"Can you get us a table?" he asked, pulling out a white shirt from one of the built-in drawers next to the closet racks.

"Certainly," she said.

The tables at the Ritz Bar were no larger than a serving tray, but they were almost impossible to come by unless one knew the management or wanted to pay the headwaiter. Taggart detested bars like this, places that pandered to Americans who needed to be able to go home and say, "Yeah. I hung out at the bar Hemingway and Fitzgerald used to drink at in London."

When they sat down, he discovered that there was almost no place to put his legs. At the long polished mahogany bar, they were standing three deep, cheek by jowl, officers in dress uniform intermingled with women in cocktail dresses. He recognized the English movie star Madeleine Carroll, talking to a young marine lieutenant.

"You prefer this to my bedroom?" asked Helen Bellayne.

"No. I hate it," said Taggart.

"Then why are we here?" she demanded. "And why are you suddenly dressing like a Fleet Street banker?"

"I knew someone was going to be here tonight," said Taggart, glancing over at a group of American officers who were sitting a few tables away. "I've been following him off and on for two weeks. Tonight I wanted to look like a civilian."

"Are you going to tell me why?" asked Helen Bellayne.

"It's personal," said Taggart.

"I can see why the generals and admirals all love you, Major Taggart," she said, leaning close and taking his gnarled hand in hers. "You're such a sociable man."

The American officers had been rewarded with a table near one of the windows looking out on Piccadilly. There were three of them, two colonels flanking a brigadier general. The general was already drunk, and brazenly eyeing a young woman in a beige dress who was sitting at the adjacent table. Taggart was close enough to hear the Americans' loud conversation. The two colonels were talking about the fighting prowess of women.

"The Russian women love combat," one of them said with open admiration in his voice. "I saw a report in Washington last week that described how they fought right alongside the men at Stalingrad . . . and thousands of them were killed, too."

The brigadier removed a cigar from his mouth, and turned his gaze from the young woman back to the others.

"I don't want to pull rank," he said sternly, "but don't underestimate the American WAC, gentlemen."

"I didn't mean to . . ." began the colonel apologetically.

"You know what a WAC is, don't you, Colonel?" the general demanded, his face seemingly clouded with anger.

The colonel looked as if he wished he could crawl under the table.

"The Women's Army Corps, General Gramm?" he answered tentatively.

The general nodded portentously before picking up his martini and finishing it in one swallow.

"The American WAC is a double-breasted GI," he said, smiling with intimate jocularity. "Except she's got a built-in foxhole."

When he began to laugh uproariously at the joke, his subordinates joined in with obsequious enthusiasm.

"I've got to take a piss," said the general, standing up. "This party is just starting, am I right?"

"Yes, sir," echoed the other two officers.

The brigadier pretended to stumble into the young woman at the adjacent table before putting his hands on her shoulders.

"Excuse me, honey," he said, grinning at her, then heading across the room to the staircase that led to the men's room. He disappeared down the stairs.

"I'll just be a few minutes," said Taggart.

"Don't leave me to this fate for very long," warned Helen Bellayne.

Taggart stood up from the table, walked across the crowded lounge, and headed down the same staircase.

There was only one person in the lavatory aside from the general: an elderly Sikh attendant with a white linen turban on his head and a freshly starched white jacket, who stood officiously next to a stack of white hand towels near the lavatory sinks. As Taggart came up to him, he picked up a towel and offered it. Taggart put a one-pound note in his tip jar and motioned him out the door. Grinning, he went.

Taggart walked over to the urinal next to the general's and unzipped his pants. General Gramm glanced over at him for a moment before returning his eyes to the wall in front of him. He had both hands at his crotch. The lit cigar was in his mouth.

Leaning closer, Taggart began staring at him, his face just a few inches away. The general felt his gaze and glared back.

"You got a problem, buddy?" he demanded, removing the cigar from his mouth with his left hand.

"I provide a service to women who like to be beaten up," said Taggart. "You know . . . masochists. We're looking for some new male recruits."

"Are you nuts or something?" said General Gramm, before putting the cigar back in his mouth and zipping up his pants.

"With something that small, I can see why you'd try to hide it."

"What did you say?"

Taggart grinned and said, "You heard me."

Gramm looked at the tailored Saville Row suit and then back at Taggart's face.

"Are you an American?" he asked.

Taggart nodded.

"Do you know who I am?" said Gramm.

"Yeah, I know what you are."

"You've got a wise mouth, fella," said Gramm, stepping away. "Good thing I'm not looking for a fight."

Taggart swung around from his urinal and drenched the general's legs with urine.

"You son of a bitch," Gramm bellowed, throwing a wild punch at the side of Taggart's jaw.

Ducking it, Taggart said, "You probably do better punching women."

As Gramm swung with his other hand, Taggart drove his fist into the bigger man's mouth, feeling the sharp, familiar pain in his knuckles as the man's front teeth caved in behind the lit cigar. Gramm dropped to the floor, his arms and legs splayed out to either side.

Still consumed by rage, Taggart kicked him in the crotch. General Gramm moaned once before he slowly rolled over to one side and clutched his genitals.

"Lloyd Barnes told me to tell you he's doing fine," said Taggart. "He'll look you up personally when he gets back to the States."

Upstairs, it was necessary to push his way through a large circle of men who were surrounding their little table.

"May we go now?" Helen asked after he worked his way into sight. "I feel as if I'm at the zoo."

"Yeah, let's go home," said Taggart.

CHAPTER 22

As she sat nervously waiting for Charlie to return to the office, Liza began to wish that she had never heard of Rawcliff or the fabled country weekend. The whole idea suddenly seemed idiotic. Liza Marantz meets the social elite of the British realm. She had already met the military elite, and the connection had not been pleasant. All she wanted to do was go back to her apartment to read the last few chapters of *Pride and Prejudice.*

At the heart of the matter was the fact that she had nothing remotely suitable to wear when she met Nicholas again. All her civilian clothing was lying inside a sunken troop transport at the bottom of the North Atlantic. When she had started packing for the weekend, it struck her that aside from one light summer dress she had inherited from a WAC who was returning to the States, there was nothing to wear but her drab uniforms.

At lunch, Liza had run out to a clothing store on Piccadilly, only to discover for the first time how ridiculously expensive women's clothes were in the London shops. The shoes in the display window started at eighteen pounds.

"I'm afraid it's the war," said the young saleslady behind the counter with a trace of bitterness in her voice. "The only ones who can afford to buy anything are you Yanks."

Liza returned to the office with a pair of brown twill slacks and a white cotton blouse. The realm's elite were not likely to be impressed, she thought, and neither would Lord Nicholas Ainsley.

It was almost four o'clock in the afternoon, and she was beginning to hope that Charlie would be detained long enough in the lair for them to miss the train. But five minutes later, he came charging into the office dragging his battered suitcase. After stuffing some papers into his briefcase, he turned to face her.

"Ready, my girl?" he asked with a grin. "I wasn't able to finish what I needed to do, but we're bloody well going anyway."

"Wonderful," said Liza without enthusiasm as he shepherded her out the door.

"I hope you brought something to wear besides that tedious uniform," he added as they stepped out onto the street.

"I have a ball gown and glass slippers in the bag," she said tartly.

"Smashing," he said. "I'm sure it's a corker."

Once he had flagged down a taxi on Pall Mall, he exhorted the driver to get them to Waterloo Station. "Flog those horses, my good man," he barked jovially.

Traffic came to a stop before they were halfway across Westminster Bridge. It took them more than ten minutes to reach the other side.

"Blast," Charlie growled, "we're going to miss the bloody train at this rate."

The side streets around the massive train station were clogged with vehicles of every shape and size. With two blocks still to go, Charlie paid off the driver, and they raced forward on foot. At the entrance to Waterloo, travelers were being funneled into one long line for a random identity check. It snaked around the building for almost two hundred feet.

"This way," Charlie called out to her as she began trudging toward the back of the line.

He had already disappeared off to the other side of the entrance façade. When she followed him around the corner, he was standing at a small white-painted door, pounding on it with his fist. It swung open to reveal a frowning little man wearing the uniform of the British Railway Service. He immediately began motioning for Charlie to return to the main entrance. Reaching into his pocket, Charlie held up his buff invitation card with the Ainsley crest. It was like holding up a cross to a movie vampire.

The man shrank back from the doorway and waved them through

before quickly slamming the door shut behind them. Inside the station, there was barely controlled pandemonium under the towering glass roof. Fish-and-chip vendors screamed their wares over the sound of shrieking train whistles as angry porters elbowed their way through the jostling crowds. But Charlie seemed to know exactly where he was going.

Long grimy trains stood waiting on almost every track. With Charlie still leading the way, they arrived at a large printed sign that read "Eastbourne–Dover." Another railway official was standing guard at the platform gate. Without slowing down, Charlie held up their invitations again and charged straight through.

The first rail carriage they came to was painted a shiny bird's-egg blue. The plate glass windows were trimmed in gold. An arched canvas canopy stood directly in front of the newly polished coach door. Two men in black swallowtail coats were standing next to it on the platform.

The coach door behind them was open, and on its polished façade Liza saw the familiar crest of a roaring lion. Surrounding the crest was a huge "A," also painted in gold. One of the men in swallowtail coats observed Charlie coming down the platform, and smiled warmly.

"Welcome back, Captain Wainwright," he said.

"Thank you, Robert," replied Charlie as the second man took his suitcase. "And this is Lieutenant Elizabeth Marantz," he added.

The porter's eyes quickly scanned his list.

"Yes, of course. Please come aboard, Lieutenant," he said as the second porter took her bag.

"The Ainsley family owns its own train?" she asked breathlessly as they stepped up into the elegant teak-trimmed passageway.

Charlie grinned and said, "Just these first two carriages. They are attached to the Eastbound Express to Dover and will be disengaged at a rail siding when we arrive at Sussex Downs."

The car was decorated like the parlor of a fine London men's club, with white lace curtains, dark teak paneling, and comfortable tapestry-covered furniture. At least fifty people were already crowded inside the car.

Liza was surprised to discover that very few of them were in military uniform. Recognizing Admiral Thomas Jellico in an oatmeal-tweed sporting rig, she realized that many had already changed into civilian clothing.

The second section of the carriage was arranged for formal dining, with a handsome Regency table and twelve matching chairs. The tabletop was anchored in the middle by a floral arrangement of long-stemmed roses. Surrounding the fresh-cut flowers were filigreed silver trays and bowls offering crab cocktail, eggs en rissoles, foie gras, marinated trout, roast guinea fowl, mushroom tartlets, and a wide selection of rolls and pastries.

A bar had been set up in the corner, and the people surrounding it were already sipping champagne and whiskey. Charlie headed straight for the bartender.

"Hello, Leftenant," came a familiar voice from off to the side.

Liza turned to see Helen Bellayne standing near the window, holding a cup of tea in her right hand. She was wearing an exquisite organdy dress that looked like it might have been fashioned during the reign of Queen Victoria.

"Mrs. Bellayne," she said. "What a lovely dress."

"It was my grandmother's," she said. "Sam Taggart sends his regards."

"Have you seen him recently?" asked Liza with genuine surprise.

"Yes," she said. "We have become good friends."

"Really," said Liza neutrally.

Helen Bellayne laughed warmly and said, "Sam thought you wouldn't believe me. I'm to give you this."

She handed Liza a sealed envelope. Inside was a short note in his familiar choppy scrawl.

It read, "Liza—You can trust her. Sam."

"I only wish he was joining us for the weekend," said Helen.

"Yes, I'm sure he would be very popular," said Liza, who was watching Admiral Jellico's eyes as they lingered on her with barely disguised contempt.

A train whistle shrieked loudly and the carriage jolted forward, stopped short for a moment, and then rolled forward again. Charlie came from the bar with two cocktails in his hand. He presented her with one.

"Let the weekend festivities begin," he said, downing half his scotch-and-soda in two swallows.

Fifteen minutes later, the eastbound express train cleared central London and was heading through the outer rim of the city. Charlie was on his second cocktail and ensconced on a Victorian sofa chatting with a girl in a purple silk dress that was slit up to her thigh. Liza stood near one of the windows, watching the unfolding spectacle inside the carriage.

"Fade me again," called out a young flyer as he loudly demanded a drink at the bar.

"Now, there's a superb dish," Liza heard someone say with an American accent. She assumed that the person was talking about one of the delicacies on the Regency dining table.

Glancing up, she saw an American navy captain staring back at her. Just beyond his shoulder, she recognized General Kilgore, who was in a heated conversation with one of his British counterparts. Like so many of the others, he was dressed in informal sporting clothes.

Turning away, Liza got a glimpse of the English countryside through the plate-glass window, and she was immediately disappointed. Perhaps it was the pall of the dark, leaden sky, but the homes within view of the train looked nothing like the countryside in *Mrs. Miniver.* They were sadly dilapidated and badly in need of paint and repair. The small gardens in front of them were weed-strewn and untended.

"That's the cost of having our young men spread far and wide across the globe," said Helen Bellayne, as if reading her mind. "They will be coming home to a very different place from the one they left."

"I hope that they will be coming home soon," said Liza.

"Yes," agreed Helen Bellayne. "Well, the die will shortly be cast, won't it?"

As Liza nodded, the train began to slow down again, finally jolting to a complete stop. A few minutes later, a troop train came hurtling past from the opposite direction. It seemed to go on forever, one carriage after another crammed with soldiers, then freight cars loaded with tanks, trucks, and artillery pieces.

When they were moving again, Charlie joined them, and they sat down at the dining table to sample the food.

At one point, Liza looked across to the other side of the car and noticed a young woman sitting in a comfortable easy chair on the opposite side of the carriage. With her strawberry-blond hair and handsome Nordic face, she projected a striking presence. But on closer examination, Liza saw that her large blue eyes seemed anesthetized. As the woman's body rocked slowly back and forth in rhythm to the jostling coach, she never moved her head, gazing blankly out at the passing countryside.

A young man about his own age clapped Charlie on the back and joined them at the table.

"Wainwright . . . I haven't seen you since I left for Burma," said the new arrival, who had tawny-blond hair, laughing eyes, and a long, crooked nose. His skin was the color of dark bronze. "Quite a guest list this year, I gather."

"Who's coming, Quentin?" asked Charlie. "I haven't been up for air for some time."

"Almost everyone . . . Let's see, the Duke of Wellington; David Niven; Edwina Mountbatten, of course, although Louis is still in Peking, holding the Gissimo's cock; Halifax; Beaverbrook; Korda; Merle Oberon; Jellico, of course," said Quentin, flashing a grin at Helen Bellayne. "And about three hundred of the rest of the faithful who aren't buried at Sidi Barrani or Mandalay or rotting here in English prisons for admiring Hitler."

"How large is this house?" asked Liza.

"Liza, it's not a house. It is one of the greatest estates in England," said Helen. "It makes Blenheim look like Shakespeare's cottage in Stratford-on-Avon."

Looking across the carriage, Liza was again intrigued by the woman who continued to stare morosely out the window.

"Who is that young woman?" she whispered into Helen's ear.

Helen glanced across the car and her smile disappeared.

"Unity," she said, with a hint of loathing.

"Unity?" repeated Liza.

"Unity Mitford," said Helen. "One of the Mitford sisters . . . Surely you've heard of them."

Liza shook her head.

"Their father is Lord Redesdale, House of Lords . . . a strange man by every account . . . raving anti-Semite," she said. "And his daughters have all turned out to be just as eccentric. Nancy is a peach, and so is Jessica—they're both raving socialists. Unity's sister Diana was the first one to become a fascist. She married Sir Oswald Mosley, the head of the Blackshirts. They're both in prison now."

"And Unity?" asked Liza.

Charlie had been listening to the conversation. He leaned in and said, "Sad story, really. God, she was smashing. But Diana took her to Germany before the war and she got besotted with Hitler . . . practically threw herself at him. Supposedly, her affections were returned. Anyway, when the war began, she became totally distraught and shot herself in the head. They brought her home after that, but she's never been right. I gather the bullet's still in her brain."

"Lord Redesdale was the peer who got Nicholas's father to join the Right Club," added Helen.

"The Right Club?" asked Liza.

"It was a secret society formed by Sir Archibald Ramsay in 1939," said Charlie. "The main object was to expose the so-called international conspiracy of organized Jewry," he added with an awkward grin.

"We're so very good at international conspiracy, aren't we?" said Liza bitingly. "What happened to this club?"

"It was eventually penetrated by MI5 agents. Later on the government passed the Defence Regulation Order, which gave the home secretary the right to imprison anybody he believed likely to endanger the realm. Most of them are now in prison."

"Lord Ainsley committed suicide," added Helen.

"Nicholas's father?" asked Liza.

As Helen nodded, the train jolted once, then again, and the rhythmic clacking of the iron wheels began to slow.

"We're here," said Charlie, standing up from the table with a glow of anticipation on his whiskey-inflamed cheeks.

CHAPTER 23

The carriage jerked to a stop in front of a little brick station surrounded by white birch trees. From the window, Liza could see nothing in the distance except rolling green pastures separated by ancient stone fences.

The two Ainsley coaches nudged forward and jerked back several times as the railway crew worked to disengage them from the rest of the train. A few minutes later, she heard the screech of a steam whistle, and the Eastbound Express rumbled out of the station, leaving them alone on a rail siding. In a minute, the air was still again.

The excited guests began milling toward the door at the front of the first carriage, several of them carrying newly opened bottles of champagne. Liza followed Helen Bellayne out onto the weathered station platform. The spring air felt surprisingly mild, and she thought she could smell the distant tang of the sea.

A small fleet of antique automobiles and horse-drawn carriages were lined up on the small country lane in front of the station. Without any apparent pecking order, the partygoers were already climbing into the vehicles.

Liza was about to follow Helen through the open door of a large Phaeton limousine when she glanced inside and saw Admiral Jellico sitting next to General Kilgore in the rear seat.

Hurriedly turning around, she stepped on the foot of the woman behind her, eliciting a small cry of pain. As she tried to apologize, Liza couldn't help noticing the scornful grin on General Kilgore's face. He leaned close to Jellico and began to whisper something.

Farther back in the line of vehicles, she saw Charlie Wainwright scramble into an almost prehistoric automobile behind his friend Quentin. It was a type she had only seen in old movies, where the driver was exposed to the elements up front and the passengers sat in silk-upholstered luxury behind him. Feeling utterly alone, she ran back to join them. There wasn't any space left next to Charlie, but she pushed in anyway, ending up on his lap.

"Well, we shall just have to make do, shan't we?" said Charlie, grinning happily as he put his arm around her shoulder.

The first car began to move slowly up the narrow country lane. The rest of the vehicles followed in a snaking line, moving just fast enough so that that the horse-drawn carriages could keep up in the long procession. Soon the caravan was deep into the lonely countryside. To Liza, it seemed they had left any trace of modern civilization behind.

At one point, they passed a farmer plowing his field behind a team of oxen. The stone farm cottage behind him looked like it had existed there since time immemorial. As the evening sky began to darken, Charlie pointed toward the distant tree line and said, "That's Rawcliff."

Their car passed between two stone pillars and entered a broad gravel lane that had been cut through a primordial forest of oaks and elms. Some of the trees were almost as big around as the redwoods Liza had seen on a childhood visit to California. The boughs of the elms formed a canopy high above them, like the ceiling of a vaulted cathedral. The silent woods went on for almost a mile.

"It's like the enchanted forest in a fairy tale," said Liza as they rolled over a small stone bridge crossing a swollen creek.

Suddenly they came out of the trees and her eyes took in the startling green of a crescent-shaped valley. In the distance, she could see a cluster of tall stone structures rising from the heath at the edge of a small blue lake. Beyond the buildings, she saw the sea.

At first, it all reminded her of the medieval castles she had read about in the *Knights of the Round Table.* But as they drew closer, she saw that it was really four different castles. The gigantic structures were connected by open courtyards and enclosed stone passageways.

The entire front wall of the first castle was covered with intertwined tendrils of ivy, a living wall of green. There was a broad stone terrace in front of it, and beyond that were acres of well-trimmed lawns that sloped down to a bluff overlooking the green sea. She could smell the moist salt air all around her.

"My God," Liza said in wonder.

"The oldest part is twelfth-century—from the days of the Saracen hordes," said Charlie, as if seeing it again for the first time. "Only a small portion of Rawcliff is even electrified."

As the wheels of their car crunched up the lane to the massive entrance doors, they passed a group of elderly workmen in navy coveralls, busily smoothing the gravel with wooden-tined rakes.

Liza looked up to see a flock of black birds cawing loudly above them as she followed Charlie toward the stone steps leading up to the entrance. Almost magically, the bronze doors swung open when the first guests arrived at the top of the stairs.

Uniformed footmen flanked the archway as they headed inside. Beyond them, a severe-looking gray-haired woman in black tweeds stood waiting to greet each guest at the entrance to the great hall. Standing behind her was Nicholas Ainsley. It was the first time she had seen him out of uniform, and he looked ruggedly handsome in a tan corduroy sports jacket and old canvas trousers.

The woman in tweeds was formally greeting each of the guests with the same simple words, delivered in a quiet reserved manner. "Welcome to Rawcliff. I hope you enjoy your stay with us."

Aside from the black-tweed suit, she wore a white blouse with a severe collar and heavy black brogans. A small gold pocket watch was pinned to the breast of her jacket. She wore no other jewelry.

As Liza approached the front of the line, Nicholas started grinning at her like a happy primate. Backing away from his mother, he stepped toward her, leaned down, and kissed her on the cheek.

"God, it's so great of you to come," he whispered.

She had reached the head of the line by then, and the gray-haired woman stood waiting to greet her. Liza saw the purple blemishes around her very pale eyes.

"Welcome to Rawcliff," Lady Ainsley said in the same monotone voice. "I hope you enjoy your stay with us."

Looking down, Lady Ainsley saw that Nicholas had not let go of Liza's right hand.

"Thank you so much for inviting me," said Liza, smiling pleasantly.

This woman has recently been very ill, she thought, noticing the sagging skin at her neck and the hollowed eyes. She was holding her left hand with the right to keep it from trembling.

"And how do you know my son?" asked Lady Ainsley as the receiving line stopped short behind her.

Her eyes seemed to take in Liza's army uniform with sudden distaste.

"We met quite accidentally," she began. "In fact, it was in my office at . . ."

"You have an exquisite figure, my dear," said Lady Ainsley, making it sound as if she were appraising a well-proportioned head of livestock. "Your uniform does not do it justice."

"Mother, please," said Nicholas very quietly. "She is my guest."

Under her fierce glare, he reluctantly let go of Liza's hand.

"Later," he whispered, before going back to stand at his mother's side.

"Welcome to Rawcliff," said Lady Ainsley to the next guest in line. "I hope you enjoy your stay with us."

Liza walked slowly into the great hall. A Flemish tapestry hung on the nearest wall. At least twenty feet high, it depicted a Christian crusader kneeling in a church in Jerusalem, surrounded by his fellow warriors. His sword was red with blood. Oil paintings on the other walls depicted various Ainsley family members, going back almost a thousand years.

Far above her, smoke-blackened oak beams vaulted across the ceiling. At the far end of the hall loomed a fireplace as large as her parents' living room on Long Island. Burning inside it were ten-foot logs suspended between enormous brass andirons.

The hall was rapidly filling with guests. Amid the indistinct buzz of distinguished, high-born accents, she walked around the vast room in wonderment. Along with an aroma of wood smoke, the smell of fresh flowers pervaded the air. They were everywhere, in vases and urns, spread across the room on almost every table, roses, lilies, even orchids in cut-glass bowls.

She passed through another archway into a magnificent library. Leather-bound books filled oak shelves that ran from the floor to the ceiling. A golden-oak gallery at the far end could only be reached by an intricately carved circular stairway.

On a plantation table in the middle of the room sat dozens of tea settings and silver trays crammed with smoked salmon, along with scones and crumpets topped with glazed vanilla icing. Nibbling on a pastry, she walked back out into the great hall and gazed at the broad marble staircase which led upstairs.

A cherubic little man in a black swallowtail suit moved to her side.

"May I show you to your room, madam?" he asked.

"That would be wonderful, but how do you know which one it is?" she asked, amid the crowd.

"We know who all our guests are, madam," he replied in a tone of almost injured pride.

Not wanting to hurt his feelings, she followed him up the broad staircase. At the first landing, she looked through the tall mullioned windows that were cut into the thick stone walls. In the waning light, she caught a glimpse of formal gardens, manicured lawns, and, in the distance, a now black sea.

The staircase parted to the left and right at the landing, and she followed the servant down a stone passageway, her army-issue shoes tapping on the flagstone floor. They passed more than a dozen doors before he stopped in the middle of the hallway.

"This is your room, madam," he said, opening the polished walnut door and standing back for her to enter. "I regret that it will be necessary for you to share a bath with several of the other ladies. It is two doors down the hall to your right."

"Thank you," said Liza as a liveried footman came into the room with her overseas bag. "I'm used to that."

The room was small but elegantly furnished, with a four-poster bed, writing desk, and mahogany dresser. A vase full of hydrangeas sat on the dresser. Blue chintz curtains framed the leaded-glass windows, and a small log fire burned cheerfully in the corner hearth.

"I hope it will be satisfactory, madam," he said, turning to leave.

"Oh yes, it will. Thank you," she said, and he gently shut the door behind him.

She went immediately to the leaded casement windows and opened them wide. It was too dark to see anything beyond the lighted terrace far below, but she could hear the distant pounding of the sea. A salt-laden haze coated the panes of the windows.

Feeling suddenly tired, she walked over to the bed. A freshly starched white counterpane stretched across it like the membrane of a drum. As she pulled it back from the pillows, there was a light knocking at the door. When she opened it, Helen Bellayne was standing in the hallway.

"I was wondering..." she began, and stopped. "Oh hell, I just wanted to make sure you had something suitable to wear to dinner tonight. Sam told me that you might not have any formal dinner clothes."

"I was going to wear my best uniform," said Liza.

"Can't allow that," said Helen, shaking her head firmly. "Not the way I saw Nicky eyeing you earlier in the great hall. You are the first woman to put the light in his eyes in a long time, my dear."

"I don't have anything else to wear," she said, "and I..."

"We're about the same size," said Helen, "and I brought one more thing than I need."

She left the room for several minutes, returning with a dark-blue silk evening dress over one arm and a pair of black pumps in her hand.

"I can't promise that this dress will even last through the evening," she said. "It's one of the last of the best. My mother wore it to a soiree with the Queen Mother at the coronation of George the Sixth. I had it altered to fit me some years ago. I think you'll fill it out nicely."

"Really, I don't know how to thank you," said Liza.

"One more piece of advice, if I may," said Helen. "As someone who has attended these parties on many occasions, you should be prepared for a very late evening. I would suggest that you take a bath while there is still some hot water left, and then take a short nap."

As soon as she was gone, Liza decided to follow her advice. Finding the bathroom down the hall, she ran a hot bath and lingered in it until someone began knocking on the door ten minutes later.

Returning to her little room, she opened the windows wide again, removed her bathrobe, and climbed naked into the four-poster bed. She fell asleep to the sound of the restless sea.

CHAPTER 24

"You look absolutely ravishing," said Charlie Wainwright, his eyes gleaming with pleasure as she came down the broad staircase in the blue silk evening gown. The dress fit as if it had been made for her, accentuating her slim, curvaceous figure in a simple, elegant way.

Liza burst out laughing when she saw the costume he had assembled for the dinner party. His black tuxedo jacket looked as if it had last been worn to a celebration of the Spanish Armada, and it didn't match the red-striped navy uniform pants. The bow tie at the neck of his rumpled white dress shirt was canary yellow with black polka dots. A long blue-and-white scarf hung across his shoulders.

"What's so funny?" he demanded with a lopsided grin.

"You are," she said.

"Well, you've missed the cocktail hour," he said in a way that made it clear he hadn't. "Everyone's already at dinner."

A thirty-piece orchestra was playing a Mozart symphony in the great hall as they went through it into the formal dining room. The three hundred guests were seated at three parallel fifty-foot-long white-damask-covered tables. Silver candelabras were set along each tabletop, providing a romantic illumination to the dramatic setting.

Lady Ainsley sat at the head of the center table, with Field Marshal Lord Alan Brooke on her right and Lord Hastings Ismay on her left. Nicholas was a few place settings down from Ismay, who was Churchill's chief of staff.

Charlie led her to a spot near the middle of the third table. At one of the two unoccupied settings, a small engraved card rested on a pewter plate. "Lieutenant Elizabeth Mintz," it read. She laughed, having seen a lot worse botchings of her name through the years.

With Charlie slouching in the adjacent seat, she glanced down the line of guests at their table, catching a brief glimpse of General Kilgore behind one of the silver candelabras. He was sitting next to the same plump young blonde woman with ringed curls Liza had seen him with at the Palace Theatre. Tonight, she was wearing a pink ruffled evening gown. Opposite him was Admiral Jellico, wearing his gold-encrusted navy dress uniform. Helen Bellayne sat at his right. Seeing Liza, she smiled and gave her a silent "thumbs up" gesture.

Directly across from Liza sat a retired British Army officer who had to be approaching ninety. His wide-lapelled scarlet military jacket was festooned with medals and decorations. He had a prominent hawk nose, and his leathery face was furrowed with lavender veins. Sitting next to him was a dowager of about seventy in an old lace-trimmed Victorian gown that revealed the swell of her ponderous breasts. Her hair was an astonishing shade of reddish orange.

"So what do you do, my dear?" she asked, exposing large predatory teeth.

"I work in the security command at Supreme Headquarters in London," said Liza.

The woman was trying to mask her double chin by holding her head very erect. It required her literally to look down her nose at the other guests.

"Sounds very important," she said.

"Not at all, I'm afraid," replied Liza.

"Don't let her mislead you," said Charlie. "She's a detective . . . and a bloody good one, if they would just let her do her job."

"A detective," said the old officer in the scarlet military jacket. "How clever of you. Like Sherlock Holmes, you mean?"

"No, General Massengale, more like Nora Charles," said Charlie.

"Nora Charles? Who is that?" the old woman demanded.

"Can you spot an evildoer just by looking at him?" demanded General Massengale, ignoring the dowager.

"No," said Liza. "I don't think anyone can."

"She spotted me," said Charlie, downing his highball as a waiter poured a ladleful of steaming consommé into his soup bowl from a silver tureen.

A legion of waiters were moving silently behind the chairs, some serving the aromatic soup, others ready to refill a guest's glass as soon as it was empty. Charlie's glass did not stay empty for long. After he had downed his third glass of claret, Liza turned to him and whispered, "Please don't drink so much, Charlie."

"Ahhh . . . the look of female disapproval . . . I have suffered under it all my life," he answered back, his cheeks as red as jam. "This is playtime, old girl. I've been cooped up in the lair for weeks."

Liza couldn't help peeking over her shoulder at Nicholas Ainsley. From the look on his face, he clearly wasn't thrilled to be there, and made no attempt to talk with the guests on either side of him. When he wasn't staring at his plate, he kept glancing at his watch.

At one point, he looked in her direction and smiled. She couldn't help smiling back at him. He picked up his wineglass and raised it in a silent toast, his eyes delivering the message, "Not much longer."

What is it about him that I find so attractive? she wondered. She had met many men since arriving in England who were more imposing, distinguished, or even classically handsome. She decided it was simply the fact that being with him gave her pleasure. Perhaps it was his melancholy eyes. Her heart simply went out to him.

The main course was beef Wellington, surrounded on the red-and-gold china plate with potatoes au gratin, creamed spinach, and braised leeks. It was served along with another vintage red wine.

"Don't know how Sylvia does it," said General Massengale. "Haven't had beef this good since before the war."

"It's from Argentina, I believe," said the old dowager. "At least that's what Sylvia told someone."

"I say . . . Wainwright."

The voice came from a thin-faced, cadaverous man farther down the table. Still in his twenties, he wore a cream-and-gold military tunic and a cute little round hat topped with a gold pom-pom. His right hand was missing.

"Is that a Trinity crew scarf you're wearing?"

"Would I wear any other?" Charlie responded belligerently.

"Just asking," said the officer, who looked quite fierce to Liza in spite of his ludicrous pom-pom hat. "No need to get in a pucker."

"Not a joking matter," said the inebriated Charlie.

"So you rowed with the Blues?" the officer asked in a nostalgic tone.

Charlie nodded. "Nicky and I both, of course," he said with unambiguous pride. "In the summer of 1938, we went over to Germany to race for the Goering Cup in Bad Ems."

"Yes, I competed for it myself the year before you did," said the other man. "That ghastly gold-plated shell casing with the Nazi eagle on it."

"Exactly," said Charlie. "Unfortunately, we were a bit hung over on the morning of the race. Too much Tokay, I'm afraid. Anyway, the German lads were all full of themselves, as you would expect—big tanned fellows, always doing calisthenics, took it for granted that we were rotten and decadent . . . quick to tell us so."

"Of course," said the crippled officer, nodding sympathetically. "I enjoyed killing several of those types at Benghazi."

"Typical rules when we got to the starting line," replied Charlie. "The starter would call out, 'Are you ready?' and if no one objected, he would fire his pistol. Well, no sooner did the starter call out, 'Are you ready?' than the five German crews were already racing up the course, oars flashing away. The starter never even fired his pistol."

"Teutonic sportsmanship," lamented the young man down the table. "So that was it, I suppose?"

"Not quite," said Charlie. "Nicky was rowing stroke, of course. . . . We were just cruising along up the course, enjoying the sights, when we came to a bridge about halfway along to the finish line. One of the Nazi swine on the bridge spit on us as we passed under it."

"In their nature," said General Massengale from across the table. "They're like bloody scorpions."

"Well, that tore it," said Charlie Wainwright. "Old Nicky cursed us up a blue streak and we took off as if the Hound of the Baskervilles was charging after us."

He paused to finish his glass of claret.

"And?" demanded General Massengale.

"And . . . we won," said Charlie, grinning fiercely.

"Good show," the general declared emphatically, as the one-handed officer thumped the table with his hook.

"Fatso Goering was by no means thrilled to give up his cup," said Charlie.

"Where is it now?" asked the young officer.

"Damned if I know," said Charlie. "We used it as an ashtray back at Trinity."

The candles on the table had burned more than halfway down by the time they finished a final course of cherries en croûte with a variety of ripe cheeses. Putting down her lace napkin, Lady Ainsley rose grandly from the head of the table, took the arm of Field Marshal Alan Brooke, and began a procession back toward the great hall.

Liza stood up with the others as they prepared to follow her. She sensed someone standing next to her, and turned to find Nicholas Ainsley at her shoulder.

"You're astonishingly lovely tonight, Liza," he said.

He was wearing a simple black tuxedo with a blood-red tie at his throat. Unlike so many of the others, he had not pinned his military decorations on his lapel. His blue eyes were incredibly somber.

"So are you," she found herself blurting back to him.

"Would you like to join me for the dancing?" he asked.

Liza turned to Charlie. He was vainly endeavoring to stay on his feet by clutching the back of his chair.

"Oh, Nicky . . . there you are. . . . Think I'll lie down in the library for a bit," he said, having trouble with the words. "Need to be ready for the sporting competitions."

"Sporting competitions?" Liza repeated as he lurched off.

"Another weekend tradition—you'll see later on," said Nicholas, offering her his arm.

The great hall was crowded with revelers, some of whom had apparently just arrived. Under the muted glow of the glass chandeliers, the orchestra began to play "Moonlight Serenade."

Nicholas took Liza in his arms and they began to dance, her cheek nestled comfortably along his right shoulder. He had a good fresh, healthy smell, leavened with lime-scented aftershave. She was surprised again at how well he danced, even with the prosthetic leg.

As they slowly moved across the floor, her eyes took in the remarkable panoply of fashions swirling around them, including silk and velvet floor-length gowns, daringly low-cut evening dresses, and old crinoline dresses with hoop skirts. Many of the women wore decorative headpieces made of feathers and fur that made them look like plumed birds. Across the floor, she saw General Massengale dancing with the old dowager, manfully moving her bulk around in a rough circle.

Her mind went back to a rainy night in New York when she had attended a Cornell mixer with a handsome boy named Howie Milstein. He had been a wonderful dancer, too. Her mother had written to her in England that he had been killed with his entire flight crew on a bombing mission over Stuttgart.

When the song ended, the orchestra leader introduced Vera Lynn, the famous London band singer, who was greeted with great applause by all the guests. The first number she sang was, "Long Ago and Far Away."

Perhaps it was the champagne she had drunk, but Liza began to feel as if she were floating in a soft romantic haze. Time seemed to slow down, and the faces of the other dancers became no more than a blur in the muted candlelight. For a while she even lost track of where she was. At the same time, she was conscious of an excitement she had never experienced before. She was in England, at a real English castle, dancing with a young English lord.

The song came to an end, and Nicholas stepped away from her. Neither of them said anything; they simply gazed into each other's eyes. As if slowly awakening to the real world, Liza could suddenly hear the happy conversational murmur of people around them, a stew of English, French, and other European tongues.

The orchestra started again. Vera Lynn began to sing "A Nightingale Sang in Berkeley Square." The strains of it were soothing as she moved back into Nicholas's waiting arms. She closed her eyes, totally content in his warm embrace.

The song went on for a long time before the orchestra effortlessly segued into "We'll Meet Again." Nicholas began to hum along to it as they danced. Liza looked up into his scarred face. She had never seen such sadness in a man's eyes. The song came to an end. This time he didn't release her.

"Perhaps I've had too much champagne," she said, "but I don't want this to end."

"It isn't the champagne," he said. "At least not for me."

The next song began, and they were dancing again, his arms still snugly around her. Liza found herself daydreaming about the future, about whether Nicholas might be the man she would spend her life with, and what that life would be like. It couldn't be living here, she quickly decided. A storybook castle was not for her. She wondered whether he might consider living in New York.

A moment later, she realized how ridiculous the whole idea was. Nicholas Ainsley was a lord of the English realm who would soon inherit one of the greatest estates in England. She would be returning to the States as soon as the war was over, to become a doctor. She smiled, trying to imagine them living together in Brooklyn Heights. But this would be a good memory, just the same.

"Would you like to take some fresh air on the terrace?" asked Nicholas.

"Very much," she said.

They went outside through the blackout curtains that cloaked the great hall, and walked across the flagstone terrace that faced the formal gardens. A tiny fringe of light was leaking past the curtains that led back into the library. Spaced along the edge of the terrace were large bronze urns full of yellow daffodils. She smelled the peppery scent of them.

"At least it's not raining for the moment," said Nicholas. "You must find our English weather abominable."

"Perhaps tomorrow will be better," she said.

"It's supposed to be miserable all weekend," he replied. "Good sleeping weather."

He had moved very close. She knew he was about to kiss her.

An angry voice bellowed through the blackout curtains covering the open library doors. "Greece was almost as big a fuckup as Gallipoli. Winston has the Balkans on the brain. I just wish he would listen to Georgie Patton. This war would be over in two months."

Liza recognized the voice. It belonged to General Everett Kilgore.

"That fellow sounds rather bellicose," said Nicholas, their romantic moment spoiled.

Liza debated whether to tell him that General Kilgore's principal contribution to the war effort consisted of fixing things for the top American brass.

From the library, an English voice responded very dryly, "I gather that Ike doesn't listen to George anymore. Field Marshal Montgomery has his ear these days, I believe."

"Montgomery," snarled Kilgore. "That sanctimonious prig . . . I'm told he set fire to one of his classmates at boarding school. If Georgie hadn't bailed him out in Sicily, he would still be stalled on the road to Messina. The goddamn faggot carries a baton!"

"I detest bellicose patriotism," said Nicholas, heading for the curtains covering the French doors.

"Now, wait just a minute, General," Liza heard the English voice come back. "You had better apologize for that remark, or we can head outside right now."

Following Nicholas, Liza reached the doors in time to see General Kilgore lurching to his feet from an easy chair near the fire. Lord Ismay was directly opposite him, angrily waving his finger in his face. The plump blonde woman who had been sitting next to Kilgore at dinner was perched on the arm of his overstuffed chair.

As General Kilgore angrily drew his arm back to knock away Ismay's offending finger, the point of his elbow struck the young woman hard on her chin, sending her flying over the arm of the chair.

Like a scalded cat, she came up on her feet with explosive fury, and belted Kilgore in the head with her heavy alligator purse. The sharp edge of it opened a cut over his right eye.

"You goddamn bastard. I've taken all I'm going to take from you," she screamed, following up the short tirade with a colorful stream of American obscenities.

Kilgore's face was full of murderous rage as he pivoted drunkenly to go after her. He was raising his fist to strike the young woman when two other American officers grabbed the general from behind and dragged him away. Still watching from the doorway, Nicholas and Liza glanced quickly at one another, and burst out laughing at the same time.

"The second front appears to have finally been launched," he said through their helpless laughter.

From inside the great hall, the orchestra began to play "Auld Lang Syne." It was apparently the signal that the dance would soon come to an end. Within a few moments, the three hundred revelers were all singing the familiar words together. As Liza came back into the hall on Nicholas's arm, she saw tears on many of the faces.

They have been fighting Germany for almost five years, she realized. For two of those years, England had fought Germany alone, losing sons, husbands, brothers. Whole families had been wiped out in the blitz. As soon as the old dirge ended, the orchestra struck up "God Save the King," bringing the more sober guests to attention

"God save the King," they shouted lustily as it came to an end.

There was a long silence after the orchestra finished playing. From the corner of her eye, Liza saw a group of young men surging madly out of the hall toward the terrace.

"Form a battle line!" one of them screamed, as if the Germans had suddenly invaded the castle grounds.

A moment later, Liza realized that the man was Charlie. As she watched, two of his friends raised him onto the shoulders of another giant, and he gleefully pitched forward toward another mounted adversary. As they came together, Charlie and the other man began grappling with one another while roaring like young lions.

"The sporting events you talked about?" said Liza, chuckling as someone else shouted, "Let the games begin!"

Nicholas nodded.

"The first of many that will go on most of the night, I'm afraid," he said as Charlie tumbled off his mount's shoulders and disappeared into the melee.

As she turned away, Liza thought she recognized someone else standing at the far edge of the terrace. He was smoking a cigarette, and watching the proceedings with obvious disgust.

"Isn't that your friend Mr. Sullivan?" she asked Nicholas, pointing in his direction.

"Yes, it is," he said immediately. "I wonder where old Des has come from."

When Sullivan looked up and saw Liza staring at him, he dropped his cigarette and disappeared into the darkness.

"We could always adjourn to one of the drawing rooms, you know," said Nicholas. "It would be a lot quieter."

"I'm actually quite tired," she said, truthfully. "Thank you for a lovely evening, Nicholas."

"Not quite the ending I had planned," he said with a rueful grin.

"It has been wonderful . . . truly," she said.

"How about a tour of the establishment tomorrow?" he asked.

"I would really like that," she said, leaning up on her toes to kiss him on the cheek.

CHAPTER 25

General Ernest Manigault stormed out of the penthouse suite, his brow furrowed with frustration. Angrily punching the elevator button, he waited impatiently for the brass-railed car to descend five floors to the lobby.

Stalking out of the elevator, he saw Sam Taggart calmly reading a morning newspaper next to one of the potted palms. Manigault's bodyguard was asleep on the chair next to him. The general glanced up at the clock over the front desk. It was four-thirty in the morning.

"Bad night?" asked Taggart, standing up to greet him.

"The worst," he snarled. "I lost eight hundred bucks. . . . Toohey Spaatz took us all over the hurdles. He must have won four grand."

"Rough," said Taggart, shaking the bodyguard awake.

"Anything hot on the threat board?" asked Manigault as they went through the lobby of the Savoy and out into the predawn darkness. His Humber Imperial was parked in the entrance circle, and the doorman rushed ahead to open the back door for him. He climbed inside, making room for Sam on the rear seat.

"Nothing new," said Taggart. "We're all set for Montgomery's planning conference this morning at Saint Paul's. I've made sure the security is as tight as can be. Several of the three-stars have complained about not being able to bring their cars closer to the school."

"Hell, don't they know the goddamn King of England is going to be there, along with Churchill? This is where everybody gets their marching orders."

"Field Marshal Montgomery has officially requested that everyone be in their chairs at 0900, double-sharp—his words," said Taggart.

The furrow in Manigault's brow grew deeper.

"Can you believe that Chief Big Wind is actually convening the invasion planning conference at his old prep school? It would be like my inviting President Roosevelt to Beverly Hills High School to launch the invasion of Japan."

"I gather he has his quirks," said Taggart.

"Quirks? That's putting it mildly," said Manigault. "Bobby . . . raise that screen, will you?"

The driver pushed a button on the dashboard, raising the thick glass screen that separated the front seat from the back compartment.

"You were with Ike this week, so you know the score. Two weeks and counting."

"Yes, sir," said Taggart.

Taggart had arranged security for one of the supreme commander's inspection tours to combat units that were landing on Omaha Beach, including V Corps at Taunton, the Fourth Division at Tiverton, and the Twenty-ninth at Tavistock.

Taggart had returned with unbridled respect for Eisenhower, who was smoking three packs of Camels a day and drinking endless cups of coffee to keep going under the pressure. While riding in the back of the staff car, the general sagged in his seat like a worn-out old man, nervously dragging on a cigarette as his eyes darted through the battle orders for each unit he was about to visit. But as soon as they arrived at a military installation, he would bound out of the car like an eager halfback. After completing a full inspection, he would always save a measure of energy for meeting the ordinary soldiers.

"Good luck and Godspeed to you," he would say after looking each one of them in the eye, seemingly brimming with confidence. As soon as he was back in the car, he would crumple into the rear seat, his hands visibly shaking as he picked up the next set of battle orders.

Manigault's Humber pulled up at the small mansion facing Hyde Park that he had requisitioned for his personal quarters. The general motioned the driver to pull over and park.

"Leigh-Mallory claims we're going to lose three-fourths of the airborne force in the first twenty-four hours," Manigault said to Taggart. "This thing could be an unmitigated disaster if it doesn't break right for us on the invasion beaches. And we learned last night, through a new ULTRA intercept, that the Jap ambassador to Germany, a guy named Oshima, just reported back to Tojo that Germany is about to launch unmanned long-range rockets at London. We still don't know what's in those payloads. It could be just blasting explosive, but at this point Hitler might be desperate enough to use poison gas."

"Someone must have already passed the word about that," said Taggart. "The Whitehall people are streaming out of London again."

"This place is a sieve, Sam. You once said it would be a miracle if the Germans didn't learn what we're doing, and I'm beginning to think you're right," said Manigault, opening the back door. "Look, I'm going to have a shower and grab a clean uniform. Take the car, and I'll see you at the conference hall in a few hours."

Fifteen minutes later, Taggart arrived at Saint Paul's. Montgomery's boyhood school looked like it had been designed by the same people who had built Buckingham Palace, with cavernous rooms, thirty-foot ceilings, and high mullioned windows. Everywhere Taggart looked there seemed to be a bronze plaque in memory of some famous alumnus, such as Samuel Pepys or Thomas Becket.

As he walked down a dark corridor to the student assembly hall, Taggart watched a three-star American general kneeling down to take a drink of water from a porcelain fountain that had obviously been designed for a ten-year-old. It's going to be a long day, Taggart concluded.

Field Marshal Montgomery had personally made all the logistical arrangements. On the floor of the stage in the assembly hall was a massive scale model of the Normandy landing beaches, as well as all the known German strong points, their long-range artillery positions, and their secondary defensive strongholds beyond the assault beaches. A gigantic relief map of the Normandy coast rose up from another platform behind the stage. Facing the maps and models were all the lower-level British, American, and Canadian generals. They sat in a semicircle of tiered platforms that had been constructed by British Army engineers.

At 0845, a procession of the senior commanders entered the lecture hall, led by Field Marshal Montgomery and Lieutenant General Omar Bradley. They took their seats in the first tier of chairs surrounding the mock-ups. Ten minutes later, they all stood as King George VI entered the hall, accompanied by Prime Minister Churchill. Sam Taggart was standing behind Manigault when General George Patton slipped through one of the rear doors and sidled up to them.

"I just shook hands with the King of England, Ernie," Patton whispered in his thin, high-pitched voice.

Manigault nodded, and whispered back, "What did he say?"

"The poor little fellow was trying so hard not to stammer that he couldn't get any words out," whispered Patton. "I'd say he's one grade above moron. Hey . . . do you know what they call the graduates of this institution?"

Manigault shook his head.

"Paulines," said Patton with a grimace. Taggart could not conceal his grin.

At precisely 0900, Field Marshal Montgomery rose from his chair, took several steps forward, and clapped his bony hands together. The buzz of conversation immediately stopped.

"Welcome to Saint Paul's School, gentlemen," he announced. "Before we start, you should know that I do not tollowate smoking at my confowences."

Lieutenant General Toohey Spaatz, commanding all the U.S. bombing forces in Europe, was sitting in the front tier of platforms. As Taggart watched, he removed a foil-wrapped cigar from his breast pocket, carefully unwrapped it, snipped the end with a cigar cutter, and planted it in his mouth. Lighting the end of it with a kitchen match, he began puffing away contentedly as Montgomery glared at him from the stage like a headmaster dealing with an unruly boy.

"Jesus, we'll be lucky to win this war," whispered Manigault to the grinning Patton.

Taggart again scanned all the entrances to the assembly hall. Each was guarded by four MPs armed with Thompson submachine guns. A battalion of Royal marines was responsible for protecting the perimeter of the school grounds.

Taking a long pointer from one of his aides, Montgomery walked down to the mammoth three-dimensional model of the Normandy landing beaches. The floor behind him was painted blue to signify the English Channel. Arranged across it were hundreds of little toy ships representing the invasion fleet. Montgomery began tapping the tip of his pointer on one of the yellow landing beaches, which had been coated with real sand.

"Some of us here know the opposing commander, Field Marshal Wommel, very well," he began with a condescending glance at General Patton. "His intention will be to deny us any penetwation."

At that moment, a young WAC with a Signal Corps badge on her shoulder came up to Taggart and handed him a message. It was marked URGENT, and read, "Request response immediately at following telephone exchange. Drummond."

Taggart left the assembly hall and walked back to the headmaster's office. After securing a telephone, he dialed the number of the exchange. Inspector Drummond picked it up on the fourth ring.

"You called me," said Taggart.

"I know we aren't supposed to be in communication with one another, but there has been another murder. I thought you would want to know about it."

"Was she young and beautiful?" asked Taggart.

"He was old and fat and a forty-five-year-old car mechanic."

"How was he killed?"

"He was strangled with piano wire."

"Did he work for Overlord?"

"No."

"Why should I be interested, Inspector?" asked Taggart.

"Have you ever heard the word ULTRA used in conjunction with our secret code-breaking apparatus at Bletchley Park?"

Taggart took a deep breath.

"I'm at Saint Paul's School, in West Kensington," said Taggart. "How far are you from me?"

"Not far . . . near Bletchley Park. I can give you directions."

Taggart wrote them down on a piece of Saint Paul's School stationery.

"I'm leaving now," he said.

When he went back into the hall to tell General Manigault that he was leaving, Field Marshal Montgomery was still at the front of the lecture hall, using his pointer to describe the anticipated British advance from Juno Beach. Taggart repeated what Drummond had said about the ULTRA connection.

"Did the murdered guy know anything about Overlord?" demanded Manigault.

"I don't know," said Taggart. "It could be just a random murder. But Bletchley Park is where they collect all the ULTRA intercepts."

"Take my car again," ordered the general as if bestowing a papal dispensation. "Find out."

The address Drummond had given him turned out to be an automobile repair garage on a dingy commercial street full of boarded-up buildings. It had obviously been closed for some time. The windows were shuttered, and two old Esso gas pumps lay in the side yard, blanketed with leaves and dirt.

Taggart told the driver to stop at the head of the weed-strewn driveway. He got out of the Humber and started walking toward the side door of the garage. Inspector Drummond came out as he approached. The two men shook hands.

"I thought you would want to see this, Sam," he said.

Before Taggart could reply, Drummond sneezed several times in quick succession and dragged a large soiled handkerchief out of the pocket of his topcoat. After blowing his nose, he briefly checked its contents.

"I'm fighting a bad cold," he said.

It was obvious to Taggart that the old man's drinking problem had gotten worse since the last time he had seen him. His angrily swollen nose resembled an overripe strawberry, and Taggart could smell the alcohol oozing out of his skin. Both of his lower eyelids hung loose, exposing the red linings and giving him the appearance of an old bloodhound.

"Sorry to hear it," said Sam.

"The dead man's name was Griffin," said Drummond, opening his notebook. "Archibald Griffin. Before the war, he owned and operated this garage. According to his wife, he hasn't been back to this place in at least a year. We're not sure at this point how or why he ended up here."

"What did he have to do with code-breaking at Bletchley Park?" asked Taggart.

"Officially, I'm not supposed to know that," said Drummond. "The Official Secrets Act, you know. I'm not supposed to know that Bletchley even exists."

"Yeah, well, you mentioned a certain word over the telephone," said Taggart.

"Unofficially, I know all about it," said Drummond. "At any rate, Griffin wasn't a code-breaker. According to his wife, he was a master automobile mechanic before the war and a technical wizard when it came to gadgetry—the kind of uneducated fellow who could repair anything."

Taggart saw that the latch on the side door of the garage had been jimmied with a pry bar. Two uniformed police officers were waiting inside for them. One of them was very young, his complexion almost lime-green.

"Please leave us alone for a few minutes, lads," said Drummond.

The younger officer seemed relieved as he went out the door.

"How long did the man work at Bletchley?" asked Taggart, smelling the familiar odor of death.

"Griffin started there about two years ago. They were in the process of constructing all the new hush-hush Enigma machinery, and it apparently needed constant servicing. You would know more about it than I do. Anyway, Griffin was one of the men who helped work out the kinks."

The garage had gray-painted brick walls and a cement floor. An old hydraulic lift that had once been used to elevate the chassis of motorcars sat in the middle of the space. The roof had obviously leaked for some time, and there was standing water in several places. The strong odor of mildew almost masked the smell of the corpse.

A tool bench ran along the far wall, next to a bank of metal shelves. In the corner sat a battered wooden desk and an old oak armchair. The dead man was strapped to the chair.

"He was found by an estate agent who came to look at the place as a possible sublet," said Drummond. "Griffin's wife had already reported him missing when he didn't come home from work."

Taggart approached the body.

"Jesus Christ," he said softly.

The man was naked. His clothes were lying on the floor behind the desk. Piano wire had been used to bind his wrists and ankles to the chair. Someone had brutally extracted four of the fingernails on his left hand. A pair of pliers sat on the cement floor next to the chair leg. At some point, the man had lost control of his bodily functions. Taggart couldn't blame him.

"Someone enjoyed doing this," said Taggart.

"How do you know?" asked Drummond.

"Because he took his time," said Taggart. "This took a good deal of time."

The man's head had been wrapped in several layers of three-inch-wide adhesive tape. It covered him like a hornet's nest. The killer had left only two small openings in the mask, one at his left ear and another at the mouth. Another length of piano wire had been twisted around his neck, and finally tightened until the wire disappeared inside the skin.

"Obviously, the killer wanted information," said Taggart. "A man is far more likely to talk if he is stripped naked first. It's a standard Gestapo interrogation technique. We should probably assume this had something to do with the code work at Bletchley."

"Do you think he got what he was looking for?"

"Hard to say," said Taggart, leaning close to examine the man's mutilated fingernails. "The killer would have finished him either way."

"There are bruises on the knuckles of both hands," said Drummond.

"Yeah," agreed Taggart. "Mr. Griffin might have marked up our killer a bit before he lost the fight."

"What now?" asked Drummond.

"Nothing that you wouldn't otherwise do—immediate autopsy, pursue every lead you can," said Taggart. "Find out who his friends were . . . whether he owed anyone money. It's always possible the murder had nothing to do with ULTRA."

"I'll put a team on it right away," said Drummond, "and I'll call you if I find out anything important."

"Thanks," said Taggart.

"Archibald Griffin must have been a very brave man," said Drummond as they both stared down at the bloated corpse. "I would have talked after the first fingernail."

"Maybe," replied Taggart. "Of course, Griffin might have talked right away, too, and the rest of it was for kicks."

"My God," said Drummond.

Taggart was walking back to his car along the driveway when his eyes were drawn to a small, brightly colored object lying on the ground. He knelt and carefully pulled back the weeds that almost covered it.

It was a tiny shard of camel-colored paper. Two more pieces were lying a few inches away. Using his pen, he flipped them over. The third one had the fragment of a gold-embossed figure on it. Picking up the pieces with his handkerchief, he turned to Drummond, who had a small evidence envelope open and ready.

"Who knows . . . these might have fallen out of the killer's car," said Taggart.

"Considering all the rain we've had, they can't have been here long," said Drummond.

"You might want to examine whatever is embossed on that one scrap," said Taggart as he climbed back into Manigault's Humber.

CHAPTER 26

Liza awoke to the constant repetitive song of a cuckoo clock. A few moments later, it struck her that the song was coming from so many cuckoos that the timepiece had to be madly out of control. She sat up.

In the warm glow of the sunlight streaming through the open casement windows, she could see a myriad of tiny dust motes swirling across the room. Sunlight. There was actual sunlight in England again, she realized, almost leaping out of bed in her excited rush to the window.

She gazed down at a small section of the formal gardens. The flowers seemed to be erupting toward her in an incredible explosion of color: pink crocuses, snowdrops, daffodils, and red azaleas, stretching all the way down to the carefully trimmed lawns.

Hearing the familiar bird cry once more, she was enthralled to discover that real cuckoos were singing from perches in the garden. She looked toward the distant sea, now an indelible blue in the glare of the unfamiliar sun.

It's heavenly, she decided.

There was utter silence in her wing of the castle as she walked down the hallway to bathe. Upon returning to her room, she found a small pot of aromatic tea waiting for her under a padded cozy. After finishing it by the window, she dressed hurriedly in the white blouse and twill slacks she had brought and headed downstairs.

A butler was waiting at the foot of the staircase.

"Breakfast is being served in the morning room, madam," he said. "Please come this way."

She could hear a radio crackling in the library as she went by, and stopped to listen for a moment as the BBC announcer described the damage from the previous night's Luftwaffe raid on London. It was hard for her to believe that the ravaged city was only about seventy miles away. At that moment, it seemed as if she was on an entirely different planet.

The morning room faced the terrace where she and Nick had been together the night before. All the French doors now stood open to take in the fresh spring air. A group of young men and women in riding clothes were serving themselves breakfast at the two sideboards along the far wall.

"Do you hunt the little red creatures?" asked a young man in a crimson riding jacket who materialized at her side.

"No, I'm afraid I don't," she said.

"Pity, it's the best hunt of the season," he said, heading back to his table with a cheese omelet.

On the sideboards she found silver urns full of coffee and tea water, pitchers of fresh juices, and a line of chafing dishes and porringers with eggs, shad, bacon, ham, pancakes, kidneys, breakfast rolls, scones, toast, and hot cereals. On a table nearby were jams, preserves, butter, and bowls of fresh fruit.

Liza discovered that she was very hungry.

After filling her plate, she adjourned to a table near one of the open French doors. It was a good place to watch the comings and goings of the guests, most of whom appeared to be preparing for the fox hunt. Several others were dressed for golfing. Everyone was clearly thrilled at the turn in the weather.

As she was finishing her breakfast, Liza happened to glance up at the white plaster ceiling towering far above her. Her eyes were immediately drawn to two garish sets of black footprints running from one end of it to the other. She was still pondering how they had come to be there when Nicholas came in from the terrace. He headed straight for her table.

"I was hoping to find you here," he said.

Before he could say any more, she pointed to the ceiling. He began to chuckle.

"One of the annual contests calls for the building of fifteen-foot-high stacks of tables and chairs. The contestants must blacken their feet in the fireplace and then compete to see who can cross the room first while lying upside down on top of the moving piles."

Liza stared at him incredulously.

"How about that tour I promised you?" he asked with a cheerful grin.

"I take it you're not going after the elusive fox this morning," she said. He was dressed in baggy green corduroys, a checked flannel shirt, and navy cashmere sweater.

"I have a confession to make," he said, sitting down next to her, his face becoming solemn. "Everyone in this corner of the realm knows how to hunt and shoot except me. I'm also afraid of horses."

She laughed.

"How can you take such pleasure in another person's inadequacies?" he asked with a hurt look on his face.

She laughed harder.

"What an insensitive creature you are," he said loudly.

This time, her laughter attracted the attention of several other diners, including Nicholas's mother, who was breakfasting with Lord Ismay. Lady Ainsley frowned in their direction. Liza immediately stopped laughing.

"Let's go explore," he said, taking her hand and standing up.

As they began walking toward the door, Liza heard Lady Ainsley call out, "Nicholas."

His mother was standing at her table, waiting for him to come back. She was dressed in the same black tweeds as the previous afternoon.

"Yes, mother?" replied Nicholas without moving toward her.

"Where are you going?" she demanded in a peremptory tone.

"I'm going to show Lieutenant Marantz a bit of the estate."

"But you have obligations to your other guests, dear," she said in a suddenly conciliatory tone.

"Yes," he replied, turning to leave. "I'm well aware of that."

"Nicholas," she cried out again.

He was grinning broadly as he led Liza out the door leading to the great hall.

"I'm sorry," said Liza. "If you need to go back, don't worry about me."

"I'm not going back," he replied evenly as they approached the foot of the staircase. "Please forget it. Do you need a coat?"

"My uniform jacket is upstairs," she said.

"Won't do," said Nicholas. "We're forgetting about the war today. Let me find you a windbreaker."

As she waited, Liza slowly strolled along the hallway. Glancing into the library, she noticed Charlie Wainwright working at one of the desks.

"You're up early," she called out cheerfully. "I'm glad to see you survived the jousting contest."

"No need to scream at me," he said with a grimace, his face a sickly yellow.

He picked up a glass of what looked like puréed tomato juice from the desk and forced down an inch of it.

"What's that?" she asked.

"Hair of the dog, my girl . . . It's the only way I'm going to be able to plow through all this."

An open notebook lay on the desktop in front of him. Scattered around his chair were various official-looking documents. One of them was a military cable written in German. It was stamped TOP SECRET in red block letters.

"Are you sure you should have brought this material with you, Charlie? It's obviously classified."

"Dear girl, I have to do a complete analysis of this traffic by tomorrow evening. I had to bring it along or I could not have come with you."

"Then you should not have come," she said, harshly.

He took another swallow of the red mixture and rolled his eyes.

"And who, pray tell, is going to steal it—Lord Ismay?"

"There are three hundred other people here, too."

"Fine," he said, grabbing up the loose papers and stuffing them in his briefcase.

"When are we heading back?" she asked.

"I'm staying until tomorrow afternoon," he said. "There is a train at three-thirty from Sussex Downs."

"I'll go with you," she said.

Nodding, he said, "Now, go off and enjoy yourself. Leave me to my misery."

When she returned to the front hall, Nicholas was waiting for her with a black leather flying jacket. He helped her put it on.

"What would you like to see first?" he asked. "Perhaps the battlements from which my ancestors poured burning oil down on the Saracen invaders?"

"All of it," she said with a bright smile.

"That could take a lifetime," he said.

Once outside, they walked across a brick courtyard and down a dark moss-covered passageway, emerging into the sunlight again near another phalanx of gray stone structures that were dominated by a tall rectangular tower. Even to Liza's untrained eye, the buildings were from a much more ancient epoch. The tower was surrounded by a shallow moat, and could only be entered by a planked drawbridge.

Approaching the drawbridge, they passed through another section of the formal gardens. Two old men were working in the beds, painstakingly snipping dead flowers from the individual stalks. She tried to imagine how long it would take them to snip their way through the countless stems, and quickly gave up.

Crossing the drawbridge, Nicholas pointed up at the tall rectangular structure and said, "Now, my dear Lieutenant Marantz, that tower you are gazing up at with such wonder is the most striking legacy of Norman castle building in the realm."

His voice had taken on the supercilious tone of a crusty English historian.

"William the Conqueror ordered the construction of this tower in 1070. Its fortifications are twelve feet thick and mortar-faced, rising from a splayed plinth, each one strengthened by flat buttresses in the center. You will certainly recognize the many similarities in masonry to Hadrian's Wall. As you probably also know, the corner buttresses set the denticular path of the battlements leading up to the turrets. Of course there are no windows, only arrow slits for the castle's defenders."

He slipped back into his own voice, said, "Am I hired?"

"Yes . . . yes, you are," said Liza. "You are quite incredible, Nicholas Ainsley."

"What a relief," he said. "I have a future, then, after the war."

As they continued the tour, the only sounds to be heard were chirping birds and the loudly buzzing bees hovering over the flower beds. He led her back across the drawbridge and across another open quadrangle, lined with sycamore trees. From beyond the high stone walls that girded the back of the castle, she suddenly heard the baying of dogs and the distant rumble of hoofbeats.

"Rather a fierce display of blood lust, I've always thought," said Nicholas.

"Does the fox ever have a chance?" she asked.

"About the same odds I used to have in my Spitfire," he said.

After going through another covered passageway, they came out on a rise of ground that led down to the bluffs overlooking the sea.

"Is that a golf course?" she asked, looking at a distant flag that was rooted to the ground.

"Yes; only three holes, though," he replied, almost apologetically.

"How sad," she said, grinning.

Beyond the last golf hole was a wide, flat pasture. A rustic stone barn stood at the far end of it. Liza could see parallel ruts bisecting the pasture, as if a horse cart had traversed the same path over and over.

"What made those peculiar tracks?" she asked.

"A Sopwith Camel," he said.

"A what?" she said.

"An old Great War biplane," said Nicholas. "My father bought it after the war. When I was thirteen, he taught me to fly it. I used to practice takeoffs and landings on that field."

"You must miss him very much," she said, remembering that Helen had told her Nicholas's father committed suicide.

"I don't, actually," he said, starting to move off again. Then he turned to her with an awkward smile and said, "Would you like to see my favorite place? It's where I loved to play as a boy."

"Of course," she said as he took her hand again.

With only a pronounced limp to remind her of his lost leg, they struck out across the open field, crossing another pasture, this one divided by low fences of piled stone. Heading back toward the sea, they went down a sloping meadow to a dense copse of woods that was thick with old maples and elms. She followed Nicholas along a narrow path that led into a dark forest lane. A hundred yards into the woods, she saw an opening in the trees up ahead.

Liza smelled them before she ever saw them. The sweet, intoxicating perfume hung in the air all around her. As they emerged from the woods, the entire tableau ahead was bathed in an aura of red, pink, and white blossoms from hundreds of wild roses that lined the crooked path to a small stone cottage overlooking the sea.

"For some reason, they've come early this year," said Nicholas happily as they walked the fragrant gauntlet.

The sun was behind them as they came to the end of the path, and it lit up his corn-colored hair like a blazing aureole. Beyond the cliff's edge, the dark-blue water stretched to the horizon.

The cottage had been built on a promontory that faced up and down the coast for several miles in both directions. Its front door was unlocked. After Nicholas swung it open, he bowed with mock formality and waved her inside.

The ground floor consisted of only one room, its big multipaned windows covering the wall that faced the sea. A stone fireplace took up the rear. Shelves filled with books and sporting equipment occupied the others. Heavy beams crisscrossed the low ceiling.

A musty smell pervaded the room.

"This place needs a good airing out," said Nicholas, opening several of the windows facing the water. "I haven't used it for a long time."

"It's quite fabulous," said Liza, gazing out across the cliff face to the sea beyond. "I feel like we're standing on the bow of a magnificent ship."

As Nicholas began rummaging through a rosewood bureau, Liza explored the rest of the cottage.

"I used to keep a good pair of binoculars in here," he said, slamming home one drawer after another.

In the rear corner of the room, a narrow set of wooden stairs led up to a small sleeping loft. A big, comfortable double bed sat under several more windows. Coming back downstairs, she was drawn to a large oil painting that hung over the fireplace.

"Who are they?" she asked, gazing up at it. In the painting, a remarkably handsome young man sat on a red divan, holding the hand of an equally beautiful young woman.

"That is the immortal Lord Byron, Liza," he said, limping over to join her. "He was my favorite Romantic poet. The woman in the painting was his mistress, Lady Caroline Lamb—a frequent guest when he lived at the estate. I gather they often met here for a secret rendezvous."

"They weren't married?" she asked.

"Not to one another," said Nicholas. "It was a rather scandalous affair, I'm afraid. Quite tempestuous while it lasted."

Taking Liza's hand, he walked her back outside and down to the edge of the cliff. His limp was becoming more pronounced as he tired from the long walk.

"This is my favorite place in the whole world," he said, looking out at the turquoise sea.

"I can understand why," she replied as the waves rolled relentlessly toward them. From the top of the cliff, the sea sounded like the shallow breathing of some vast, primordial being.

"You really are quite beguiling to me, Liza," said Nicholas, moving close to her as a flock of gulls began wheeling and diving toward the rocks below. "If I wasn't a cripple I might actually think you could come to appreciate me someday."

"You are not a cripple," she said angrily. "What an absurd thing to say."

"I am," he said, his voice hoarse against the wind. "But thank you for saying that."

When he didn't move to kiss her, she placed her hand behind his neck and slowly drew him down to her. His lips were soft and gentle. For as long as it lasted, the kiss erased her awareness of everything else around her. She actually shuddered for a moment before he pulled away from her.

"Your mouth is like sweet fire," he said.

"Did Lord Byron write that?" asked Liza.

"No," he replied. "Just Nicholas Saint John Ainsley, I'm afraid."

"I . . . dreamed of you last night," she said truthfully.

Nicholas shook his head wistfully before staring out at the sea again.

"I have dreams because without them I would not be able to bear the truth," he said.

"Are you ever happy?" she demanded in an exasperated voice. "Truly happy?"

"Right now I am," he said, gazing into her eyes.

"I don't mean that."

"I know," he said. "Well, no, actually."

He leaned down and kissed her again, this time with an almost fierce intensity.

"I think you're very special, Lord Ainsley," she said after they parted again.

"If that is the case, why don't we go away together?" he said.

Knowing he was joking, she said, "An island in the South Seas, perhaps?"

"No," he said. "Most of those are still held by the Japanese. I was thinking more along the lines of South America—Buenos Aires, perhaps."

Laughing, she leaned up on her toes to kiss him again.

"Really . . . would you go with me?" he asked.

"I'm afraid the United States Army would frown on the idea," said Liza.

"Resign your commission, then," he said.

"I know you're not serious, Nicholas Ainsley," she said, laughing. "There is no place to run to in this world. The whole world is at war."

"I'm so tired of it all," he said.

She looked at him quizzically.

"I'm serious," he said. "Do you know the conservative estimate of Chinese dead since the Japanese invaded in 1937? Ten million—mostly women and children—and it's probably more. Do you know how many Russians have been killed? Another fifteen to twenty million so far. Add in about five million Germans, and all for what?"

"To save the world from the greatest evil that has ever existed," she said.

"It all depends on how you define evil," said Nicholas. "Liza, the predators are going to be in business for a long time. Do you think it will end with the Germans and the Japanese? Stalin is *our* murderer for now, but as soon as this war ends he'll be striking out on his own. Wait and see how much of the world he tries to gobble up. The Chinese are going to have the biggest civil war in the history of creation, and God knows where that will lead. And wait until the British Raj ends in India. See what the Hindus and Muslims do to one another in that bloodbath. I don't want any part of it. I just want to live the rest of my life in a place of peace and contentment."

"If that is true, Nicholas, you never have to leave home," said Liza, pointing back toward the distant battlements of Rawcliff.

He shook his head no.

"I want to find a place where life is worth living again . . . and I would like you to go with me."

She gazed into his somber eyes.

"I know you've had a hard time, Nick. . . . you've been through a lot," said Liza. "I think you just need to take a long break. You've already done your part."

"And you?"

"I don't believe in war . . . at least in the abstract," said Liza. "If I ever have children, I will bring them up to abhor war as a way of solving problems."

"Then why won't you go with me?"

"Why?" she responded. "Good question, I suppose. Why am I fighting this war, in my own small way?"

Liza walked over to the edge of the cliff and gazed down at the small nest that one of the seabirds had burrowed between the cliff rocks. Inside it she saw a small purple egg.

"Everyone might have their own reason," she said. "Mine is simple: because Adolf Hitler and his acolytes set out to destroy whole peoples—Jews, Czechs, Poles, Russians—people he called subhuman. He has perpetrated the worst evil this world has ever witnessed, and he needs to be eradicated along with every person who shares his ideas."

"Well, that is a very passionate view," said Nicholas.

"Anyone who fights Hitler and what he stands for is a hero in a just cause."

"I see."

"You're a hero, Nicholas. You did your part . . . and paid dearly for it."

"I had hoped . . ." he began, and then stopped. "It was ridiculous, really. Please, forget I ever brought it up."

His hands suddenly felt very cold.

"Perhaps we ought to get back," she said.

"Yes, you're right," he said.

They closed the door of the cottage and walked back up the rose-lined path toward the castle.

CHAPTER 27

Charlie Wainwright was waiting for them in the front hall, a goblet of amber liquid in his right hand. Apparently, the hair of the dog had settled his stomach enough so he could begin another round of drinking.

"We were about to send out a search party for you two," he said. "Where have you been?"

"Exploring my realm," said Nicholas with a grin. "Why? What is so important?"

"The King, my lord," replied Charlie, raising his glass in a mocking toast. "King George the Sixth has arrived with his retinue of fawning noblemen and not-so-noble women. They have armed themselves to the teeth and gone out to shoot anything with wings and a heartbeat. I regret that there will be less birdsong in these parts by tomorrow morning."

"Lord Ismay told me last night that he might be coming today," mused Nicholas.

A manservant in black approached them, bowed his head once to Nicholas, and said, "My lord, I regret to inform you that your mother has had another attack, and was taken to hospital an hour ago."

From his body language, Liza concluded that it was probably a familiar refrain. "Dr. Thackaberry has asked you to join him there as quickly as possible."

The servant bowed his head again and stepped back two paces.

"Yes . . . well, she has had them before, hasn't she, Derrick?" said Nicholas.

"Dr. Thackaberry said he thought it was very serious this time," persisted the manservant.

"Unlike the last few times, I suppose," said Nicholas with a trace of bitterness in his voice.

"You have to go, old man," said Charlie, who was standing close enough to hear the exchange.

"Yes, of course," replied Nicholas.

Turning to Liza, he said, "I shan't be long if I can help it. Have them bring my car around, will you?" said Nicholas to the manservant.

"Yes, my lord," he said.

"Charlie," said Nicholas, putting his hands on the bigger man's shoulders, "please see to this extraordinary creature. Make sure she doesn't get into any trouble after dinner."

"I shall take that oath gladly," said Charlie with mock gravity.

Nicholas gave Liza a rueful smile and said, "Well, my dear Liza . . . enjoy the evening. The King awaits you."

As he began limping toward the front entrance, Liza wondered whether she should offer to go with him. Then she remembered his mother's hostile attitude toward her that morning, and remained silent as he went out the door.

She followed Charlie down the hall into the library. The fox hunters were back, their scarlet jackets blazing red in the glow of the big fire. One of them was triumphantly waving a piece of bloody fur above his head. She saw that the champagne and whiskey were flowing again as booming laughter echoed toward her through clouds of cigar smoke.

While Charlie headed off to get a drink, she noticed Des Sullivan standing at the edge of the boisterous crowd. Just as on the previous night, he was watching the revelers with obvious disdain. Feeling very much out of place, Liza headed upstairs to her room.

Tired after the long walk, she lay down on her bed and quickly dozed off. When she awoke, it was dark outside and someone was knocking on the door. She opened it to find Helen Bellayne standing in the hallway with a lovely fawn-colored dress over her arm.

"This is the dress I wore last night," she said. "If we exchange them, no one will notice the difference."

"Of course," said Liza, with a grateful smile. "You are a very wise woman."

"No, I'm just a survivor," said Helen Bellayne.

Going to the closet, Liza retrieved the blue evening dress she had worn the night before, and exchanged it for the other.

"Are you finding our typical English country weekend much fun?" asked Helen.

"It almost seems like a Hollywood movie," said Liza, "with everyone delivering rehearsed lines."

"That's actually a fairly good analogy," said Helen. "But I hope it isn't true of Nicky. He seems very smitten with you."

"No, he is quite unrehearsed," agreed Liza, smiling as she thought of their time together.

"Charlie told me to tell you he'll pick you up for dinner at eight," said Helen. "Right now, he's sleeping off his afternoon revelry."

"I wish he wouldn't drink so much," said Liza. "It seems so pointless."

"Charlie is a very unhappy young man," said Helen, opening the door to leave. "He was in love with my niece, Jocelyn, you know."

"Yes, I know," said Liza.

It was nearing eight-thirty when she finally heard Charlie's ferocious knock on the door. Opening it, she saw that he was hung over again, although this time he had put on proper evening clothes.

"Sorry I'm late. I was told I would be banned from dinner if I wasn't dressed appropriately for His Majesty," he said as they made their way downstairs. "Had to hunt up this outfit from Quentin."

When they arrived in the dining room, Liza saw that the King and his retinue were sequestered at a separate table. The King was wearing the navy, gold-braided uniform of an admiral of the fleet, and his entourage seemed to laugh uproariously at every witticism he shared with them. She looked around for Nicholas, but he was not at any of the tables.

The rest of the guests were on their best behavior, indulging in low, muted conversations as if they were chastised children afraid to upset their parents. Charlie barely said a word to her, renewing his attachment to the claret bottle as they worked their way through the interminable courses.

Liza kept glancing toward the parted entrance doors, hoping to see Nicholas come limping through. As dessert was being served, Lord Ismay rose to his feet at the King's table. A hush fell over the room.

After first apologizing for the unavoidable absence of Lord and Lady Ainsley because of her sudden illness, he expressed his gratitude for the King's "bestowal of his presence on this simple gathering of old friends at Rawcliff."

The King stood for a moment to accept their hearty applause before sitting down again to finish his chocolate soufflé. A half-hour later, the orchestra in the great hall struck up a Strauss waltz.

The King and his consorts rose from their table and began to saunter slowly toward the great hall. As the last member of his party went out the door, there was a pent-up roar from the rest of the guests, and they rushed to follow the exodus like excited schoolchildren after school lets out.

Liza stayed close to Charlie as he followed the rest of the throng into the hall. Suddenly realizing that his glass was empty, he began looking around for the closest bar. Liza chose that moment to slip into his arms. With a red-faced grin, he began bearishly moving her around the crowded dance floor. The first song hadn't ended when someone tapped him on the back and moved to cut in.

"My turn, Wainwright," said Des Sullivan.

As Charlie reluctantly let her go, Sullivan took her in his arms and effortlessly swung her off. Whatever else he was, the man was a good dancer, Liza conceded. Looking up at him, she noticed a small bruise over his left eye, along with a raw scrape across his left jaw line. He had tried to cover the abrasions with face powder.

"Did you say the wrong thing to someone, Mr. Sullivan?" she asked.

"Someone chose to say the wrong thing to me," he said in his familiar lilting brogue while pulling her uncomfortably closer. The fingers of his right hand slid slowly down her back.

"Don't hold me so tightly," she demanded.

"You've been spoiled by Nicky . . . impoverished as he is, or soon will be."

"Impoverished?" she asked, bewildered.

"Don't tell him I told you," he said. "In spite of everything, the poor idiot still believes in love."

"You don't believe in love?" asked Liza.

"Love is a disease . . . a weakness . . . nothing more than an invention of the poets," said Sullivan. "Do you think our caveman ancestors chose their women based on love?"

"You would know," she said.

He gave her a leering grin.

"You're a Jew," he said, "not a stupid captive to two thousand years of self-righteous Christian morality."

"Even a Jew has a sense of morality on occasion," she said.

"Fidelity is contrary to the laws of nature . . . and so is monogamy," he went on. "The ancients had it right, you know. Bacchus and Dionysus—Gods for drinking and screwing."

"With your attitude toward women, Mr. Sullivan, you should be at least a field marshal," she said, her face inclined toward his.

"I don't understand why so many men in this war are tormented by the thought of their women back home enjoying another man," said Sullivan. "It's the giving and taking of pleasure, that's all. Why don't you and I enjoy some?"

"You're a pig, Mr. Sullivan," said Liza as she struggled to free herself from his arms.

He was far too strong for her, keeping her locked in his embrace as they continued to move around the floor, slowly weaving through the crowd.

"Let me go," she said, her voice becoming shrill with anger.

"I hope you're not going to cause an ugly scene in front of the King of England," said Des Sullivan, "rattle-skulled idiot that he is."

Raising her pointed heel, Liza brought it down hard on the instep of his ankle. She knew the pain had to be excruciating, but all it accomplished was to pull the corners of his mouth down as he continued to dance.

"You'll regret that, you bitch," Sullivan whispered hoarsely in her ear.

He was staring down at her with almost palpable hatred. Still trapped in his arms, she involuntarily trembled. A few moments later,

Charlie came lurching toward them. From the look on his face, Liza could see that he knew what was happening. He tapped Sullivan hard on the back.

"My turn, Des," he said.

Sullivan gave him a venomous look before slowly releasing her. For a second, Liza thought he was going to strike the bigger man, but as they stood confronting one another, the King swayed past in the smoky haze, his simpering dance partner gowned in bright-orange silk. Charlie's fists were still clenched as the King smiled benevolently over at them.

Sullivan nodded, as if deciding there would be a better time to settle accounts. Walking away, he disappeared into the crowd. Like a crusading knight with his newly rescued damsel, Charlie opened his arms wide, and Liza stepped into his bearlike hold again.

"Des was always a bastard," he said, carefully leading her across the floor.

When the waltz ended, there were tears in his eyes.

"He and Joss . . ." he began and stopped. "God . . . she let him have her, too. Goddamn Des. Why? Why?"

"Charlie, you can't be responsible for the way another person leads her life," she said gently.

Taking his big calloused hand in hers, Liza led him back to their small table near the terrace. As she slowly sipped her tea, a waiter brought him a new whiskey. Every few minutes, she would stand up to survey the gathering, hoping to see Nicholas's corn-colored hair towering over the shorter guests as he came searching for her.

"Please don't," she said as Charlie ordered still another drink. Taking his hand, she turned him around to face her. "I'm asking you not to drink anymore tonight."

"Already too late, old girl," he replied sadly, his eyes almost vacant. "I'm at the promised land."

As it had the night before, the orchestra struck up "Auld Lang Syne," signaling that the formal part of the evening's entertainment was coming to an end. Charlie sat through the song with maudlin tears streaming down his face. When the dirge ended, he got up from their table without a word and started reeling across the floor.

"Charlie, come back," Liza called out as he disappeared through one of the blackout curtains covering the doors to the terrace.

She quickly glanced about for someone to help bring him back, but most of the guests were already heading toward the entrance doors. The few partygoers who remained behind were as helplessly drunk as Charlie.

Liza rushed after him through the blackout curtains. As her eyes slowly adjusted to the darkness, she looked both left and right. The flagstone walk was deserted, and the only sound she heard came from the tree branches swaying in the wind above her. A moment later, she heard the tinkle of broken glass.

Running to the edge of the terrace, she gazed out into the night. In the dimness, Liza could see a hint of movement on the stone staircase that led down to the formal gardens. She started running toward it.

"Charlie," she called out once more.

The shadowy figure slowed to a stop, appearing to lean against the stone balustrade for support. Reaching the staircase and following it down, she was relieved to see that it was indeed Charlie. He was still crying.

"She's here," he moaned in a strange, almost incoherent voice.

"Who is here?" asked Liza.

"Joss," he said.

"Joss is dead, Charlie. She is dead."

"No," he shouted madly, whipping his head back and forth. "Pale she is . . . dreadful in the night."

Liza felt his boozy breath on her cheek as she grabbed him by the arms and began to turn him around on the staircase.

"What are you talking about, Charlie?" she said, attempting to steer him back up the steps.

"She's not dead. Oh God . . . Joss," he cried, collapsing to his knees.

Liza was bending down to help him regain his feet when she felt a sharp, jagged pain in the back of her head, and the sky tilted above her. As she fought to keep her balance, the distant walls of the castle seemed to be shifting. The ground was sliding back and forth between her feet. She was falling forward into a pool of darkness. It had no bottom.

CHAPTER 28

It was well past midnight when the telephone started ringing in the narrow hallway of Taggart's apartment. Dozing in the darkness, he listened to the rumble of far-off thunder and waited for the nightly wail of the London air-raid sirens that would signal the next Luftwaffe attack.

As the ringing continued, Taggart realized the thunder was coming from the northwest, and concluded it was nothing more than a storm front sweeping down from the Hebrides. When it became obvious the caller wasn't going to hang up, he wearily got out of bed and went to the hallway, grabbing the telephone earpiece from its wall cradle.

"Yeah," he said into the mouthpiece.

"This is Corliss," said a male voice at the other end of the line.

"Corliss?" repeated Taggart.

"Corliss Drummond," said the old inspector.

"Your first name is Corliss?" asked Taggart.

There was a pause.

"I have some news," said Drummond. "If you are interested."

"Shoot," said Taggart.

"It's probable that whoever murdered our Mr. Griffin paid a physical price for it," he said. "Griffin had commando training at the beginning of the war. Based on his defensive wounds, our pathologist believes he probably inflicted physical injuries on the person who killed him."

"Very good . . . Anything else?" asked Taggart.

"About those scraps of paper you found," he said. "It appears that one section included a portion of the Ainsley family crest."

"What is that?" asked Taggart.

"The Ainsleys are one of the oldest families in England. The current ancestral heir is Lord Nicholas Ainsley. He is a Battle of Britain RAF hero."

"I know who he is," said Taggart. "Helen Bellayne is spending the weekend at his country house right now. And Lieutenant Marantz as well."

Taggart suddenly remembered Liza telling him that Lord Ainsley had a silver key to the Royal Natatorium. He tried to recall whether anyone had reported a connection between him and J.P. Barnes.

"I need a telephone number for Ainsley's country house immediately," said Taggart.

"I assumed you might," said Drummond. "Here it is."

Taggart wrote down the exchange.

"Where is this house?" he asked.

"It's called Rawcliff. In the Sussex Downs—about seventy miles southeast of London, and right on the coast," he said. "It's a little more than a house, Sam. In fact . . ."

"Do you know how to get there, Corliss?" interrupted Taggart.

"Yes," said Drummond. "Everyone does. It's a national landmark."

"Can you meet me in about twenty minutes at our MP barracks on Tunnicliff Road?"

"I'll be there," said the old man, hanging up.

Taggart immediately dialed the number Drummond had given him. It was busy. He waited a minute and tried again. It rang several times before a voice responded, "Rawcliff."

"I need to speak to one of your weekend guests . . . Lieutenant Elizabeth Marantz," he said.

"We have more than a hundred guests at this time, sir, but if you leave your name and trunk exchange, I will give her the message as quickly as possible," said the pompous voice.

"I need to speak to her now," Taggart demanded. "This is General Ernest Manigault speaking, and it is vitally important that I speak to her right away."

"Sir, we have only one telephone line. Surely you must understand that I cannot allow the telephone to be occupied for the length of time necessary to locate Lieutenant Marantz. In fact, sir, Field Marshal Nemes is waiting to use it right now."

"It is urgent that I speak to her," said Taggart. "Please give her the message to call me right away."

"I assure you that I will do my best under the circumstances," came back the voice, clearly perturbed. "Is that all, sir?"

"One more thing," he said. "You have another guest staying there, named Helen Bellayne. Please give her the same message. And tell her that I'm on my way with the goddamn cavalry."

"'With the goddamn cavalry,'" he repeated. "Yes, sir, I will tell her."

The next call Taggart placed was to the MP barracks on Tunnicliff Road. It took the sergeant who answered several minutes to find the duty officer. The man was yawning when he picked up the phone.

"Lieutenant Darlow," he said.

"This is General Ernest Manigault," Taggart lied again. "I need a squad of MPs armed with light infantry weapons to be ready and deployed when I arrive there in fifteen minutes. And requisition two trucks for us. Have you got that, Lieutenant Darlow?"

"Yes, sir," he barked back. "They'll be ready, sir."

Taggart went to his room and threw on his uniform. Before leaving, he grabbed his .45-caliber Colt pistol from under the pillow and jammed it into the pocket of his topcoat. Back in the hallway, he was about to pick up the phone to call General Manigault when it began ringing again.

It was General Manigault.

"Sam, this is Ernie," he said. "All hell is breaking loose over at MI5. Apparently, one of their code analysts took off with several important ULTRA intercepts that were supposed to go back in the vault before he signed out for the weekend."

"What is his name?" asked Taggart.

"Charles Wainwright," said Manigault.

"I know him," said Sam, "and I think I know where he is. Something's up, General. I think we're close to solving those murders. I just hope it isn't too late."

Taggart took several minutes to fill him in on the third murder, and the possible connection to both ULTRA and the invasion plans.

"If the Germans get hold of those intercepts, they'll have a brand-new encryption code in twenty-four hours," said Manigault. "And I don't have to tell you what will happen if the invasion plan is compromised."

"I'll do my best, General," said Taggart.

CHAPTER 29

Liza lay beneath the infinite weight of a black basalt mountain, breathing very weakly, as her mind continued to struggle against the oppressive mass above her. It was impossible to raise her arms. The black mountain encased her like a granite tomb. She thought she could hear someone humming an ancient requiem to her from the summit of the mountain.

She was fearful that if she opened her eyes and actually saw the impervious black mass entombing her she would lose her mind forever. Then she heard the voice chanting to her again and recognized the melody. Taking a deep breath, she opened her eyes.

She lay in the four-poster bed in her room that overlooked the garden. It was dark outside the windows. She slowly turned her head to the side. Helen Bellayne was sitting at the desk across the room. She was playing Solitaire and quietly humming "Barbara Allen."

"Helen," said Liza, the word coming out like a dying croak.

Helen Bellayne dropped the cards and went to the mahogany dresser. After pouring a glass of water from the pitcher on the tray, she came to the side of the bed, gently lifted Liza's head, and helped her sip it.

"What time is it?" whispered Liza.

"A little after two," said Helen.

She went back to the dresser and returned with a bottle of aspirin. Liza swallowed two of them with the rest of the water.

"How did I get here?"

"One of the servants found you on the stone staircase leading down to the garden. He thought you had fallen . . . or were possibly . . ."

"I didn't fall," she said. "And I wasn't drunk. Someone attacked me."

"There is a fair-sized lump on the back of your head," said Helen. "I wasn't sure how . . ."

"Where is Charlie Wainwright?" Liza asked.

"I have no idea."

"He was with me."

"You were alone when they found you," said Helen, stroking her hand.

"Please ask someone to find him," said Liza. "It's very important."

Helen stood up and went to the other side of the bed. A tasseled rope hung from a small round hole in the ceiling. Grasping the tasseled end, she pulled on it. There was no sound.

"What is that?" Liza asked.

"A bell rope," said Helen. "It's a signal to the servants."

Within a minute, someone knocked lightly on the door. Helen opened it.

"Yes, madam?" asked one of the floor maids.

"Please go to Captain Wainwright's room immediately," Helen ordered. "He is staying in the suite next to Lord Ainsley. If he is asleep, wake him. Tell him to come here right away."

Liza thought she heard the sound of thunder. A few seconds later, a long sliver of lightning divided the black sky through the casement window. Feeling nauseous, she closed her eyes and drifted off again. She came awake to the muffled sound of more voices at the door. Helen came back to her.

"Charles is not there," she said. "Apparently, he left a note saying that he had to return to London immediately."

"I don't believe it," said Liza. "He was too drunk to write anything."

"The butler said his luggage was gone . . . all of his personal things as well."

"What about his briefcase?" she demanded.

"I have no idea," said Helen. "What are you implying?"

"He would never have gone back without telling me," she said. "I'm sure of it."

When Liza tried to sit up, she immediately felt faint once more. Lying back, she tried desperately to will the stuporous weakness away, but only drifted off to sleep again. Another rumble of thunder brought her up from the blackness. Helen was standing by the dresser, glancing down at several articles Liza had removed from her purse after arriving the previous afternoon.

"How long was I out?" she asked.

"Just ten minutes," said Helen, coming toward her. "Tell me . . . why do you have these cards?"

She was holding the two index cards on which Liza had copied the lines originally written in blood that Sam had found in Joss Dunbar's apartment.

"They are part of an unsolved mystery," said Liza. "One of too many, I'm afraid."

"Why are they a mystery?" asked Helen Bellayne.

"The mystery lies in who authored the words," said Liza.

Holding up the first index card, Helen read it aloud.

"'I asked you not to send blood but Yet do—because if it means love I will have it. I cut the hair too close & bled much more than you need—I pray that you put not the knife blade near where quei capelli grow.'"

"Yes," said Liza. "Those words."

"Were they originally written in blood?" asked Helen.

"Yes," Liza said, astonished. "How could you know that?"

"The mystery is solved," said Helen Bellayne.

"You know who wrote those words?" Liza demanded.

Helen nodded, smiling.

"They were written more than a hundred years ago," she said. "I happen to have a soft spot for Caroline Lamb."

Liza recognized the name, but couldn't remember why.

"Lady Caroline Lamb," said Helen, seeing her confusion. "She was the mistress of Lord Byron. He made her life a living hell. She wrote those words in blood to prove her love and then sent the letter to him with shavings of her pubic hair."

"And the other one?" asked Liza.

"'My God, you shall pay for this. I'll wring that obstinate little heart. . . . Noel,'" read Helen, aloud.

"Yes."

"Byron wrote that to her," she said. "He had a clubfoot, you know. . . . The man needed complete adoration. It was not enough for a woman to become his lover. He wanted her to love him above all other things in life. Once a woman surrendered to him, he would lose interest and move on to the next one. What he never anticipated was that Caroline was his equal in every way. It was when she refused to concede to him that Byron wrote his note."

In her mind's eye, Liza could see the dramatic painting of Byron and his mistress over the fireplace in the cliff cottage. Another peal of thunder rent the sky, and the lace curtains began billowing in through the casement window.

"'Noel' was his familiar name to his friends," said Helen. "George Gordon Noel Byron."

"Were Joss and Nicholas ever lovers, Helen?" Liza demanded.

Helen's face reflected her shock at the question.

"Why would you even . . . ?"

"Were they lovers, Helen?" Liza demanded again.

"I don't know."

"Did they know one another growing up?"

"Of course," said the older woman. "The Dunbar estate is only a few miles from Rawcliff. They both spent their summers down here when they were children. As to their relationship in those days, I have no idea. Joss was a very secretive creature, even as a little girl."

No, Liza's mind silently screamed. It couldn't be. Not Nicholas. With everything he had come to mean to her, it was impossible to conceive that he was a double murderer. But Joss had written one of the notes in blood that mimicked Caroline Lamb. Nicholas had almost certainly written the other one. Liza was gripped by another wave of nausea as she struggled to erase a lurid mental image of Nicholas and the dying Joss from her reeling imagination.

"Are you all right, Liza?" asked Helen with sudden concern. "You've gone completely white."

The nausea slowly ebbed away.

"Nicholas murdered her," she said, as if proclaiming the horrid truth aloud would allow her to actually believe it.

"That's absurd," said Helen. "Joss took her own life, Liza. She was desperately unhappy in the weeks before her death. I believe I told Sam that her father abused her when she was a child."

"She was pregnant with Nicholas's child."

Helen's eyes widened in disbelief as Liza pulled back the covers and slowly tried to sit up again. The pain in her head slowly subsided to a dull ache. Once on her feet, she walked tentatively to the closet.

"What are you doing?" demanded Helen. "You can't get up yet."

"I have to," she said.

Removing her slip, she began to put on her uniform. There was another knock at the door, and Helen went to answer it, this time opening it just a crack. A butler was standing in the hallway.

"I was asked to deliver this," he said, handing Helen a folded note. She closed the door and brought it back to the chair where Liza was tying her shoes.

"It is from a General Ernest Manigault," she said after reading it. "What a remarkably odd message."

"What does it say?" asked Liza, standing up again.

"It just says . . . the goddamn cavalry is coming."

When Liza grinned, the back of her head hurt.

"That's Sam," she said. "He is on his way."

She took Helen's hand in her own.

"I have something very important to tell you," said Liza. "I haven't any idea who can be trusted in this menagerie, but Sam said I can trust you, so I will. As ridiculous as this will probably sound, the future course of the war might be at stake."

"I don't understand," she said.

"I don't have time to explain it all. When Sam arrives, tell him that I believe Nicholas Ainsley is involved in a plot to betray both the ULTRA secret and Overlord to the Germans. The key to his plan is Charlie Wainwright. Nicholas, along with Desmond Sullivan, has kidnapped him. They are taking him to Germany."

"Are you sure that the injury to your head hasn't temporarily . . ."

"Stop it," demanded Liza. "Just give the message to Sam. Do you remember it?"

"Yes," she said. "You believe they are planning to betray ULTRA and Overlord to the Germans."

"They probably have an escape route planned across the channel. Tell Sam to alert the Royal Navy and the Royal Air Force," she said.

Helen seemed to sag toward her for a moment.

"Oh God, it can't be true," she said.

"I'm counting on you, Helen," said Liza, heading for the door.

"Where are you going now?" asked Helen, her voice taut with fear.

"To try to find Charlie," she said. "It's possible they haven't left yet."

"Why don't you wait until Sam arrives?" asked Helen. "If what you say is true, you have no chance to stop them alone."

"That might be too late. Tell him that I went to Nicholas's cottage down by the sea. Oh . . . and tell him there is a landing strip on the field near the golf course."

"You don't even have a weapon," said Helen.

Liza stopped and quickly glanced around the room, her eyes alighting on the billfold-sized surgical kit she had carried since the first bombing raid she had survived in London. Tucking the flat leather pouch inside her uniform coat, she opened the bedroom door and started down the corridor.

"God be with you," Helen called out to her from the open doorway.

At the foot of the front staircase, a group of people in nightclothes were milling about in the hallway as she rushed toward the massive entrance door. Several of their faces registered shock and incredulity.

"Lord Ismay told me himself," Liza heard one of them say as she ran out into the night. "Lady Ainsley died late this afternoon."

CHAPTER 30

Liza felt the first drop of rain on her cheek as she reached the edge of the formal gardens. She was following the same path that Nicholas had taken her on during their tour of the castle grounds.

Still groggy, she walked unsteadily across the brick-faced courtyard, past the old wooden drawbridge, and through the covered passageway. Emerging onto the rise of ground that overlooked the expanse of lawns, she heard another peal of thunder and waited for the subsequent flash of lightning to light up the sky.

In its incandescent glare, she could see the coal-black sea far in the distance. Off to the left was the little golf course. Directly ahead of her was the flat pasture where Nicholas said he had practiced his takeoffs and landings as a boy. With her head still aching, she began to walk across the field.

Why? she kept repeating in her mind. Why would Nicholas betray his country? He had lost his leg in the Battle of Britain to help save his country. In betraying England he would be giving up his title and vast estates. None of it made sense to her. Could it be an act of insanity?

But if it was, how could she have been so wrong about him? All through her medical training, she had won a well-deserved reputation for unbiased critical reasoning. One of her classmates had once half-seriously accused her of sorcery. Another girl jokingly suggested that Liza would never fall in love with a man as long as she looked at men as human guinea pigs. Perhaps that was it. Nicholas was the first man she had failed to subject to her ruthlessly objective scrutiny.

She suddenly remembered Des Sullivan's words to her on the dance floor. Nicky would soon be impoverished, he had said. What could that mean? Nicholas was one of the richest men in England. She started to run.

Her brain transmitted an acute jolt of pain with each pounding step, but she didn't slow down until she had crossed the last stone fence and was able to reorient herself. The smell of the sea was stronger as she arrived at the copse of elms and maples that bordered the path leading to the cottage. She plunged ahead into the woods.

The storm began as a gentle hum of tiny raindrops, a thin pattering against the leaves of the trees lining the path. A few moments later, it was coming down in a raging torrent that forced her to slow down again.

Emerging from the woods, Liza knew she was close to the cottage when she smelled the fragrant power of the wild roses. A harsh wind was coming off the sea as she slowly made her way along the crooked path. Now she could hear the booming of heavy surf as big rollers cascaded into the base of the cliff.

In another arc of lightning, she saw the little stone cottage, dark and forbidding against the raging black sea. They've already gone, she concluded, just before seeing the monstrous shadow off to the left of the path. Liza stopped short, momentarily convulsed by a tremor of fear.

The light went out of the sky and she was blinded again. Shielding her eyes from the rain, she took a halting step toward the dark, shadowy outline. It appeared to be some kind of vehicle. Stepping closer, she felt the cold metal rim of its fender.

As her eyes adjusted to the darkness, she saw that it was an old farm truck, its freight bed made of raw wooden planks. What looked like a rolled-up carpet was lying on the bed. In touching it, she realized that was exactly what it was—a section of carpet, tightly wound and tied with heavy rope.

Liza shuddered with horror as it suddenly rolled toward her and she heard a loud groan. A head was protruding from the edge of the carpet. It was Charlie Wainwright, his face a dark mask.

"Oh God," she cried out.

"He's not here," came back the harsh brogue of Des Sullivan as he enveloped her arms from behind. "Somehow I thought you might be along."

Dragging her away from the truck, he forced her down the path to the cottage, opened the front door, and shoved her inside. The cottage was dark and cold. In the light of a guttering candle, she could barely make out a recumbent form lying on the couch in front of the fireplace. It was Nicholas. He was gazing up at the painting of Byron and Lady Caroline Lamb. An open bottle of champagne sat on the low table next to his elbow.

"Wainwright's on the truck," said Des Sullivan as raindrops ferociously lashed the windows. "She found us, just as I told you she would."

"I was hoping you wouldn't come," said Nicholas laconically.

The hideous truth became a reality to her for the first time.

"If she could find us here," said Des, "we have to assume that others are on the way."

"Perhaps," said Nicholas, without moving from the couch. "What time is it?"

Sullivan checked his watch. "Ten before three," he said. "The flight path across France will be open to us in about twenty minutes."

"Nicholas . . . what have you done?" cried Liza as rainwater dripped from her uniform onto the old pine floor.

"Why don't you go and monitor the latest weather report," he said to Des. "I'll be along."

"What about her?"

"I'll see to her."

"We can't leave her here alive," said Sullivan.

"I said I would see to her," said Nicholas, his tone sharp.

Sullivan stalked out into the rain, slamming the door behind him.

It was quiet again except for the sound of raindrops hissing on the red coals in the fireplace.

"You already know what I have done," he said.

"I know," she said, shivering against her will. "Just please tell me why."

Getting up from the couch, he began limping toward her. He was wearing his black leather flying jacket over a tan flight suit. It was the same jacket he had lent her during their walk around the estate.

"When Joss first confided the ULTRA secret to me, I had no plans to do this," he said. "Even later, when she learned the Overlord plans from Jellico, it never entered my mind."

"So that's why you killed Joss?" asked Liza. "Because she threatened to tell on you?"

Nicholas's voice remained surprisingly mild.

"I didn't kill Joss," he said.

"You expect me to believe that?"

"No, I suppose not," he replied. "But I don't have time to convince you one way or the other."

He went past her to the table under the front window. A leather briefcase was sitting on it. It was Charlie's. Lifting the latched cover, Nicholas put his hand inside and withdrew a semi-automatic pistol. He slid back the bolt to inject a bullet into the chamber.

"Then why are you doing this? Tell me the truth."

"The truth?" he repeated. "The truth is, I don't really care who wins this war anymore. I'm part German to begin with, as you know—bad mix of blood, I suppose."

Releasing the hammer of the pistol with his thumb, he put it into the pocket of his flying jacket.

"But why?" she demanded again.

"Do you have any idea what my German cousins will pay for the Normandy plans and the knowledge that we have broken their most secret military code?" he asked. "It's enough for me to disappear to a safe haven with about ten million pounds sterling."

"What is money to you?" she said. "You already have a vast fortune."

"I'm as rich as Jacob Marley's ghost, Liza," he said. "My father plundered it all. Quite a piece of work he was . . . coward, swindler, pedophile, alcoholic, embezzler, collaborator—you name it—they all applied. It took my family a thousand years to accumulate its wealth, and just thirty for him to throw it all away. I am not looking forward to being dragged into debtors' court. That would be quite pathetic, really."

"But all your estates . . ."

"Mortgaged to the hilt, and the house of cards is about to fall," he said with a laugh. "It's all a bloody façade—a pathetic gold-plated façade. My mother continued the pretense right up until the bill collectors were at her door. They were going to serve her on Monday. This last house party was her swan song. She poisoned herself this afternoon."

"Oh . . ."

"My father preferred the shotgun in his mouth," he added with a sardonic grin, picking up Charlie's briefcase. "Shall we be on our way?"

"You're not a traitor, Nicholas," said Liza. "You were a hero in the Battle of Britain."

"I wasn't a hero," he said forcefully as he limped toward her again. "Not like the real ones in this war. To be truthful, it was no more than a lark at the beginning. A lot of us in the Oxford squadron looked on Spitfires as a throwback to the days of jousting knights—kill or be killed—I enjoyed it—very stimulating, shooting down my obnoxious German cousins, actually."

He picked up a fleece-lined mackintosh from the back of the couch and handed it to her.

"You're going to need this for a bit," he said.

"Why are you taking Charlie with you?" she asked.

"Des paid someone a great deal of money to secure one of the ULTRA code-breaking devices," he said, "but that didn't work out. In the end, the man couldn't deliver, or so Des says."

"So how will you convince them?" she asked, trying to buy time, already knowing the answer.

"The Germans are such thickheaded clots," he said. "If I simply told them about ULTRA and the Overlord secret, they wouldn't believe me. Adolf apparently remains convinced by his soothsayer that we are going to invade at Calais. But Charlie is the living proof of ULTRA and all it represents. He was even kind enough to supply me with several German military cables, along with his impressive interpretive analysis of them. That should be enough to convince them."

"When they are finished interrogating Charlie, they will kill him."

"No, they won't," said Nicholas. "You'll have to trust me on that."

She laughed harshly.

"We really have to go now," he said, firmly taking her arm and leading her to the door. "Don't worry. No harm will come to you."

"Not if Des Sullivan has his way."

"Des is a paid agent of the German Abwehr—rather handsomely

paid, I might add," said Nicholas, opening the door for her. "He has been working for them since the war began. Like so many Irishmen, he continues to take fervent umbrage at the subjugation of his race by my forebearers over the last few hundred years."

The rain and wind had strengthened considerably in the short time she had been in the cottage. Liza pulled the mackintosh tightly around her as Nicholas helped her up into the cab of the farm vehicle. Sullivan appeared surprised to see her, glowering at Nicholas before putting it in gear and turning on the masked headlamps. Letting out the clutch, he ran the truck forward through the mass of rosebushes.

Liza suddenly heard the crackle of a foreign voice followed by a long burst of static. Looking down, she saw a small shortwave receiver sitting on the floor of the cab. Two wires ran from the metal unit into the engine compartment. As the voice continued speaking, Liza realized his language was German. The man was delivering a weather forecast for southern France.

A rough cart track ran along the edge of the cliff and through the trees that led back to the open pastures below the castle. A few minutes later, they pulled up next to the large stone barn that Liza had seen at the edge of Nicholas's boyhood airstrip.

Leading her to a small padlocked side door, Nicholas opened the lock with a key and led Liza inside. The barn was dark and reeked of gasoline. Sullivan followed behind them, dragging the massive rolled rug with Charlie in it. He dropped his burden just inside the door. Charlie moaned once and was still again.

"I hope you didn't hit him too hard," said Nicholas disapprovingly. "He is going to need all his faculties when we get there."

"And where is that?" asked Liza as Sullivan flipped a wall switch, illuminating four bare lightbulbs spaced across the interior of the barn.

"Since you're not going with us, I would prefer you not to know that," said Nicholas.

Liza gazed across the dark, cavernous interior. Old metal farm implements had been shoved against the walls to make room for the airplane. It was painted entirely black and had no numbers or markings on the fuselage or the wings.

"Is that the Sopwith Camel?" she asked.

Nicholas laughed and said, "No. That old girl is gathering dust up in the loft, I'm afraid. This is a DeHavilland Tiger Moth, a little more appropriate for our present purposes. It's more than ten years old, but still quite serviceable now that I configured it for our needs. Charlie will ride comfortably in the cabin bay with Des."

The airplane had two parallel wings on each side, like the First World War planes she had seen at Mitchell Field on Long Island. It was about twenty feet long, with a small enclosed cockpit for the pilot and a separate cabin underneath and behind it. The cabin seats had been removed and were lying on an old threshing machine off to the side of the plane.

Still carrying Charlie's briefcase, Nicholas climbed up on the lower wing and stowed it in the pilot's compartment. She heard the quick snap of switches being thrown as he leaned into the cockpit.

"Ignition off," he called out.

Sullivan moved around to the front of the plane and pulled the propeller through several revolutions before stepping back.

"Contact," shouted Nicholas.

Sullivan placed his fingers on one blade of the propeller and pulled it downward in one quick motion, jumping back from the whirling propeller as the engine sparked to life.

Nicholas adjusted the controls in the cockpit, and the engine slowed to a low snarl. A few moments later, he climbed down from the wing to help Sullivan lift the rolled rug holding the still-unconscious Charlie into the cabin bay.

"Well, I guess we're ready to leave," said Nicholas. "Liza, it's time to say goodbye. No ceremony. I wish you a good life. Believe that."

"You can't be serious," said Sullivan. "You can't just let the bitch go."

"She has no idea where we are going," said Nicholas. "Besides, once we're airborne they'll never find us in this storm. I'll be on instruments all the way."

"She will go straight to the authorities," said Sullivan.

"They will know everything soon enough anyway," said Nicholas.

"Not about me . . . not about the murders," said Sullivan. "I had to take care of Griffin."

"You didn't tell me about your latest handiwork," said Nicholas.

"I'm not going to swing for any of it," Sullivan said, pulling a knife from his jacket and flipping open the long blade. "We're heading for Lake Maggiore in Switzerland, love," he said to Liza with a braying laugh. Then, turning to Nicholas: "Now she knows where we are going."

"Yes," said Nicholas.

"You just fly the plane," said Sullivan. "I'll handle the rest."

Walking straight toward her, Des said, "I'll make this painless for you, since the good Lord Ainsley appears to be so squeamish about it."

Seeing the cold menace in his black eyes, Liza knew it would be impossible to reason with him. She slowly backed away as he came toward her, glancing left and right for a place to escape. Sullivan watched her every move like a hunter waiting for his rabbit to break for cover. When she tried to run for the door, he grabbed her easily with his left hand, raising the knife toward her throat with his right.

"Des," shouted Nicholas over the growl of the engine.

It was no longer the voice of the Nicholas she had once known. It was as cold and hard as an executioner. The knife stopped in midair. Des slowly turned to face him. Nicholas was pointing his pistol at Des's back. As she watched, he cocked the hammer of the automatic with his thumb.

"Drop the knife," he demanded. "Now!"

Sullivan grinned at him.

"As you wish, my lord," he said, letting it fall from his hand.

"Get in the plane," Nicholas ordered.

Des slowly led her back to the cabin bay.

"I think Charlie might need medical attention," said Nicholas, helping her inside. "Please see to him."

"If you succeed tonight, the war could go on for years," she said, kneeling on the floor next to Charlie. "Don't do this, Nicholas."

Ignoring her, he pointed to a circular rubber diaphragm in the corner of the cabin and said, "That is a Gosport tube. If you need to talk to me during the flight, just shout through it and I'll hear you."

As Des climbed in after her, Nicholas grabbed his shoulder.

"She had better be safe and unharmed when we arrive in Switzerland," he said, his eyes deadly earnest.

Des grinned at him again before following her into the little cabin.

Nicholas shut the door to the bay, and Des drove home the bolt. Still kneeling on the floor, Liza quickly glanced around the fuselage. The frame appeared to be made of wood and stretched canvas. Two pillows and a blanket lay against the far bulkhead. A bamboo food-hamper sat next to the near bulkhead, along with a rack holding several glass bottles of water. There was a square glass porthole in the front of the cabin, and one on each side of the fuselage. Charlie's head was resting by her feet. The rug that enclosed him disappeared toward the tail.

"A brief reprieve," said Sullivan with a cobra's smile. "Perhaps you'll be a useful addition to the trip after all, Liza. We have many hours to kill until we reach Switzerland."

Through the glass nose-port, she watched Nicholas go to the two barn doors in front of the plane. He swung the first one open, anchored it against the wind with a large block of stone, and then went to the second, swinging it wide before securing it with another block.

Across the dark meadow, she could see a small section of the castle grounds in the distance. For some reason, the lawns were lit up like a football field. At least a dozen vehicles were parked sideways along the gravel drive, their headlights pointed across the field toward the barn. In the glow of the lights, she could see the shadows of tiny figures coming toward them on the run. A large truck was rumbling ahead of the men, moving straight for the makeshift runway.

A shot rang out, and she heard a bullet clang off an old tractor parked alongside the aircraft. She watched Nicholas come limping back toward the plane, as unruffled as if he were heading out for a Sunday ride after church. He disappeared for a moment below the glass porthole. When she saw him again, he was pitching aside the wooden chocks that had blocked the front of the wheels.

The plane was creeping forward on its own. As it rolled past him, Nicholas clambered onto the wing, and climbed into the cockpit. The engine noise suddenly increased from a low snarl to a throaty roar. The airplane rolled quickly through the open doors and out into the stormy night.

Staring through the right port, she prayed that the men running toward them could disable the plane before Nicholas was able to take off. The Tiger Moth was vibrating and shuddering as if it was about to come apart as it gathered speed across the rutted field, the tail bouncing violently behind them. Up ahead, she could see the truck headlights racing across the muddy pasture in a converging line with their takeoff path.

Liza heard the faint crack of gunshots in the distance. Des shoved her toward the rear of the compartment and removed a large revolver from his belt. He slammed the butt of it against the right port, shattering the glass.

A young American soldier was running toward them, raising his rifle as he came. He was only twenty feet away when Des shoved the barrel of his revolver through the open port and fired. The soldier went down headfirst in the grass.

Liza glanced at Charlie. He was still unconscious, his head bumping up and down on the wooden deck as the Tiger Moth leapt and bounced. Kneeling next to him, she cradled his head in her arms as the staccato crack of massed rifle fire momentarily drowned out the engine.

Jagged holes suddenly appeared in the wooden frame alongside her shoulder, the same bullets making instantaneous exit holes in the opposite bulkhead. Another bullet whined past her ear and smashed one of the water bottles. Des was firing back at them when she heard a dull thud and he dropped the gun out the window. The force of the bullet carried him backward until he came up hard against the far bulkhead and was still.

Up ahead, she could see the truck's headlights. They were no longer moving. It had come to a stop directly in their path. Men were scrambling out the open doors of the cab and diving to safety.

From the closed cockpit, Nicholas adjusted the throttle control to maximum pitch. With its petrol tanks crammed to the brim with fuel, the Tiger Moth was reacting very sluggishly to the joystick as he fought to keep it on the rutted path. There was no way to turn the plane to avoid the truck, not if he still hoped to escape. It was a big one, a troop carrier. They would have to go over it or through it.

Taggart had been driving the truck. Now he stood at the edge of the makeshift runway, watching the small plane careening wildly toward him. When he saw the rapidly narrowing distance between the plane and truck, he knew it had no chance to clear the obstacle. Taggart was mouthing a silent prayer of gratitude that he had had gotten there in time when the realization struck him that Liza might well be aboard the doomed plane.

Nicholas felt the deadening shock of a rifle bullet graze his right arm as the airplane jounced once, and then again, before finally beginning to lift off the ground. The huge truck was less than twenty feet ahead. If he kept his wings level, he knew that the fixed landing gear below the fuselage would never clear it. The Tiger Moth would become a flaming fireball.

With the resolute calm and athletic finesse that had made him the finest stroke in Oxford crew history, he expertly banked the plane slightly to the left. Giving another instinctive nudge to the joystick, he watched through the cockpit window as the tip of the left wing lightly kissed the meadow grass at the far edge of the flight path.

A moment later, the canted nose of the airplane cleared the front end of the truck by an inch or two. He felt a loud thump, and the plane shuddered momentarily as the right wheel carriage sheered off after striking the cab. With the Moth's engine screaming in torment, Nicholas banked right again to level the wings, and the plane soared up into the darkness.

A white dagger of lightning lit the sky for several seconds, and Taggart watched the tiny plane become a speck over the black sea in the distance. He was standing with his men near the troop carrier when Helen Bellayne caught up to him. From behind the stone fence at the edge of the field, a handful of weekend visitors in soggy nightclothes stood gaping at them.

"Whoever is flying that plane is the best goddamn pilot I've ever seen," said Taggart.

"What can you do now?" asked Helen.

"The RAF will try to intercept it using radar," he said, "but in this weather who knows. The navy will send out fast torpedo boats, in case our bullets might have damaged his engine or hit a fuel line. One of them is meeting me down in the cove."

Helen took his hand in hers.

"When you ordered them to open fire, Sam, did you know that Liza is probably on that plane?" she asked, staring hard at him.

"It wouldn't have mattered if the King of England was on it," he said. "I had no choice but to try to bring it down."

"The King is the one standing over there in the royal-purple night-dress," she said, pointing at the bedraggled group behind the stone fence.

CHAPTER 31

Soaking a handkerchief with cold water from the bullet-shattered bottle, Liza carefully cleaned the dried blood away from the wound on Charlie's head. He had a deep gash along his right temple, just above the hairline.

In the dim light of the one small bulb fixed to the bulkhead, she removed the surgical pouch from her uniform coat and unfolded its two leather halves. Opening a tube of sulfa, she sprinkled powder into the gash and fitted a small surgical dressing over the wound with a strip of adhesive. As Charlie slowly regained consciousness, his upturned head was cradled in Liza's lap.

"Am I in heaven?" he asked, gazing up at her with his familiar grin.

"No, Charlie," she said harshly.

"This place reeks of petrol," he said woozily.

"That's because we're in an airplane on our way to Switzerland."

"The last thing I remember was Des Sullivan employing his unique form of Gaelic charm on my head," he said.

"He's lying over there," said Liza, using her scalpel to cut the ropes binding the carpet that enclosed his body.

"Did you . . . do it?" he asked.

"He was shot as we were taking off," she said. "I just had a look at him. His wound isn't fatal. It went through his shoulder and broke the collarbone. He's still out cold."

Pulling back the edges of the rug, she helped Charlie crawl out of it.

"Why Switzerland?" he asked, his eyes focusing for the first time.

"Nicholas is turning you over to the German Abwehr."

"I don't believe it."

"Believe it," she said. "It's true. He told me so himself."

"But why . . ."

"This is not the time to explain it all, Charlie," she said furiously.

"Where are we now?" he asked.

"We took off a few minutes ago from Rawcliff," she said. "I assume we are out over the English Channel."

"Without trying to sound lurid, Liza, I'll have to kill myself before I'm turned over to the Germans," said Charlie. "I simply know too much."

Staring down at his big homely face, she shuddered involuntarily, knowing he was right.

"I'll try not to make a mess of it," he said, eyeing the scalpel.

"As Dr. Abramowicz used to say at medical school," she said, "let's keep that one in our back pocket for now."

Charlie sat up on the deck and glanced around the tiny cabin. The engine had settled into an even pitch, but the plane continued to buck and leap in the turbulence of the storm. Looking through the side port, he saw only the black night.

"I'm sorry to say that Nicholas also has your briefcase with the ULTRA cables," said Liza.

"Then I'm afraid both our lives must be forfeit," he said. "We have to do whatever is required to stop him."

"Yes," she agreed.

They felt the plane bank to the right, on a new course setting.

"We have to bring the plane down before he reaches the continent," she said.

He nodded and said, "The English Channel is only about twenty miles wide here. We'll be over German-occupied France in less than ten minutes."

"Do you know anything about airplanes?" she asked.

"Only what I've read, which isn't much, I'm afraid. This bulkhead separates us from the cockpit, so there is no way for us to reach the joystick. His hand and foot controls are connected to the rudder and elevator flaps with wire cables . . . like those over there," he said pointing to several braided strands of wire that ran back along the wall of the fuselage toward the rear of the plane.

Charlie leaned across to examine them more closely. They were about the same diameter as a drinking straw, and formed of many interconnected wire strands.

"It would take a file or a wire cutter to sever these things," he said, "and we would have to know which one to cut. If I severed the elevator cable, he would immediately lose control. The rudder is less crucial, but I have no idea which one it is."

"Could we make the engine fail?" she asked.

"Wizard idea if I had some way to disable it," he said. "We're sealed off from the engine compartment, and I can't reach the fuel lines."

"What else?" she demanded, her voice rising for the first time. "We need to do it now."

Charlie glanced at his watch and shrugged.

"As much as I hate to say it, I think we need a fire," he said, touching the fabric skin of the fuselage. "These things are made of wood and canvas. The canvas fabric is sealed with dope to make it impervious to water. If I put a flame to it, the plane will become a bloody blowtorch in less than a minute. He'll have to put it down then . . . if he can."

Reaching into the surgical kit, she pulled out a small foil packet of waterproof matches that could be used to sterilize the instruments.

"I was afraid you might have some of those," he said, grinning, as he tore the packet open.

"Where will you start it?" she asked.

"Toward the rear—as far away from the gas tanks as possible," he said. "That will give us the best chance. The slipstream will carry the flames away from the tanks. Nicholas will see that the fuselage is on fire, and will hopefully have time to put us down safely before the tail burns off."

He glanced out the side port again.

"I hope we're not higher than one or two thousand feet," he said as the plane bucked wildly in the unstable air. "Any higher than that and we won't make it. The plane will burn up before he can ditch it in the water."

"Do it," she demanded. "Don't wait any longer."

Ripping a cloth strip off one of the pillow covers, Charlie dropped to the deck on his stomach and started inching headfirst down the narrow fuselage toward the tail.

"There's one more thing," he said, stopping a last time to look back at her. "This plane has a fixed landing gear. The wheels don't retract. Chances are when we hit the sea she'll flip right over. Be sure to brace yourself against the bulkhead before we go in."

"Don't you have anything positive to say?" she asked him with a nervous grin.

"It's my own stupidity that put us in this predicament," he said, his eyes becoming liquid. "I just pray that you survive this, Liza."

He started his slow crawl back to the tail. Liza watched him until she could no longer see the soles of his feet. A moment later, she suddenly felt a painful pressure on her left shoulder. Turning, she saw Des Sullivan behind her, his pain-wracked face outlined in the murky light. His left arm hung by his side, blood-soaked and useless.

"Where is Wainwright, you bitch?" he shouted, breaking his hold on her shoulder to pick up the top section of the broken water bottle from the cabin deck. Grasping its neck in his fist, he extended the jagged edge toward her.

Liza scrambled back, extending her legs at him as she came up against the bulkhead wall a few feet away from him. As he started crawling toward her, she saw a tiny gout of flame erupt at the tail of the fuselage.

As the fire quickly grew, she could see Charlie desperately trying to back away from the flames in the constricted tunnel. His huge shoulders filled the space on both sides, and he could only edge back an inch or two at a time.

Liza struck out violently with her legs at Sullivan, temporarily keeping him at bay.

Above them in the cockpit, Nicholas saw the sudden glare in the sky behind him. Loosening the brackets that held the cockpit cover in place, he shoved upward on it. A deafening gale of wind ripped the cockpit cover away from the brackets, and it disappeared into the darkness. Looking back, he saw the fire spreading along the canvas-covered ribs of the fuselage.

He had less than a minute before the fire burned away the elevator. Pulling the throttle to idle, he pushed the nose over into a steep descent. According to the altimeter, they were just under two thousand feet above sea level. It would be a race for time as he headed down to find a place to ditch.

He lowered the left wing and nudged the stick to the right, causing the plane to slip left, and keeping the flames away from the tailplane. Staring into the blackness below, he grabbed the radio mike.

"Achtung . . . Achtung," Liza heard him shouting through the Gosport tube as he transmitted his estimated position in German over the radio. Still braced against the bulkhead, she heard him report that he was about eight miles west of the French coast, and fourteen miles southwest of Manseur.

One of her violent kicks found Sullivan's wounded left shoulder and he fell backward again. A moment later, Charlie began screaming in mortal agony. Seeing the soles of his shoes finally appear, Liza grabbed his ankles and began pulling him toward her. The screams abruptly stopped.

Wiping the lashing rain from his eyes, Nicholas could just make out the foamy lather of a cresting wave fifty feet below him. When he glanced back, he saw that the rear half of the fuselage was raging with fire.

He had to come down on top of one of the swells, so that the airship would slide down the back side of it and come to rest in the trough before the next wave flipped them over. He wouldn't have a second chance.

Liza was still trying to pull Charlie toward her when Nicholas hit the swell perfectly, the following wave snuffing out the flames behind him as if blowing out a match. When the Tiger Moth hit the water, its fire-weakened airframe broke in two at the wing struts. As the plane came to a stop, both sections began to wallow in the trough of the wave.

Climbing out of the cockpit onto the wing, Nicholas could see a narrow breach in the cabin compartment just below him. Liza and Des were already through the opening. Charlie still had to be inside.

The weight of the engine was dragging the front section of the plane under the surging waves. As he watched, the narrow breach was rapidly disappearing as the compartment overflowed with seawater. While Liza was still desperately trying to haul Charlie out by his feet, Des headed for the other piece of floating wreckage, awkwardly using his right arm to propel himself forward.

Liza could feel Charlie's body slipping away as the front section went under. Suddenly Nicholas was in the water beside her. Together, they dragged Charlie through the breach as the front end of the aircraft disappeared under the surface.

Struggling to keep Charlie's head above the heaving sea, Liza smelled the appalling odor of his badly charred flesh. Fortunately, he was still unconscious as Nicholas helped her convey him over to the remaining section of floating wreckage.

It consisted only of the denuded skeleton of the fuselage along with one of the tail stabilizers, but the wood-ribbed frame was riding higher than the teeming waves around it. Des was holding on to the far edge with his right hand as Nicholas reached the near side and pulled Charlie toward it.

"We've got to get him out of the water," cried Liza.

Together, they worked to hoist his shoulders over the top strut of the fuselage, but as soon as his bulk was added to the skeletal framework, it dipped below the surface, pulling them all under. When they came up again, Sullivan screamed, "It can't hold all of us."

Abandoning the wreckage, Liza attempted to tread water in the turbulent sea while still helping to hold Charlie's head up. Again and again she found herself being dragged under, gagging as she took saltwater into her lungs. She felt herself weakening with each desperate scissor kick back to the surface.

As her face emerged once more from the sea, Liza felt a stinging blow to the side of her head. She opened her eyes to see Des Sullivan, his face contorted with terror. With another well-delivered blow, he drove her under again. Her strength almost gone, she let go of Charlie and fought her way up through the black turbulence.

Without the wreckage to hold on to, she knew she would drown. Hanging on was her only hope of survival. As she swam toward the far end of the fuselage, Sullivan moved to intercept her. He let go of the wreckage with his good arm just long enough to raise it for the coup de grâce.

Liza heard the crack of a pistol, strangely thin over the roar of the sea. A puzzled expression registered on Sullivan's face as his arm dropped weakly to his side. He stared sightlessly at her for a moment before slowly vanishing beneath the surface.

Liza grabbed the edge of the fuselage and held on as another savage wave engulfed them. Holding her breath for as long as she could, she came out of it to see Charlie still draped over the frame of the fuselage, his body safe in the arms of Nicholas. The pistol had disappeared.

"I'm reminded of that line from *Macbeth,*" shouted Nicholas, spitting out sea water. "'Nothing in his life became him like the leaving it.'"

Struggling along the edge of the fuselage, she joined him next to the still-unconscious Charlie. As the minutes passed, they discovered that, if each of them kept one hand on Charlie's shoulder while holding on to the frame with the other, both his head and the fuselage remained just above the surface of the surging waves.

"Charlie," Liza called out to him in the darkness.

There was no response.

Nicholas switched on the small flashlight that was hanging from a leather lanyard around his neck and trained the beam on Charlie's face. Most of the big man's hair was gone, and his lips were swollen up like inner tubes. Through a mask of shock, his open, childlike eyes stared downward. Picking up his hand from the water, Liza saw that the skin had peeled away in shreds and most of the flesh underneath was burned black.

Nicholas switched off the flashlight.

They floated in the sea for a long time without saying anything. Liza had lost her sense of direction. She had no idea from where rescue might come, if it ever came. She only knew that Charlie would live no more than an hour or two unless they got him medical attention. Her bitterness at Nicholas and what he had done suddenly exploded.

"I know why you helped me to save Charlie back there," she shouted over the wind. "Without him you have nothing to give your German cousins."

"You may think what you like," said Nicholas calmly.

He switched on the flashlight again, illuminating a small hand compass he had removed from his pocket. Turning away from her, he stared into the darkness, then switched the light off again.

They continued to drift in the cold, boiling sea. Every few minutes, she would take Charlie's pulse to make sure he was alive. As the rain steadily pummeled her face, she began to lose track of time. Her mind went back to the last conversation she had had with Nicholas in the cliff cottage.

"So you didn't murder Joss," she said, as if there had been no interruption.

"She took her own life," he came back in a conversational tone.

"But you were kind enough to help her, is that it?" she said acidly. "I was there, Nicholas. I saw it all."

In the darkness, she could just make out the shape of his head above the crashing waves. He was obviously looking at her, but remained silent.

"Didn't you?" she shouted at him.

"You don't know anything about us, Liza . . . about Joss and me. We grew up together alone . . . the two of us united against our hideous parents."

A wave rolled over both of them before he continued again.

"We were fourteen during the summer we decided to become Lord Byron and Lady Caroline. She thought we could go through the rest of our lives playing those roles. But that wasn't the reality, Liza. Actually, I was always kind to her. I would like you to believe that."

"Yes, what a Good Samaritan you were," Liza shouted. "I also happened to be with her at the moment she discovered she was pregnant with your child."

"She had hoped it was mine," he said, taking in another mouthful of seawater and hacking it out. "But I can never have children, Liza . . . one more legacy from my sainted parents. That was another reason she wanted to take her life—realizing it was Jellico's or Kilgore's or Des Sullivan's."

"You were there," shouted Liza over the biting wind. "You made no effort to save her."

"I was there," he said. "We had made love for a last time, and then the air-raid sirens went off, and I went upstairs to the roof to watch the raid. When I came back down to the pool, she was . . . she had . . ."

"So that's when you tied her to the tile machine?"

"She had already fastened the cord herself," he said. "Joss was always very melodramatic—just ask her aunt Helen."

"So you helped her by shoving the tile machine into the pool."

"She was going, Liza. It was like watching an animal die by the road after it has been hit by a car."

"How noble of you," she shouted as they continued to drift in the stormy darkness.

There was silence again. A few minutes later, Nicholas said, "She was already quite old in many ways, Liza . . . just as I am."

"She was in love with you and you killed her," pronounced Liza for the last time.

"So be it."

"And what about J.P.?" she demanded. "Did you drive the hatpin through her brain to put her out of her misery?"

"Des murdered her," he said. "I had no idea he was planning to do it. Afterwards, he claimed he had done it to protect me."

Charlie's chin had dipped lower into the water, and Nicholas carefully lifted it onto the edge of the wreckage again.

"From what?"

"One night we were all together at Des's apartment . . . the four of us . . . Joss, J.P., Des, and I. It was a . . . You wouldn't understand."

"I understand," she said.

"You and I had very different upbringings, Liza," he said then.

"If that's what you want to call it," she said coldly. "So what happened then?"

"In the course of the evening, I got fairly drunk, as usual," said Nicholas. "I gather that at one point Joss was talking to me about the proposed date of Overlord and the fact that Normandy would be the landing site, and that she hoped her favorite hotel would survive the invasion."

"So?" Liza demanded after another wave rolled over them.

"Des said that J.P. heard Joss talking to me about it and that she would eventually connect Joss's death to us—at least, that is what he said."

Staring across at the shadowy outline of his face, Liza realized she no longer felt the constant lash of the rain. She looked up to see the sliver of a crescent moon through the ragged storm clouds, and a small patch of starry sky.

"The sea is beginning to moderate," said Nicholas, checking his pocket compass with the flashlight again.

"So you're completely innocent," she said, "the victim of an unhappy childhood."

"Hardly," he said, staring out again into the distance.

For the first time, Liza could detect a hint of predawn illumination from one horizon, and realized that France had to be in that direction. She remembered Nicholas radioing the message, before the plane went down, that he was within eight miles of the French coast. It was impossible for her to tell if they were drifting toward it or away from it. A few minutes later, she could definitely make out a dark outline of land against the leaden sky.

Charlie began to moan aloud as the shock of his burns began to wear off. The first glimmer of dawn turned his grotesquely swollen face into an image of horror. His cries grew steadily louder.

"He isn't going to make it much longer without help," said Liza.

"I know," said Nicholas.

Liza thought she heard the distant growl of engines. The sound stopped for a few seconds and then came again, slightly louder. Nicholas had obviously heard it, too. He was gazing into the distance. Liza suddenly realized the sound was coming from the dimly lit landmass over his shoulder. France.

"Well, Liza, you survived a ship being torpedoed in the North Atlantic, and now you have survived the crash landing of a plane," said Nicholas, his voice steady. "What a remarkable tale you will have to tell your grandchildren someday. It certainly proves you're one of the chosen people."

"Not if your German cousins have their way," she said.

The sound of the marine engines was definitely louder now. Although she could not see the craft's running lights, it seemed to be heading directly toward them. Soon she could actually make out its rakish lines against the dark horizon. It was low and sleek and very fast.

"I know you won't believe this, Liza," he said, "but I loved you from the first moment I met you."

"Goddamn you, Nicholas," she shouted. "Where is that boat coming from?"

"It's an E-boat," Liza," he said, "a German patrol craft, and it's coming to pick us up. They will take good care of Charlie. And I will make certain that you both are returned safely to England in a month or two."

Liza had already decided what she had to do. She had begun thinking about it long before the sound of the engines, and had already transferred the scalpel to the breast pocket of her uniform. After she finished slitting Charlie's throat, she would kill Nicholas, or die trying.

As Nicholas let go of the wreckage and switched on his pocket flashlight again, she tugged the scalpel out of her pocket. The German patrol craft was about a half-mile away, and moving toward them with astonishing speed. She had no more than a minute before it arrived. Removing her other hand from Charlie's shoulder, Liza tugged his head back, exposing his neck.

"Not so fast, my darling," said Nicholas, pulling Charlie's body out of her grasp.

A moment later, Liza heard a tremendous blast. It sounded like the roar of a cannon, followed by a long, ear-piercing whine. As she watched, a huge splash erupted within a dozen yards of the German patrol craft that was racing toward them.

She heard another blast, quickly followed by several more. Two geysers of water erupted near the E-boat, the first on one side and the second on the other. Still it raced on toward them at an incredible rate of speed, not veering an inch from its original path.

"They've got her bracketed," said Nicholas calmly.

The front deck of the German craft suddenly appeared to glow bright red for a moment. A split second later, the E-boat blew up in a massive tower of flame and wreckage that rose fifty feet into the air. The ensuing fire lit Nicholas's tranquil face for several seconds before fading into the gloom.

"Our immortal English navy," he said admiringly. "That destroyer is still at least two miles away from us. It must be equipped with radar-controlled guns."

As Charlie continued to groan in agony, Liza wondered how Nicholas could remain so composed when his one chance for rescue had just been obliterated. The low snarl of other powerful engines came toward them, borne on the wind from the opposite direction of the E-boat.

"English motor torpedo boats," he said. "Well, Liza, if I'm the man you think I am, I guess it's time to get rid of the both of you."

"Go ahead and try," she said fiercely, the scalpel extended in her hand.

In the murky light, she could now see on his face the familiar endearing grin that she had once found so compelling.

"They'll never find you in time to save Charlie without this," he said, holding up the lit flashlight. After removing the lanyard from around his neck, he secured it to the central rib of the fuselage.

"Where are you going?" she demanded as the rain came again, harder than ever.

"I'm swimming for it," he said, as if the French coast were just a few hundred yards away.

"You'll never make it, Nicholas. It's eight miles."

"Piece of cake," he said jauntily. "See you in Biarritz when the war is over."

He had already let go of the wreckage and was slowly drifting away from them, but then appeared to look back at her once with enduring intensity.

"I did love you, you know," came his voice across the open water.

He began to swim in a crude attempt at a sidestroke, but, given his prosthetic leg, he couldn't generate any momentum against the turbulent sea. The iron harness was already weighing him down.

Liza kept him in the beam of the flashlight for almost a minute as he rose and fell on the crest of the waves. By then he was humming a tune, as if setting off for a romantic holiday at the beach. She recognized the song. It was Bunny Berrigan's "I Can't Get Started with You."

A savage breaker rolled over the fuselage and momentarily drove her underwater. By the time she was able to train the flashlight on him again, the humming had stopped and Nicholas had disappeared.

CHAPTER 32

Liza came up out of the foaming sea into the pitiless rain, shivering uncontrollably as powerful hands pulled her into the motor torpedo boat and draped a blanket around her shoulders.

She opened her eyes experimentally. A flask of brandy was suddenly at her lips, and she felt its fire going deep inside her. Someone picked her up in his arms and carried her across the deck and down a short set of steps.

"Charlie," she cried out, her salt-inflamed eyes almost shut.

"Don't you worry, miss. We got the big bloke first," a man called out after her.

"You're both safe now, Liza," said a familiar voice very close to her ear. It was Sam's.

He carried her into the captain's cabin and placed her on a warm, dry bunk. She could not stop shivering. Quickly pulling off her soaked uniform, he wrapped her in two more blankets and began briskly rubbing her feet, first one and then the other, a minute at a time. She felt sharp needles of pain as the numbness in them slowly receded and circulation returned.

"Rest easy for a moment," he said. "I'm going to check on Wainwright."

Burrowing deeper in the blankets, she closed her swollen eyes and drifted away.

"Miss," she heard someone calling out to her. "Miss."

Opening her eyes, she saw an English sailor standing next to the bunk, wearing rain-slicked oilskins. He had a chest-long gray beard, and was holding a mug of steaming tea. After he helped her to sit up, she grasped it with both hands and took the first sip. Almost scalding hot, it had been spiked with a healthy measure of rum.

"It's a good cupper, lass," said the man with a grin. "Put my grog ration in it for you."

"Thank you so much," she said, taking another wonderful swallow as he headed back up on deck.

Her head felt thick and frozen as she looked down absently at her hands, which were still wrapped around the warm china mug. Blood was dripping from the rim onto the woolen blanket.

Removing her right hand from the mug, she saw that her fingers and palm were badly shredded from clutching the splintered framework of the wrecked fuselage. She heard the compartment door bang open, and Sam came back in carrying a handful of gauze bandages and a tube of sulfa ointment. She couldn't help smiling up at him.

"You did well, Liza," he said, unwrapping a gauze bandage.

"I tried, Sam," she said.

"They think Wainwright is going to make it," he said, squeezing some ointment onto the palm and fingers of her right hand.

"Thank God," said Liza.

"You saved his life. . . . You've saved a hell of a lot of lives," said Taggart, gently wrapping the bandages over the raw areas and taping them into place.

The warm cabin smelled strongly of the captain's aromatic pipe tobacco. It reminded her of the blend her father had often smoked in his book-lined study. It smelled like home.

"Things got a little complicated at the end, Sam," she said as he started on her other hand.

"Yeah, I figured," he said. "What happened to Ainsley?"

The last image of him trying to swim away from her on his prosthetic leg flickered in her mind, and she felt a sudden stab of sorrow.

"He didn't make it," she said, keeping her voice steady as Taggart finished taping the second dressing. Dropping the extra bandages on the captain's chart table, he came around behind her and began to massage her aching shoulders through the blanket. She felt the soreness and pain slowly ebbing away.

"You have found another important calling," said Liza gratefully.

"I also have a lot of questions," said Taggart.

"I think I have most of the answers," she said.

Liza was about to tell him what had happened to Joss and J.P. when he said, "Those deaths can wait until we're ashore. Did you see Ainsley drown?"

As was so often the case, he had divined what she was going to say.

"I'll tell the Royal Navy to call off its search if you saw him die," he said.

She could still hear Nicholas nonchalantly humming the song as he struggled to stay afloat long enough to disappear from her view. He had not wanted her to see him die.

"He drowned," she said, feeling a final shiver of regret.

"Good," he came right back.

In her mind's eye, she saw Nicholas once more. He was standing in the snow outside the Savoy on the first night they had dinner together. The first night they had danced to Glenn Miller in the little piano bar upstairs.

"Liza?" Taggart said, interrupting her thoughts.

"Yes?"

"Did you care for him?"

"Do you mean did I love him?" she asked.

He nodded.

The bulkhead next to her shoulder heeled over as the boat changed course before speeding up again.

"I don't know," she said.

He nodded again.

"You shouldn't have tried to take him and that other bastard alone," he said. "I would never have forgiven myself if you hadn't made it through."

"I think it's time you began forgiving yourself for a lot of things," said Liza.

"Yeah . . . maybe," he said. "Someday."

"What happens to us now?" she asked, as he eased her head back down to the pillows.

"I don't know," he said. "When we tell them what happened, the King will probably call his security chief, Colonel Gaines, and he will

call the King's retainer in the House of Lords, and he will call Churchill, and when they're all through, Lord Nicholas Ainsley will have died a hero's death fighting against the Axis forces of evil."

"And after that?"

"They will hopefully have something useful for us to do."

"Yes," she said. "I hope so."

"Try to get some rest now," he said, turning out the light over her bunk.

After he left her, Liza lay in the darkness in a state of languorous torpor, wrapped tightly in the cocoon of the warm woolen blankets. She fell asleep to the steady, reassuring drone of the boat's powerful engines.

She was back in the sea again, although it was no longer the violent maelstrom in which she had fought to survive. She had left the raging surface behind and was descending through its dark, tranquil depths, falling deeper and deeper into the silent abyss. On and on she slid into the unfathomable void. Time and space had long ceased to have meaning when her feet finally touched the soft, yielding ocean floor.

Making a slow, easy pirouette, she began to search for a sign of life in the blackness. When she had come almost full-circle, she suddenly sensed a faint gleam of light in the distance. She slowly glided toward it, till she saw that the shimmering glow was emanating from a silver candelabra, suspended high above her in the darkness. It yielded one small cone of light directly beneath it.

She could now hear an orchestra playing, although the music was distorted by the horrific depth of the sea. Beneath the cone of light, a figure was slowly moving in and out of the shadows.

It was Nicholas. He was dancing alone, leisurely moving with exquisite grace to the orchestra's sad, disembodied requiem in a macabre minuet that would last for eternity.